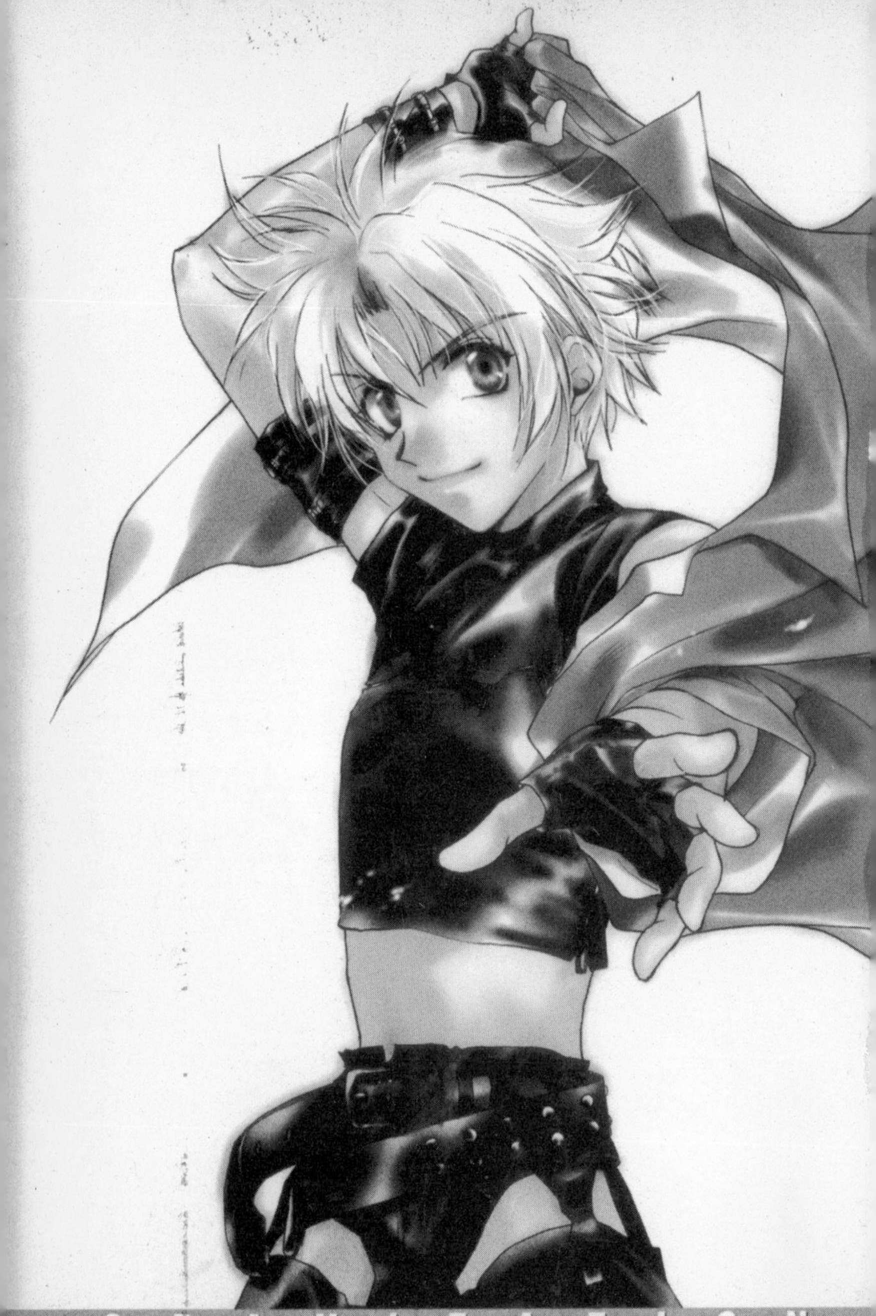
GRAVITATION

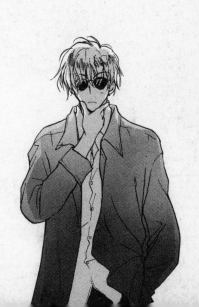

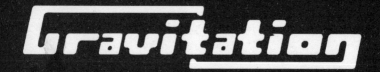

Volume 9

By
Maki Murakami

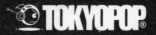

HAMBURG // LONDON // LOS ANGELES // TOKYO

Gravitation Vol. 9
Created by Maki Murakami

Translation - Ray Yoshimoto
English Adaptation - Jamie S. Rich
Copy Editor - Peter Ahlstrom
Retouch and Lettering - Vicente Rivera, Jr.
Production Artist - James Dashiell
Cover Design - Raymond Makowski

Editor - Paul Morrissey
Digital Imaging Manager - Chris Buford
Pre-Press Manager - Antonio DePietro
Production Managers - Jennifer Miller and Mutsumi Miyazaki
Art Director - Matt Alford
Managing Editor - Jill Freshney
VP of Production - Ron Klamert
President and C.O.O. - John Parker
Publisher and C.E.O. - Stuart Levy

A 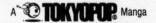 Manga

TOKYOPOP Inc.
5900 Wilshire Blvd. Suite 2000
Los Angeles, CA 90036

E-mail: info@TOKYOPOP.com
Come visit us online at www.TOKYOPOP.com

ISBN: 1-59182-341-2

First TOKYOPOP printing: December 2004
10 9 8 7 6 5 4
Printed in the USA

THE MEMBERS OF THE GRAVITATION BAND

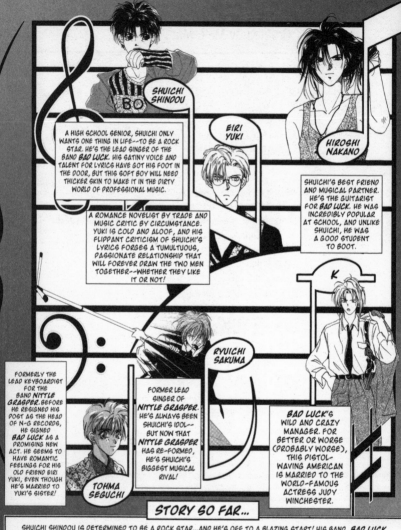

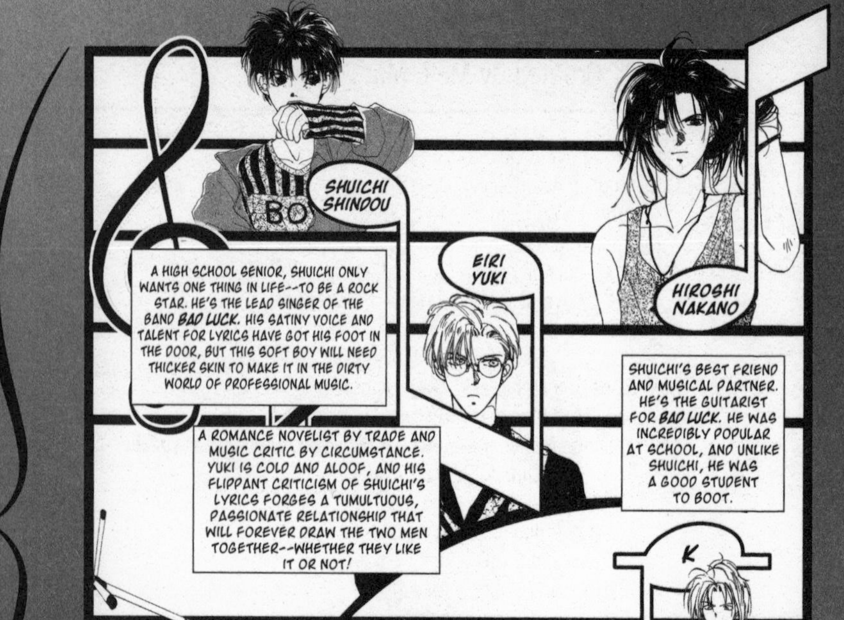
SHUICHI SHINDOU
A HIGH SCHOOL SENIOR, SHUICHI ONLY WANTS ONE THING IN LIFE--TO BE A ROCK STAR. HE'S THE LEAD SINGER OF THE BAND ***BAD LUCK***. HIS SATINY VOICE AND TALENT FOR LYRICS HAVE GOT HIS FOOT IN THE DOOR, BUT THIS SOFT BOY WILL NEED THICKER SKIN TO MAKE IT IN THE DIRTY WORLD OF PROFESSIONAL MUSIC.
HIROSHI NAKANO
SHUICHI'S BEST FRIEND AND MUSICAL PARTNER. HE'S THE GUITARIST FOR ***BAD LUCK***. HE WAS INCREDIBLY POPULAR AT SCHOOL, AND UNLIKE SHUICHI, HE WAS A GOOD STUDENT TO BOOT.
EIRI YUKI
A ROMANCE NOVELIST BY TRADE AND MUSIC CRITIC BY CIRCUMSTANCE. YUKI IS COLD AND ALOOF, AND HIS FLIPPANT CRITICISM OF SHUICHI'S LYRICS FORGES A TUMULTUOUS, PASSIONATE RELATIONSHIP THAT WILL FOREVER DRAW THE TWO MEN TOGETHER--WHETHER THEY LIKE IT OR NOT!
K
BAD LUCK'S WILD AND CRAZY MANAGER. FOR BETTER OR WORSE (PROBABLY WORSE), THIS PISTOL-WAVING AMERICAN IS MARRIED TO THE WORLD-FAMOUS ACTRESS JUDY WINCHESTER.
RYUICHI SAKUMA
FORMER LEAD SINGER OF ***NITTLE GRASPER***. HE'S ALWAYS BEEN SHUICHI'S IDOL--BUT NOW THAT ***NITTLE GRASPER*** HAS RE-FORMED, HE'S SHUICHI'S BIGGEST MUSICAL RIVAL!
TOHMA SEGUCHI
FORMERLY THE LEAD KEYBOARDIST FOR THE BAND ***NITTLE GRASPER***. BEFORE HE RESIGNED HIS POST AS THE HEAD OF N-G RECORDS, HE SIGNED ***BAD LUCK*** AS A PROMISING NEW ACT. HE SEEMS TO HAVE ROMANTIC FEELINGS FOR HIS OLD FRIEND EIRI YUKI, EVEN THOUGH HE'S MARRIED TO YUKI'S SISTER!

STORY SO FAR...

SHUICHI SHINDOU IS DETERMINED TO BE A ROCK STAR...AND HE'S OFF TO A BLAZING START! HIS BAND, ***BAD LUCK***, IS SIGNED TO THE N-G RECORD LABEL, AND THEIR ALBUM HAS JUST GONE PLATINUM! WITH THE ADDITION OF HIS NEW MANAGER--THE GUN-TOTING AMERICAN MANIAC NAMED "K"--SHUICHI IS POISED TO TAKE THE WORLD HOSTAGE! BUT THINGS ARE THROWN INTO DISCORD WHEN THE LEGENDARY BAND ***NITTLE GRASPER*** ANNOUNCES THEY ARE REUNITING! NOW SHUICHI WILL HAVE TO GO HEAD-TO-HEAD WITH HIS IDOL, RYUICHI SAKUMA. ALL THE WHILE, SHUICHI COPES WITH HIS ROLLER-COASTER RELATIONSHIP WITH THE MYSTERIOUS WRITER EIRI YUKI. THEIR SECRET ROMANCE HAS HIT A FEW JARRING NOTES, PROVING THAT LOVE ISN'T ALWAYS HARMONIOUS. HOW LONG CAN THEY REMAIN INEXORABLY INTERTWINED, HELD TOGETHER BY A FORCE AS STRONG AS GRAVITY? CONFRONTED BY A VORACIOUS PACK OF REPORTERS, YUKI SURPRISINGLY ADMITS TO A SHOCKED WORLD THAT HE AND SHUICHI ARE INDEED LOVERS! FUELED BY JEALOUSLY, SEGUCHI ORDERS SHUICHI TO BREAK UP WITH EIRI. SHUICHI CONTEMPLATES LEAVING N-G IN ORDER TO SALVAGE HIS ROMANCE, BUT ALL IS FOR NAUGHT--IN A SHOCKING MOVE, EIRI DUMPS ***HIM***! K TRIES IN VAIN TO HELP A DEVASTATED SHUICHI RECOVER, BUT THE SURPRISES JUST KEEP COMING: SHUICHI IS KIDNAPPED...AND PUT ON A PLANE TO R-O-C-K IN THE U.S.A.!

CONTENTS

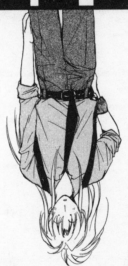

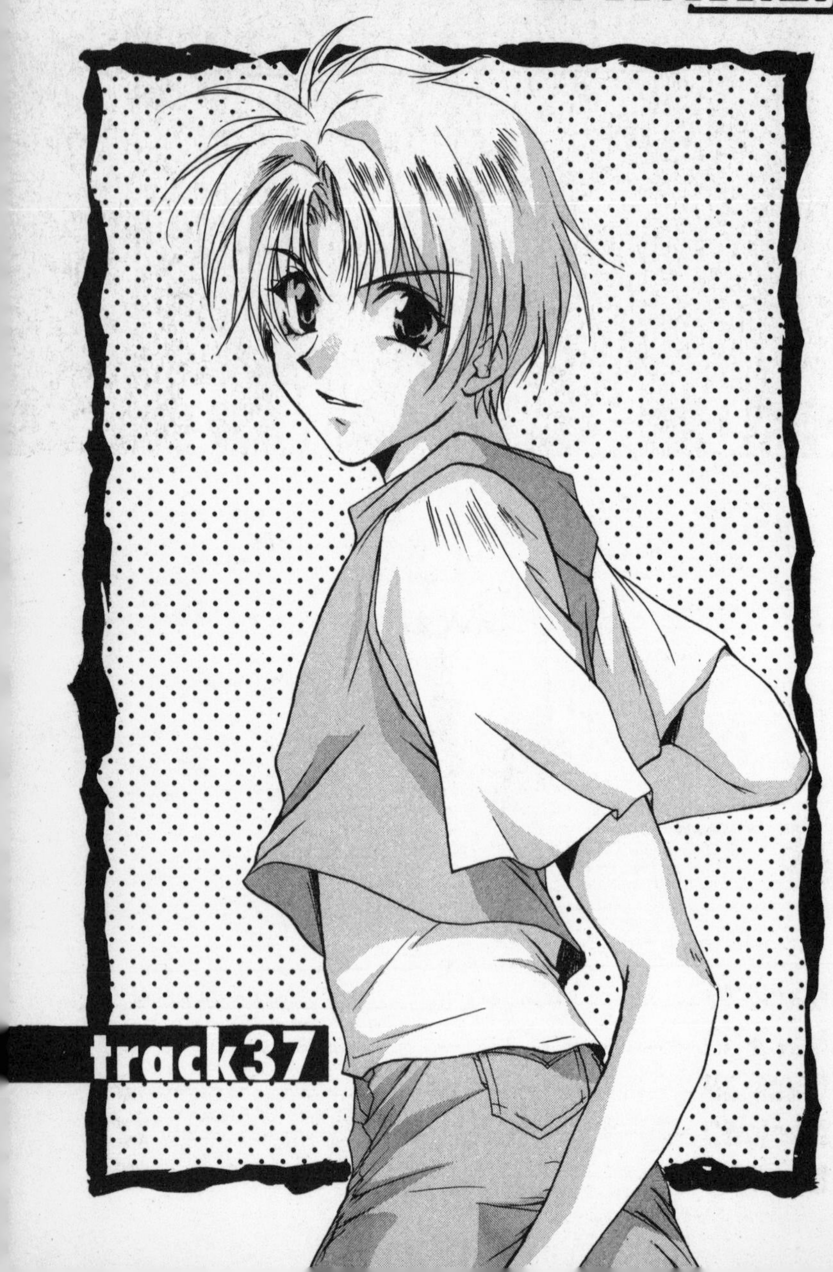

track 37

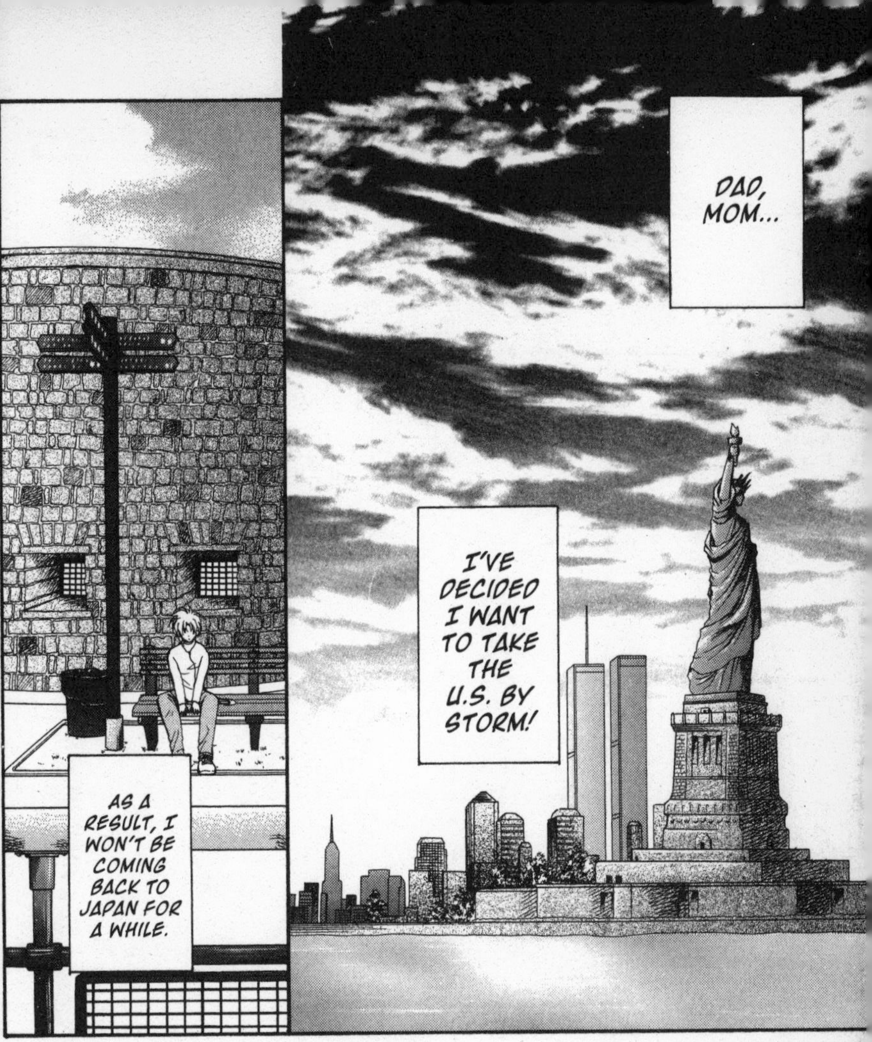
DAD, MOM...
I'VE DECIDED I WANT TO TAKE THE U.S. BY STORM!
AS A RESULT, I WON'T BE COMING BACK TO JAPAN FOR A WHILE.

ABOUT GRAVITATION TRACK 37

Hello, everyone. Long time no see. Welcome to the rather ominous ninth volume of the boy-loves-boy manga I like to call *Gravitation*. We are in the New York phase now. I know it *sounds* cool, but trust me, it isn't all that and a bag of chips. As usual, I'm having my butt saved by my fabulous assistants. It's almost as if I'm their assistant and not the other way around. That strange girl Reiji, who showed up at the end of volume 8, is going to play a big role in volume 9. Have you gotten used to Shindou's blonde hair yet? This is Murakami Maki, the queen of debt, the queen of homeowner troubles, always relying on the fabulous artistic talent of my assistants, delivering to you, volume 9. (I guess nobody needs to care about my drawings...)

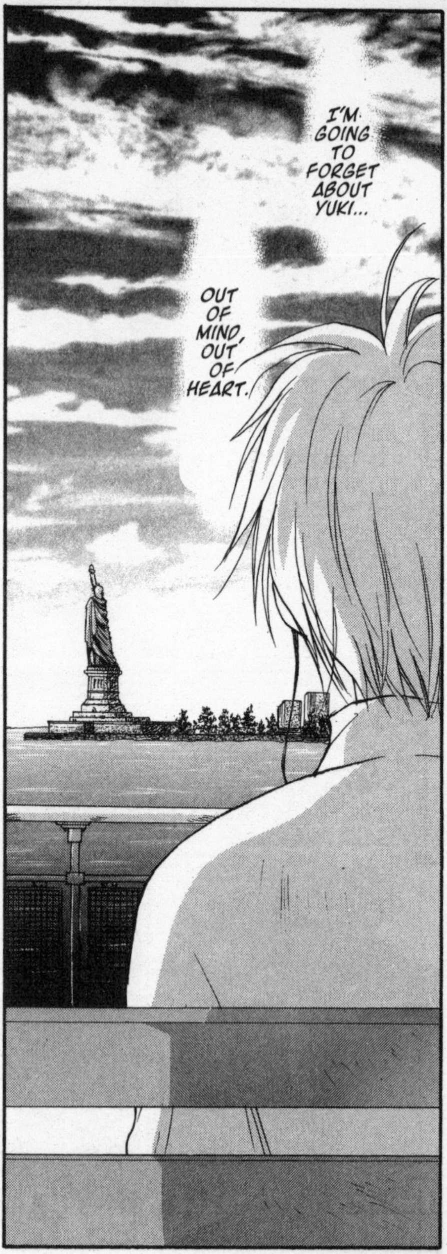
I'M GOING TO FORGET ABOUT YUKI...
OUT OF MIND, OUT OF HEART.

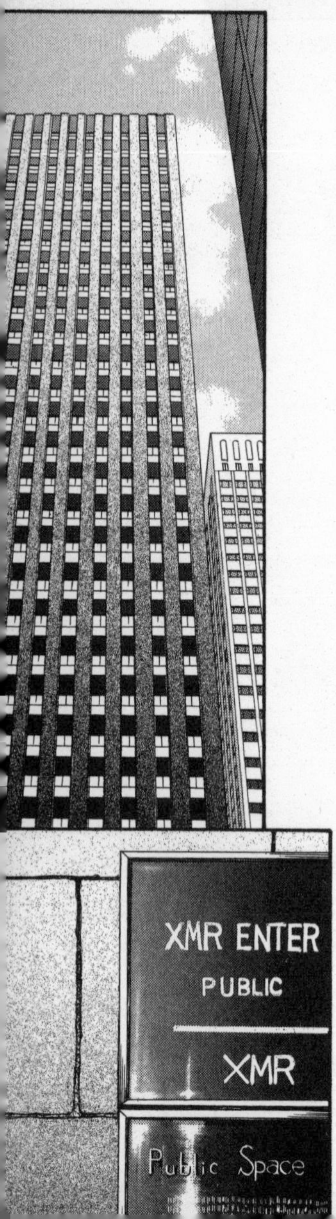
XMR ENTER
PUBLIC
XMR
Public Space

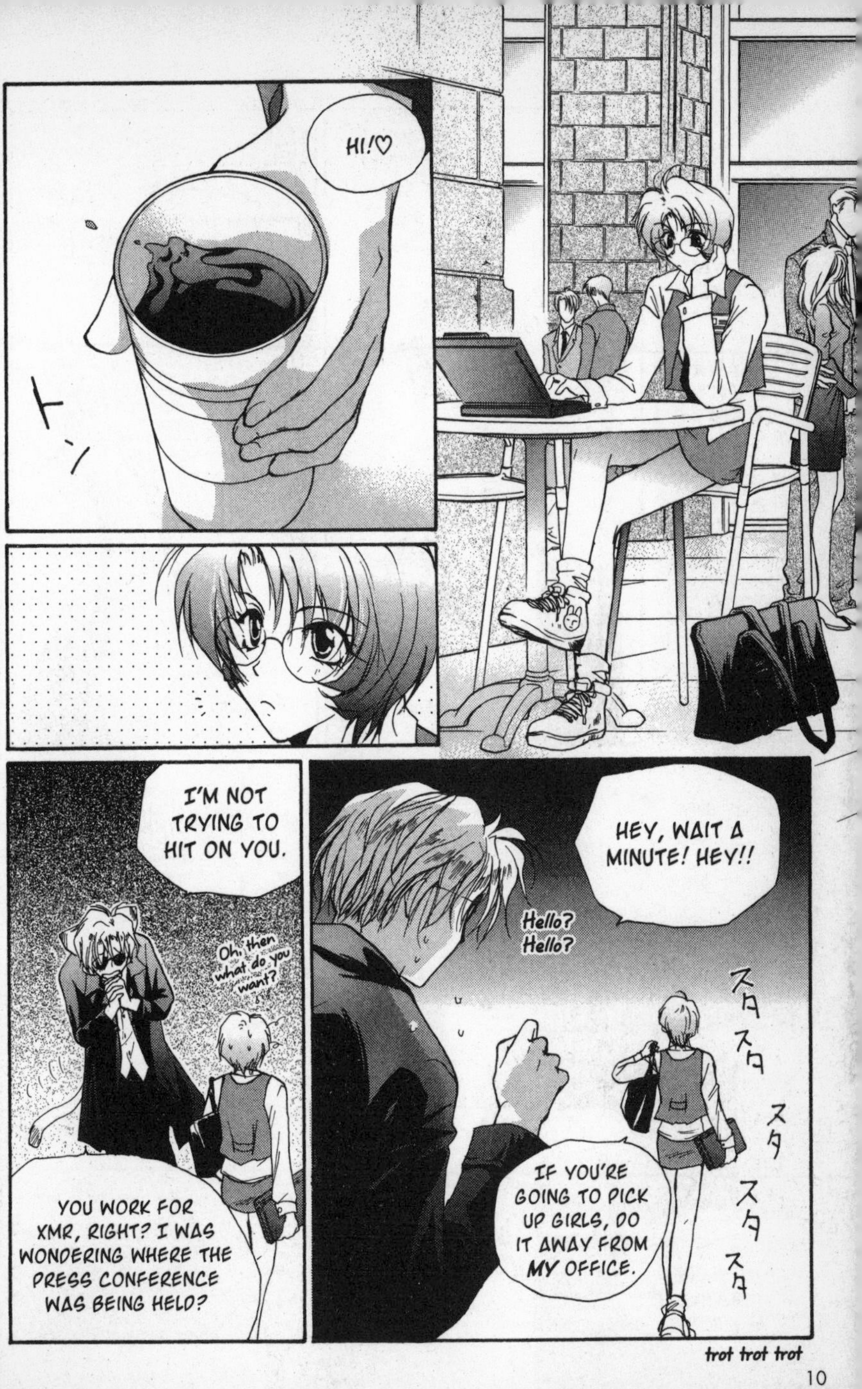
HI!♡
トン
HEY, WAIT A MINUTE! HEY!!
Hello? Hello?
スタ スタ スタ スタ スタ
IF YOU'RE GOING TO PICK UP GIRLS, DO IT AWAY FROM MY OFFICE.
I'M NOT TRYING TO HIT ON YOU.
Oh, then what do you want?
YOU WORK FOR XMR, RIGHT? I WAS WONDERING WHERE THE PRESS CONFERENCE WAS BEING HELD?
trot trot trot

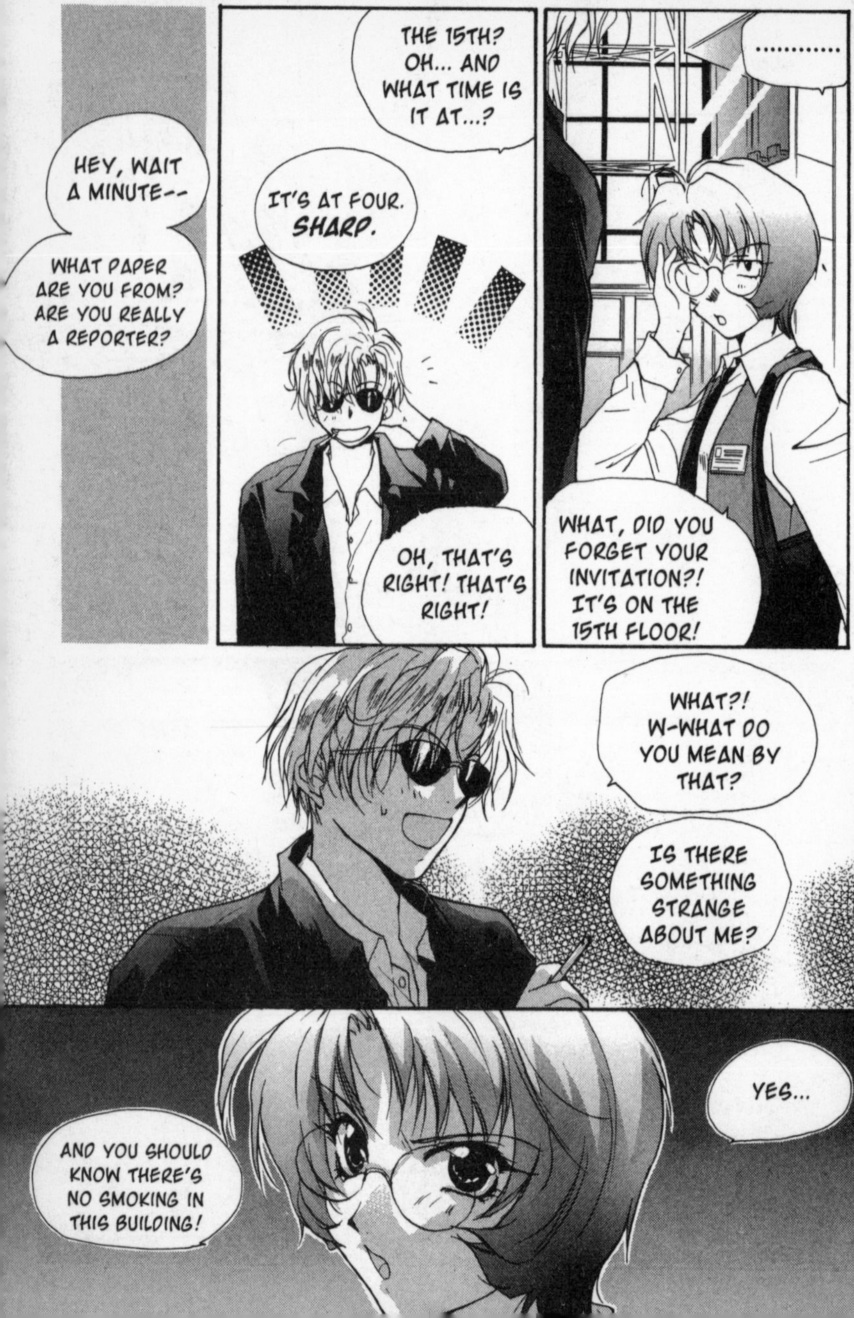
....
WHAT, DID YOU FORGET YOUR INVITATION?! IT'S ON THE 15TH FLOOR!
THE 15TH? OH... AND WHAT TIME IS IT AT...?
IT'S AT FOUR. SHARP.
OH, THAT'S RIGHT! THAT'S RIGHT!
HEY, WAIT A MINUTE--
WHAT PAPER ARE YOU FROM? ARE YOU REALLY A REPORTER?
WHAT?! W-WHAT DO YOU MEAN BY THAT?
IS THERE SOMETHING STRANGE ABOUT ME?
YES...
AND YOU SHOULD KNOW THERE'S NO SMOKING IN THIS BUILDING!

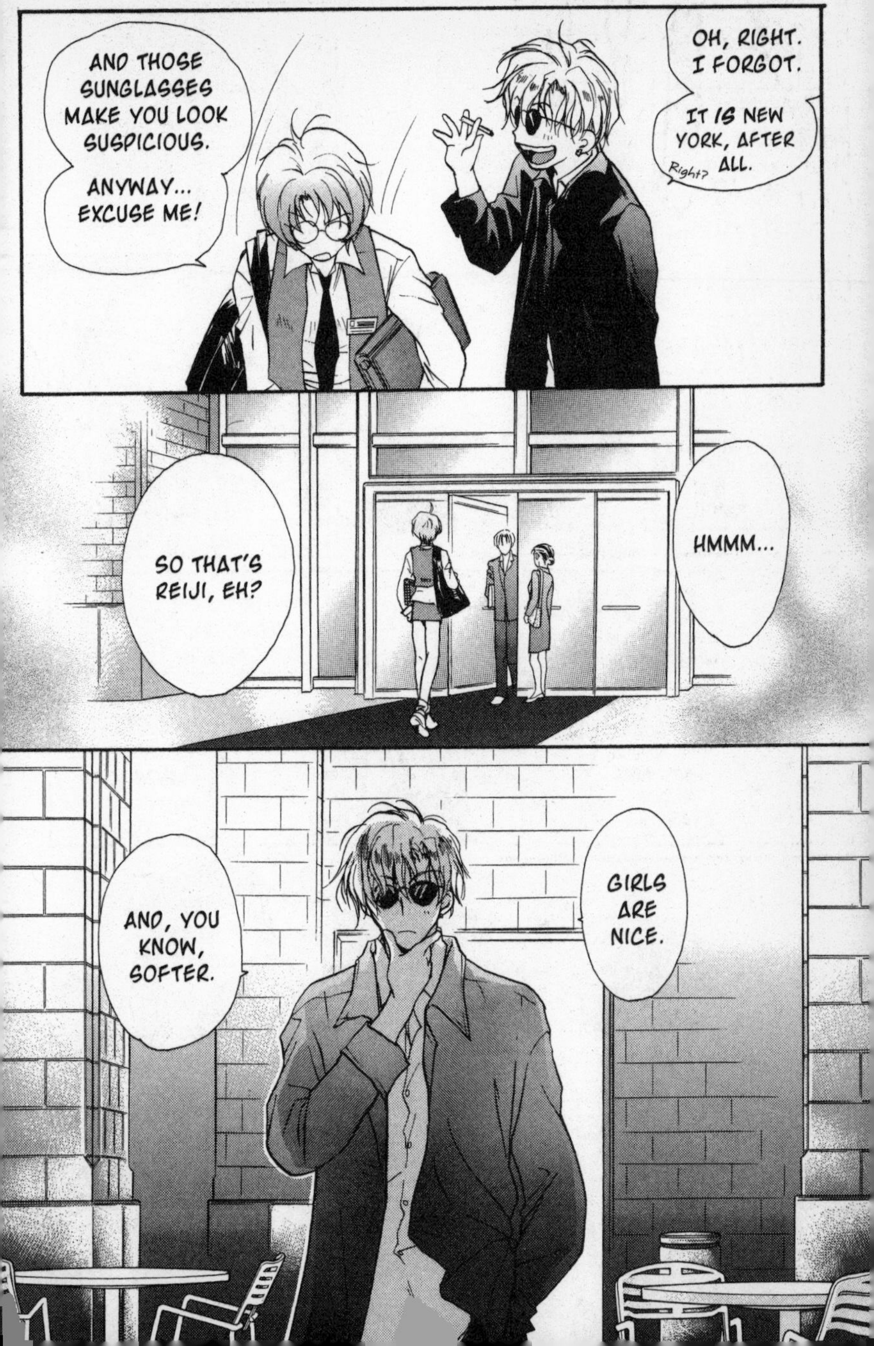
OH, RIGHT. I FORGOT.
IT IS NEW YORK, AFTER ALL.
Right?
AND THOSE SUNGLASSES MAKE YOU LOOK SUSPICIOUS.
ANYWAY... EXCUSE ME!
HMMM...
SO THAT'S REIJI, EH?
GIRLS ARE NICE.
AND, YOU KNOW, SOFTER.

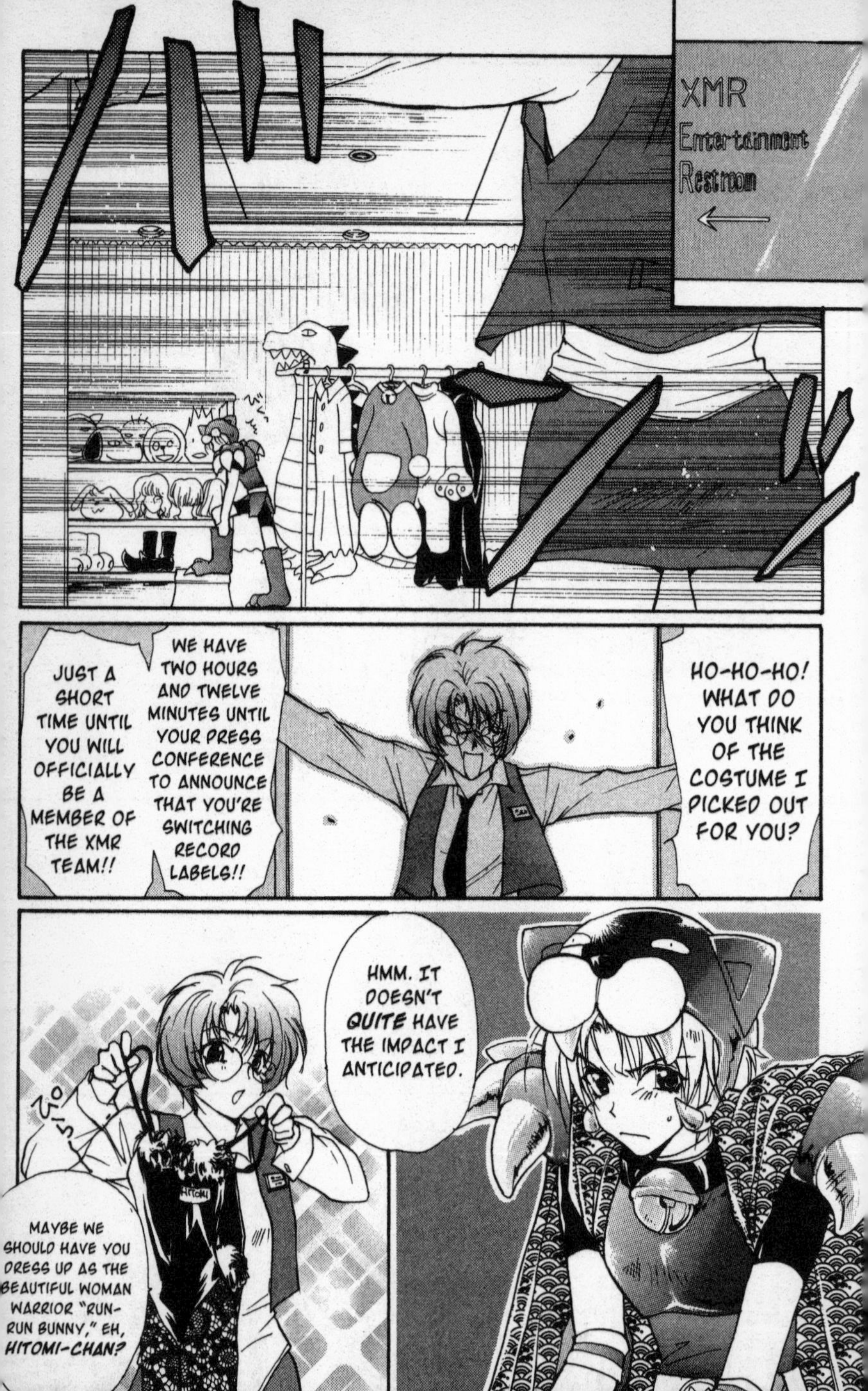
XMR
Entertainment
Restroom
HO-HO-HO! WHAT DO YOU THINK OF THE COSTUME I PICKED OUT FOR YOU?
WE HAVE TWO HOURS AND TWELVE MINUTES UNTIL YOUR PRESS CONFERENCE TO ANNOUNCE THAT YOU'RE SWITCHING RECORD LABELS!!
JUST A SHORT TIME UNTIL YOU WILL OFFICIALLY BE A MEMBER OF THE XMR TEAM!!
HMM. IT DOESN'T *QUITE* HAVE THE IMPACT I ANTICIPATED.
MAYBE WE SHOULD HAVE YOU DRESS UP AS THE BEAUTIFUL WOMAN WARRIOR "RUN-RUN BUNNY," EH, *HITOMI-CHAN*?

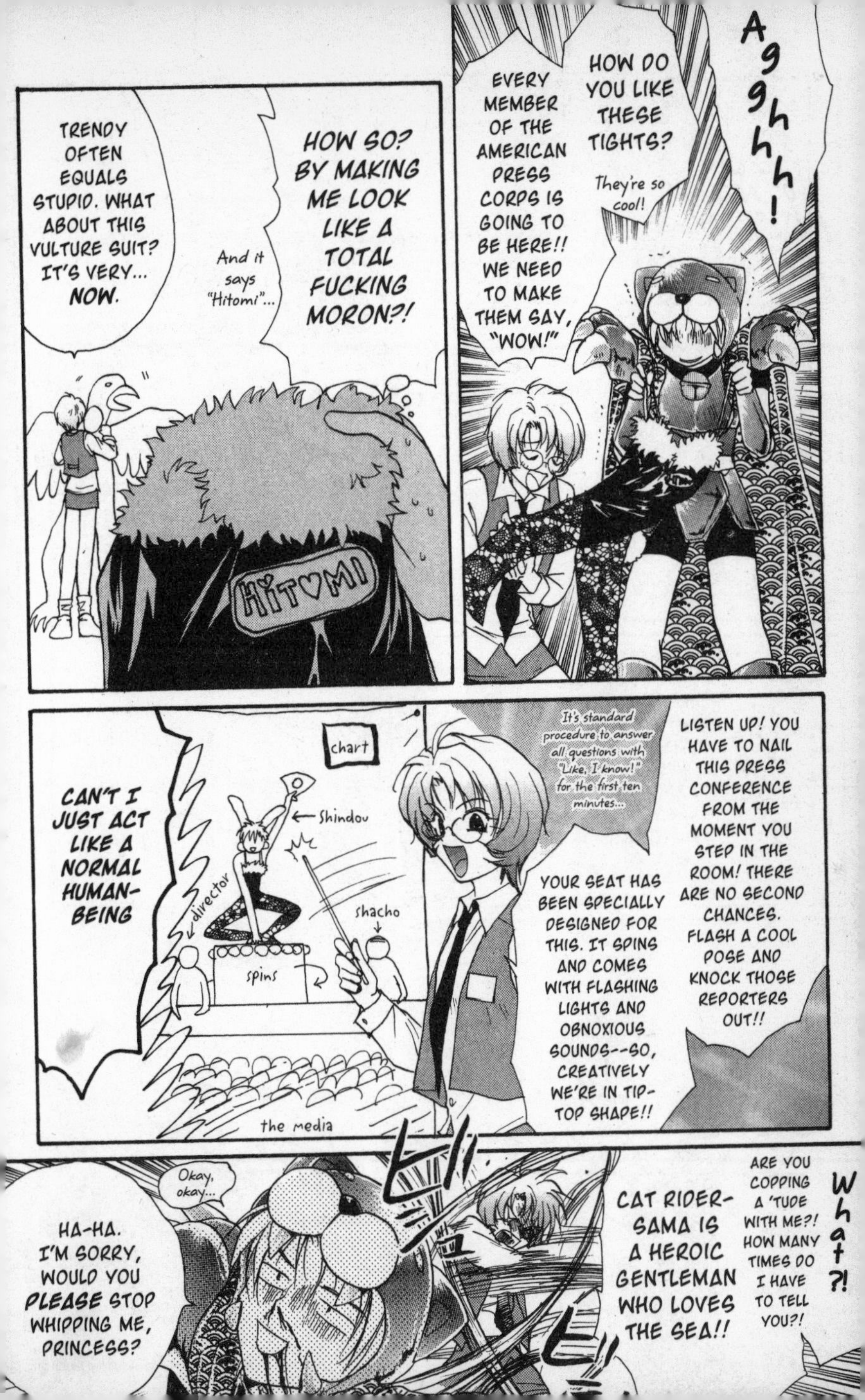
Agghhh!
HOW DO YOU LIKE THESE TIGHTS?
They're so cool!
EVERY MEMBER OF THE AMERICAN PRESS CORPS IS GOING TO BE HERE!! WE NEED TO MAKE THEM SAY, "WOW!"
HOW SO? BY MAKING ME LOOK LIKE A TOTAL FUCKING MORON?!
And it says "Hitomi"...
TRENDY OFTEN EQUALS STUPID. WHAT ABOUT THIS VULTURE SUIT? IT'S VERY... NOW.
HITOMI
LISTEN UP! YOU HAVE TO NAIL THIS PRESS CONFERENCE FROM THE MOMENT YOU STEP IN THE ROOM! THERE ARE NO SECOND CHANCES. FLASH A COOL POSE AND KNOCK THOSE REPORTERS OUT!!
It's standard procedure to answer all questions with "Like, I know!" for the first ten minutes...
YOUR SEAT HAS BEEN SPECIALLY DESIGNED FOR THIS. IT SPINS AND COMES WITH FLASHING LIGHTS AND OBNOXIOUS SOUNDS--SO, CREATIVELY WE'RE IN TIP-TOP SHAPE!!
chart
Shindou
shacho
director
spins
the media
CAN'T I JUST ACT LIKE A NORMAL HUMAN-BEING
What?!
ARE YOU COPPING A 'TUDE WITH ME?! HOW MANY TIMES DO I HAVE TO TELL YOU?!
CAT RIDER-SAMA IS A HEROIC GENTLEMAN WHO LOVES THE SEA!!
Okay, okay...
HA-HA. I'M SORRY, WOULD YOU PLEASE STOP WHIPPING ME, PRINCESS?

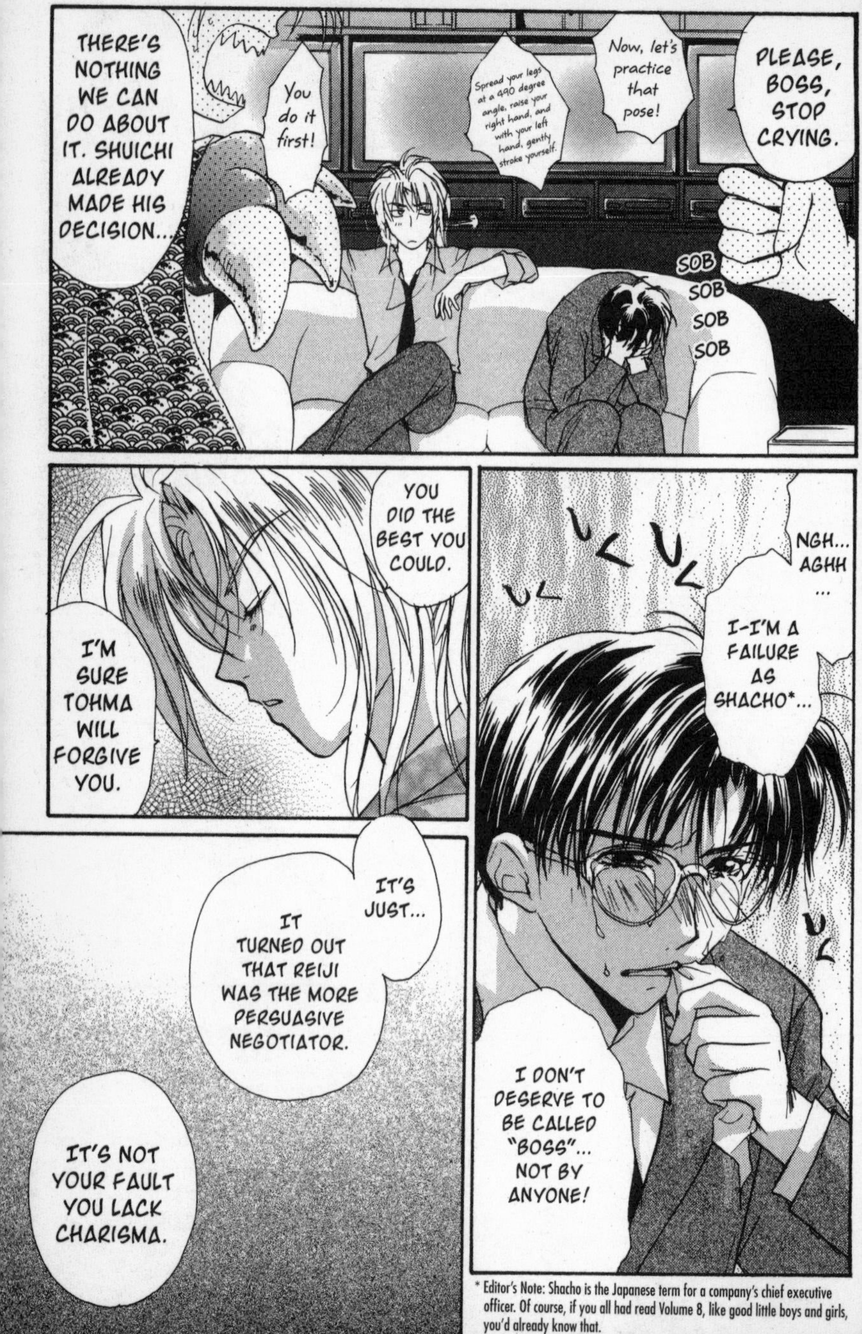
PLEASE, BOSS, STOP CRYING.
SOB SOB SOB SOB
Now, let's practice that pose!
Spread your legs at a 490 degree angle, raise your right hand, and with your left hand, gently stroke yourself.
You do it first!
THERE'S NOTHING WE CAN DO ABOUT IT. SHUICHI ALREADY MADE HIS DECISION...
NGH... AGHH ...
I-I'M A FAILURE AS SHACHO*...
I DON'T DESERVE TO BE CALLED "BOSS"... NOT BY ANYONE!
YOU DID THE BEST YOU COULD.
I'M SURE TOHMA WILL FORGIVE YOU.
IT'S JUST...
IT TURNED OUT THAT REIJI WAS THE MORE PERSUASIVE NEGOTIATOR.
IT'S NOT YOUR FAULT YOU LACK CHARISMA.

* Editor's Note: Shacho is the Japanese term for a company's chief executive officer. Of course, if you all had read Volume 8, like good little boys and girls, you'd already know that.

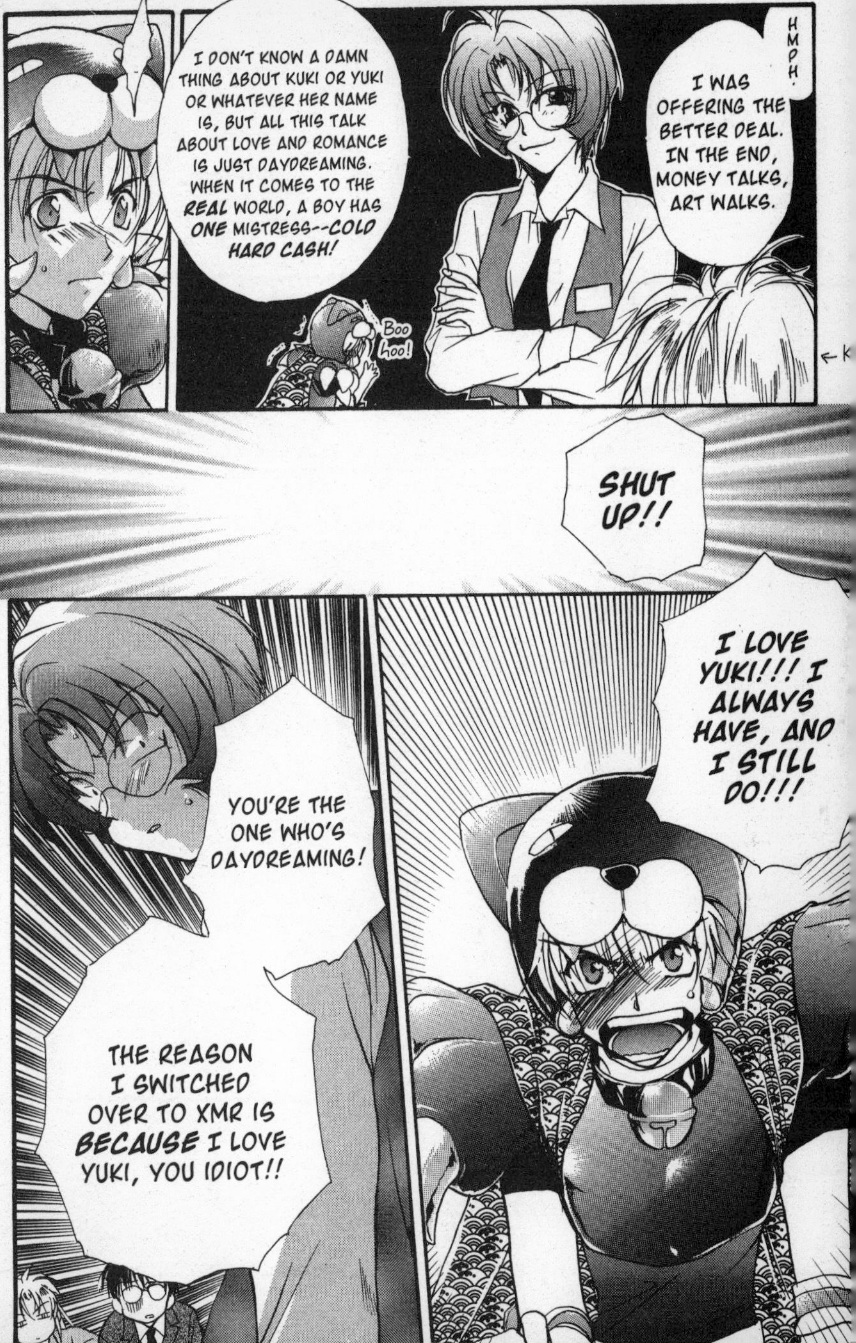
HMPH.
I WAS OFFERING THE BETTER DEAL. IN THE END, MONEY TALKS, ART WALKS.
I DON'T KNOW A DAMN THING ABOUT KUKI OR YUKI OR WHATEVER HER NAME IS, BUT ALL THIS TALK ABOUT LOVE AND ROMANCE IS JUST DAYDREAMING. WHEN IT COMES TO THE *REAL* WORLD, A BOY HAS *ONE* MISTRESS--*COLD HARD CASH!*
Boo hoo!
SHUT UP!!
I LOVE YUKI!!! I ALWAYS HAVE, AND I STILL DO!!!
YOU'RE THE ONE WHO'S DAYDREAMING!
THE REASON I SWITCHED OVER TO XMR IS *BECAUSE* I LOVE YUKI, YOU IDIOT!!

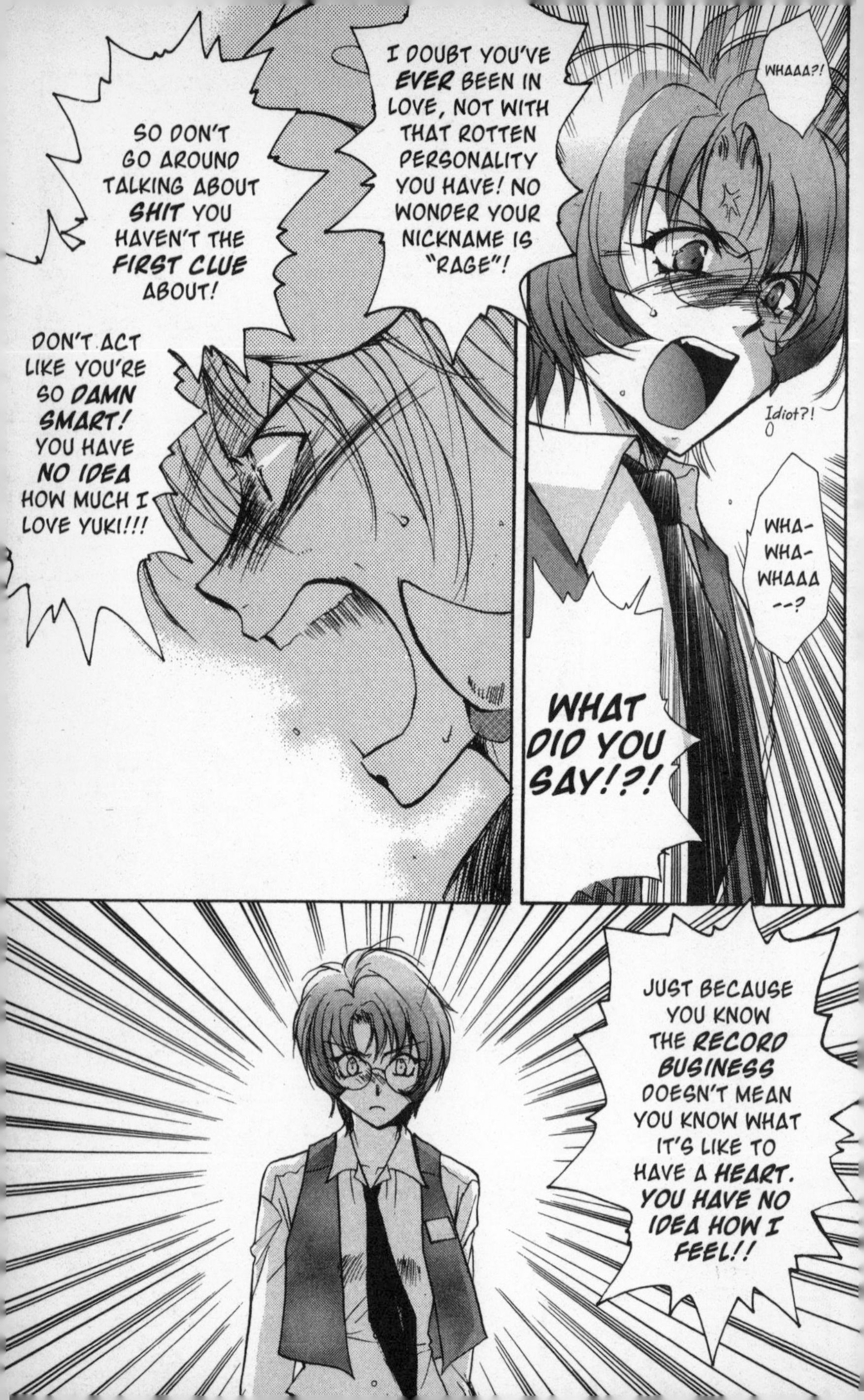

WHAAA?!
Idiot?!
WHA-WHA-WHAAA--?
WHAT DID YOU SAY!?!
I DOUBT YOU'VE EVER BEEN IN LOVE, NOT WITH THAT ROTTEN PERSONALITY YOU HAVE! NO WONDER YOUR NICKNAME IS "RAGE"!
SO DON'T GO AROUND TALKING ABOUT SHIT YOU HAVEN'T THE FIRST CLUE ABOUT!
DON'T ACT LIKE YOU'RE SO DAMN SMART! YOU HAVE NO IDEA HOW MUCH I LOVE YUKI!!!
JUST BECAUSE YOU KNOW THE RECORD BUSINESS DOESN'T MEAN YOU KNOW WHAT IT'S LIKE TO HAVE A HEART. YOU HAVE NO IDEA HOW I FEEL!!

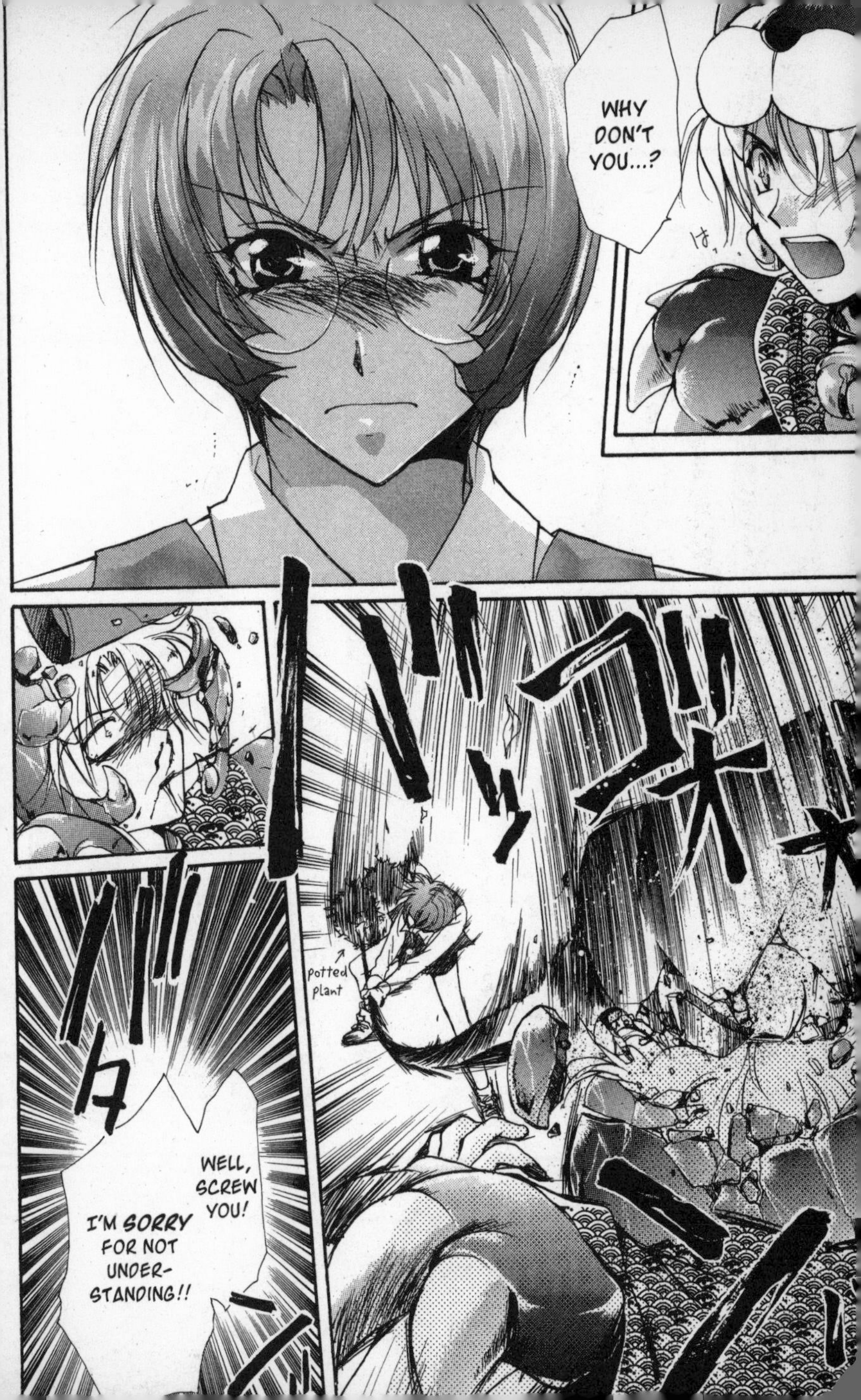
WHY DON'T YOU...?
は、
potted plant
WELL, SCREW YOU!
I'M **SORRY** FOR NOT UNDER-STANDING!!

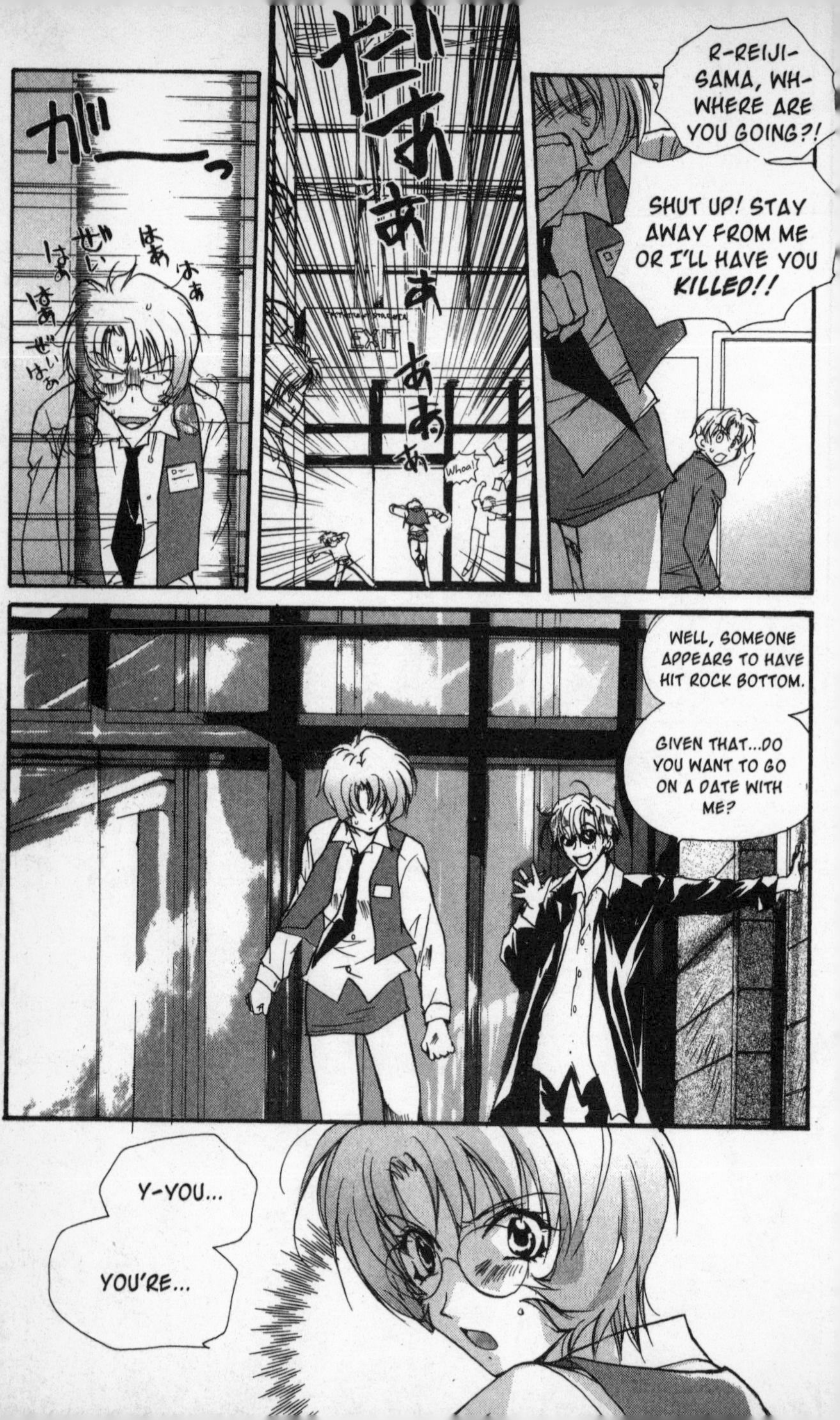
R-REIJI-SAMA, WH-WHERE ARE YOU GOING?!
SHUT UP! STAY AWAY FROM ME OR I'LL HAVE YOU KILLED!!
EXIT
Whoa!
WELL, SOMEONE APPEARS TO HAVE HIT ROCK BOTTOM.
GIVEN THAT...DO YOU WANT TO GO ON A DATE WITH ME?
Y-YOU...
YOU'RE...

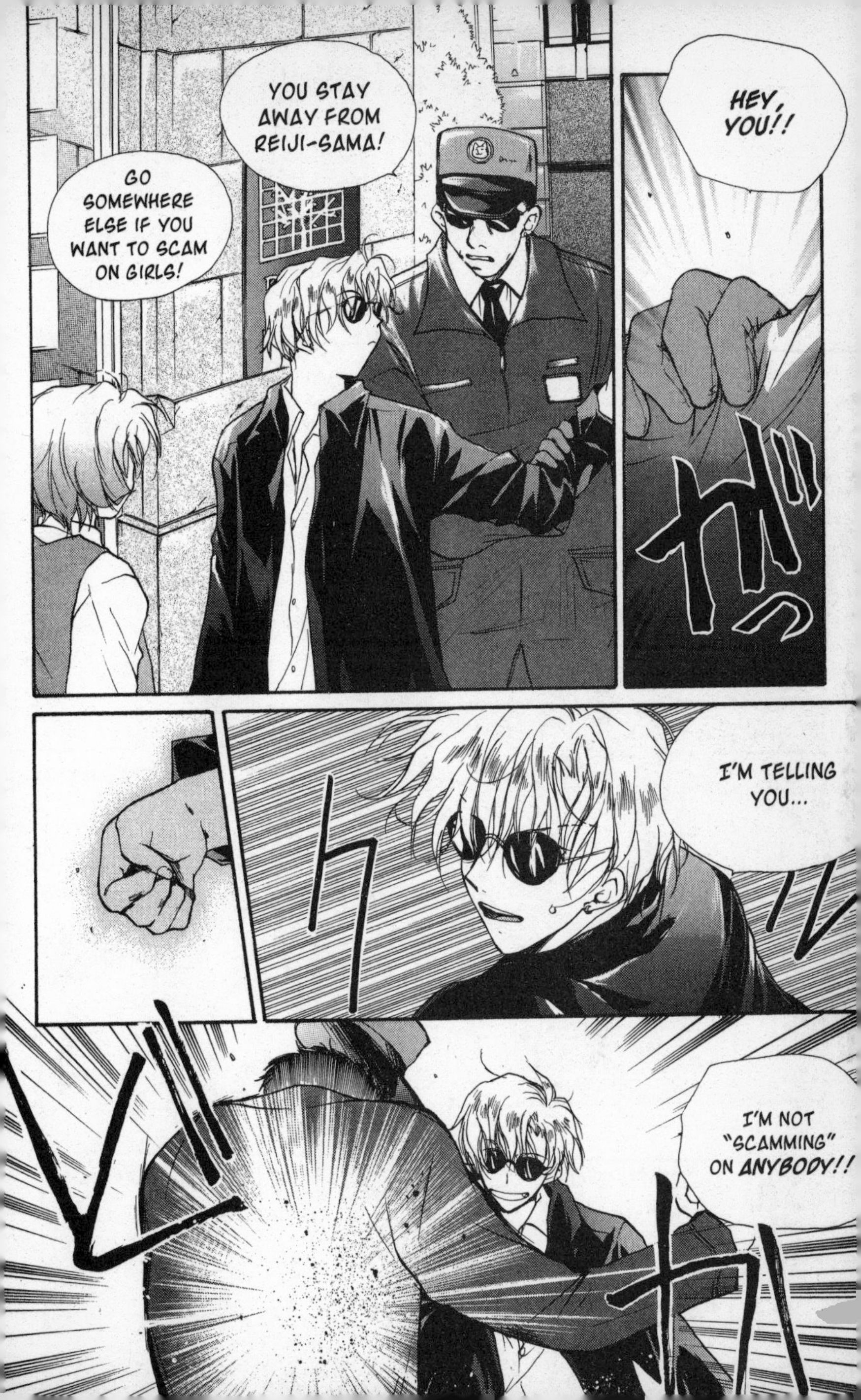
HEY, YOU!!
ガッ
YOU STAY AWAY FROM REIJI-SAMA!
GO SOMEWHERE ELSE IF YOU WANT TO SCAM ON GIRLS!
I'M TELLING YOU...
I'M NOT "SCAMMING" ON ANYBODY!!

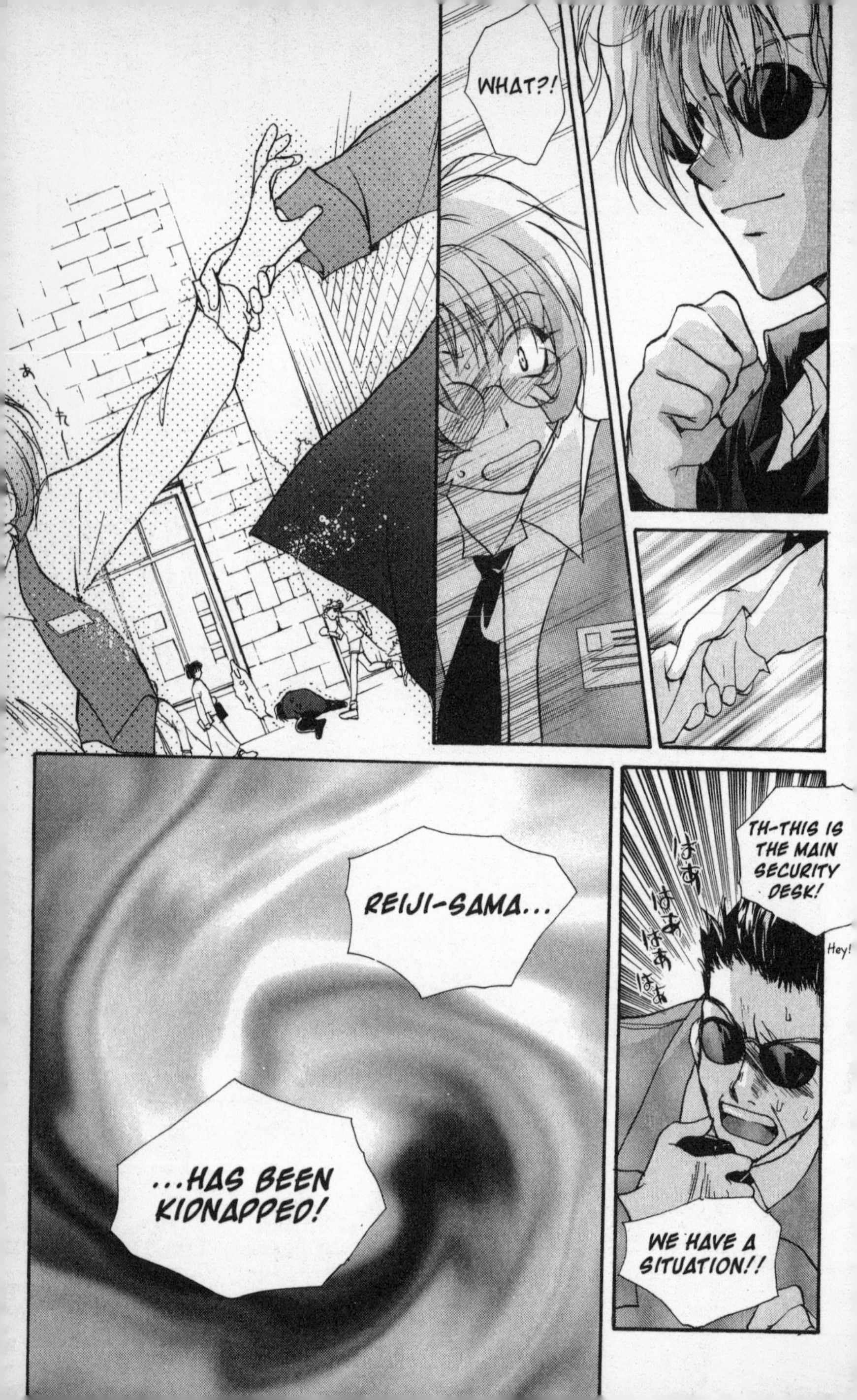
WHAT?!
TH-THIS IS THE MAIN SECURITY DESK!
Hey!
WE HAVE A SITUATION!!
REIJI-SAMA...
...HAS BEEN KIDNAPPED!

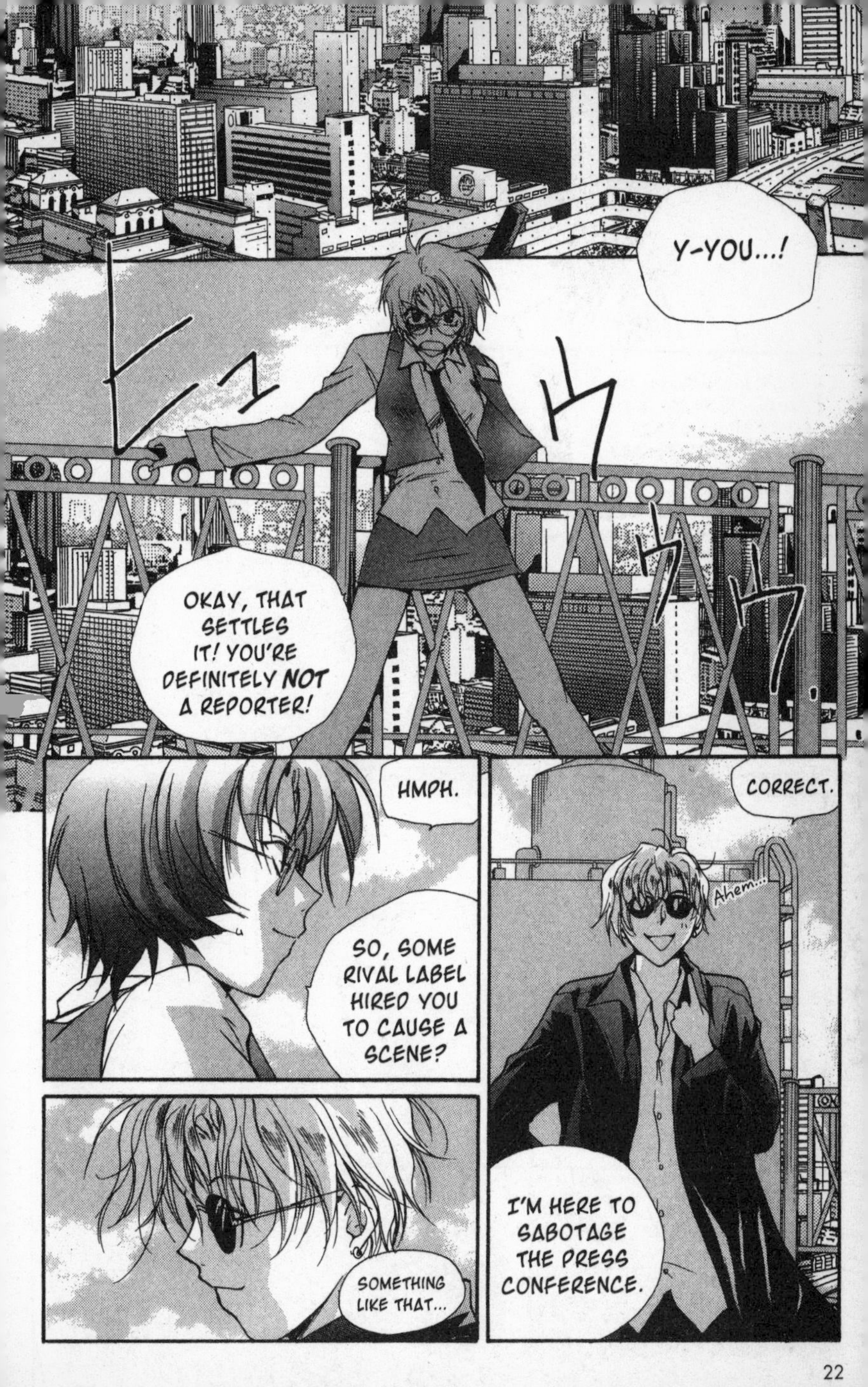
Y-YOU...!
OKAY, THAT SETTLES IT! YOU'RE DEFINITELY **NOT** A REPORTER!
CORRECT.
Ahem...
I'M HERE TO SABOTAGE THE PRESS CONFERENCE.
HMPH.
SO, SOME RIVAL LABEL HIRED YOU TO CAUSE A SCENE?
SOMETHING LIKE THAT...

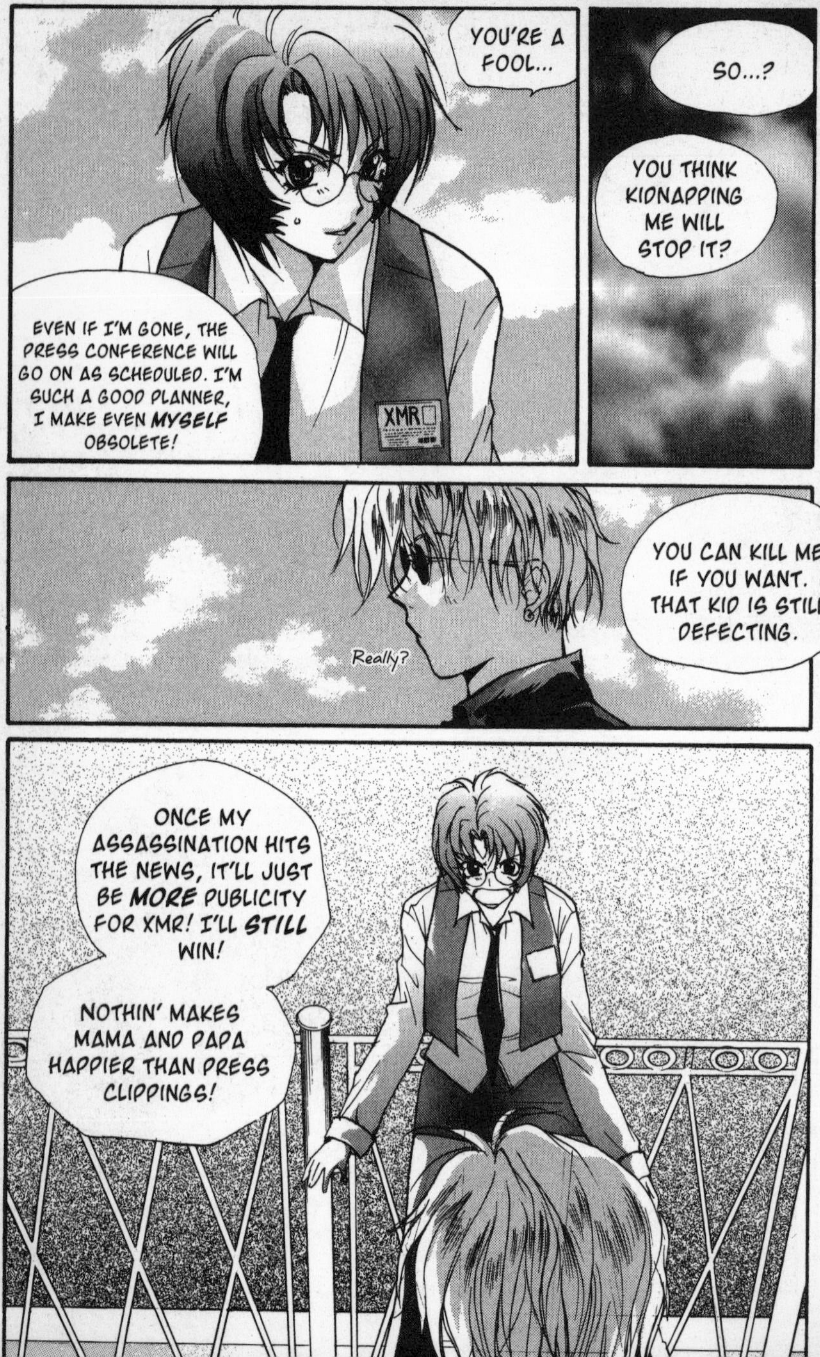
SO...?
YOU THINK KIDNAPPING ME WILL STOP IT?
YOU'RE A FOOL...
XMR
EVEN IF I'M GONE, THE PRESS CONFERENCE WILL GO ON AS SCHEDULED. I'M SUCH A GOOD PLANNER, I MAKE EVEN *MYSELF* OBSOLETE!
YOU CAN KILL ME IF YOU WANT. THAT KID IS STILL DEFECTING.
Really?
ONCE MY ASSASSINATION HITS THE NEWS, IT'LL JUST BE *MORE* PUBLICITY FOR XMR! I'LL *STILL* WIN!
NOTHIN' MAKES MAMA AND PAPA HAPPIER THAN PRESS CLIPPINGS!

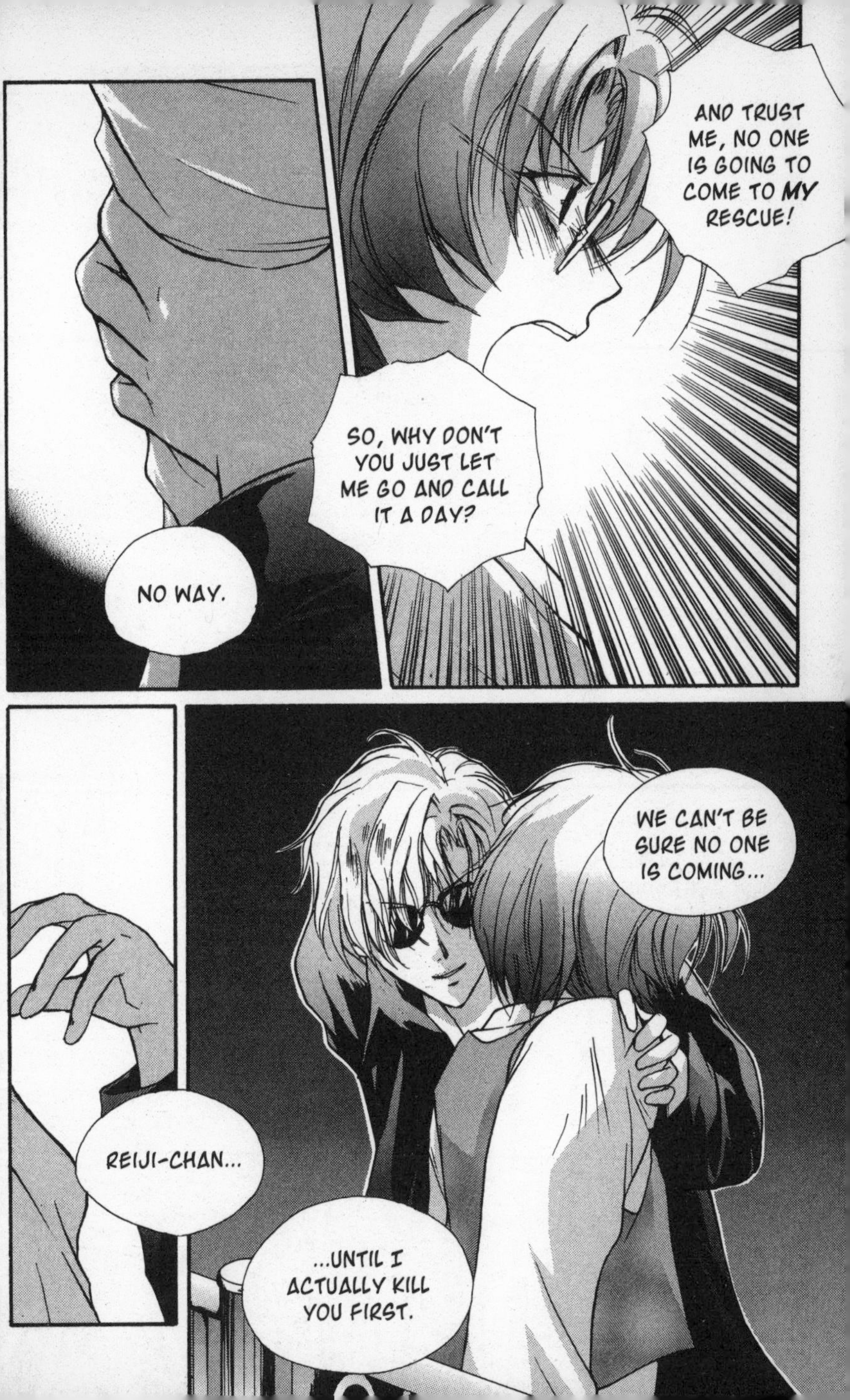
AND TRUST ME, NO ONE IS GOING TO COME TO MY RESCUE!
SO, WHY DON'T YOU JUST LET ME GO AND CALL IT A DAY?
NO WAY.
WE CAN'T BE SURE NO ONE IS COMING...
...UNTIL I ACTUALLY KILL YOU FIRST.
REIJI-CHAN...

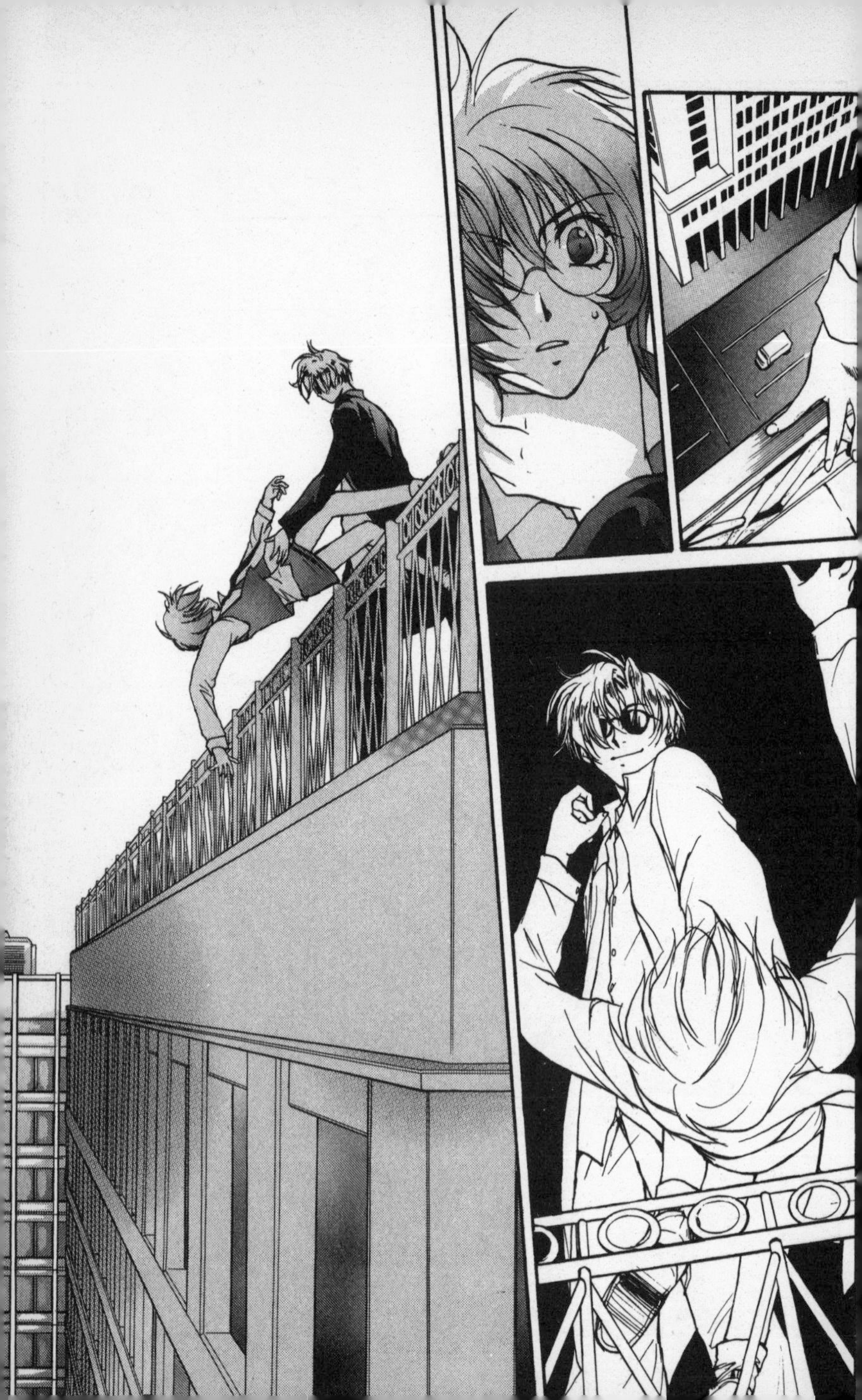

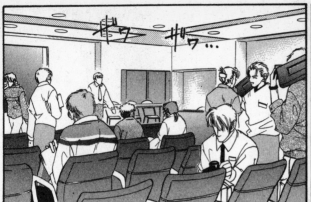

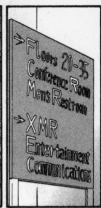

>Floors 20-35
Conference Room
Men's Restroom
>XMR
Entertainment
Communications
ザワ ザワ…
HMM, LOOKS LIKE A FULL HOUSE.
I GUESS XMR HAS A LOT OF JUICE.
YEAH...
THIS IS ALL GOING BETTER THAN EXPECTED. NOW ALL I HAVE TO DO IS SCORE A TIE-IN COMMERCIAL STARRING YOUR WIFE, AND I'LL BE IN THE BIG TIME.
HA-HA-HA! DON'T WORRY, I'LL SET YOU UP WITH MY WIFE!
ぽ～んっ
OWWW!

SLAP!

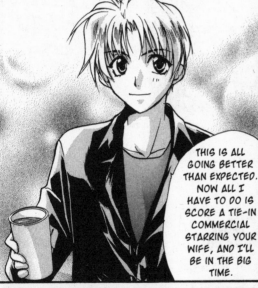

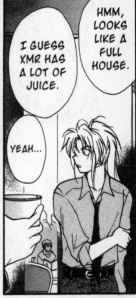

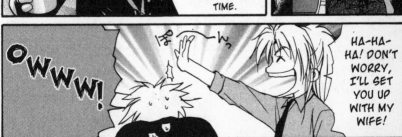

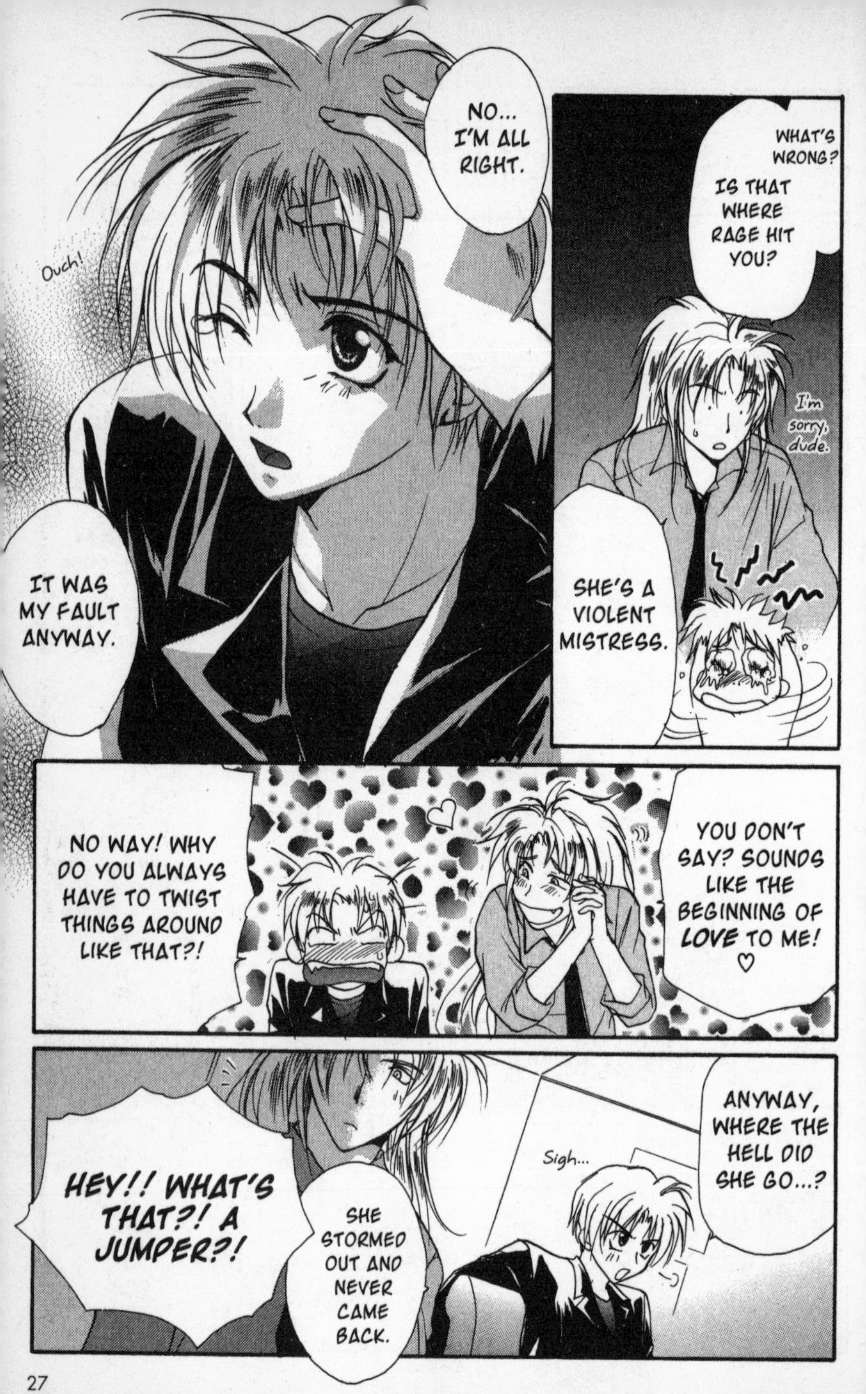
WHAT'S WRONG?
IS THAT WHERE RAGE HIT YOU?
I'm sorry, dude.
SHE'S A VIOLENT MISTRESS.
NO... I'M ALL RIGHT.
Ouch!
IT WAS MY FAULT ANYWAY.
YOU DON'T SAY? SOUNDS LIKE THE BEGINNING OF LOVE TO ME! ♡
NO WAY! WHY DO YOU ALWAYS HAVE TO TWIST THINGS AROUND LIKE THAT?!
ANYWAY, WHERE THE HELL DID SHE GO...?
Sigh...
SHE STORMED OUT AND NEVER CAME BACK.
HEY!! WHAT'S THAT?! A JUMPER?!

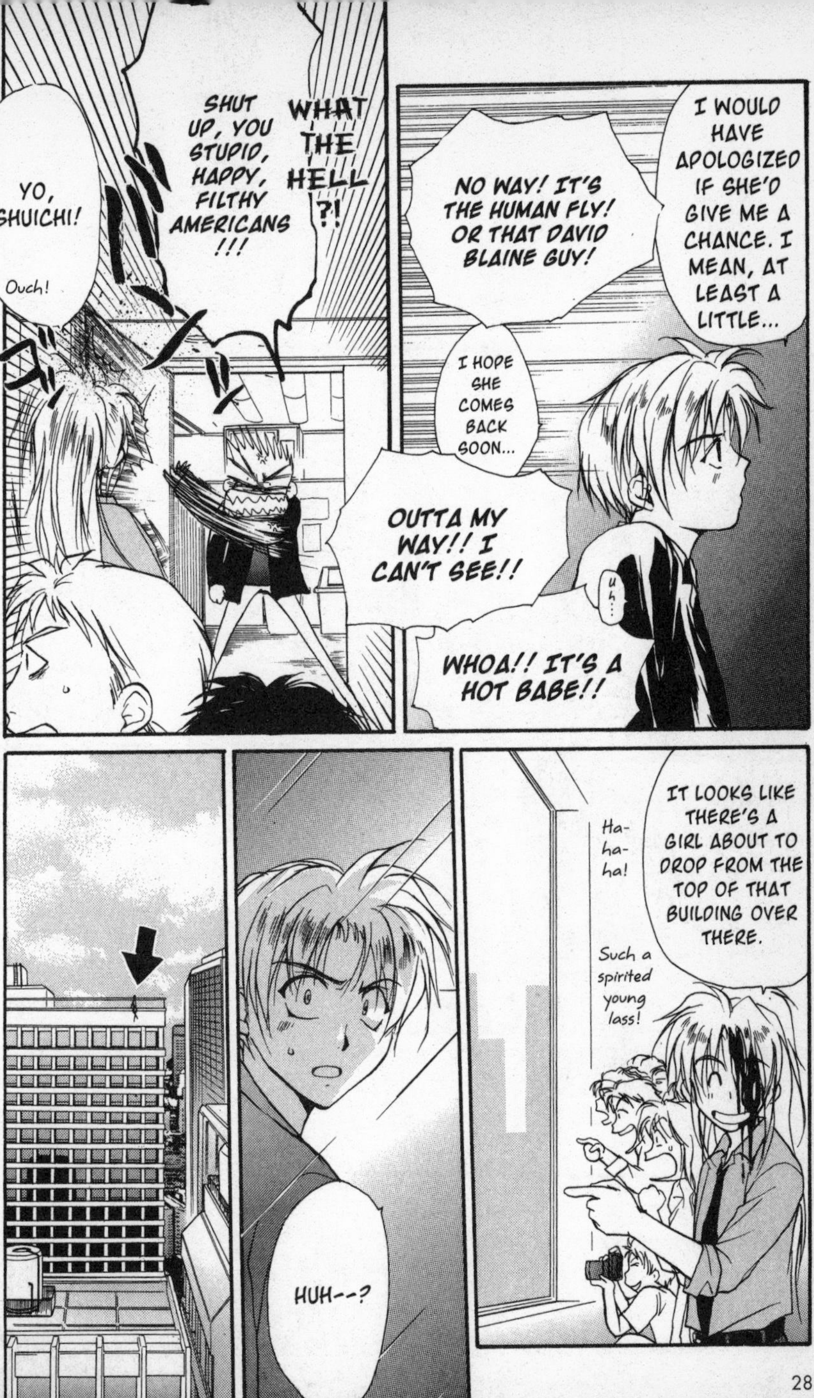
I WOULD HAVE APOLOGIZED IF SHE'D GIVE ME A CHANCE. I MEAN, AT LEAST A LITTLE...
NO WAY! IT'S THE HUMAN FLY! OR THAT DAVID BLAINE GUY!
I HOPE SHE COMES BACK SOON...
OUTTA MY WAY!! I CAN'T SEE!!
uh...
WHOA!! IT'S A HOT BABE!!
WHAT THE HELL ?!
SHUT UP, YOU STUPID, HAPPY, FILTHY AMERICANS !!!
YO, SHUICHI!
Ouch!
IT LOOKS LIKE THERE'S A GIRL ABOUT TO DROP FROM THE TOP OF THAT BUILDING OVER THERE.
Ha-ha-ha!
Such a spirited young lass!
HUH--?

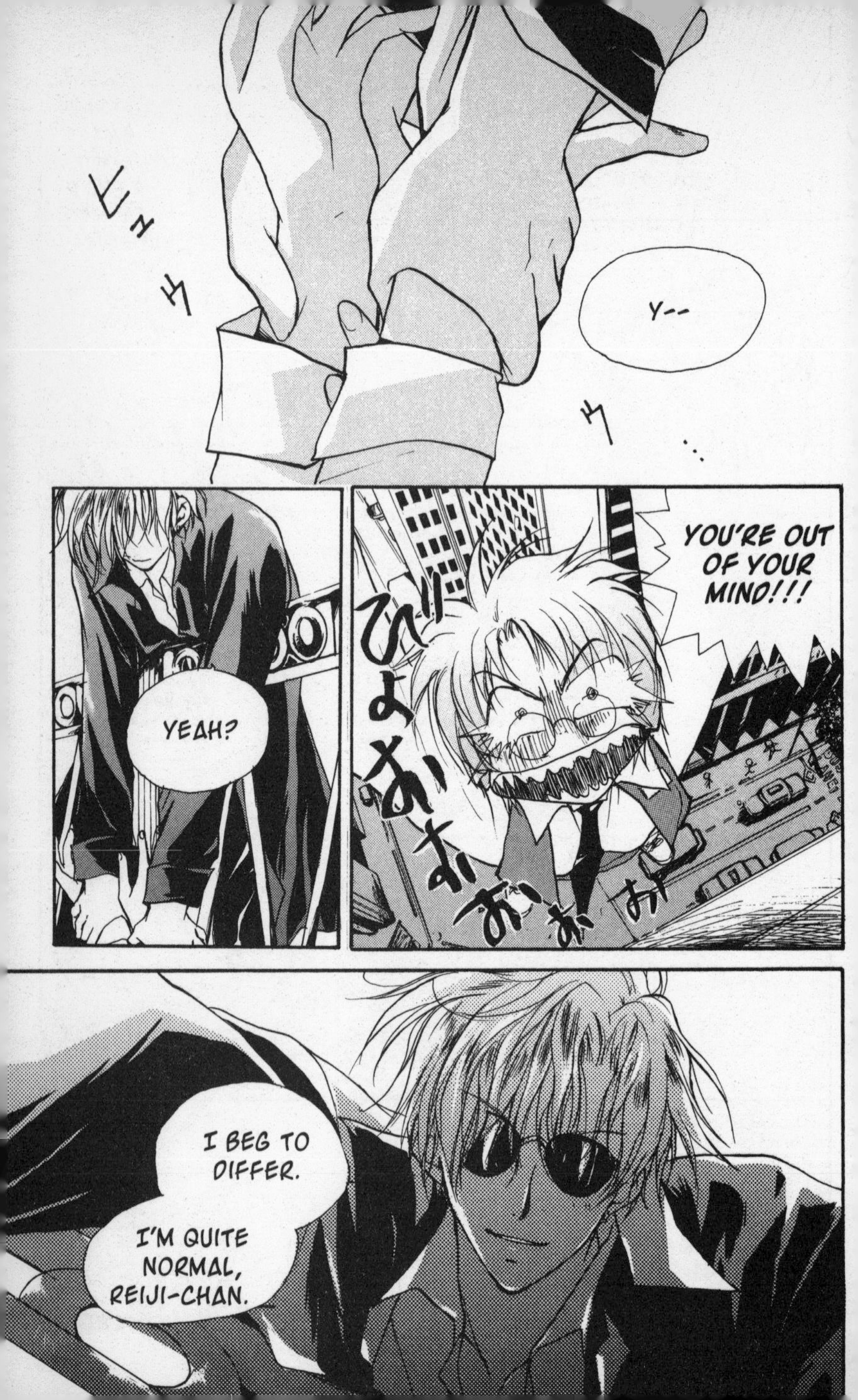
Y--
YOU'RE OUT OF YOUR MIND!!!
YEAH?
I BEG TO DIFFER.
I'M QUITE NORMAL, REIJI-CHAN.

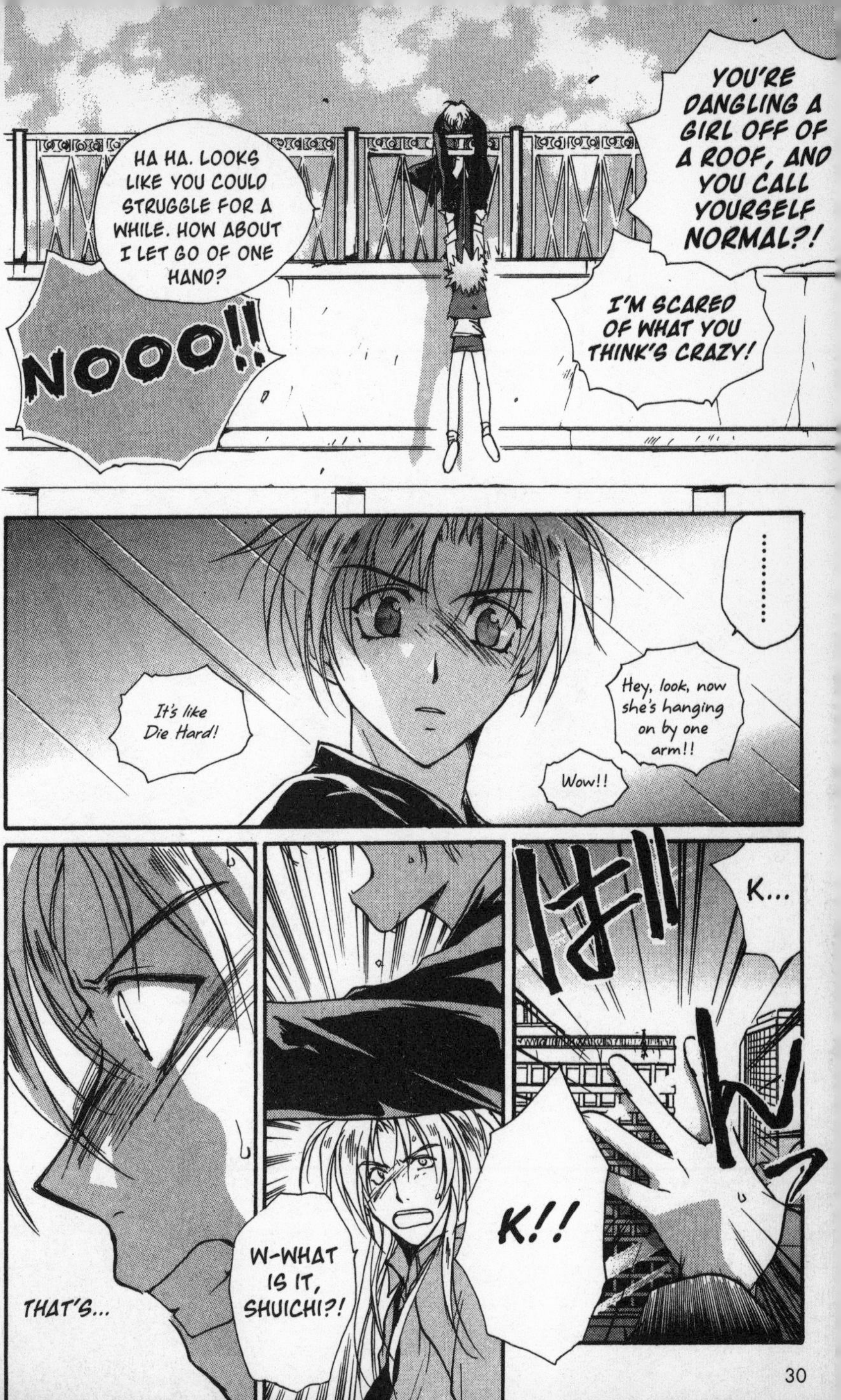
YOU'RE DANGLING A GIRL OFF OF A ROOF, AND YOU CALL YOURSELF NORMAL?!
HA HA. LOOKS LIKE YOU COULD STRUGGLE FOR A WHILE. HOW ABOUT I LET GO OF ONE HAND?
I'M SCARED OF WHAT YOU THINK'S CRAZY!
NOOO!!
......
Hey, look, now she's hanging on by one arm!!
Wow!!
It's like Die Hard!
K...
K!!
W-WHAT IS IT, SHUICHI?!
THAT'S...

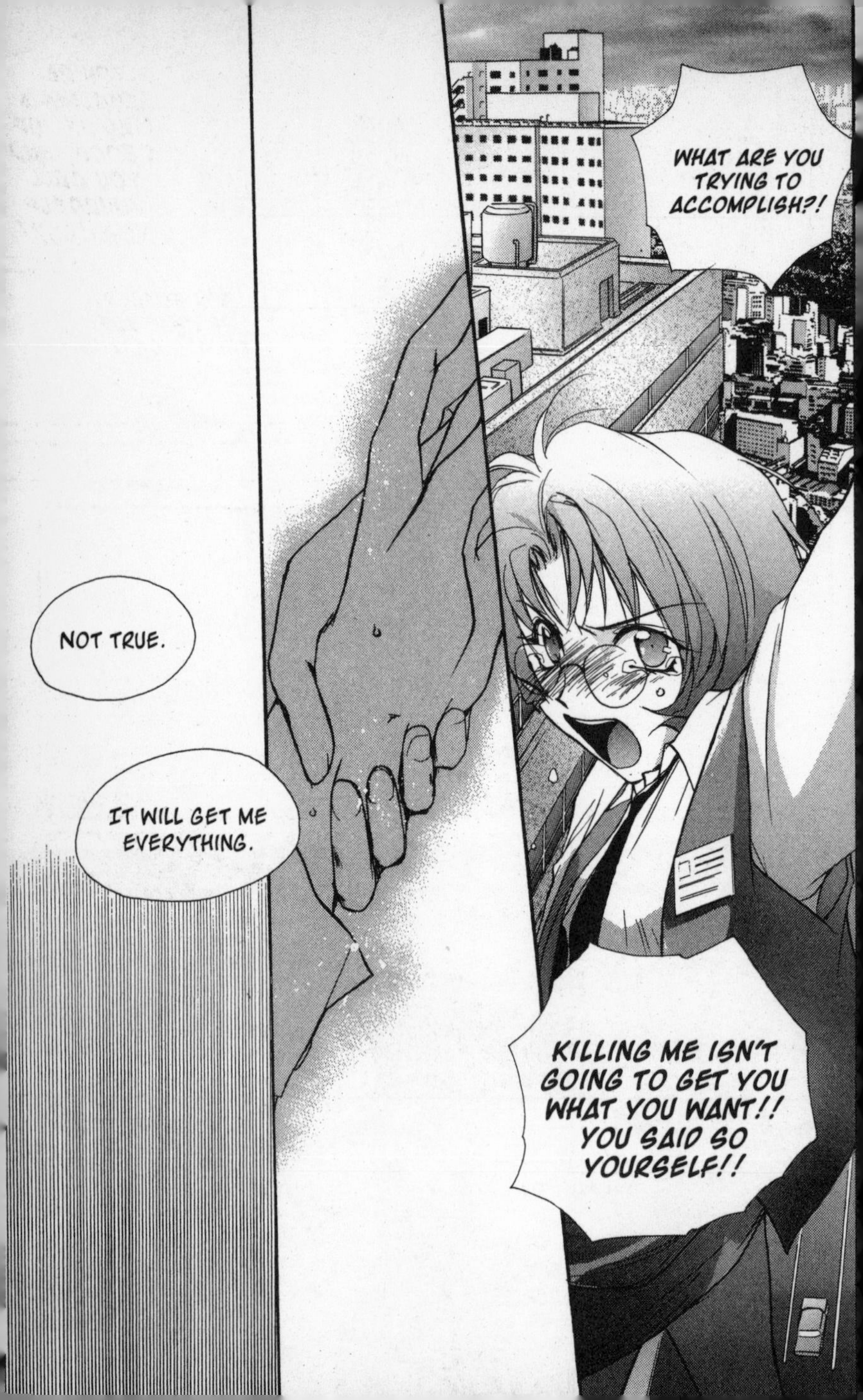
WHAT ARE YOU TRYING TO ACCOMPLISH?!
KILLING ME ISN'T GOING TO GET YOU WHAT YOU WANT!! YOU SAID SO YOURSELF!!
NOT TRUE.
IT WILL GET ME EVERYTHING.

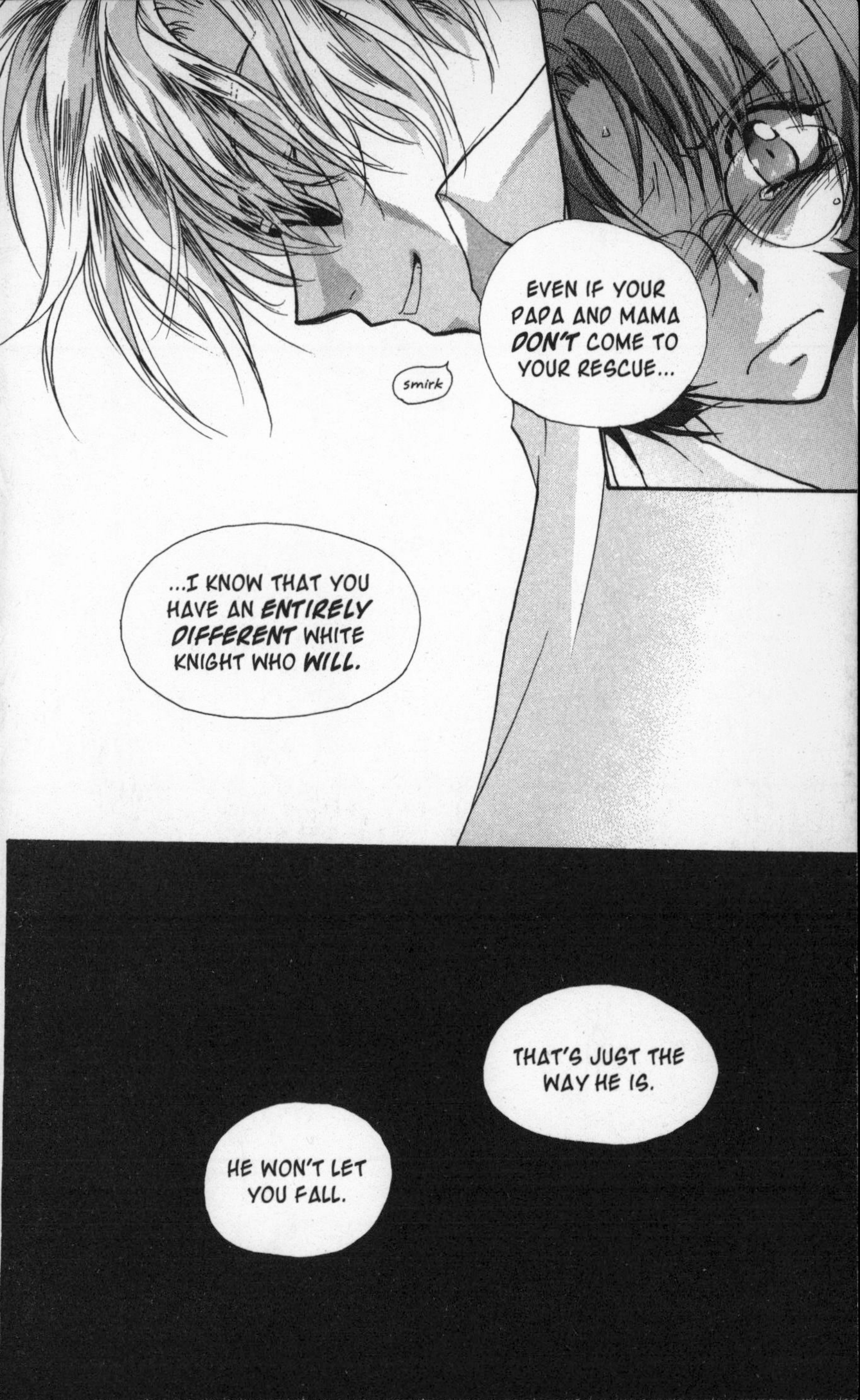
EVEN IF YOUR PAPA AND MAMA DON'T COME TO YOUR RESCUE...
smirk
...I KNOW THAT YOU HAVE AN ENTIRELY DIFFERENT WHITE KNIGHT WHO WILL.
THAT'S JUST THE WAY HE IS.
HE WON'T LET YOU FALL.

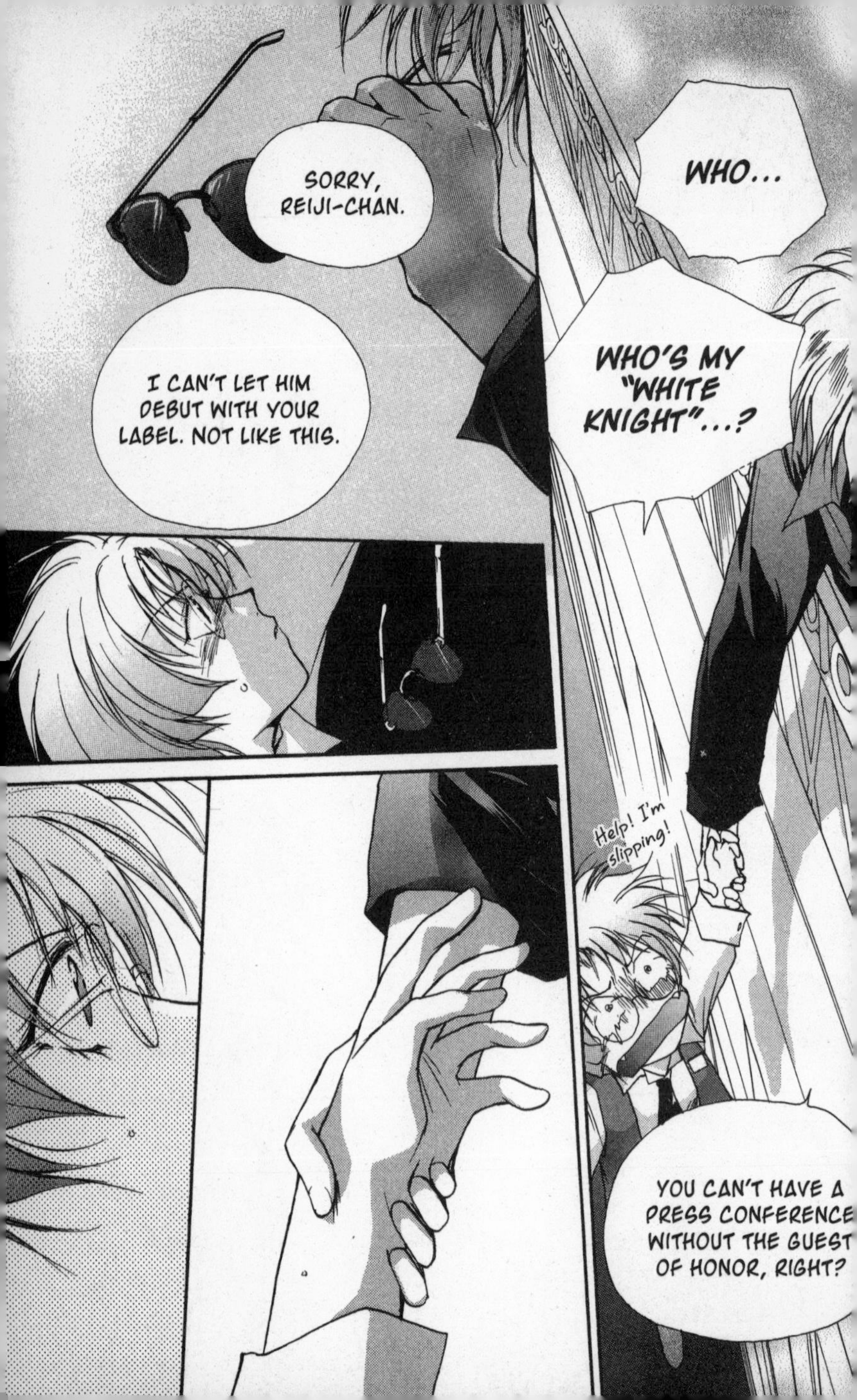
WHO...
WHO'S MY "WHITE KNIGHT"...?
Help! I'm slipping!
YOU CAN'T HAVE A PRESS CONFERENCE WITHOUT THE GUEST OF HONOR, RIGHT?
SORRY, REIJI-CHAN.
I CAN'T LET HIM DEBUT WITH YOUR LABEL. NOT LIKE THIS.

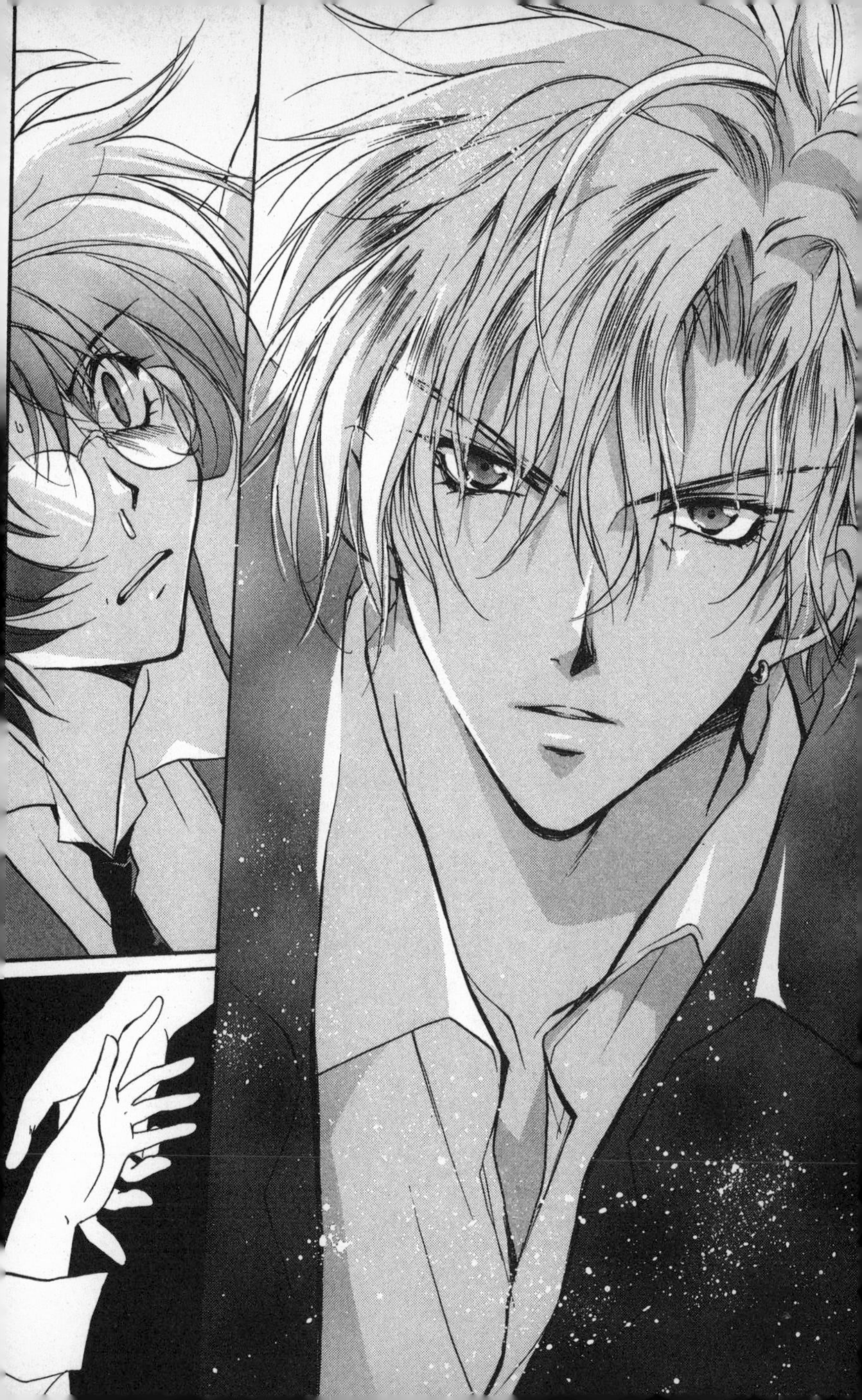

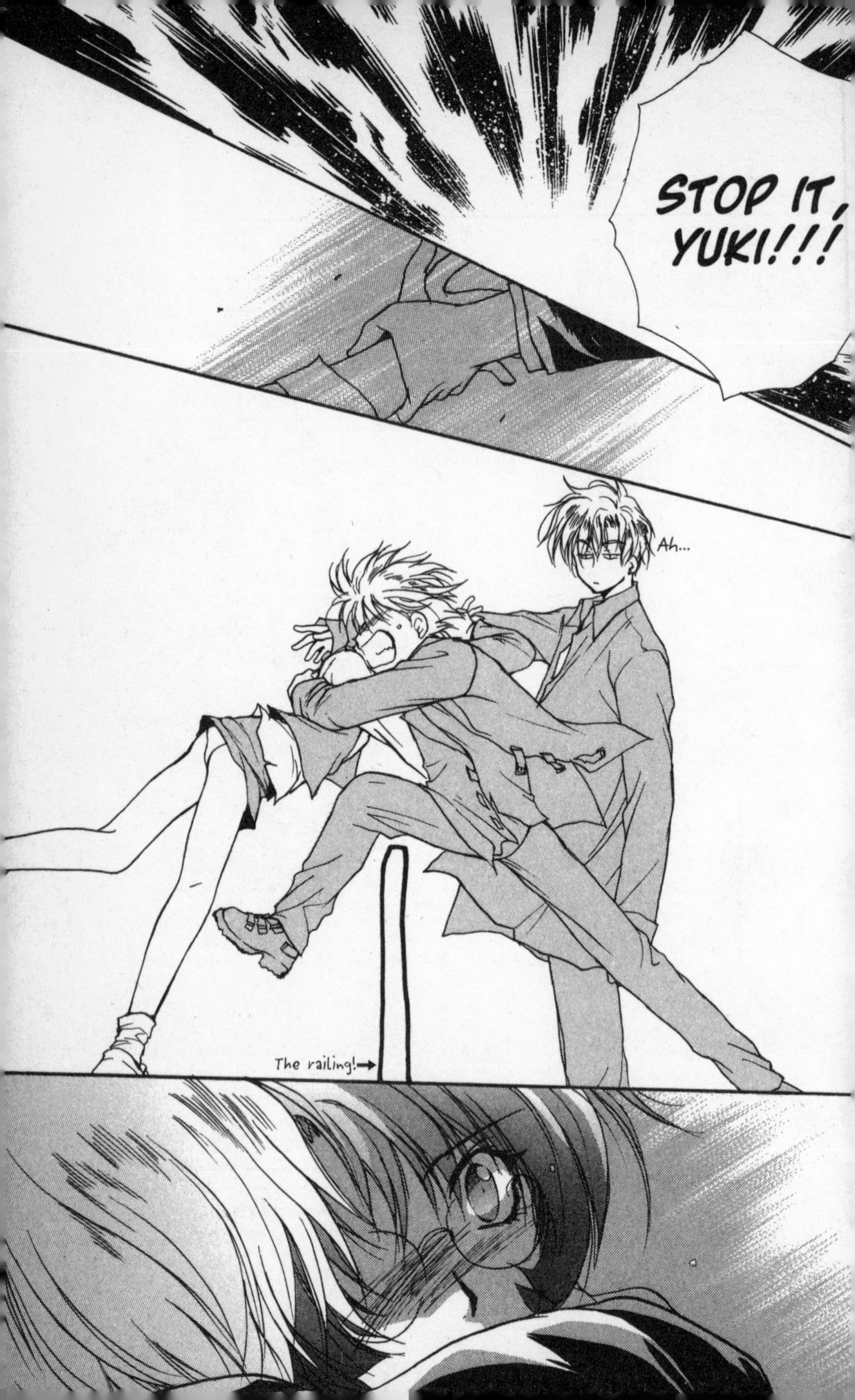
STOP IT, YUKI!!!
Ah...
The railing!

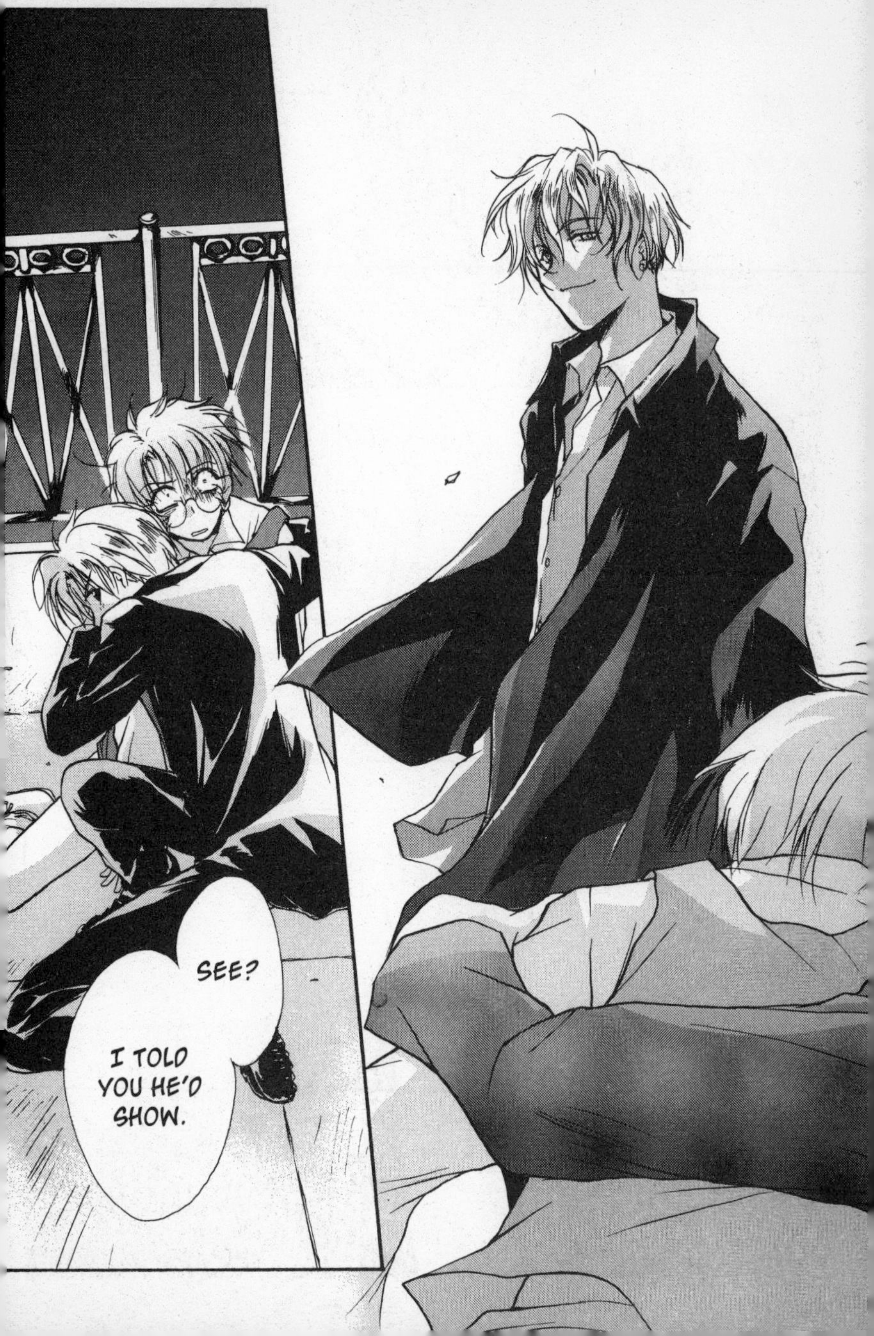
SEE?
I TOLD YOU HE'D SHOW.

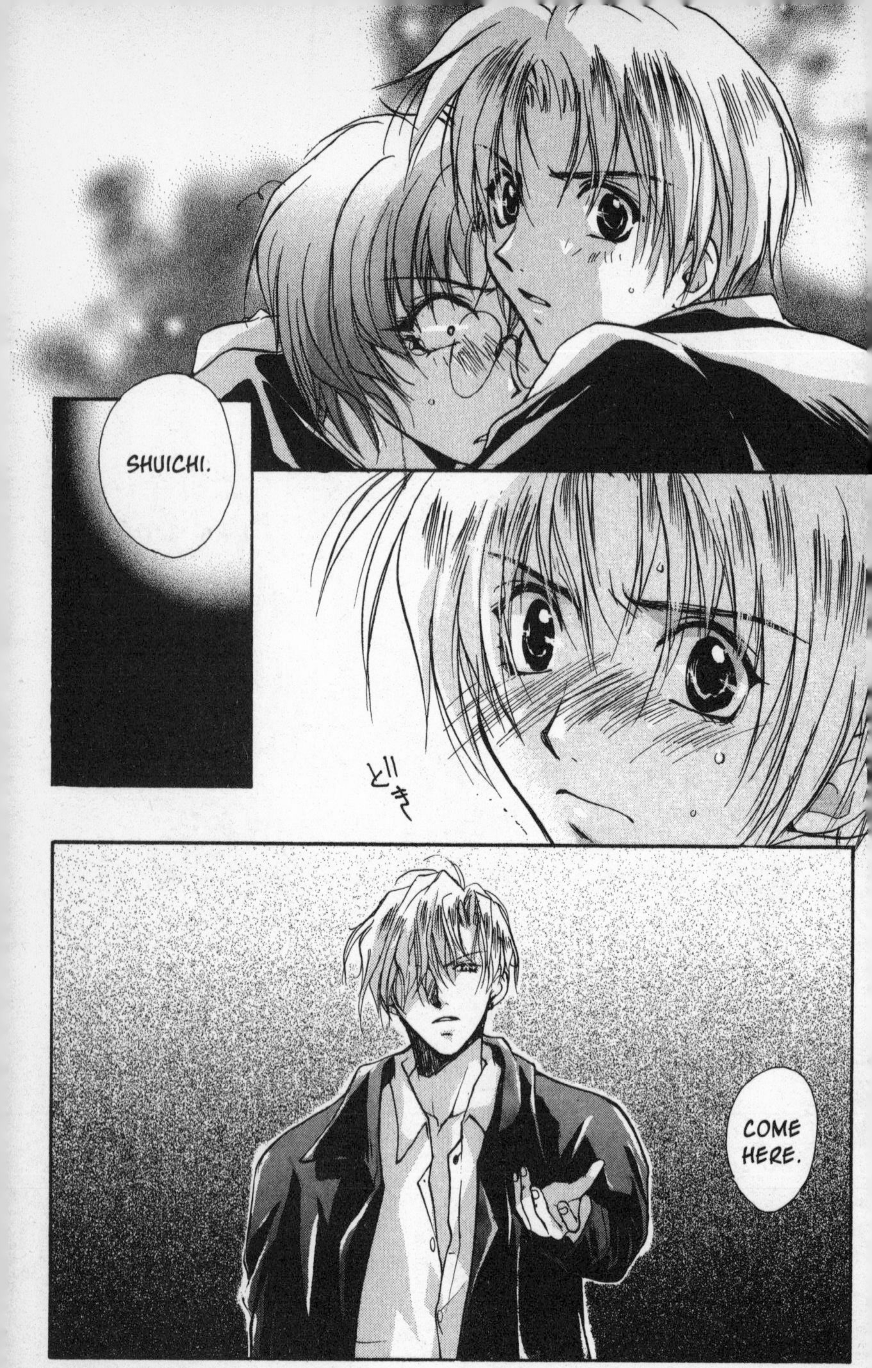
SHUICHI.
どき
COME HERE.

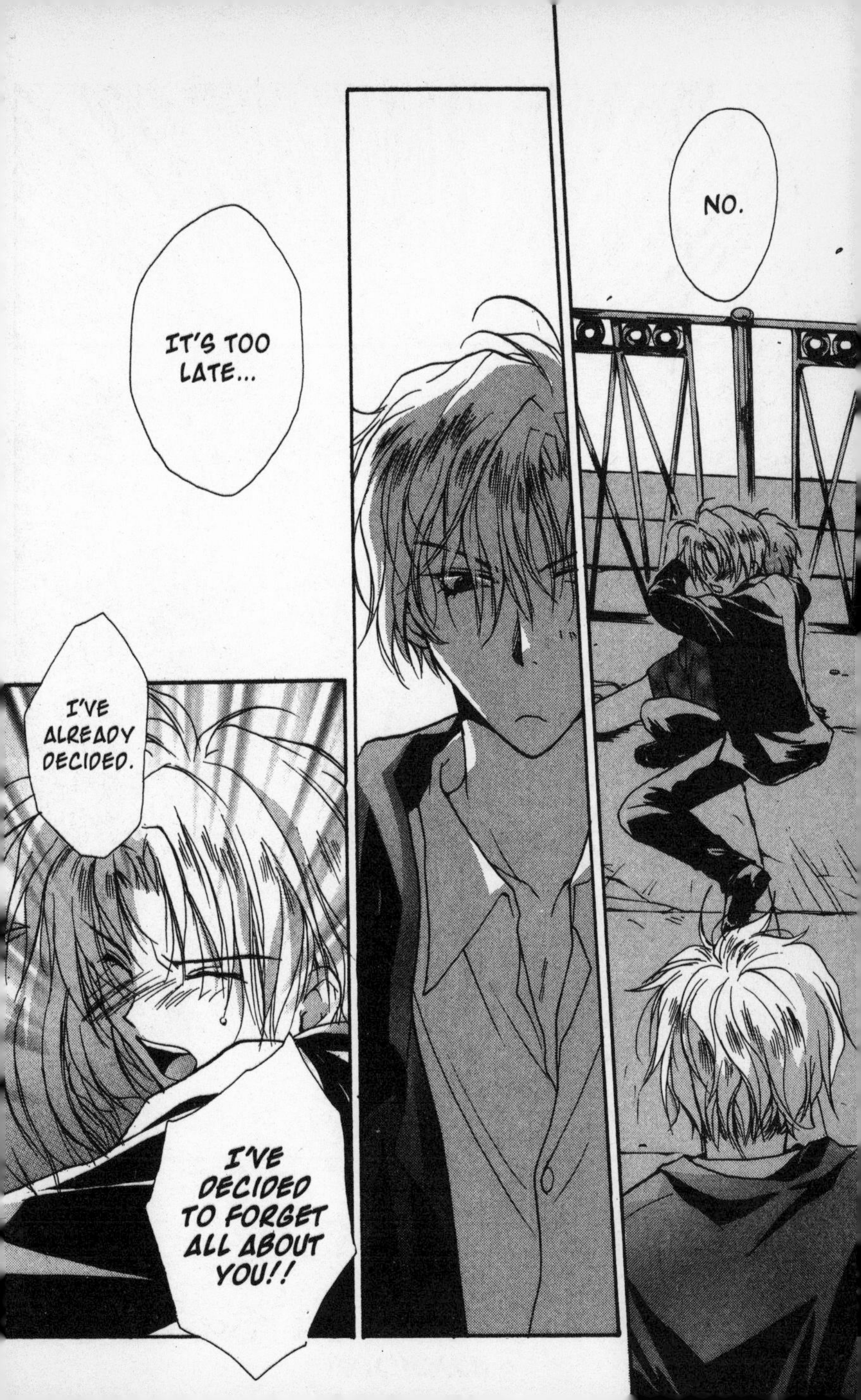
NO.
IT'S TOO LATE...
I'VE ALREADY DECIDED.
I'VE DECIDED TO FORGET ALL ABOUT YOU!!

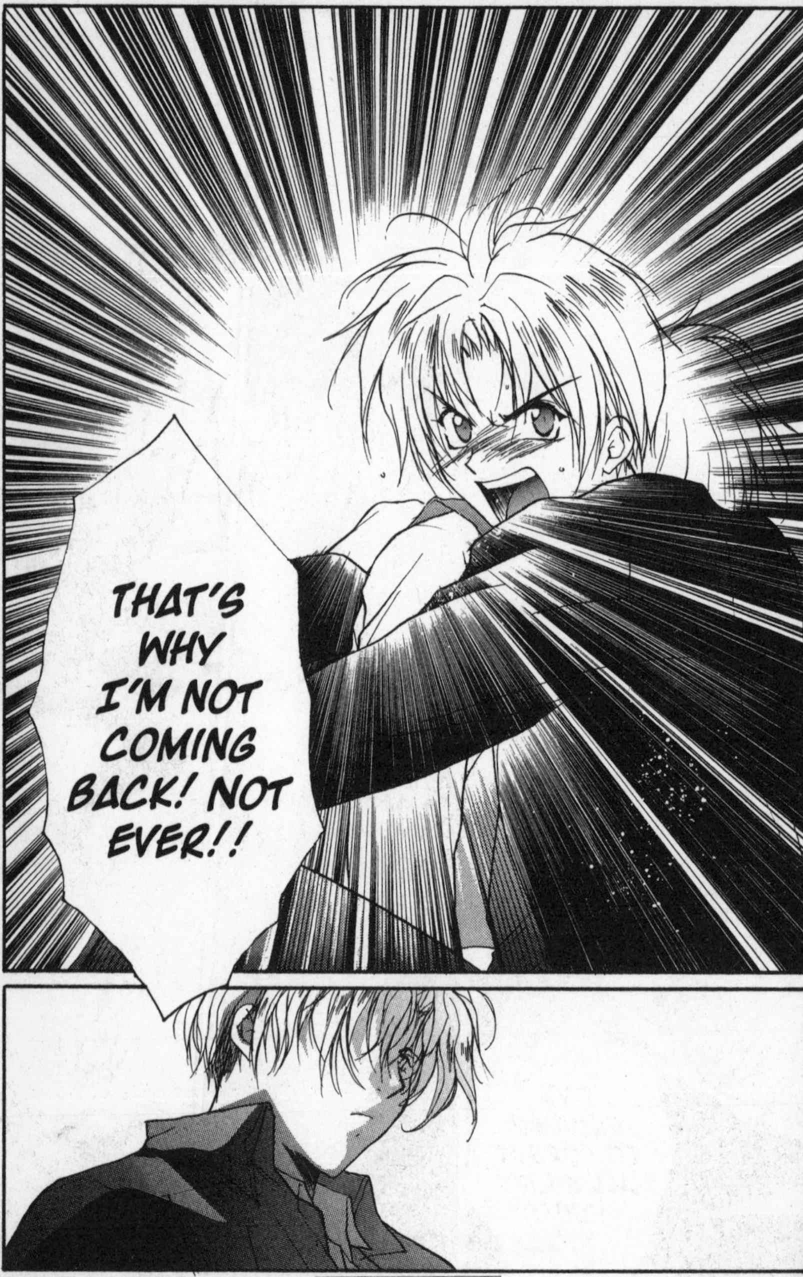
THAT'S WHY I'M NOT COMING BACK! NOT EVER!!

track37▶END

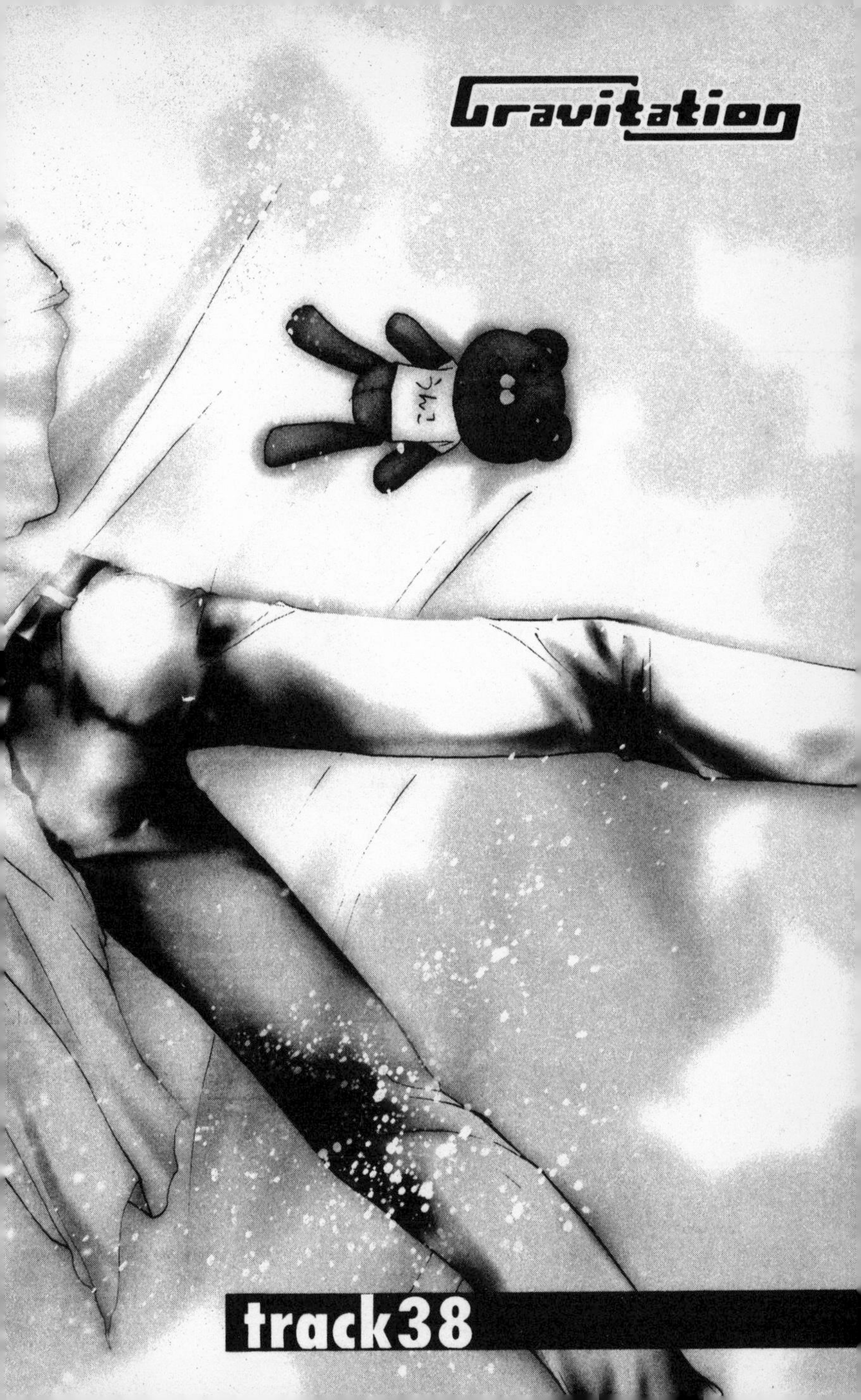
Gravitation
track38

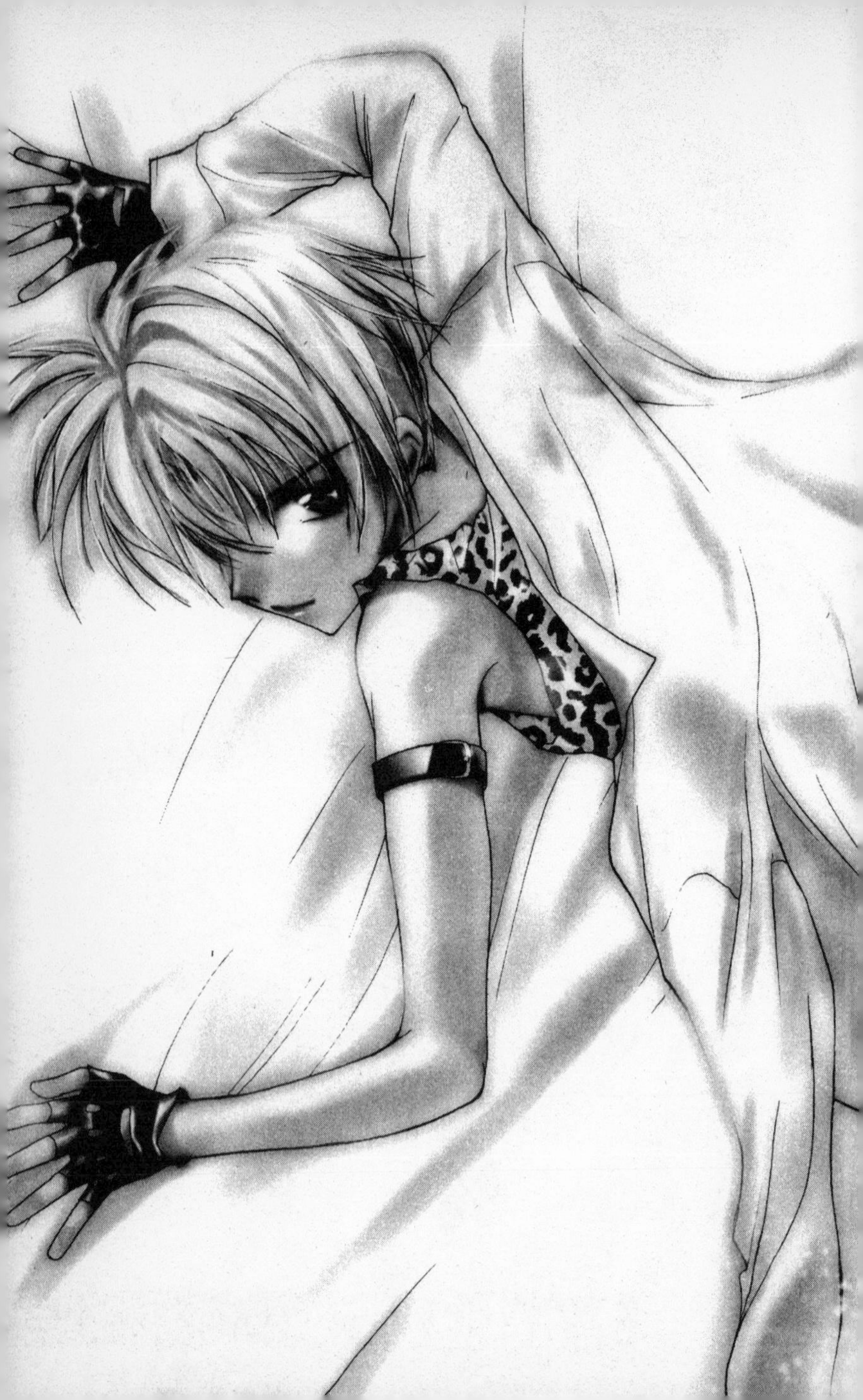

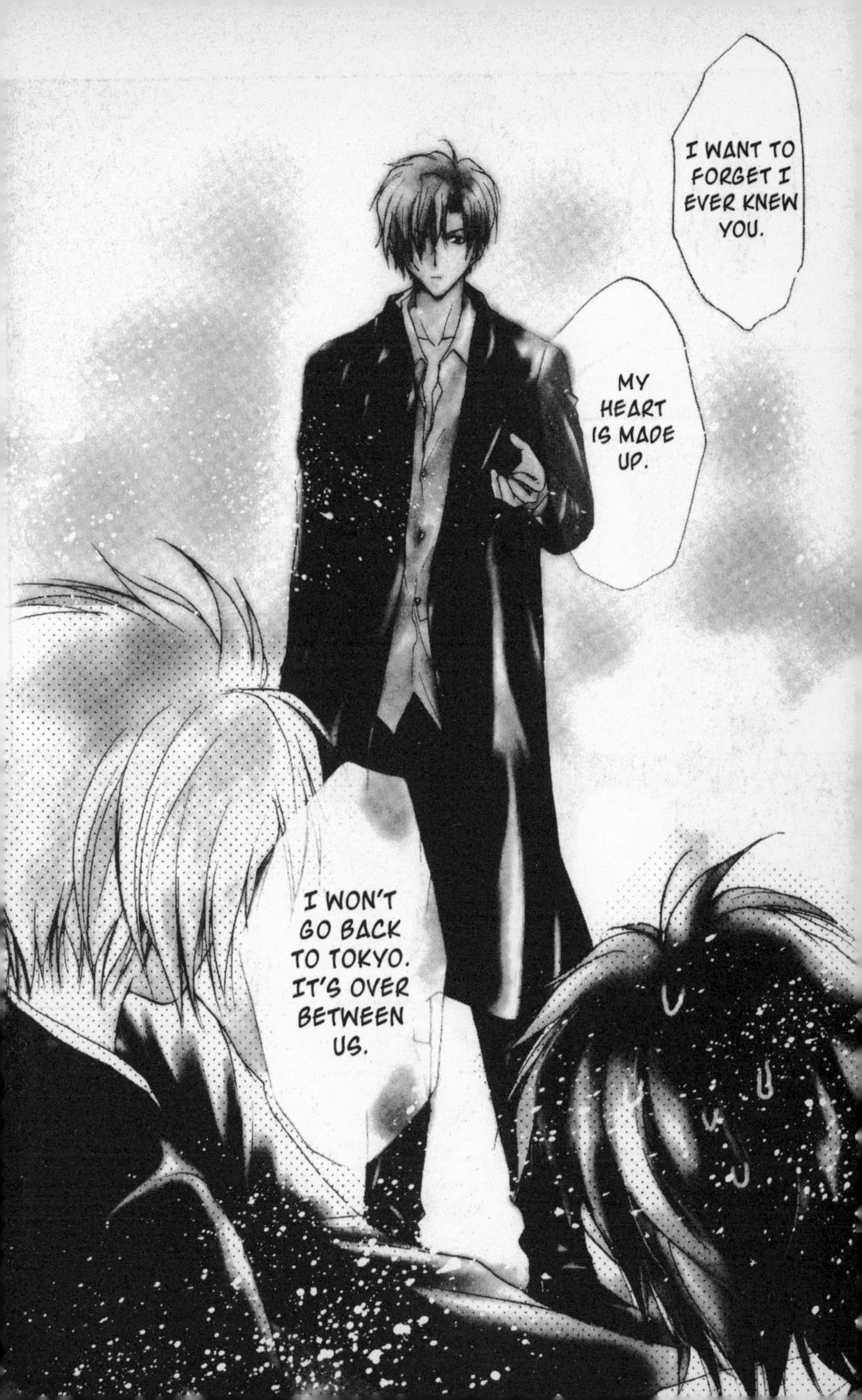
I WANT TO FORGET I EVER KNEW YOU.
MY HEART IS MADE UP.
I WON'T GO BACK TO TOKYO. IT'S OVER BETWEEN US.

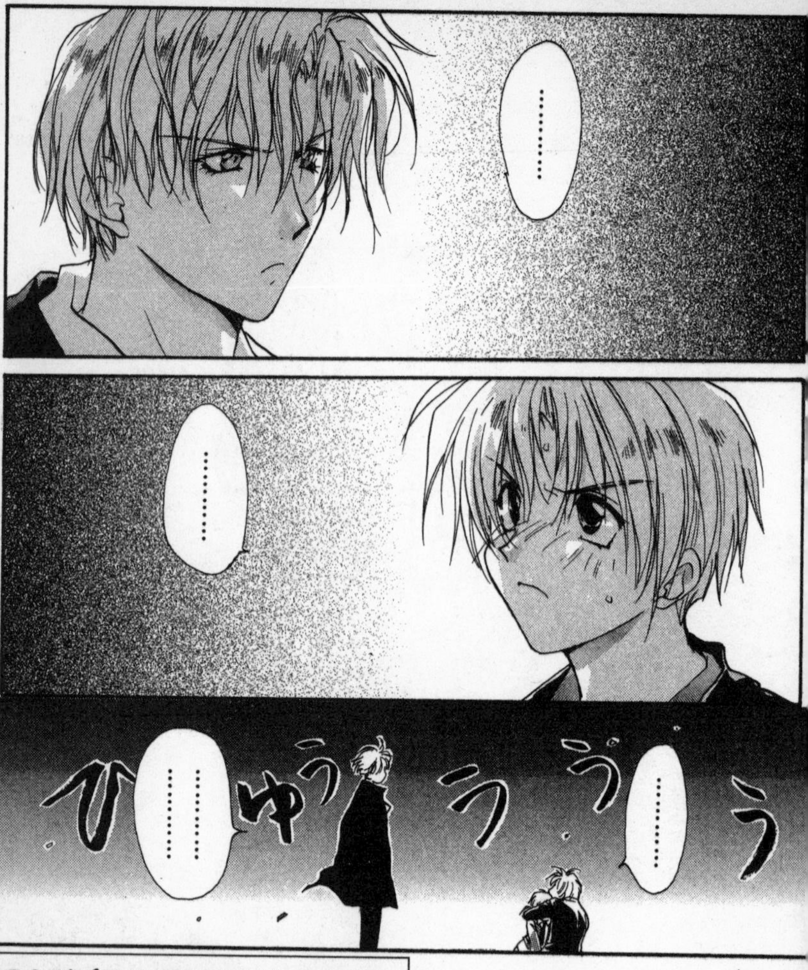
……
……
……
……
ひゅうううう

ABOUT GRAVITATION TRACK 38

If I continued on at this rate and drew a picture of Eiri, I think that would be bad, so I'll end here. Speaking of starvation, S-san's cooking is very delicious, and even though we're in a bit of a pinch and burn a lot of energy working, it's still enough to make you fat. But no one believes us when we say we're in a pinch.

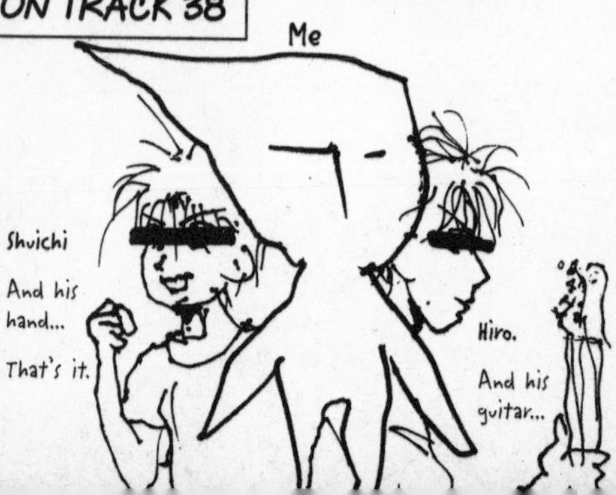
Me
Shuichi
And his hand...
That's it.
Hiro.
And his guitar...

Since Murakami-san is on the verge of death (from starvation, most likely), I, Run-chan, shall insert some illustrations here.

I'm drawing seriously here, really.

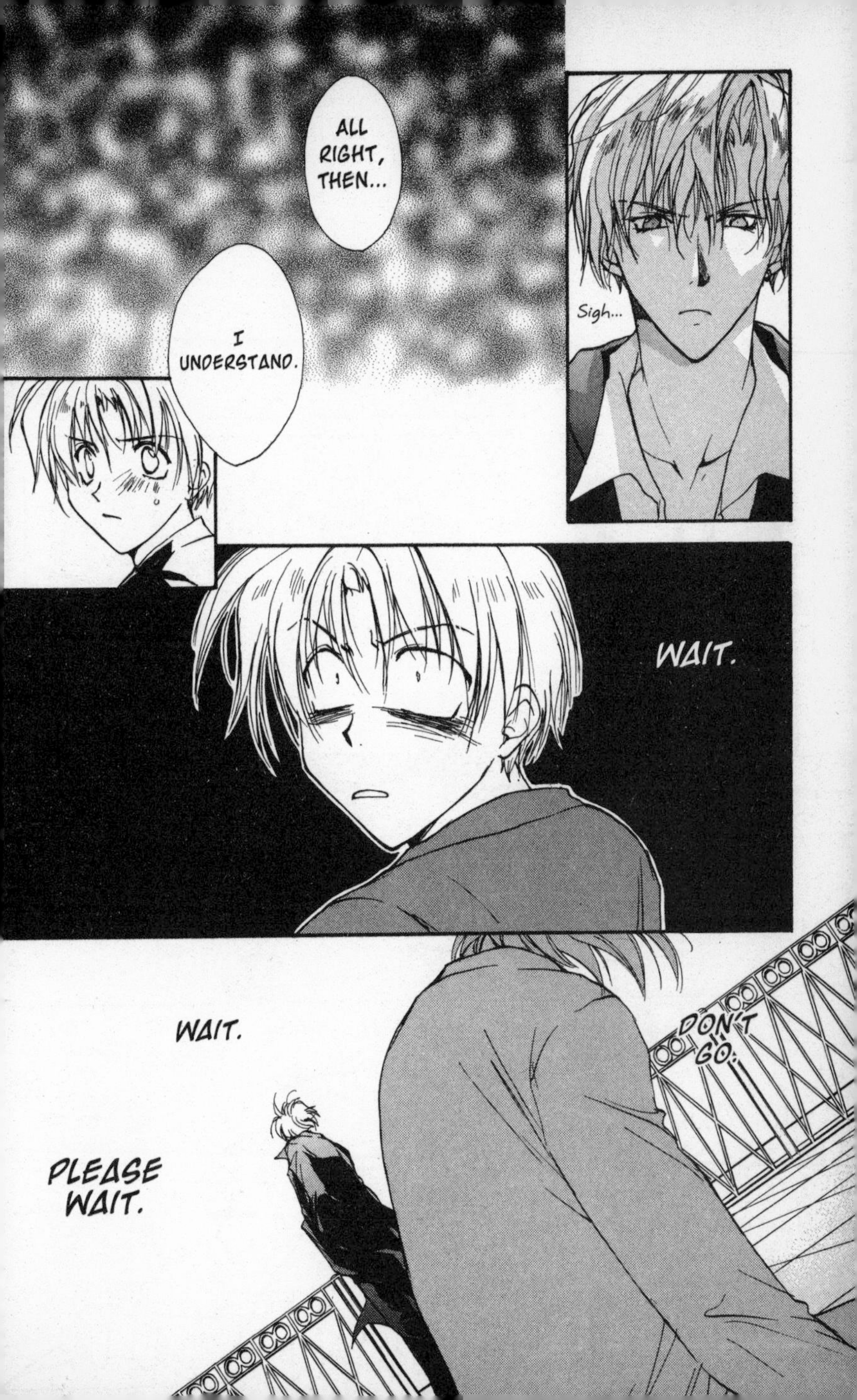
Sigh...
ALL RIGHT, THEN...
I UNDERSTAND.
WAIT.
DON'T GO.
WAIT.
PLEASE WAIT.

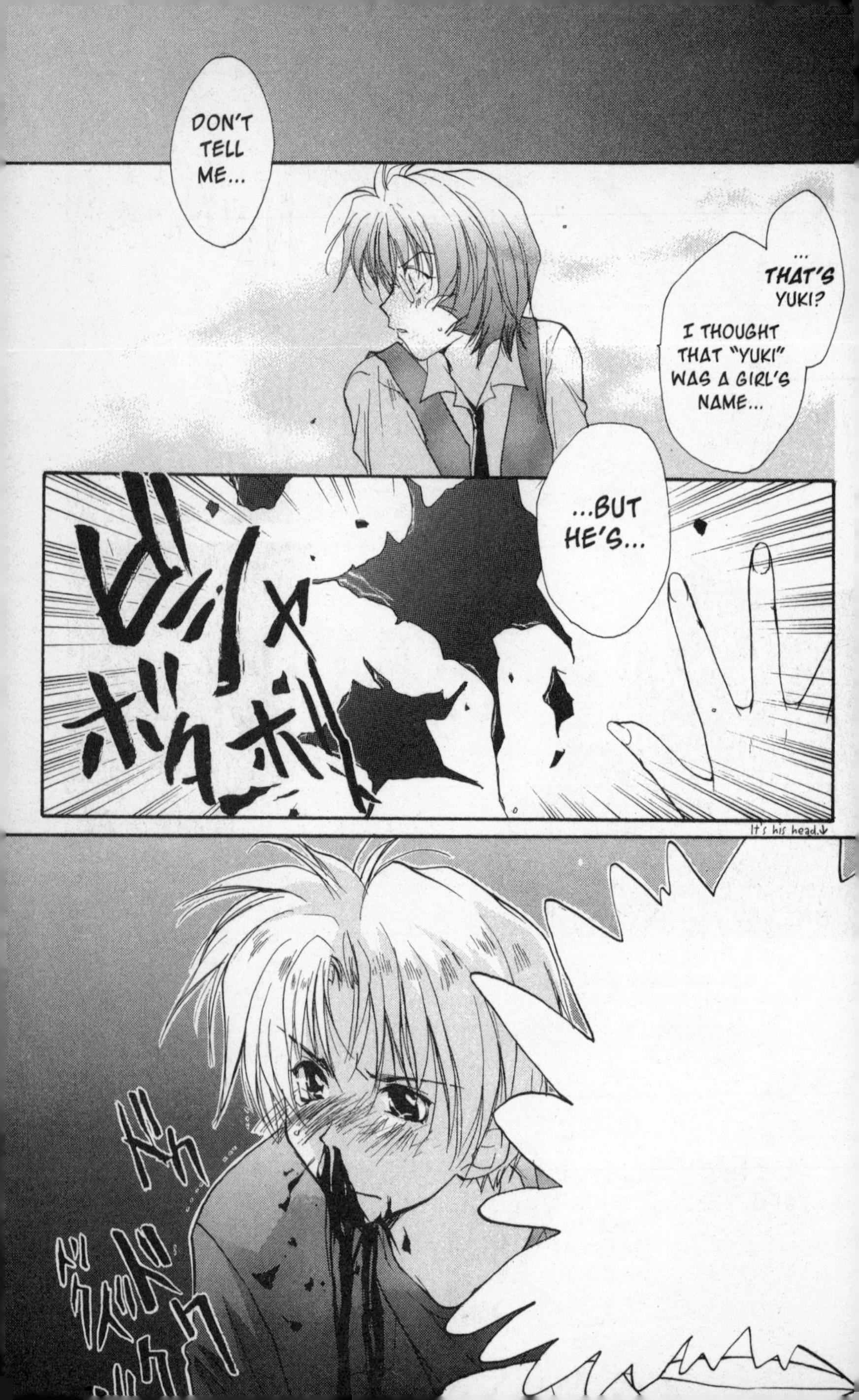
DON'T TELL ME...
...THAT'S YUKI?
I THOUGHT THAT "YUKI" WAS A GIRL'S NAME...
...BUT HE'S...
It's his head.↓

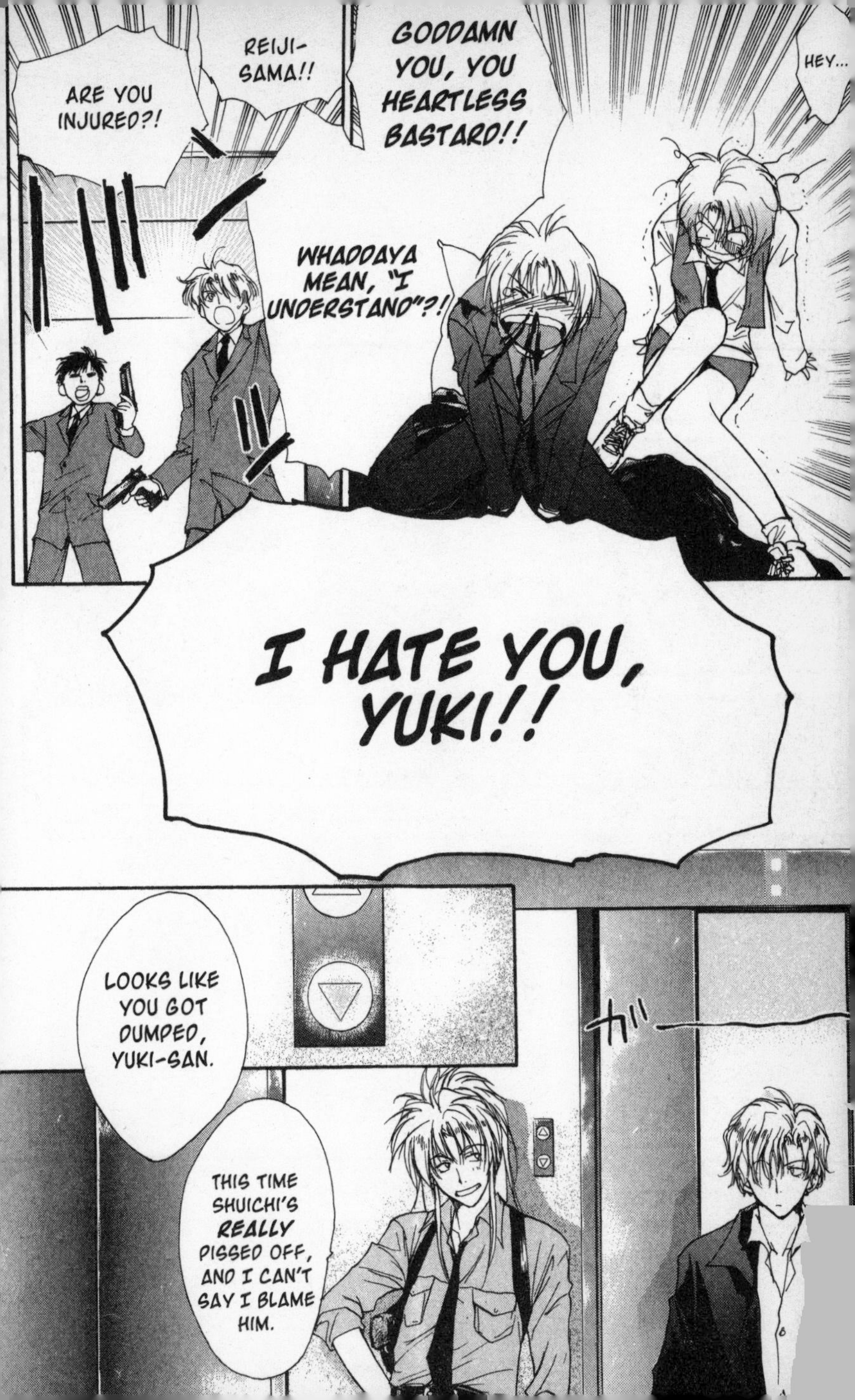
HEY...
GODDAMN YOU, YOU HEARTLESS BASTARD!!
REIJI-SAMA!!
ARE YOU INJURED?!
WHADDAYA MEAN, "I UNDERSTAND"?!
I HATE YOU, YUKI!!
ガ
LOOKS LIKE YOU GOT DUMPED, YUKI-SAN.
THIS TIME SHUICHI'S **REALLY** PISSED OFF, AND I CAN'T SAY I BLAME HIM.

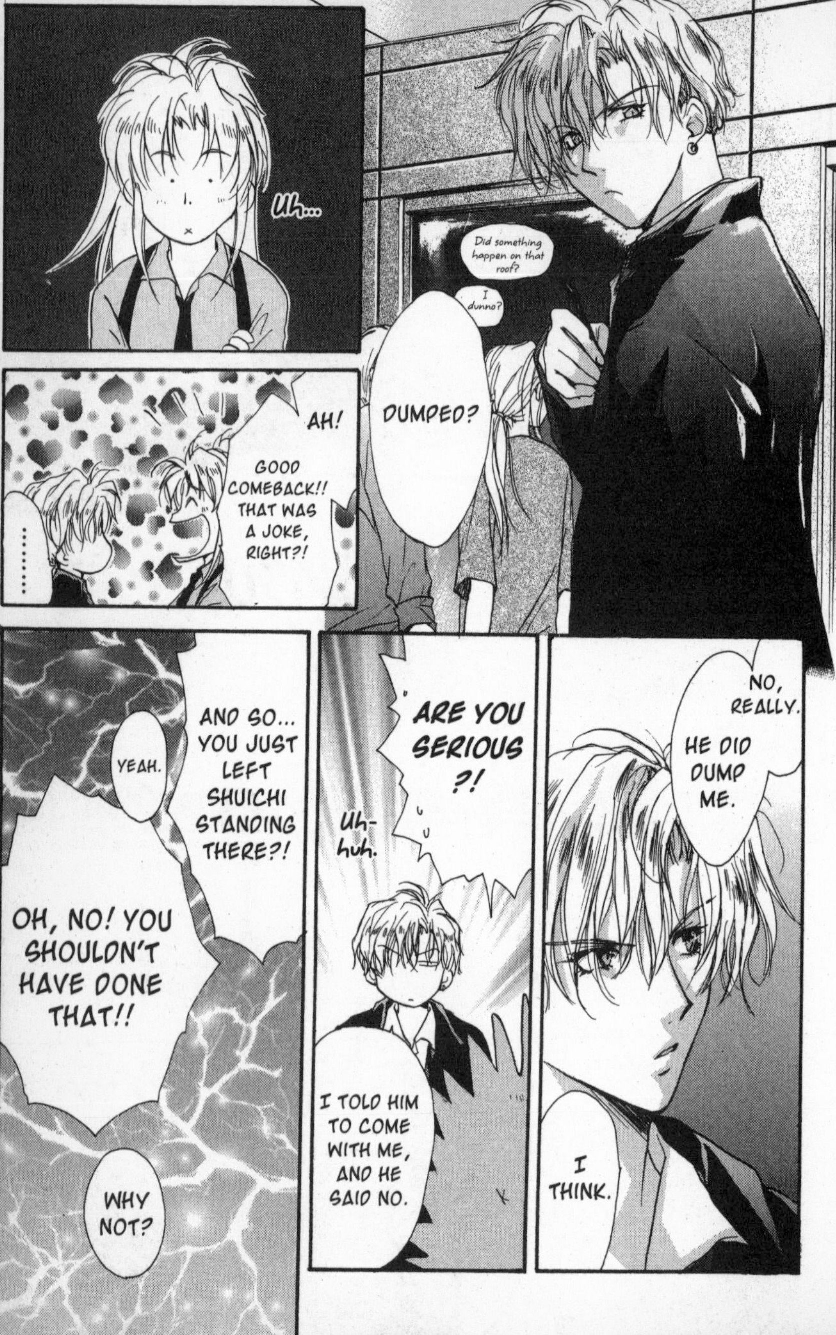

Did something happen on that roof?
I dunno?
DUMPED?
Uh...
AH!
GOOD COMEBACK!! THAT WAS A JOKE, RIGHT?!
......
NO, REALLY.
HE DID DUMP ME.
I THINK.
ARE YOU SERIOUS?!
Uh-huh.
I TOLD HIM TO COME WITH ME, AND HE SAID NO.
AND SO... YOU JUST LEFT SHUICHI STANDING THERE?!
YEAH.
OH, NO! YOU SHOULDN'T HAVE DONE THAT!!
WHY NOT?

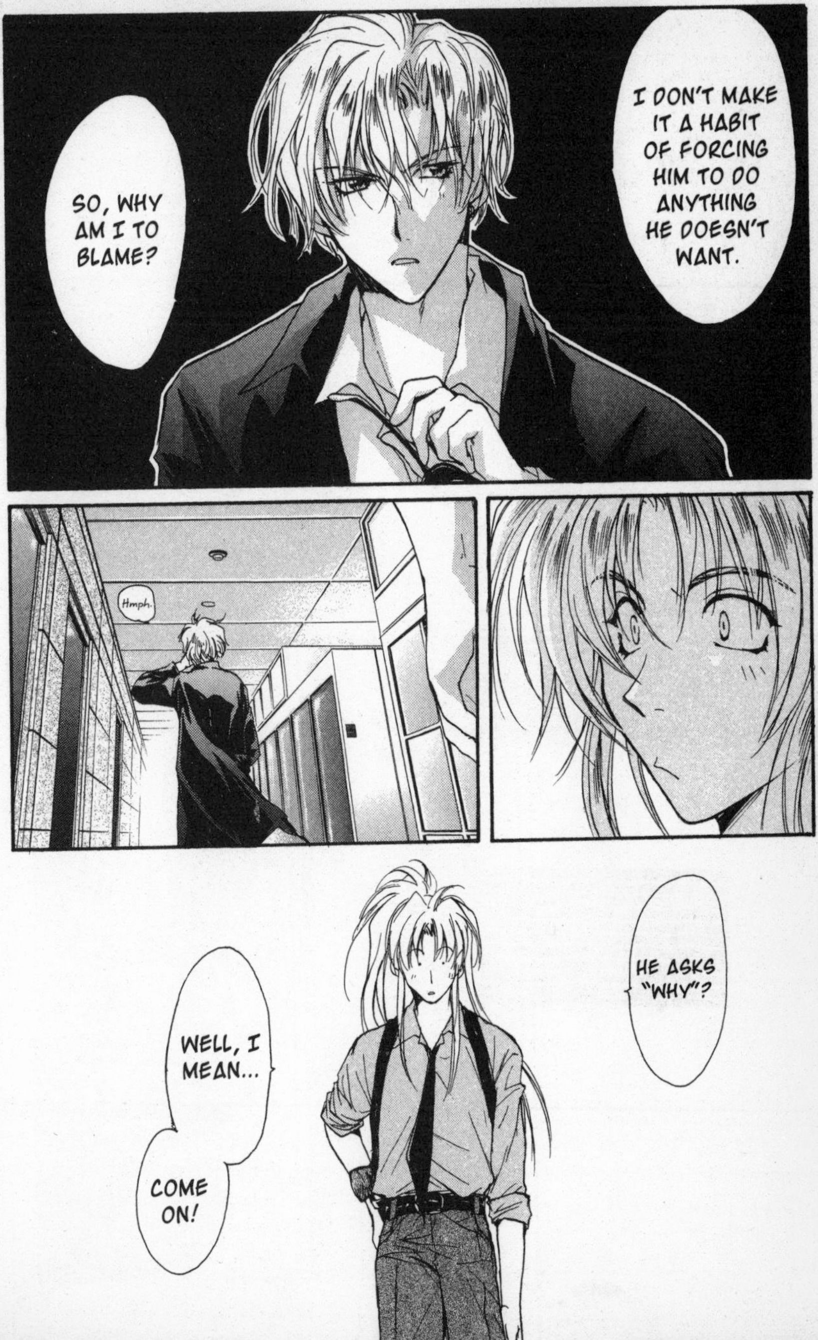
I DON'T MAKE IT A HABIT OF FORCING HIM TO DO ANYTHING HE DOESN'T WANT.
SO, WHY AM I TO BLAME?
Hmph.
HE ASKS "WHY"?
WELL, I MEAN...
COME ON!

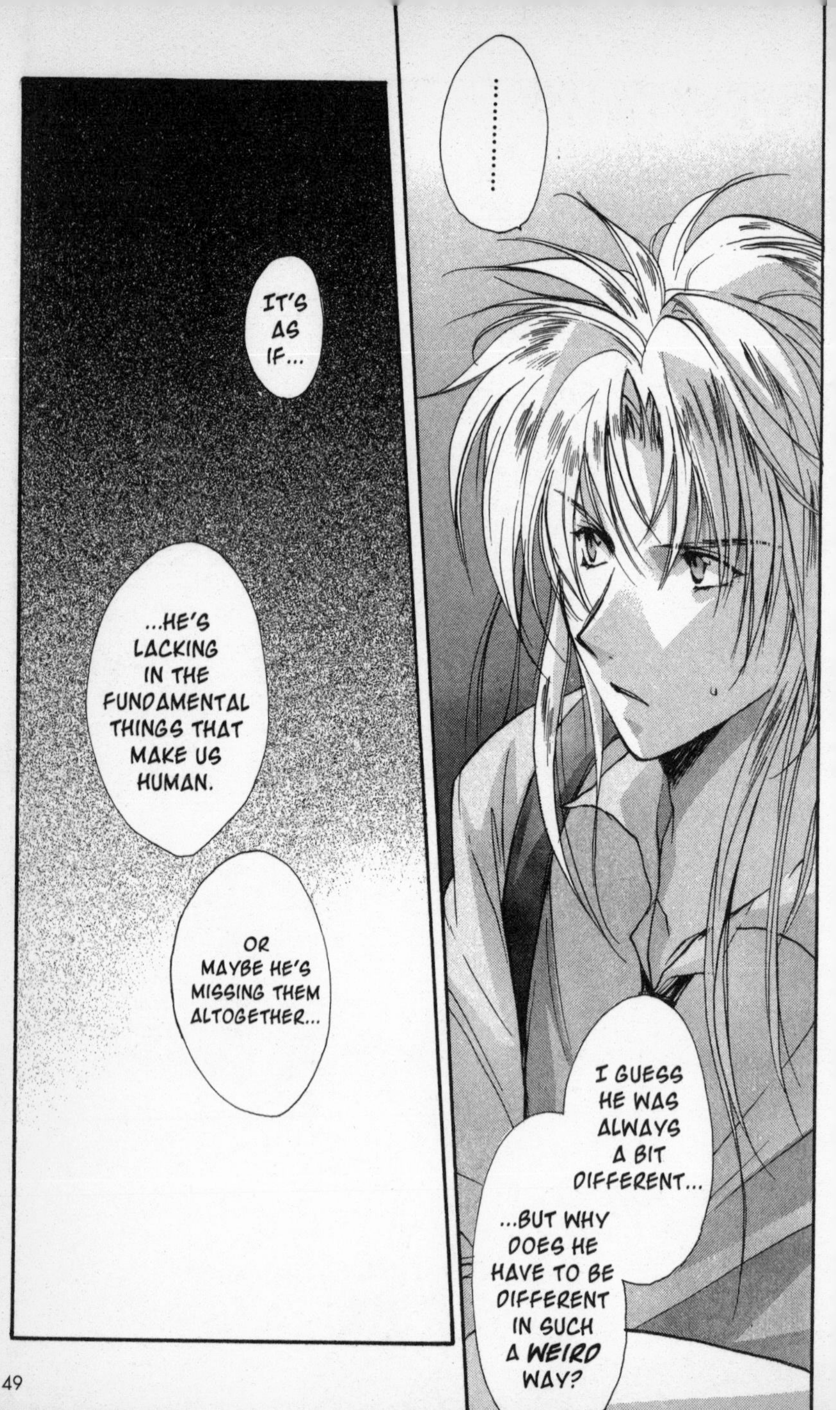
……
I GUESS HE WAS ALWAYS A BIT DIFFERENT...
...BUT WHY DOES HE HAVE TO BE DIFFERENT IN SUCH A **WEIRD** WAY?
IT'S AS IF...
...HE'S LACKING IN THE FUNDAMENTAL THINGS THAT MAKE US HUMAN.
OR MAYBE HE'S MISSING THEM ALTOGETHER...

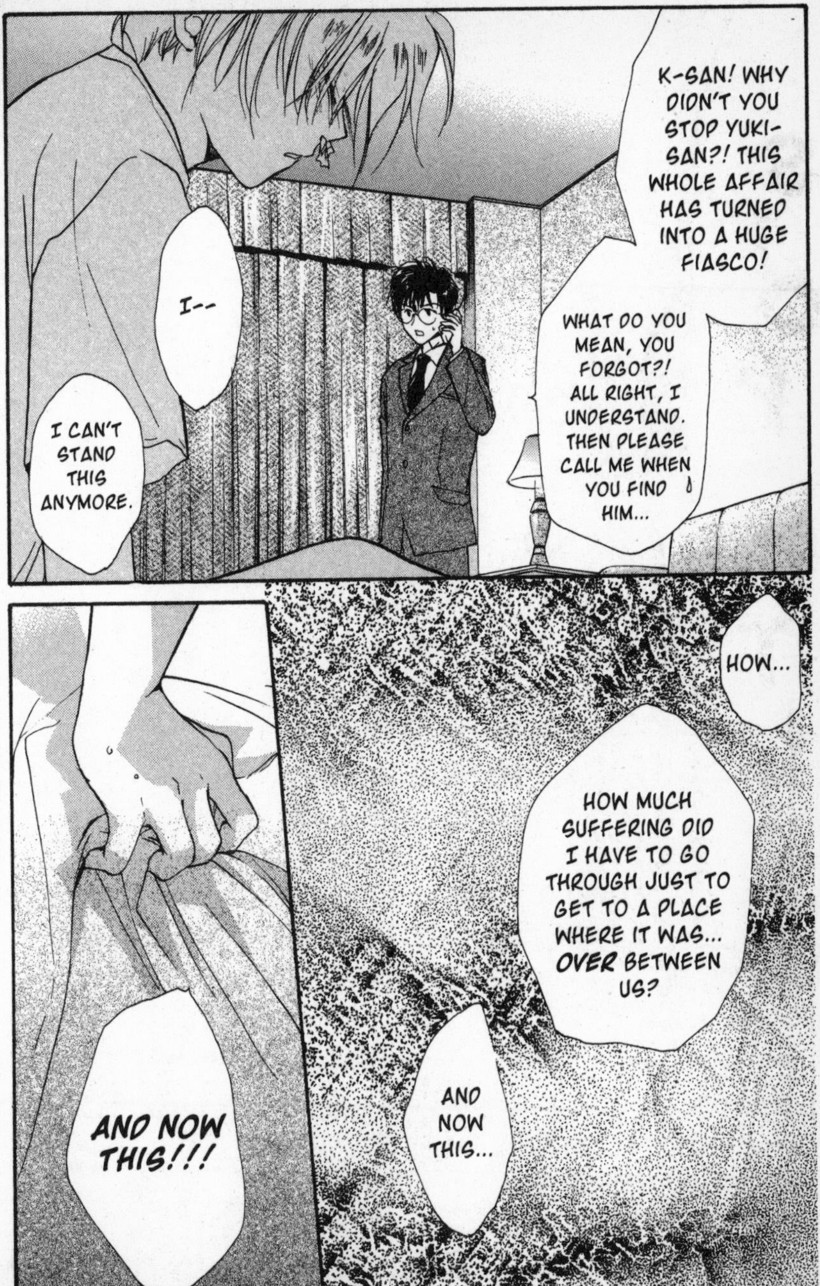
K-SAN! WHY DIDN'T YOU STOP YUKI-SAN?! THIS WHOLE AFFAIR HAS TURNED INTO A HUGE FIASCO!
WHAT DO YOU MEAN, YOU FORGOT?! ALL RIGHT, I UNDERSTAND. THEN PLEASE CALL ME WHEN YOU FIND HIM...
I--
I CAN'T STAND THIS ANYMORE.
HOW...
HOW MUCH SUFFERING DID I HAVE TO GO THROUGH JUST TO GET TO A PLACE WHERE IT WAS... ***OVER*** BETWEEN US?
AND NOW THIS...
AND NOW THIS!!!

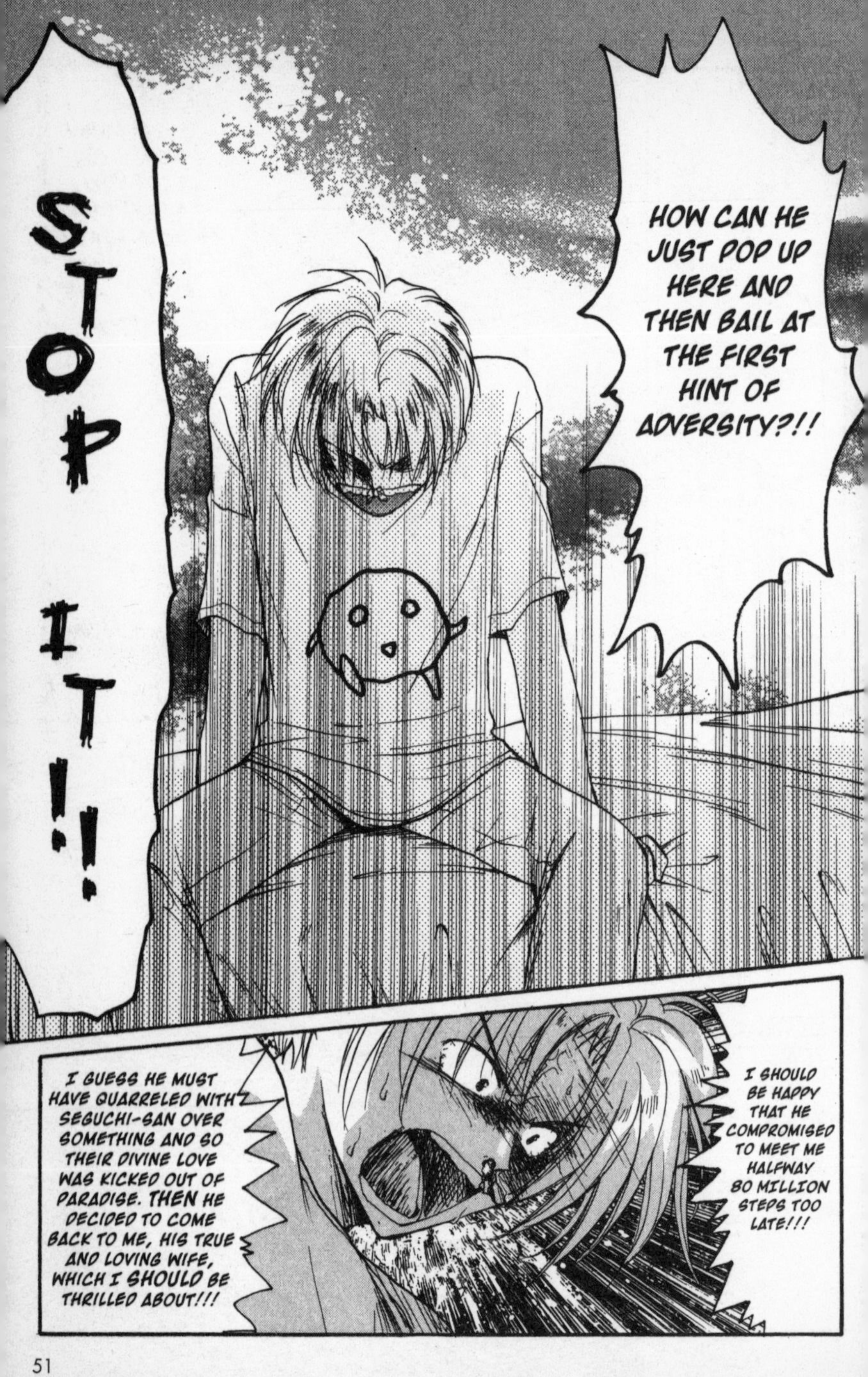
HOW CAN HE JUST POP UP HERE AND THEN BAIL AT THE FIRST HINT OF ADVERSITY?!!
STOP IT!!
I SHOULD BE HAPPY THAT HE COMPROMISED TO MEET ME HALFWAY 80 MILLION STEPS TOO LATE!!!
I GUESS HE MUST HAVE QUARRELED WITH SEGUCHI-SAN OVER SOMETHING AND SO THEIR DIVINE LOVE WAS KICKED OUT OF PARADISE. THEN HE DECIDED TO COME BACK TO ME, HIS TRUE AND LOVING WIFE, WHICH I SHOULD BE THRILLED ABOUT!!!

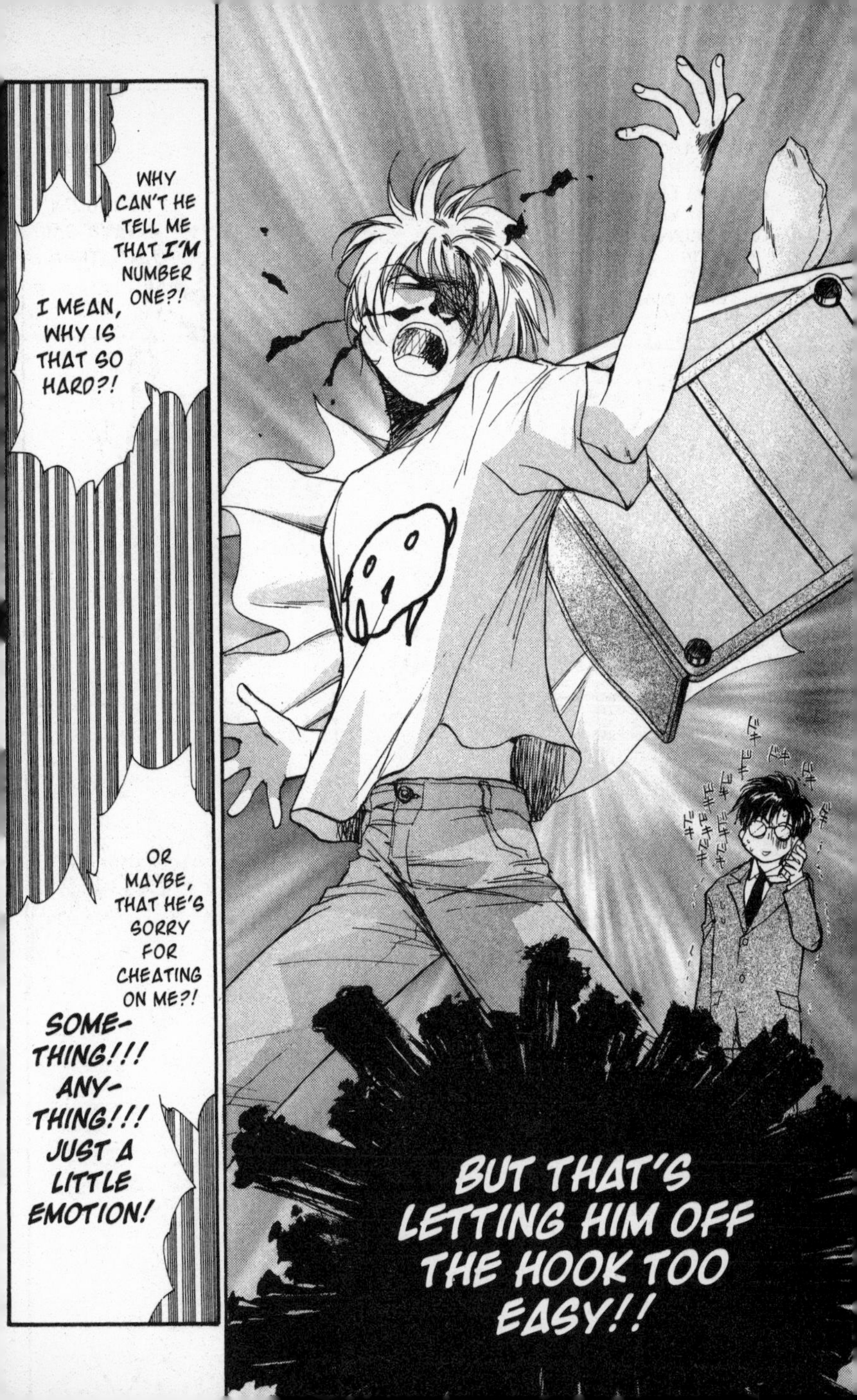
BUT THAT'S LETTING HIM OFF THE HOOK TOO EASY!!
WHY CAN'T HE TELL ME THAT I'M NUMBER ONE?!
I MEAN, WHY IS THAT SO HARD?!
OR MAYBE, THAT HE'S SORRY FOR CHEATING ON ME?!
SOME-THING!!! ANY-THING!!! JUST A LITTLE EMOTION!

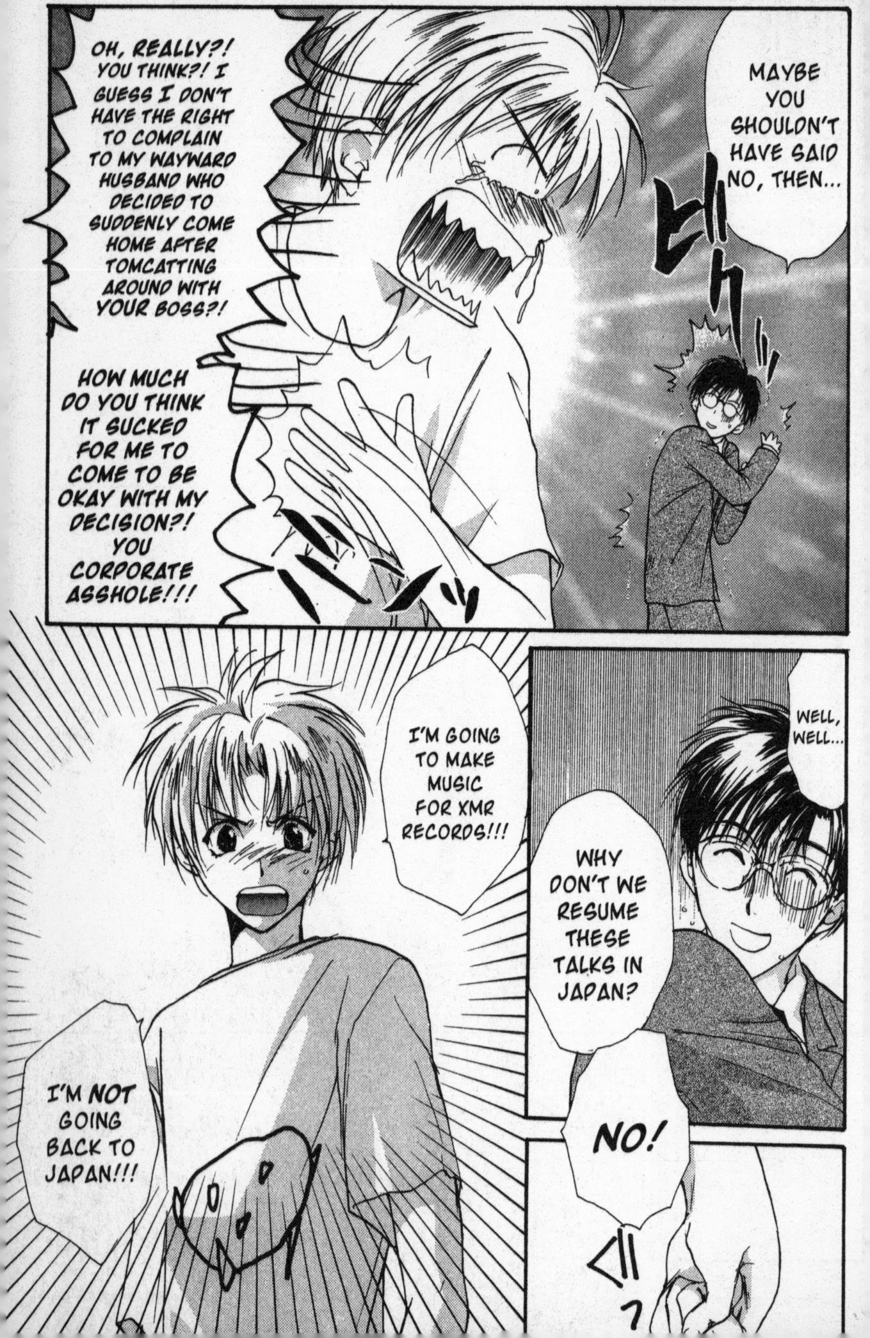
MAYBE YOU SHOULDN'T HAVE SAID NO, THEN...
OH, REALLY?! YOU THINK?! I GUESS I DON'T HAVE THE RIGHT TO COMPLAIN TO MY WAYWARD HUSBAND WHO DECIDED TO SUDDENLY COME HOME AFTER TOMCATTING AROUND WITH YOUR BOSS?!
HOW MUCH DO YOU THINK IT SUCKED FOR ME TO COME TO BE OKAY WITH MY DECISION?! YOU CORPORATE ASSHOLE!!!
WELL, WELL...
WHY DON'T WE RESUME THESE TALKS IN JAPAN?
NO!
I'M GOING TO MAKE MUSIC FOR XMR RECORDS!!!
I'M **NOT** GOING BACK TO JAPAN!!!

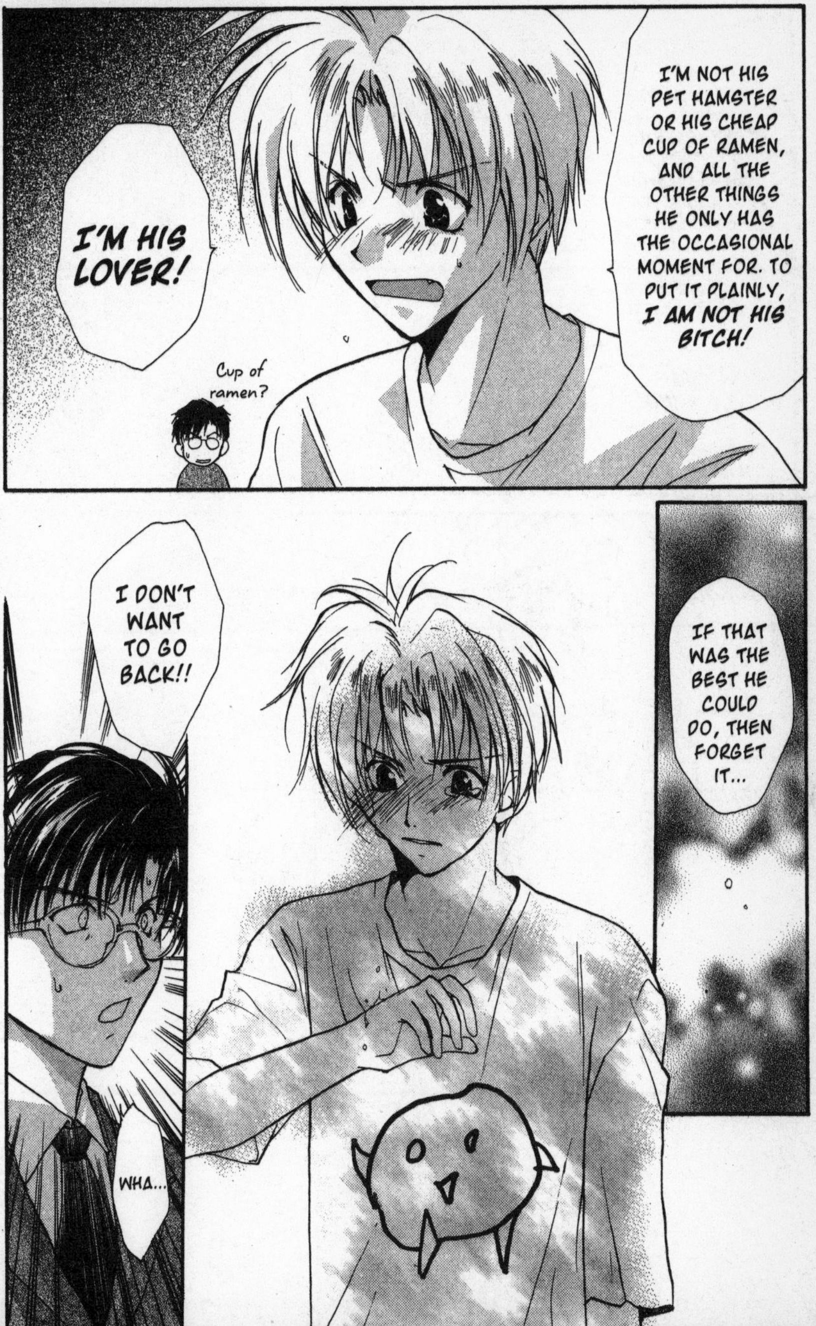
I'M NOT HIS PET HAMSTER OR HIS CHEAP CUP OF RAMEN, AND ALL THE OTHER THINGS HE ONLY HAS THE OCCASIONAL MOMENT FOR. TO PUT IT PLAINLY, I AM NOT HIS BITCH!
I'M HIS LOVER!
Cup of ramen?
IF THAT WAS THE BEST HE COULD DO, THEN FORGET IT...
I DON'T WANT TO GO BACK!!
WHA...

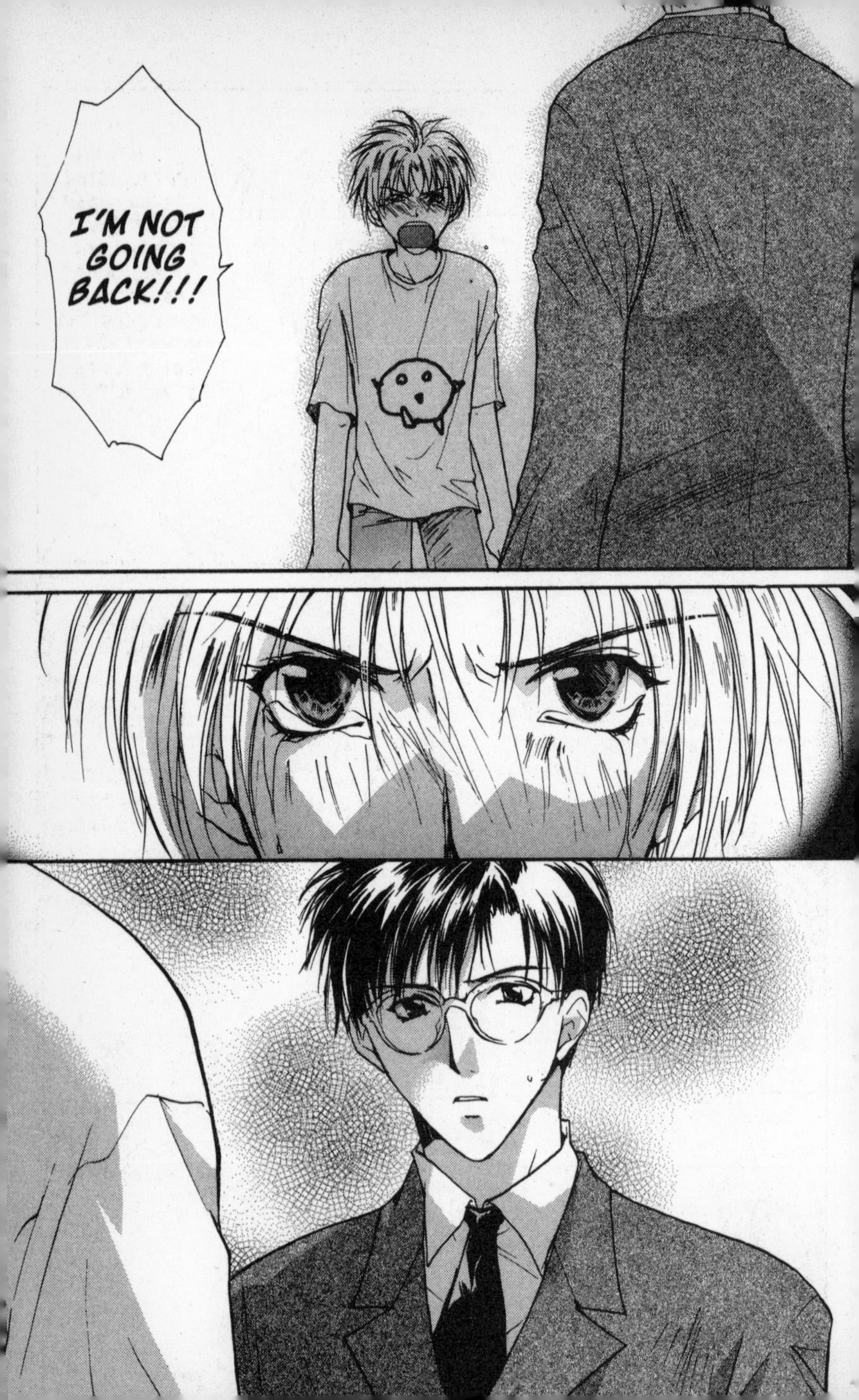
I'M NOT GOING BACK!!!

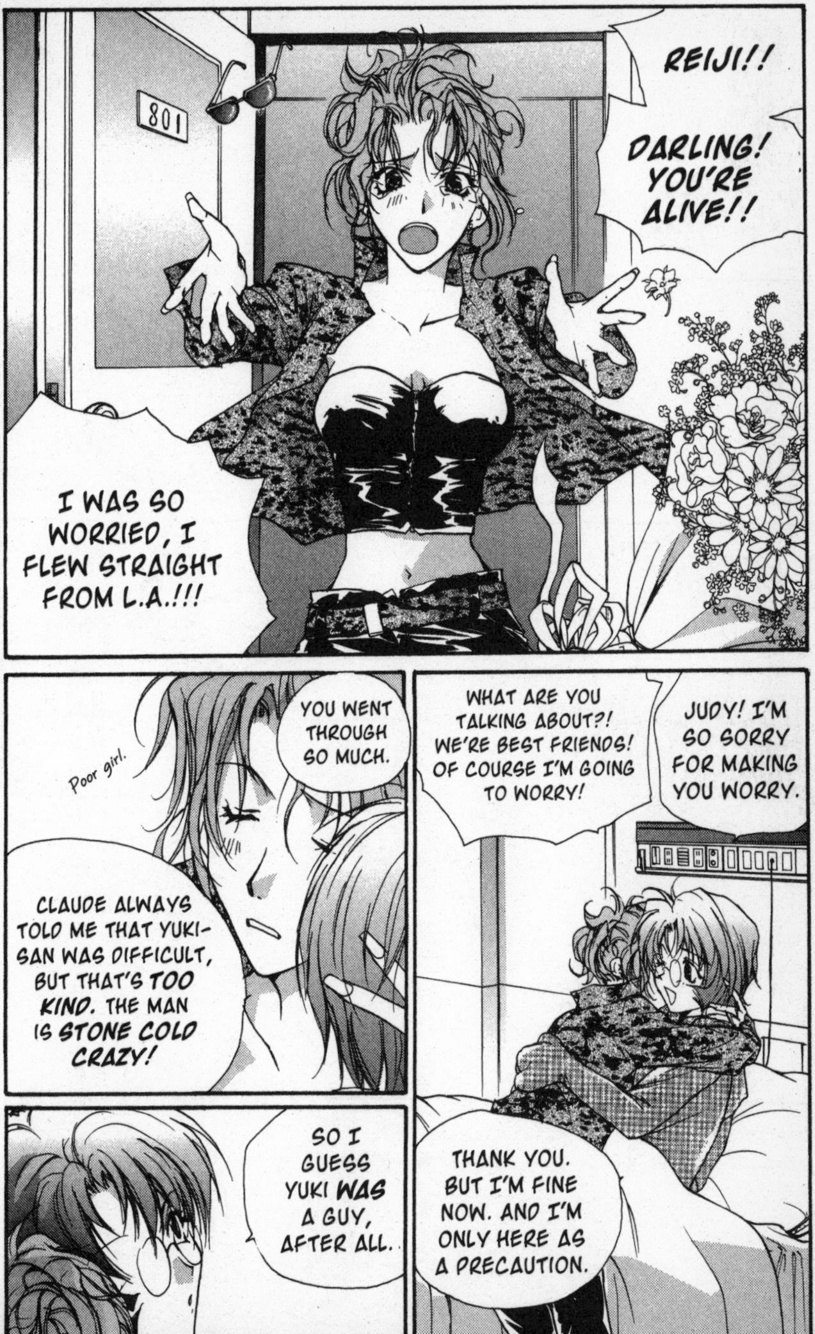
REIJI!!
DARLING! YOU'RE ALIVE!!
I WAS SO WORRIED, I FLEW STRAIGHT FROM L.A.!!!
JUDY! I'M SO SORRY FOR MAKING YOU WORRY.
WHAT ARE YOU TALKING ABOUT?! WE'RE BEST FRIENDS! OF COURSE I'M GOING TO WORRY!
THANK YOU. BUT I'M FINE NOW. AND I'M ONLY HERE AS A PRECAUTION.
YOU WENT THROUGH SO MUCH.
Poor girl.
CLAUDE ALWAYS TOLD ME THAT YUKI-SAN WAS DIFFICULT, BUT THAT'S TOO KIND. THE MAN IS STONE COLD CRAZY!
SO I GUESS YUKI WAS A GUY, AFTER ALL.

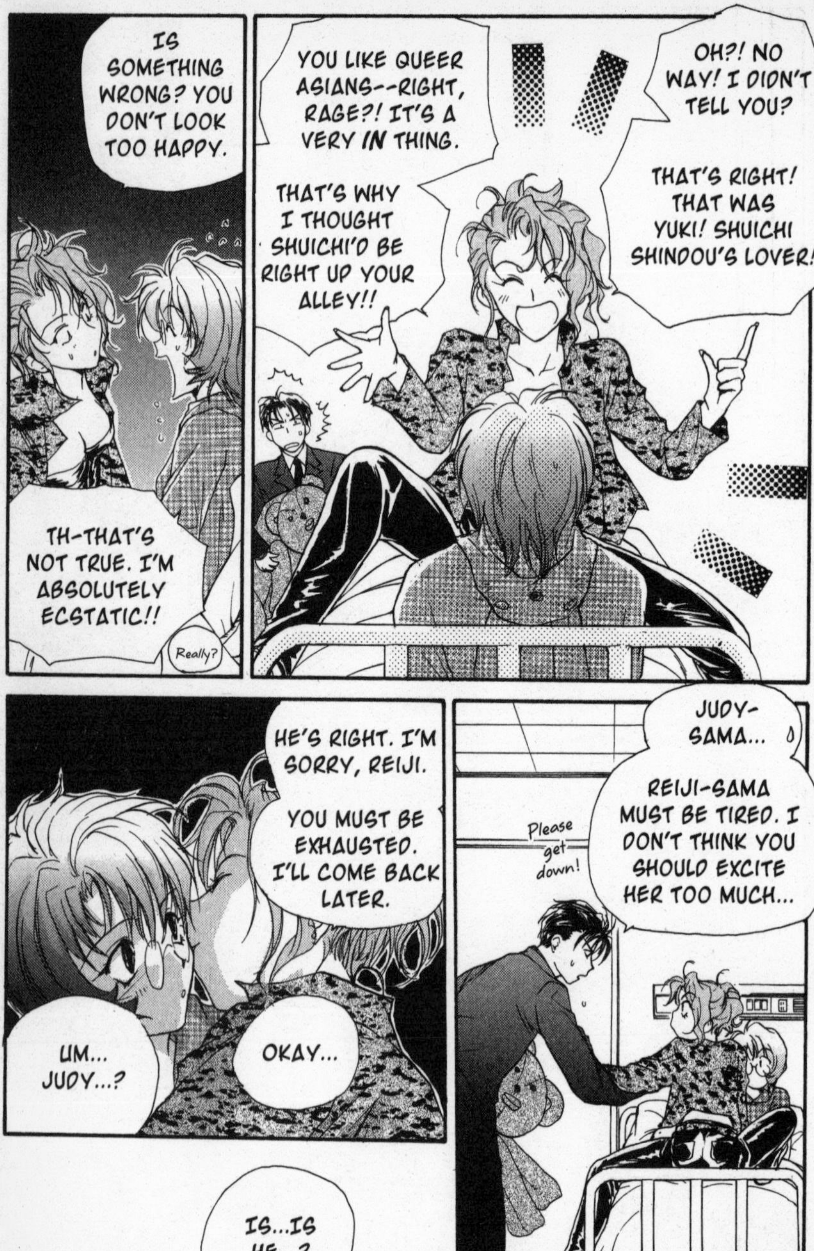
OH?! NO WAY! I DIDN'T TELL YOU?
THAT'S RIGHT! THAT WAS YUKI! SHUICHI SHINDOU'S LOVER!
YOU LIKE QUEER ASIANS--RIGHT, RAGE?! IT'S A VERY *IN* THING.
THAT'S WHY I THOUGHT SHUICHI'D BE RIGHT UP YOUR ALLEY!!
IS SOMETHING WRONG? YOU DON'T LOOK TOO HAPPY.
TH-THAT'S NOT TRUE. I'M ABSOLUTELY ECSTATIC!!
Really?
JUDY-SAMA...
REIJI-SAMA MUST BE TIRED. I DON'T THINK YOU SHOULD EXCITE HER TOO MUCH...
Please get down!
HE'S RIGHT. I'M SORRY, REIJI.
YOU MUST BE EXHAUSTED. I'LL COME BACK LATER.
OKAY...
UM... JUDY...?
IS...IS HE...?

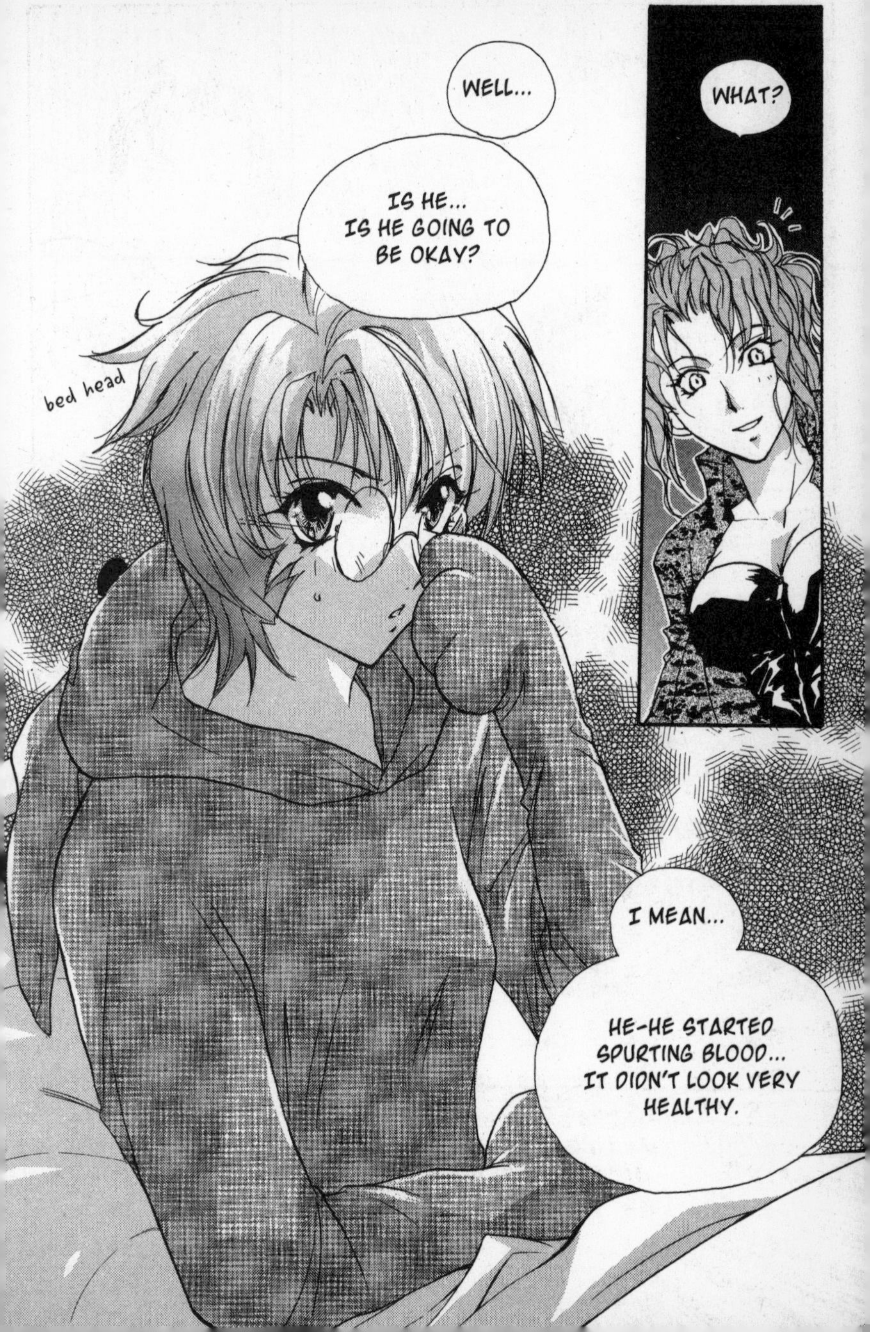
WHAT?
WELL...
IS HE... IS HE GOING TO BE OKAY?
bed head
I MEAN...
HE-HE STARTED SPURTING BLOOD... IT DIDN'T LOOK VERY HEALTHY.

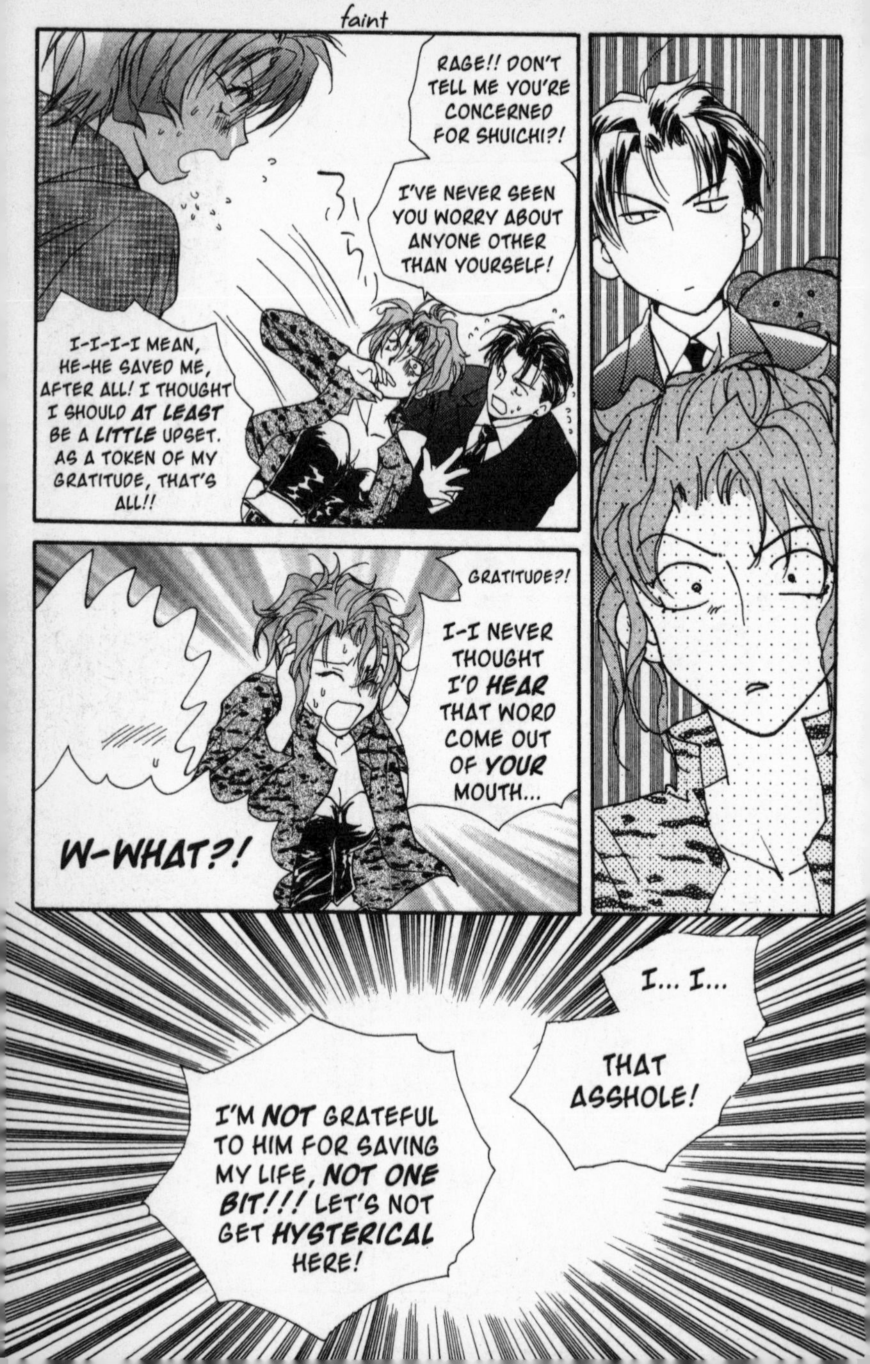

faint
RAGE!! DON'T TELL ME YOU'RE CONCERNED FOR SHUICHI?!
I'VE NEVER SEEN YOU WORRY ABOUT ANYONE OTHER THAN YOURSELF!
I-I-I-I MEAN, HE-HE SAVED ME, AFTER ALL! I THOUGHT I SHOULD AT LEAST BE A LITTLE UPSET. AS A TOKEN OF MY GRATITUDE, THAT'S ALL!!
GRATITUDE?!
I-I NEVER THOUGHT I'D HEAR THAT WORD COME OUT OF YOUR MOUTH...
W-WHAT?!
I... I...
THAT ASSHOLE!
I'M NOT GRATEFUL TO HIM FOR SAVING MY LIFE, NOT ONE BIT!!! LET'S NOT GET HYSTERICAL HERE!

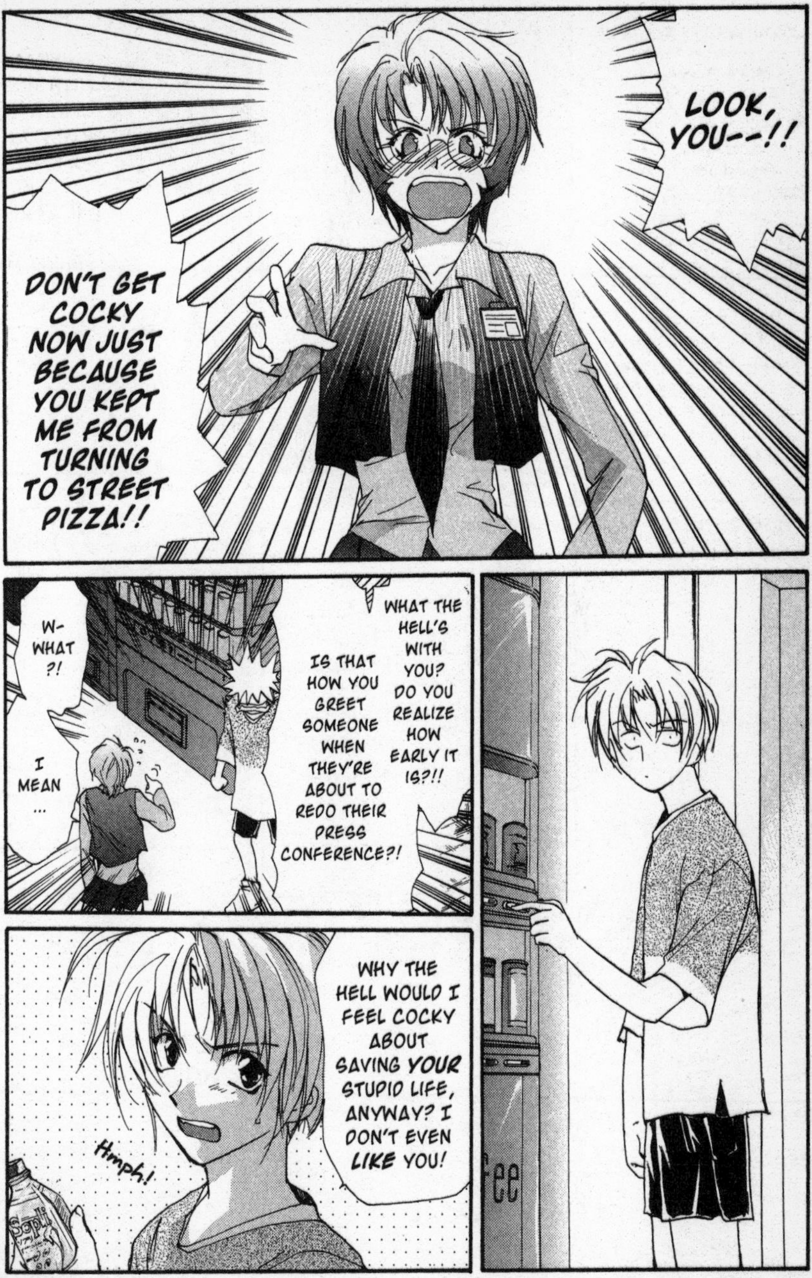
LOOK, YOU--!!
DON'T GET COCKY NOW JUST BECAUSE YOU KEPT ME FROM TURNING TO STREET PIZZA!!
WHAT THE HELL'S WITH YOU? DO YOU REALIZE HOW EARLY IT IS?!!
IS THAT HOW YOU GREET SOMEONE WHEN THEY'RE ABOUT TO REDO THEIR PRESS CONFERENCE?!
W-WHAT?!
I MEAN ...
WHY THE HELL WOULD I FEEL COCKY ABOUT SAVING YOUR STUPID LIFE, ANYWAY? I DON'T EVEN LIKE YOU!
Hmph!

MORE ABOUT TRACK 38

I've recovered from my hunger pangs. I apologize for Run-chan's ugly drawings, which should never have defiled your precious eyes. As revenge, I shall draw, with my left hand... In one stroke?! No way!! This is what you call a professional job! With just shading tones!!

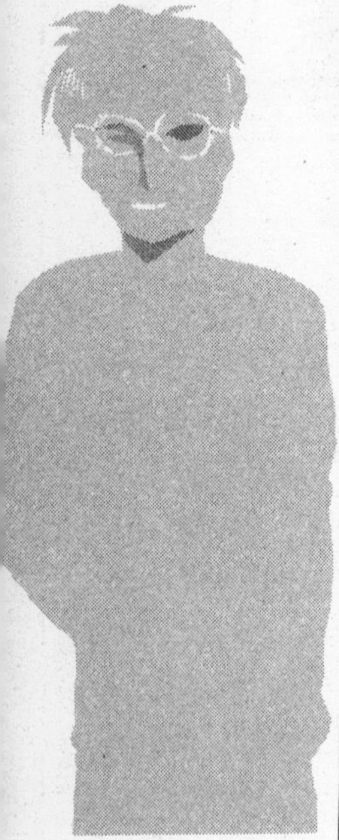

So who is this?
(I give up...)

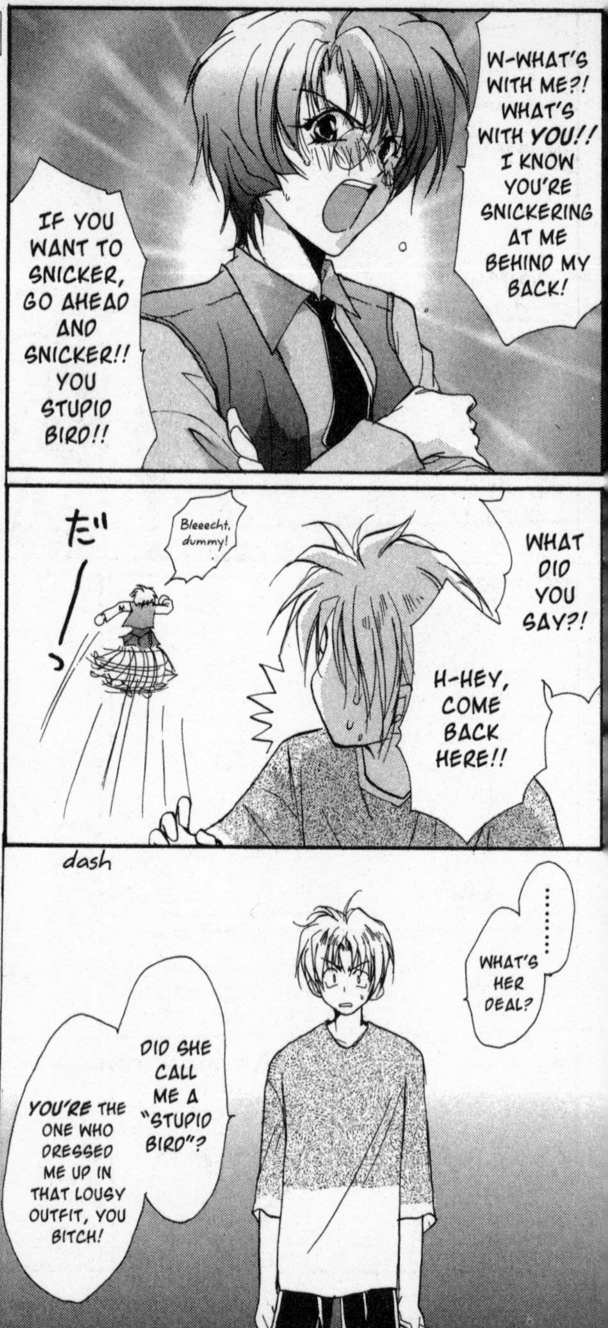
W-WHAT'S WITH ME?! WHAT'S WITH YOU!! I KNOW YOU'RE SNICKERING AT ME BEHIND MY BACK!
IF YOU WANT TO SNICKER, GO AHEAD AND SNICKER!! YOU STUPID BIRD!!
WHAT DID YOU SAY?!
H-HEY, COME BACK HERE!!
Bleeecht, dummy!
だ
dash
......
WHAT'S HER DEAL?
DID SHE CALL ME A "STUPID BIRD"?
YOU'RE THE ONE WHO DRESSED ME UP IN THAT LOUSY OUTFIT, YOU BITCH!

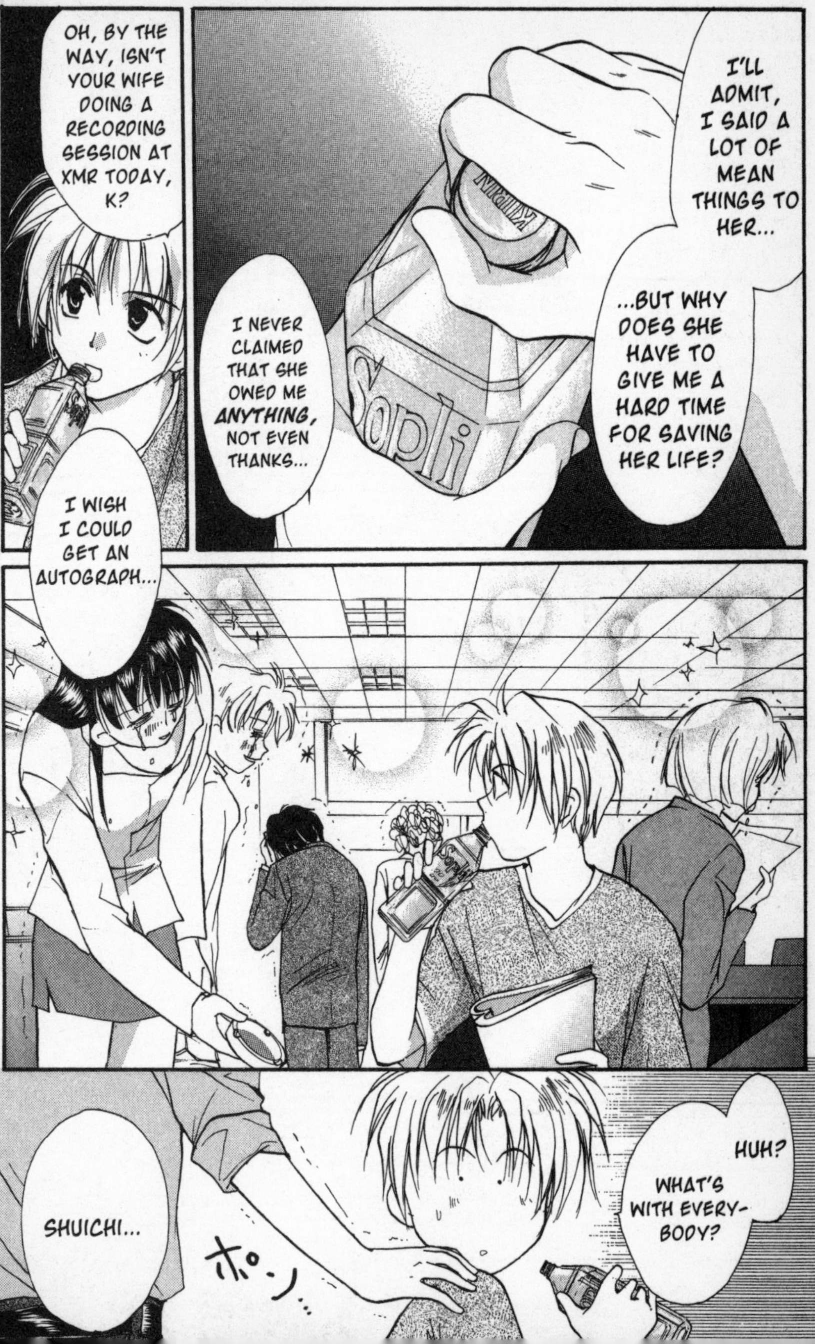
I'LL ADMIT, I SAID A LOT OF MEAN THINGS TO HER...
...BUT WHY DOES SHE HAVE TO GIVE ME A HARD TIME FOR SAVING HER LIFE?
I NEVER CLAIMED THAT SHE OWED ME ANYTHING, NOT EVEN THANKS...
OH, BY THE WAY, ISN'T YOUR WIFE DOING A RECORDING SESSION AT XMR TODAY, K?
I WISH I COULD GET AN AUTOGRAPH...
HUH?
WHAT'S WITH EVERY-BODY?
SHUICHI...
ポン…

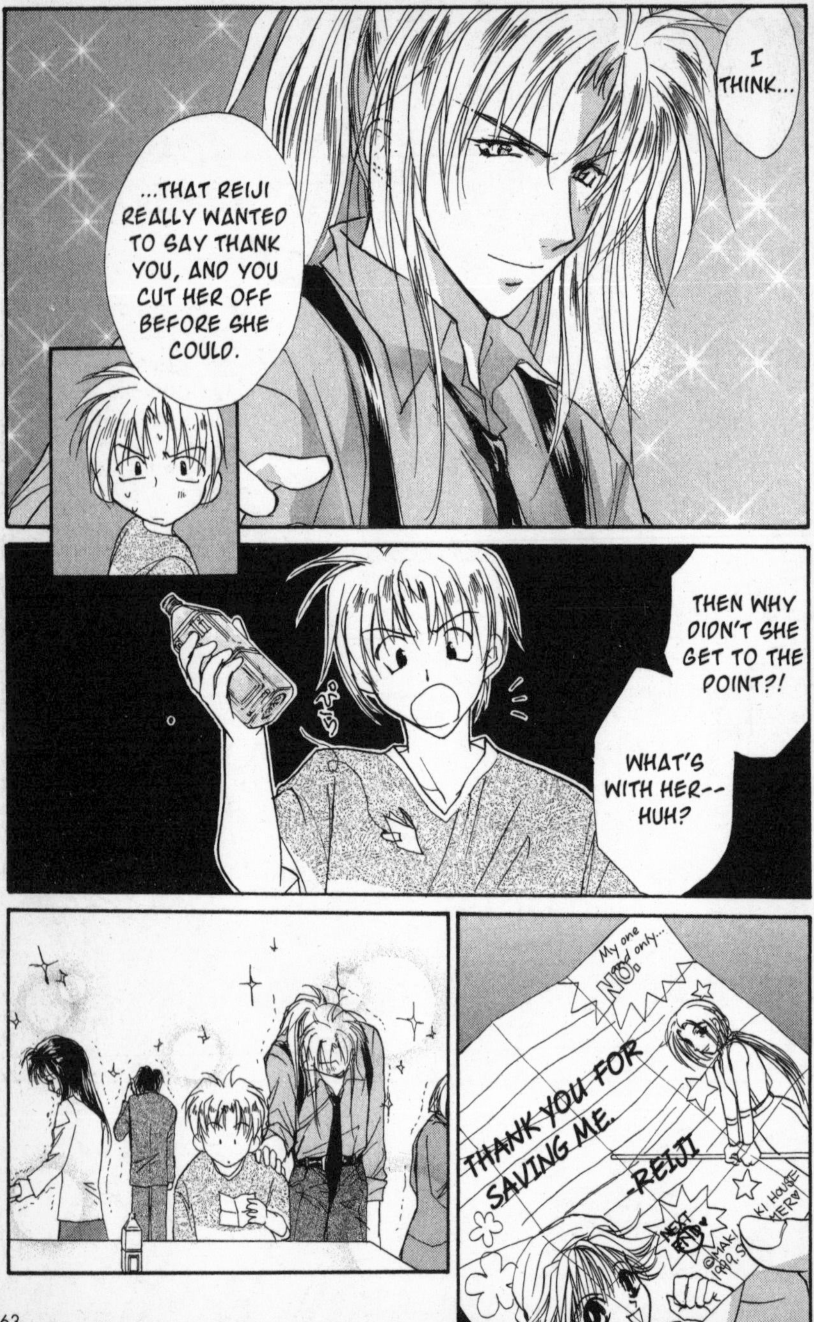
I THINK...
...THAT REIJI REALLY WANTED TO SAY THANK YOU, AND YOU CUT HER OFF BEFORE SHE COULD.
THEN WHY DIDN'T SHE GET TO THE POINT?!
WHAT'S WITH HER--HUH?
My one and only...
NO
THANK YOU FOR SAVING ME.
-REIJI

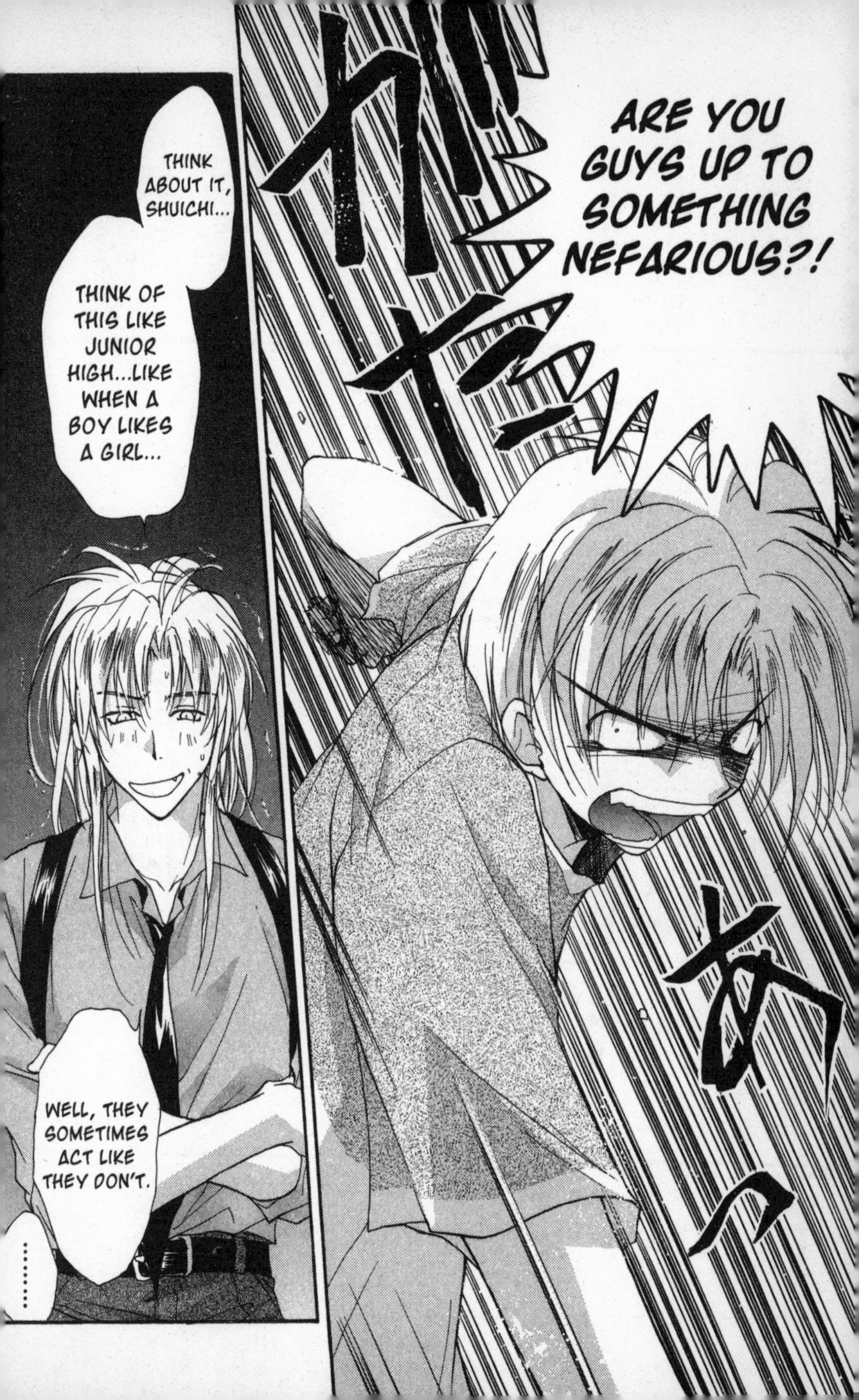
ARE YOU GUYS UP TO SOMETHING NEFARIOUS?!
THINK ABOUT IT, SHUICHI...
THINK OF THIS LIKE JUNIOR HIGH...LIKE WHEN A BOY LIKES A GIRL...
WELL, THEY SOMETIMES ACT LIKE THEY DON'T.
....

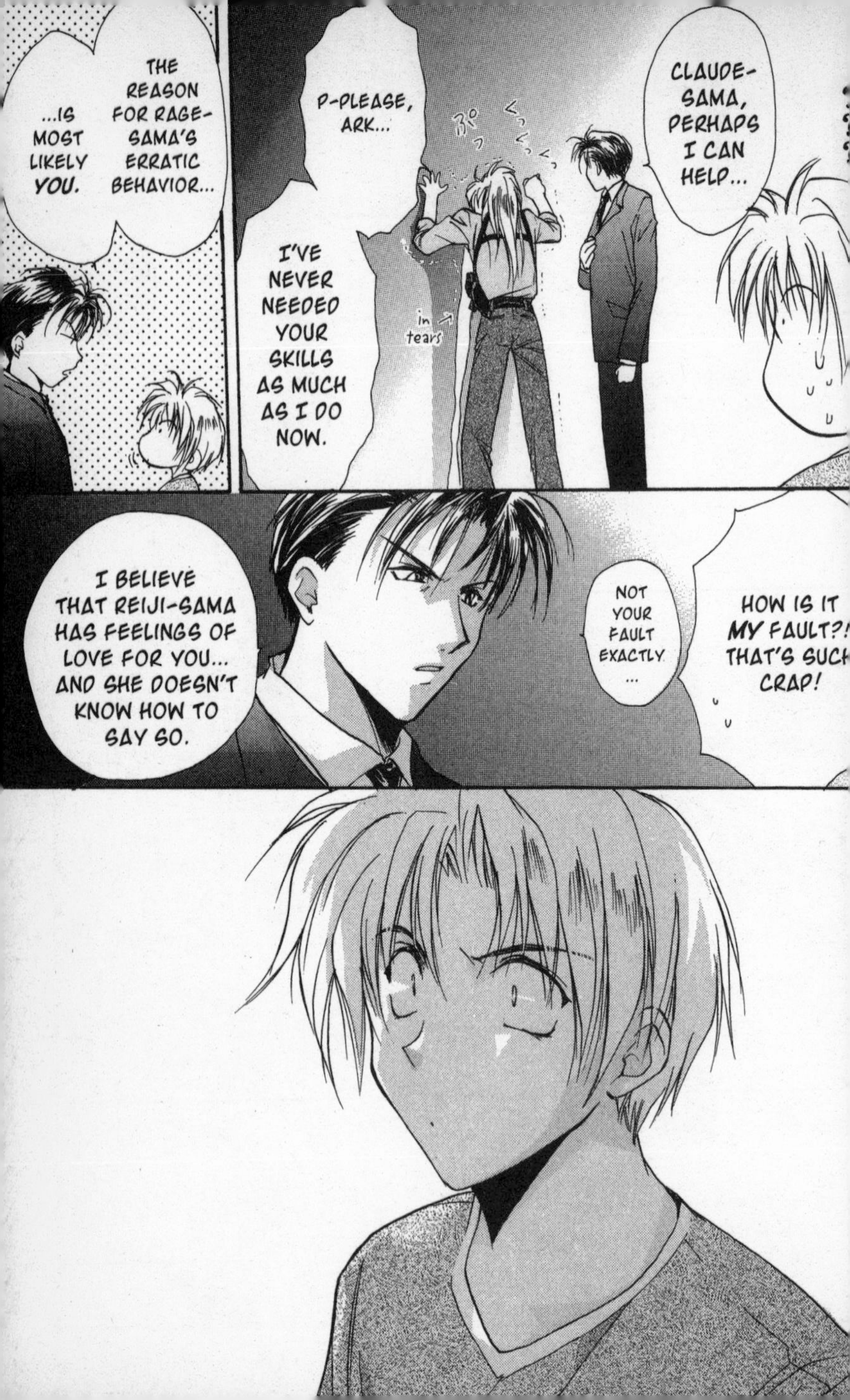
CLAUDE-SAMA, PERHAPS I CAN HELP...
P-PLEASE, ARK...
I'VE NEVER NEEDED YOUR SKILLS AS MUCH AS I DO NOW.
in tears
THE REASON FOR RAGE-SAMA'S ERRATIC BEHAVIOR...
...IS MOST LIKELY *YOU.*
HOW IS IT *MY* FAULT?! THAT'S SUCH CRAP!
NOT YOUR FAULT EXACTLY...
I BELIEVE THAT REIJI-SAMA HAS FEELINGS OF LOVE FOR YOU... AND SHE DOESN'T KNOW HOW TO SAY SO.

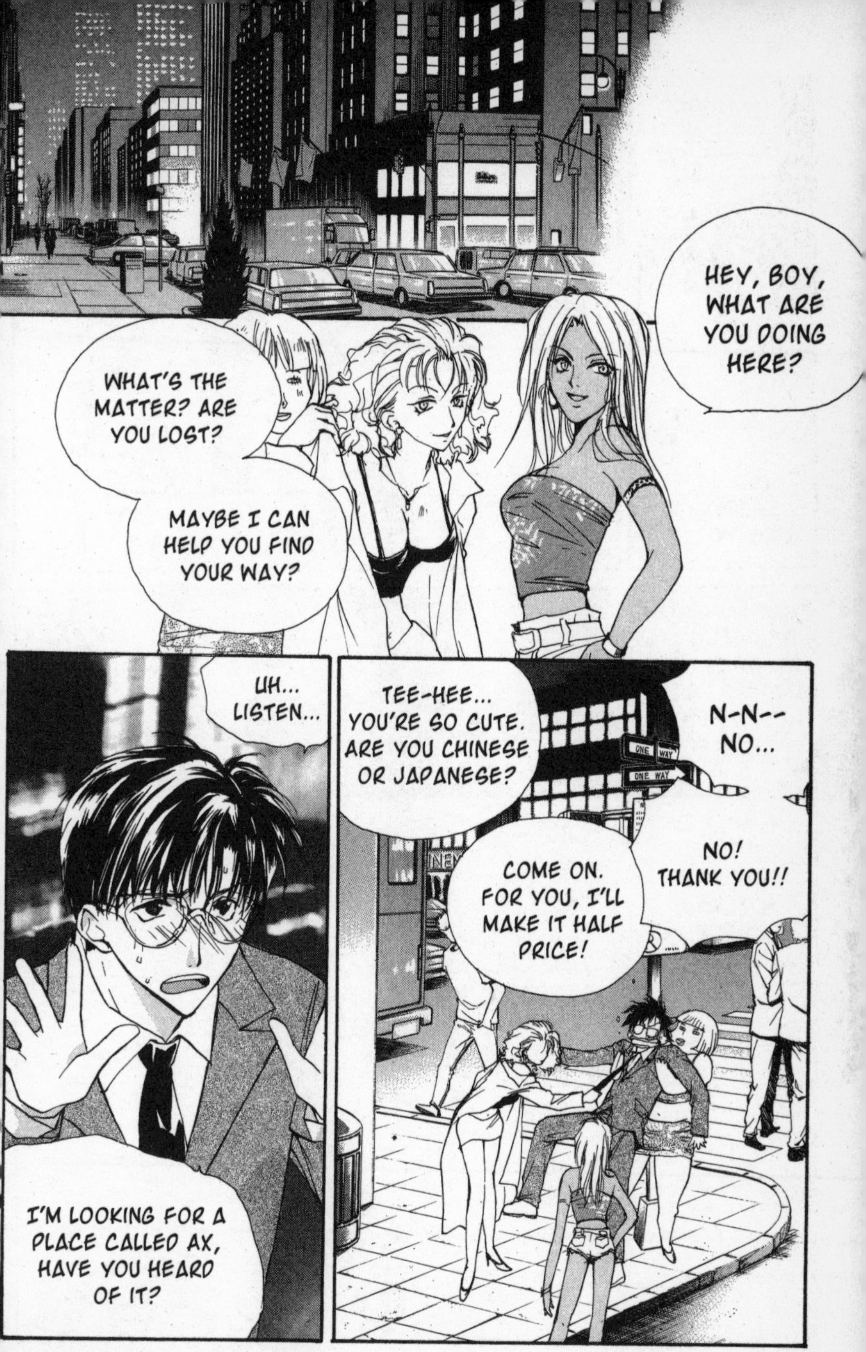
HEY, BOY, WHAT ARE YOU DOING HERE?
WHAT'S THE MATTER? ARE YOU LOST?
MAYBE I CAN HELP YOU FIND YOUR WAY?
TEE-HEE... YOU'RE SO CUTE. ARE YOU CHINESE OR JAPANESE?
N-N--NO...
COME ON. FOR YOU, I'LL MAKE IT HALF PRICE!
NO! THANK YOU!!
ONE WAY
ONE WAY
UH... LISTEN...
I'M LOOKING FOR A PLACE CALLED AX, HAVE YOU HEARD OF IT?

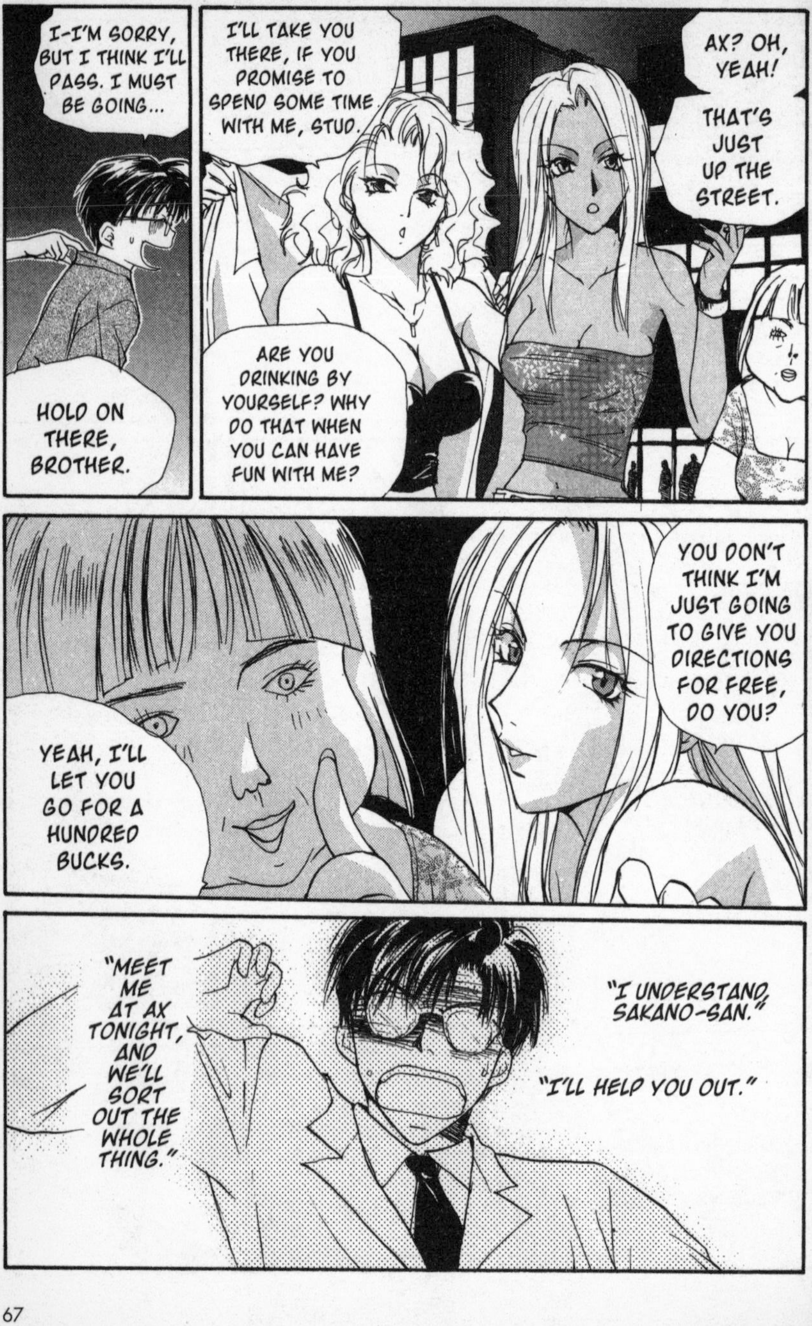
AX? OH, YEAH!
THAT'S JUST UP THE STREET.
I'LL TAKE YOU THERE, IF YOU PROMISE TO SPEND SOME TIME WITH ME, STUD.
ARE YOU DRINKING BY YOURSELF? WHY DO THAT WHEN YOU CAN HAVE FUN WITH ME?
I-I'M SORRY, BUT I THINK I'LL PASS. I MUST BE GOING...
HOLD ON THERE, BROTHER.
YOU DON'T THINK I'M JUST GOING TO GIVE YOU DIRECTIONS FOR FREE, DO YOU?
YEAH, I'LL LET YOU GO FOR A HUNDRED BUCKS.
"I UNDERSTAND, SAKANO-SAN."
"I'LL HELP YOU OUT."
"MEET ME AT AX TONIGHT, AND WE'LL SORT OUT THE WHOLE THING."

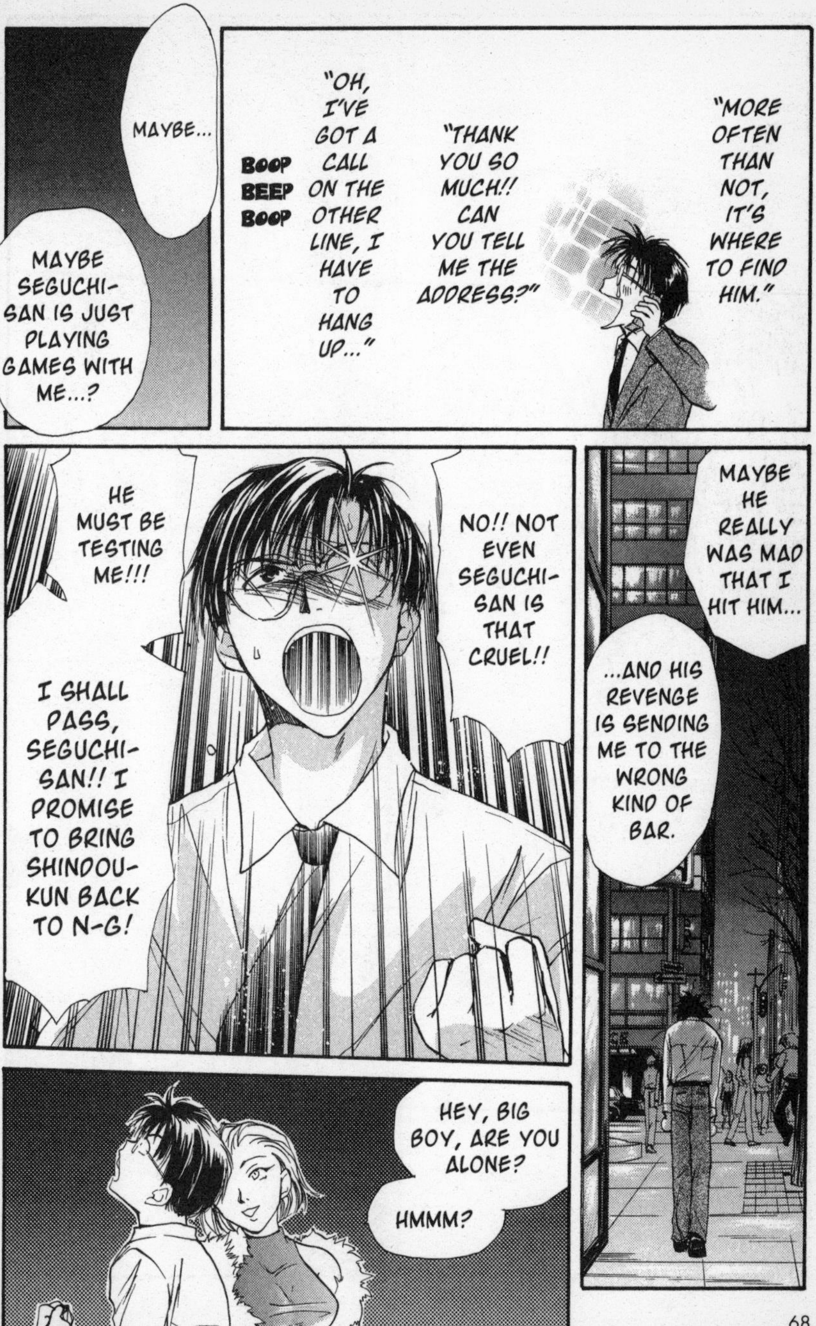
"MORE OFTEN THAN NOT, IT'S WHERE TO FIND HIM."
"THANK YOU SO MUCH!! CAN YOU TELL ME THE ADDRESS?"
"OH, I'VE GOT A CALL ON THE OTHER LINE, I HAVE TO HANG UP..."
BOOP BEEP BOOP
MAYBE...
MAYBE SEGUCHI-SAN IS JUST PLAYING GAMES WITH ME...?
MAYBE HE REALLY WAS MAD THAT I HIT HIM...
...AND HIS REVENGE IS SENDING ME TO THE WRONG KIND OF BAR.
NO!! NOT EVEN SEGUCHI-SAN IS THAT CRUEL!!
HE MUST BE TESTING ME!!!
I SHALL PASS, SEGUCHI-SAN!! I PROMISE TO BRING SHINDOU-KUN BACK TO N-G!
HEY, BIG BOY, ARE YOU ALONE?
HMMM?

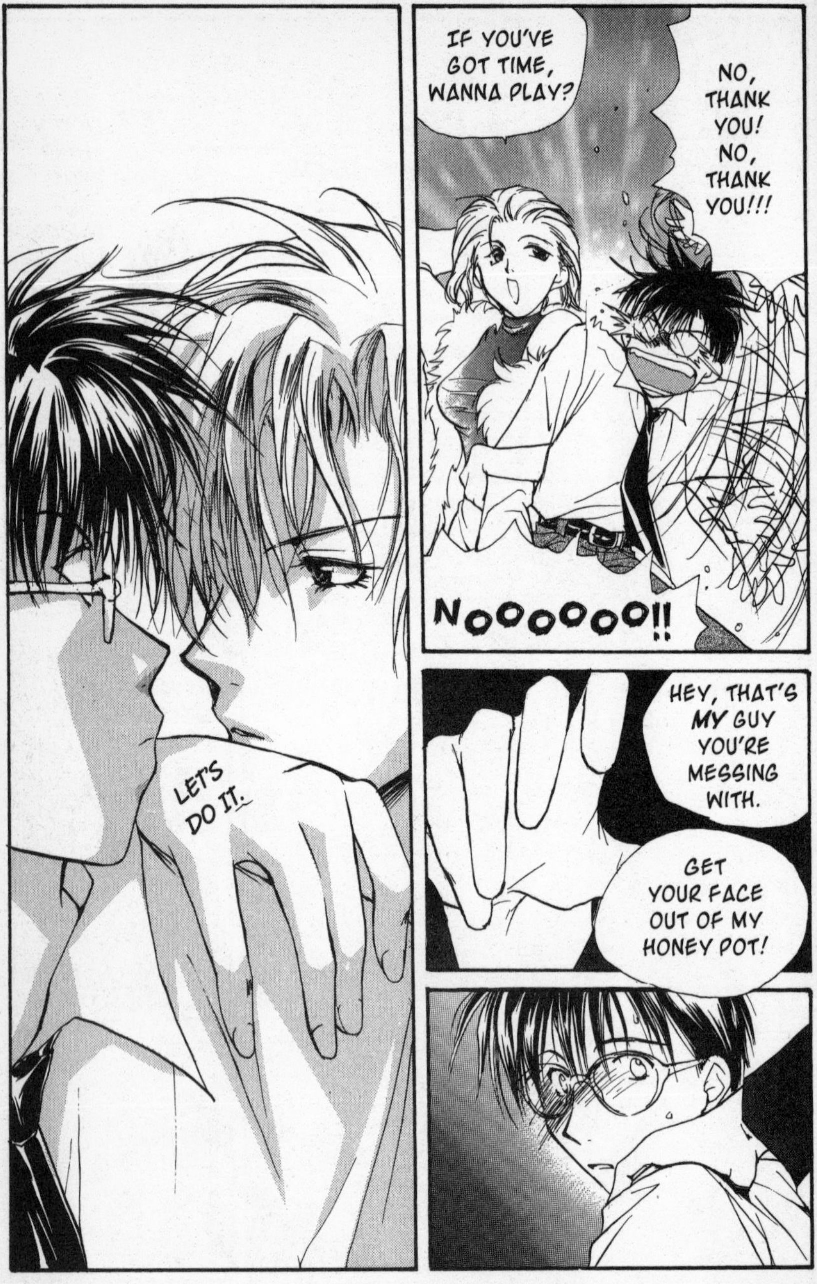
IF YOU'VE GOT TIME, WANNA PLAY?
NO, THANK YOU! NO, THANK YOU!!!
NOOOOOOO!!
HEY, THAT'S MY GUY YOU'RE MESSING WITH.
GET YOUR FACE OUT OF MY HONEY POT!
LET'S DO IT.

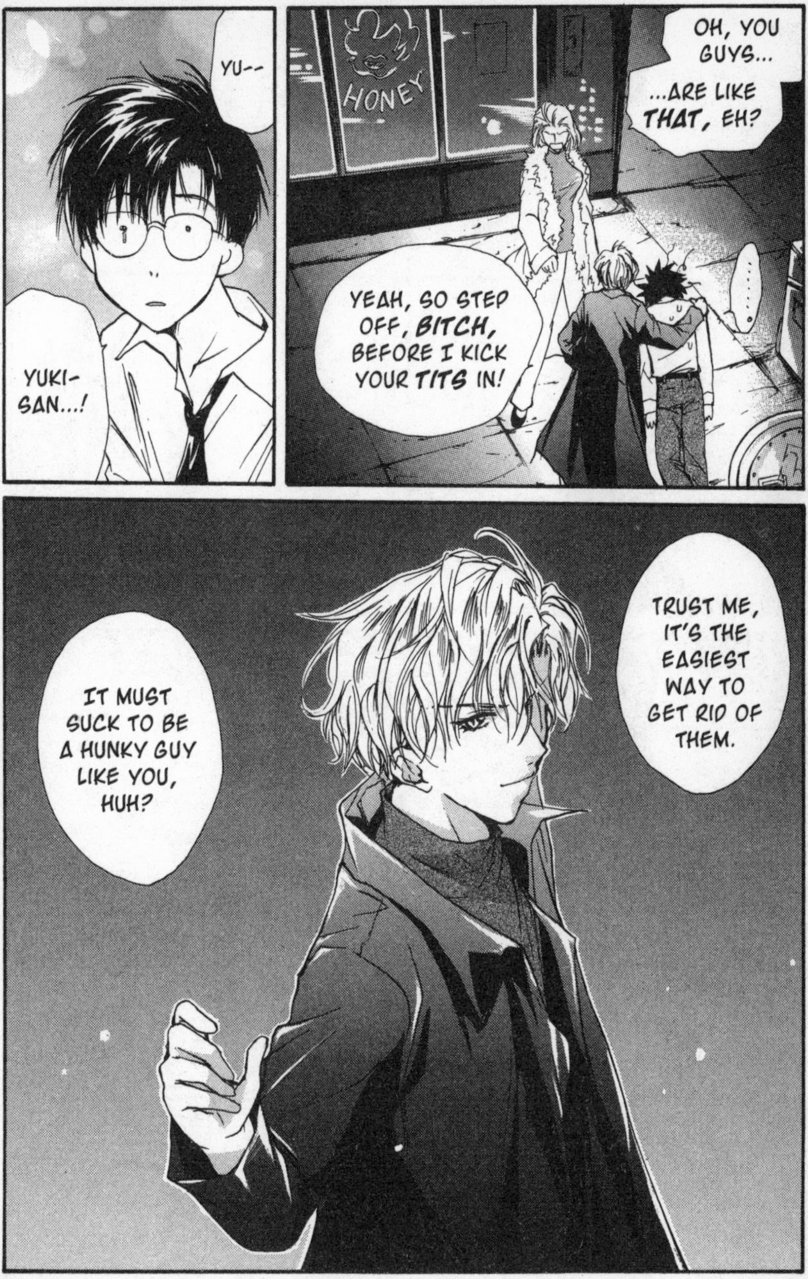
OH, YOU GUYS...
...ARE LIKE THAT, EH?
......
YEAH, SO STEP OFF, BITCH, BEFORE I KICK YOUR TITS IN!
YU--
YUKI-SAN...!
TRUST ME, IT'S THE EASIEST WAY TO GET RID OF THEM.
IT MUST SUCK TO BE A HUNKY GUY LIKE YOU, HUH?

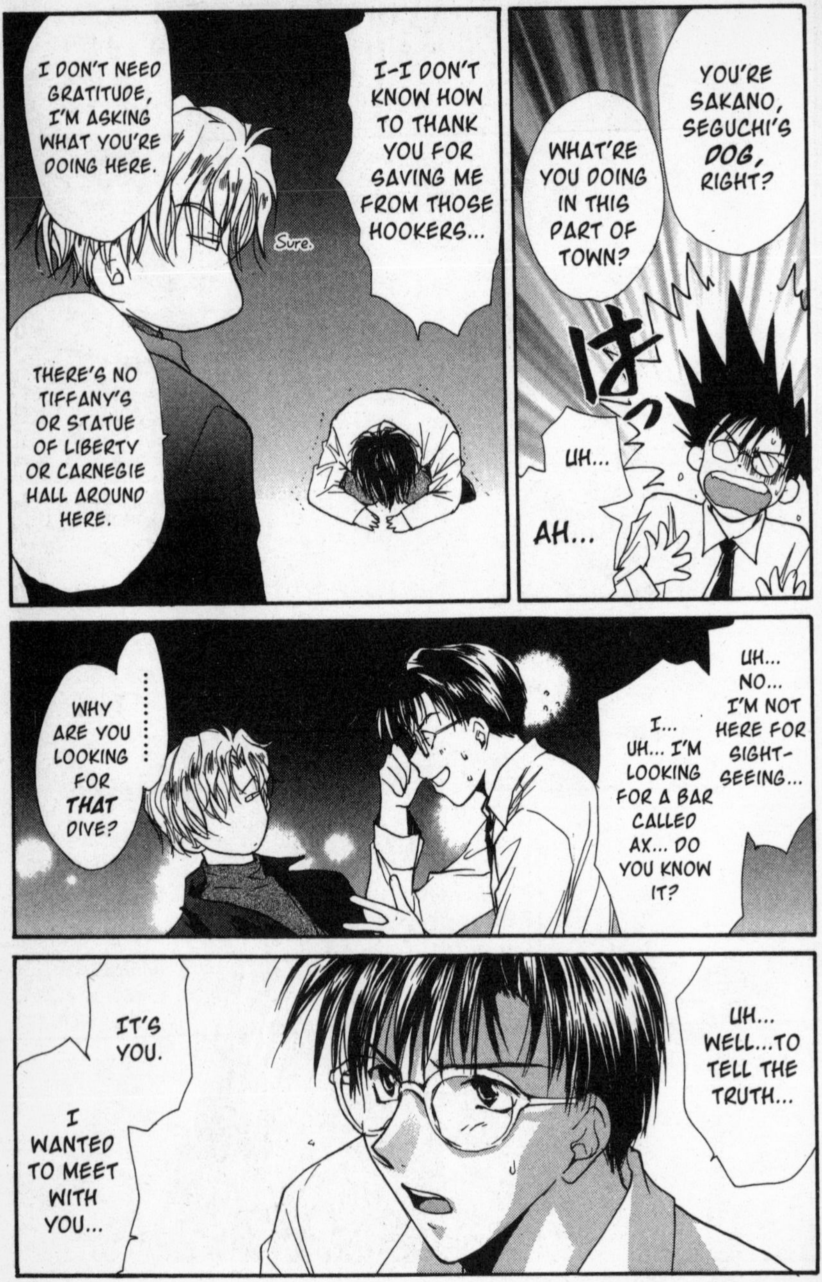
YOU'RE SAKANO, SEGUCHI'S DOG, RIGHT?
WHAT'RE YOU DOING IN THIS PART OF TOWN?
はっ
UH...
AH...
I-I DON'T KNOW HOW TO THANK YOU FOR SAVING ME FROM THOSE HOOKERS...
Sure.
I DON'T NEED GRATITUDE, I'M ASKING WHAT YOU'RE DOING HERE.
THERE'S NO TIFFANY'S OR STATUE OF LIBERTY OR CARNEGIE HALL AROUND HERE.
UH... NO... I'M NOT HERE FOR SIGHT-SEEING...
I... UH... I'M LOOKING FOR A BAR CALLED AX... DO YOU KNOW IT?
......
WHY ARE YOU LOOKING FOR **THAT** DIVE?
UH... WELL...TO TELL THE TRUTH...
IT'S YOU.
I WANTED TO MEET WITH YOU...

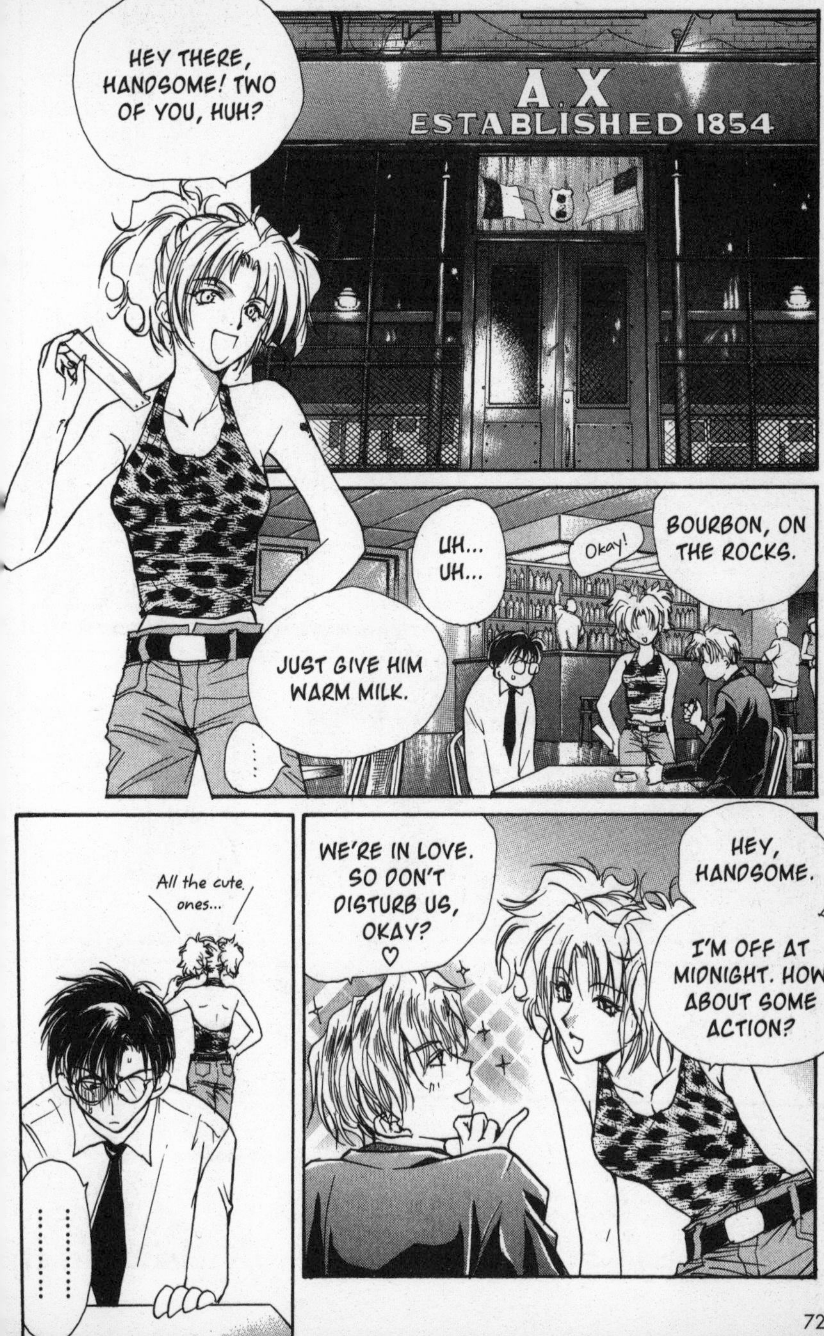
HEY THERE, HANDSOME! TWO OF YOU, HUH?
A.X
ESTABLISHED 1854
BOURBON, ON THE ROCKS.
Okay!
UH... UH...
JUST GIVE HIM WARM MILK.
......
HEY, HANDSOME.
I'M OFF AT MIDNIGHT. HOW ABOUT SOME ACTION?
WE'RE IN LOVE. SO DON'T DISTURB US, OKAY? ♡
All the cute ones...
......

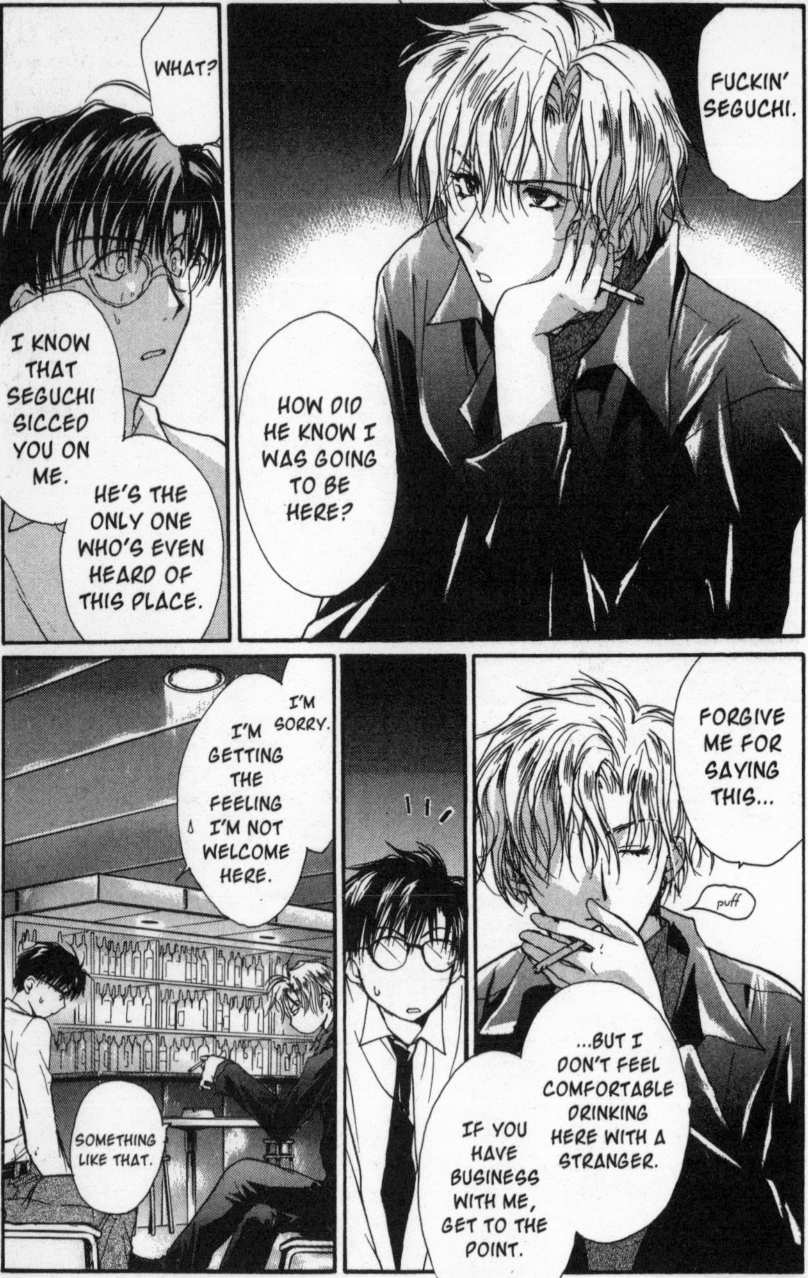
FUCKIN' SEGUCHI.
HOW DID HE KNOW I WAS GOING TO BE HERE?
WHAT?
I KNOW THAT SEGUCHI SICCED YOU ON ME.
HE'S THE ONLY ONE WHO'S EVEN HEARD OF THIS PLACE.
FORGIVE ME FOR SAYING THIS...
puff
...BUT I DON'T FEEL COMFORTABLE DRINKING HERE WITH A STRANGER.
IF YOU HAVE BUSINESS WITH ME, GET TO THE POINT.
I'M SORRY.
I'M GETTING THE FEELING I'M NOT WELCOME HERE.
SOMETHING LIKE THAT.

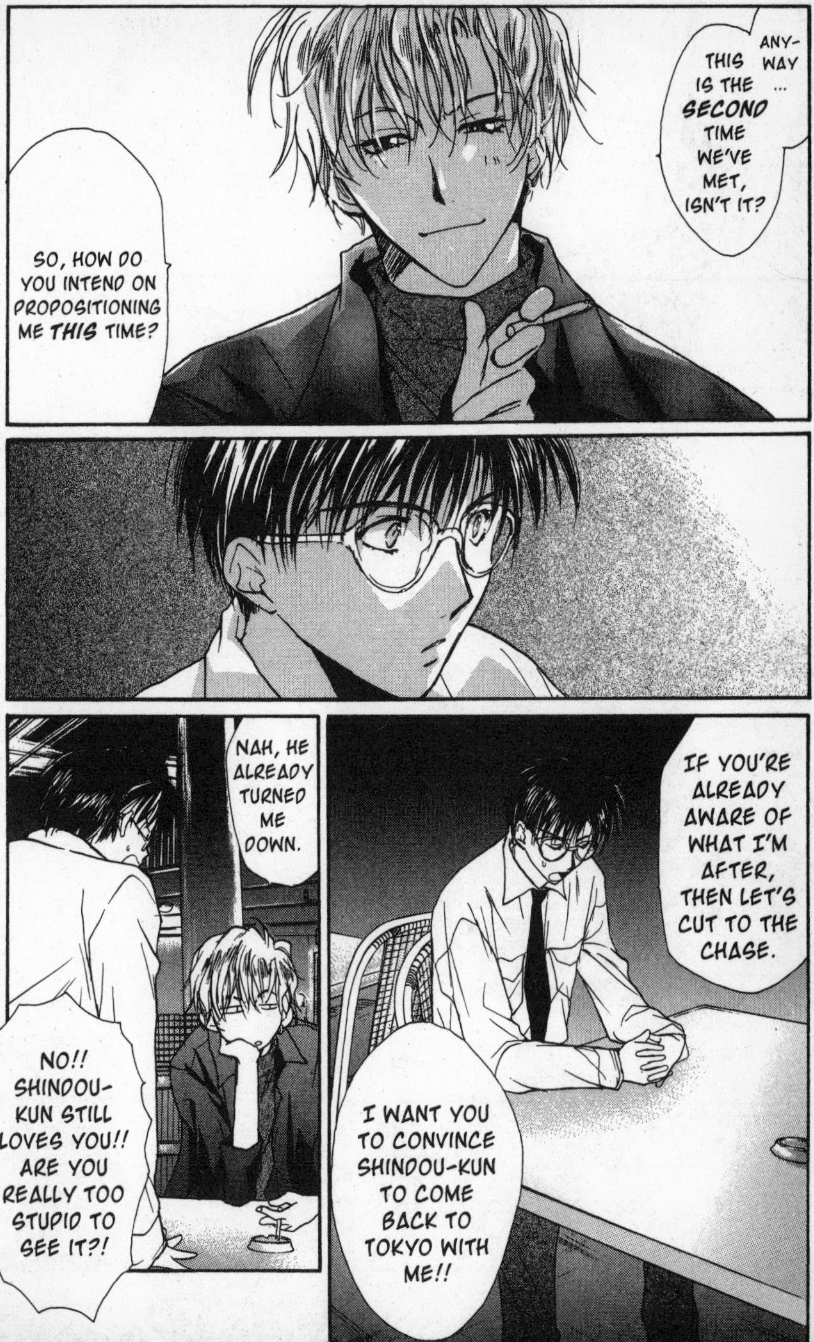
ANYWAY... THIS IS THE SECOND TIME WE'VE MET, ISN'T IT?
SO, HOW DO YOU INTEND ON PROPOSITIONING ME THIS TIME?
IF YOU'RE ALREADY AWARE OF WHAT I'M AFTER, THEN LET'S CUT TO THE CHASE.
I WANT YOU TO CONVINCE SHINDOU-KUN TO COME BACK TO TOKYO WITH ME!!
NAH, HE ALREADY TURNED ME DOWN.
NO!! SHINDOU-KUN STILL LOVES YOU!! ARE YOU REALLY TOO STUPID TO SEE IT?!

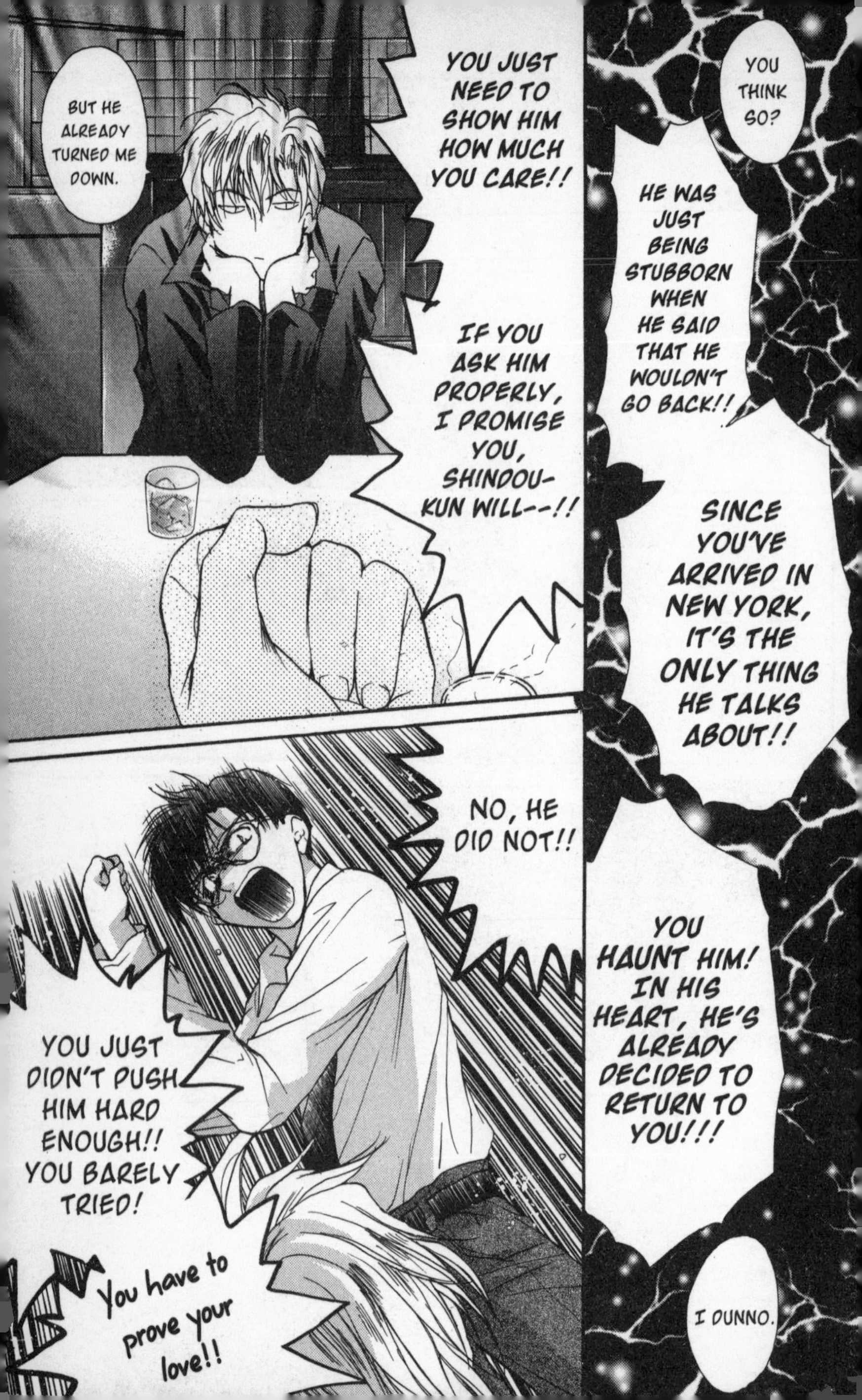
YOU THINK SO?
HE WAS JUST BEING STUBBORN WHEN HE SAID THAT HE WOULDN'T GO BACK!!
SINCE YOU'VE ARRIVED IN NEW YORK, IT'S THE ONLY THING HE TALKS ABOUT!!
YOU HAUNT HIM! IN HIS HEART, HE'S ALREADY DECIDED TO RETURN TO YOU!!!
I DUNNO.
YOU JUST NEED TO SHOW HIM HOW MUCH YOU CARE!!
BUT HE ALREADY TURNED ME DOWN.
IF YOU ASK HIM PROPERLY, I PROMISE YOU, SHINDOU-KUN WILL--!!
NO, HE DID NOT!!
YOU JUST DIDN'T PUSH HIM HARD ENOUGH!! YOU BARELY TRIED!
You have to prove your love!!

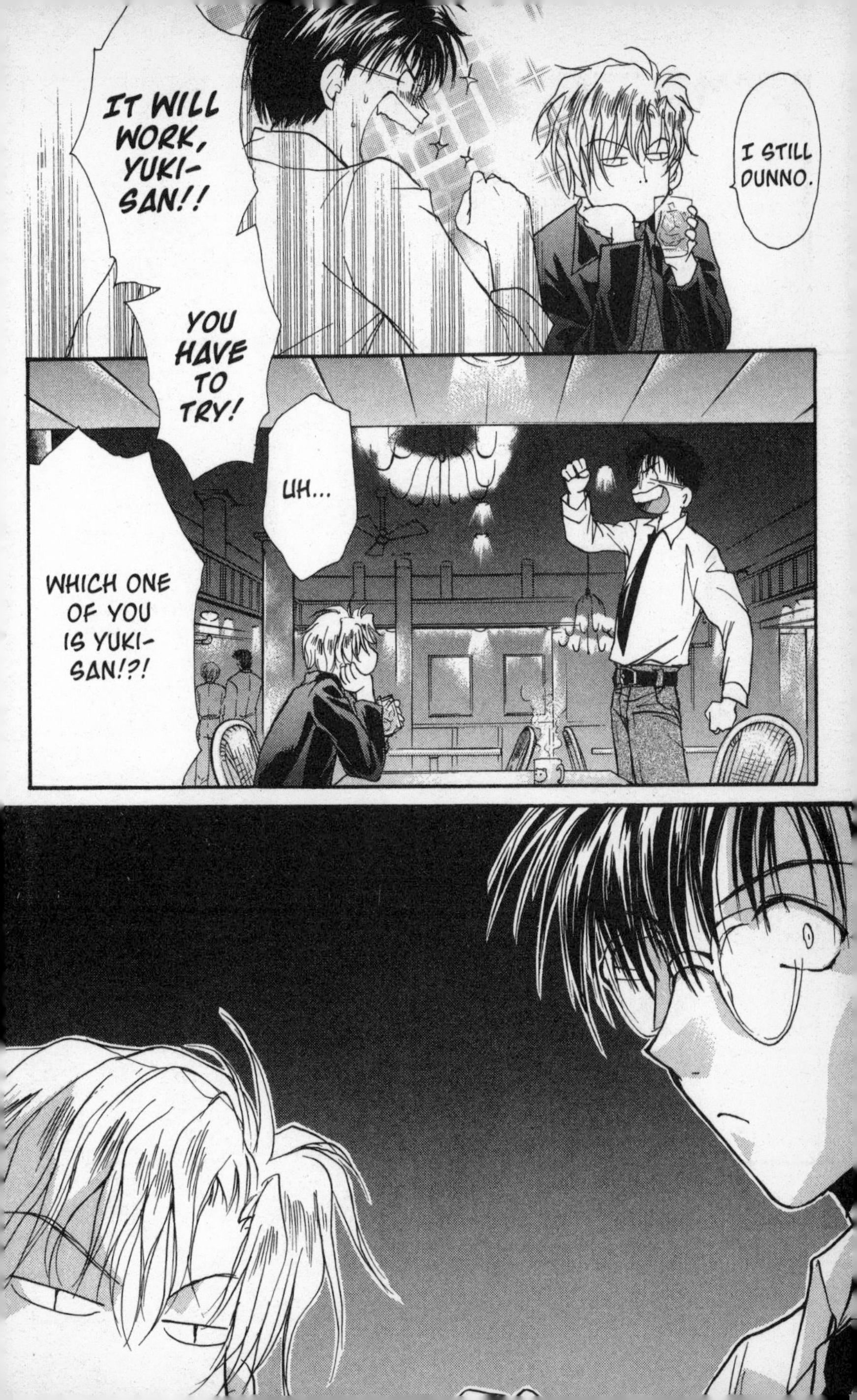
I STILL DUNNO.
IT WILL WORK, YUKI-SAN!!
YOU HAVE TO TRY!
UH...
WHICH ONE OF YOU IS YUKI-SAN!?!

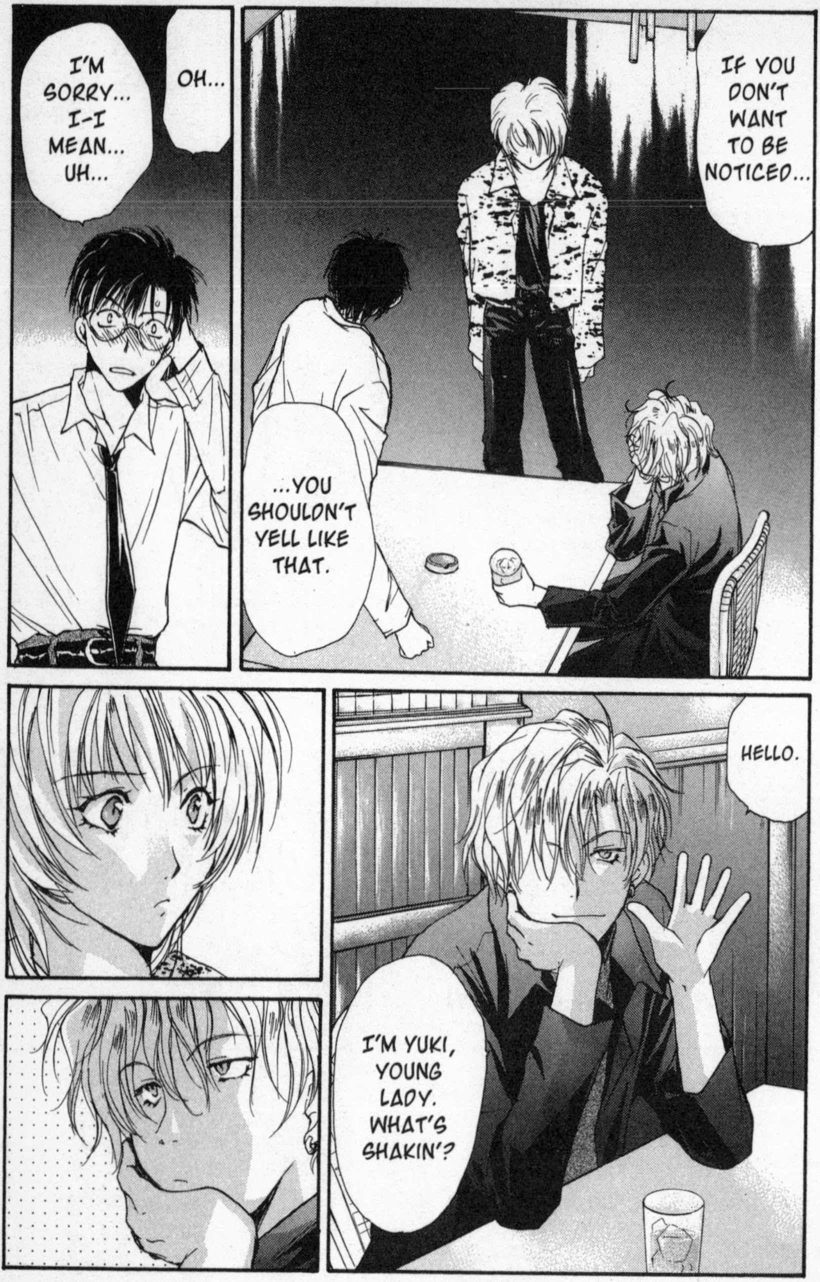
IF YOU DON'T WANT TO BE NOTICED...
...YOU SHOULDN'T YELL LIKE THAT.
OH...
I'M SORRY... I-I MEAN... UH...
HELLO.
I'M YUKI, YOUNG LADY. WHAT'S SHAKIN'?

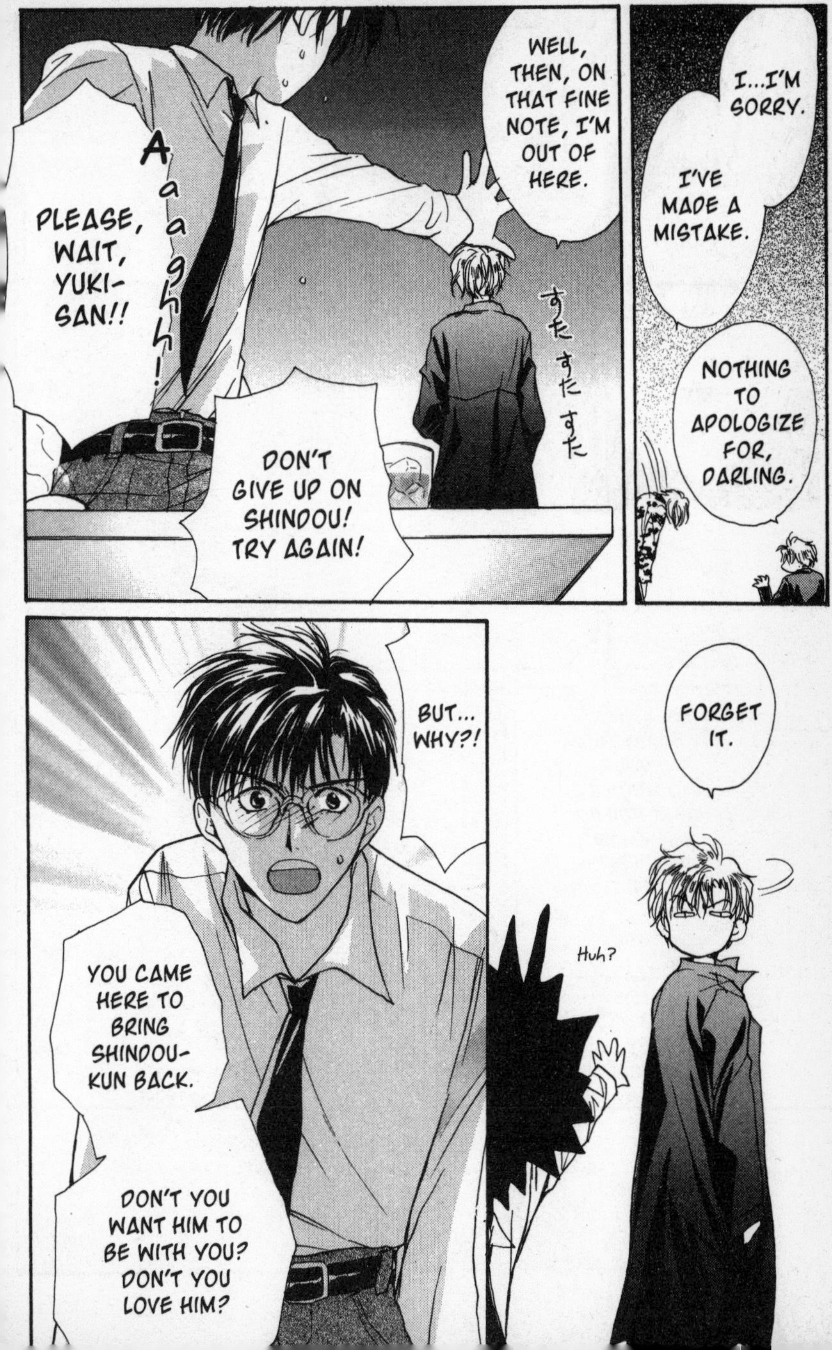
I...I'M SORRY.
I'VE MADE A MISTAKE.
NOTHING TO APOLOGIZE FOR, DARLING.
WELL, THEN, ON THAT FINE NOTE, I'M OUT OF HERE.
すたすたすた
Aaaghh!
PLEASE, WAIT, YUKI-SAN!!
DON'T GIVE UP ON SHINDOU! TRY AGAIN!
FORGET IT.
BUT... WHY?!
Huh?
YOU CAME HERE TO BRING SHINDOU-KUN BACK.
DON'T YOU WANT HIM TO BE WITH YOU? DON'T YOU LOVE HIM?

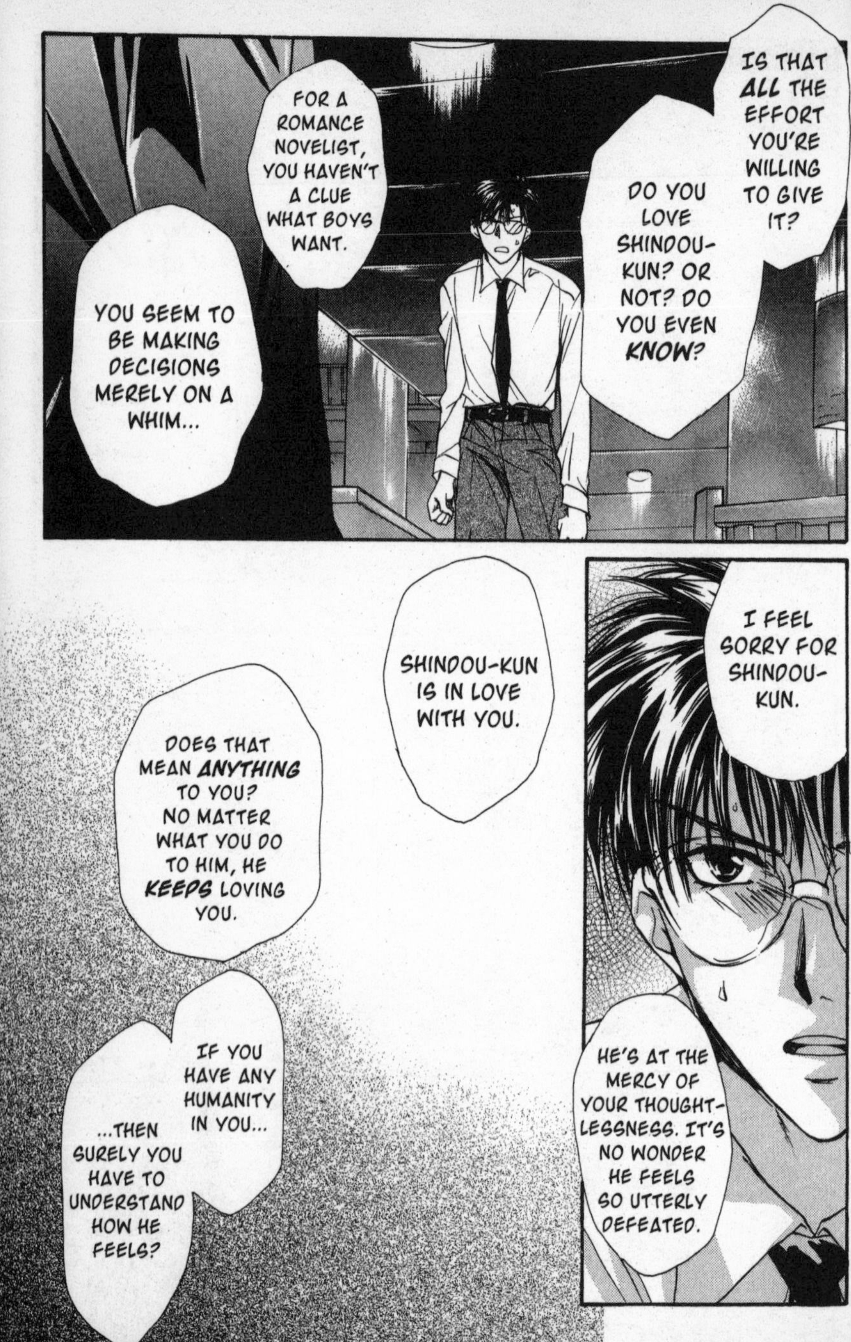
IS THAT ALL THE EFFORT YOU'RE WILLING TO GIVE IT?
DO YOU LOVE SHINDOU-KUN? OR NOT? DO YOU EVEN KNOW?
FOR A ROMANCE NOVELIST, YOU HAVEN'T A CLUE WHAT BOYS WANT.
YOU SEEM TO BE MAKING DECISIONS MERELY ON A WHIM...
I FEEL SORRY FOR SHINDOU-KUN.
HE'S AT THE MERCY OF YOUR THOUGHT-LESSNESS. IT'S NO WONDER HE FEELS SO UTTERLY DEFEATED.
SHINDOU-KUN IS IN LOVE WITH YOU.
DOES THAT MEAN ANYTHING TO YOU? NO MATTER WHAT YOU DO TO HIM, HE KEEPS LOVING YOU.
IF YOU HAVE ANY HUMANITY IN YOU...
...THEN SURELY YOU HAVE TO UNDERSTAND HOW HE FEELS?

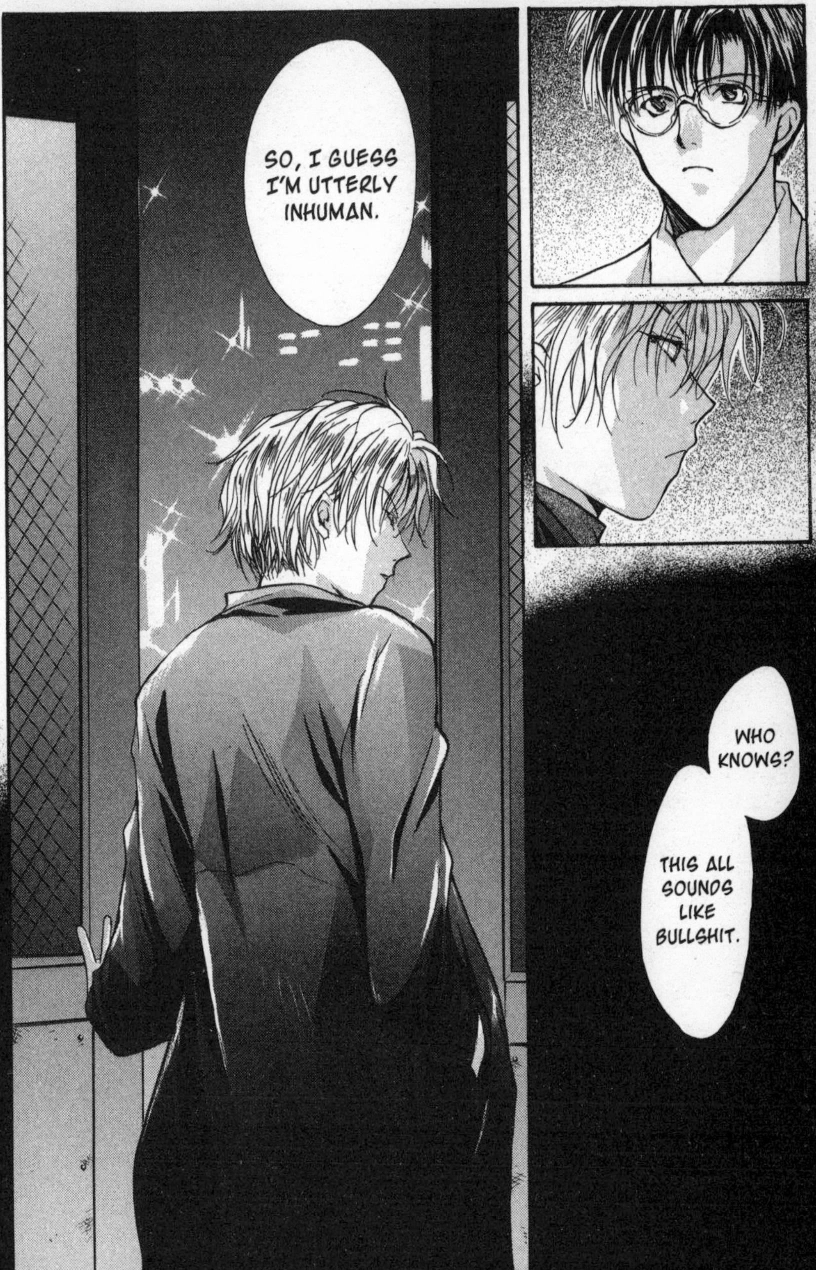
SO, I GUESS I'M UTTERLY INHUMAN.
WHO KNOWS?
THIS ALL SOUNDS LIKE BULLSHIT.

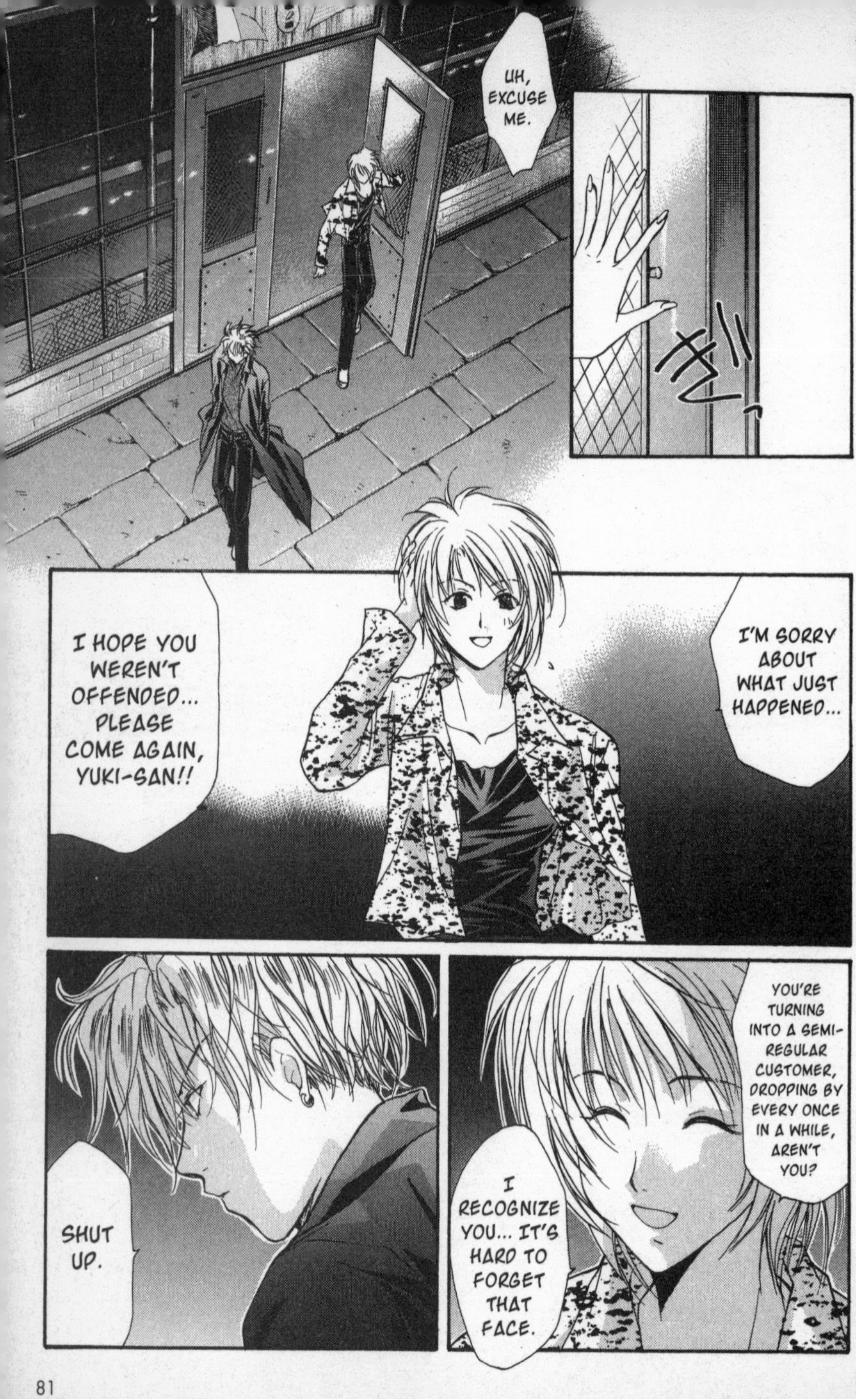
UH, EXCUSE ME.
I'M SORRY ABOUT WHAT JUST HAPPENED...
I HOPE YOU WEREN'T OFFENDED... PLEASE COME AGAIN, YUKI-SAN!!
YOU'RE TURNING INTO A SEMI-REGULAR CUSTOMER, DROPPING BY EVERY ONCE IN A WHILE, AREN'T YOU?
I RECOGNIZE YOU... IT'S HARD TO FORGET THAT FACE.
SHUT UP.

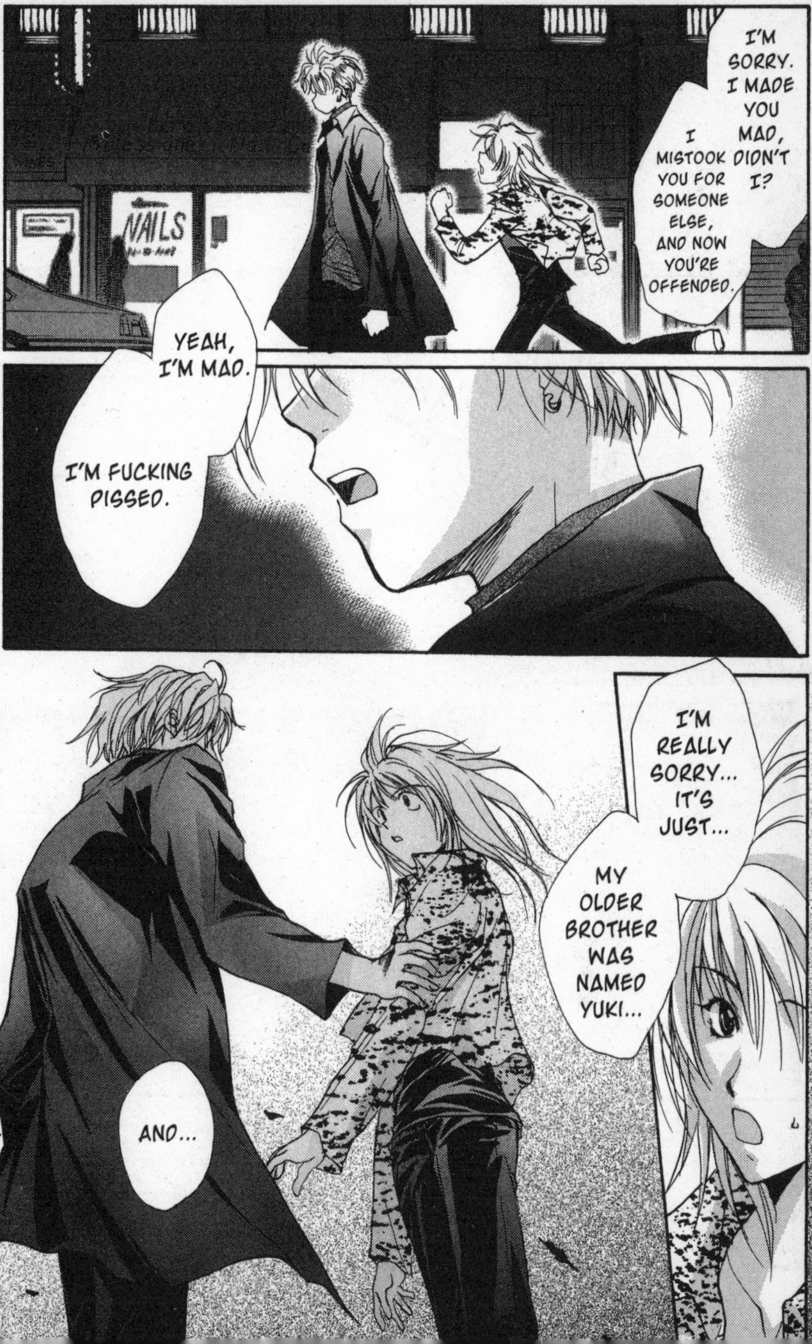
I'M SORRY. I MADE YOU MAD, DIDN'T I?
I MISTOOK YOU FOR SOMEONE ELSE, AND NOW YOU'RE OFFENDED.
NAILS
YEAH, I'M MAD.
I'M FUCKING PISSED.
I'M REALLY SORRY... IT'S JUST...
MY OLDER BROTHER WAS NAMED YUKI...
AND...

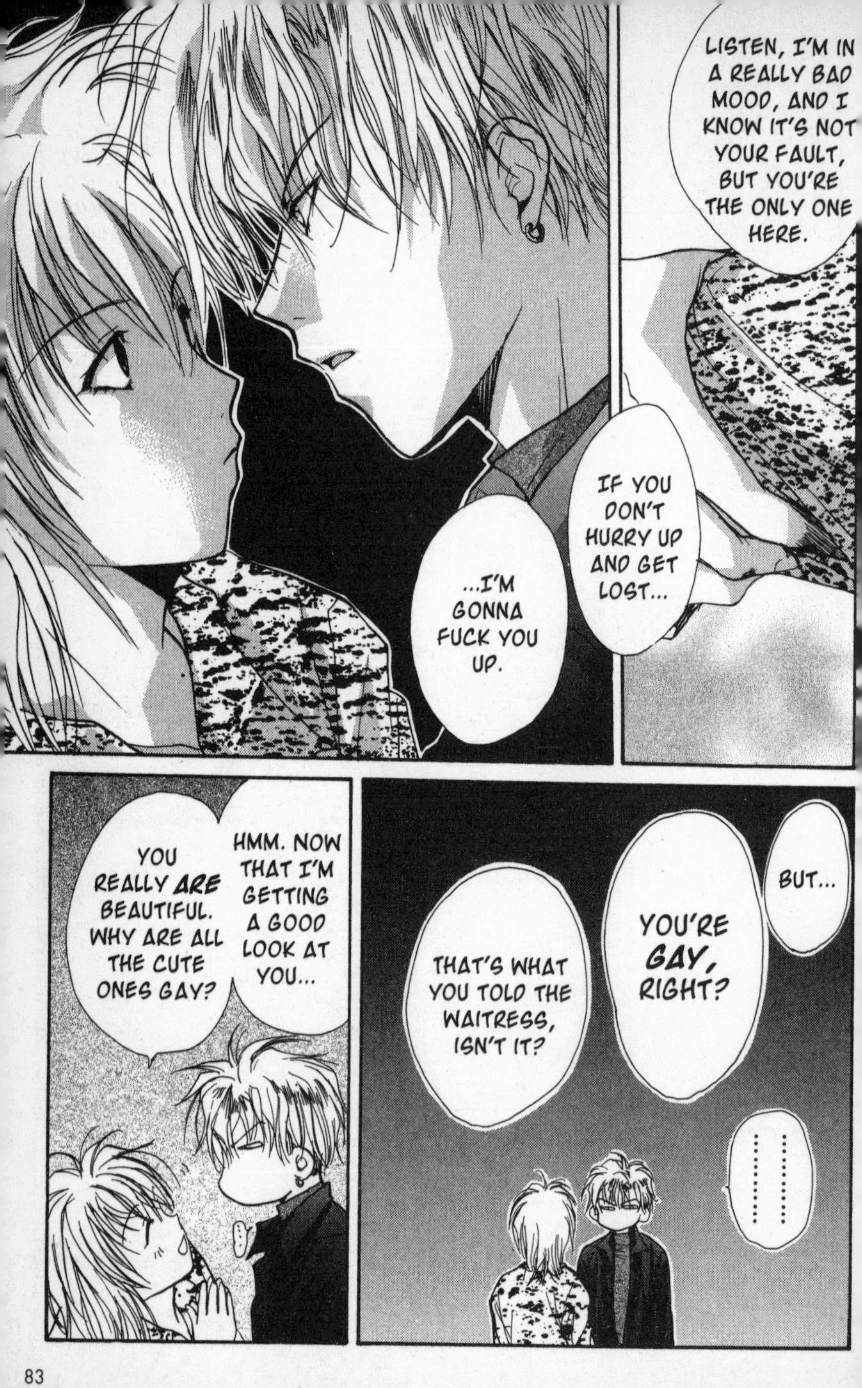
LISTEN, I'M IN A REALLY BAD MOOD, AND I KNOW IT'S NOT YOUR FAULT, BUT YOU'RE THE ONLY ONE HERE.
IF YOU DON'T HURRY UP AND GET LOST...
...I'M GONNA FUCK YOU UP.
BUT...
YOU'RE **GAY**, RIGHT?
THAT'S WHAT YOU TOLD THE WAITRESS, ISN'T IT?
......
HMM. NOW THAT I'M GETTING A GOOD LOOK AT YOU...
YOU REALLY **ARE** BEAUTIFUL. WHY ARE ALL THE CUTE ONES GAY?
...

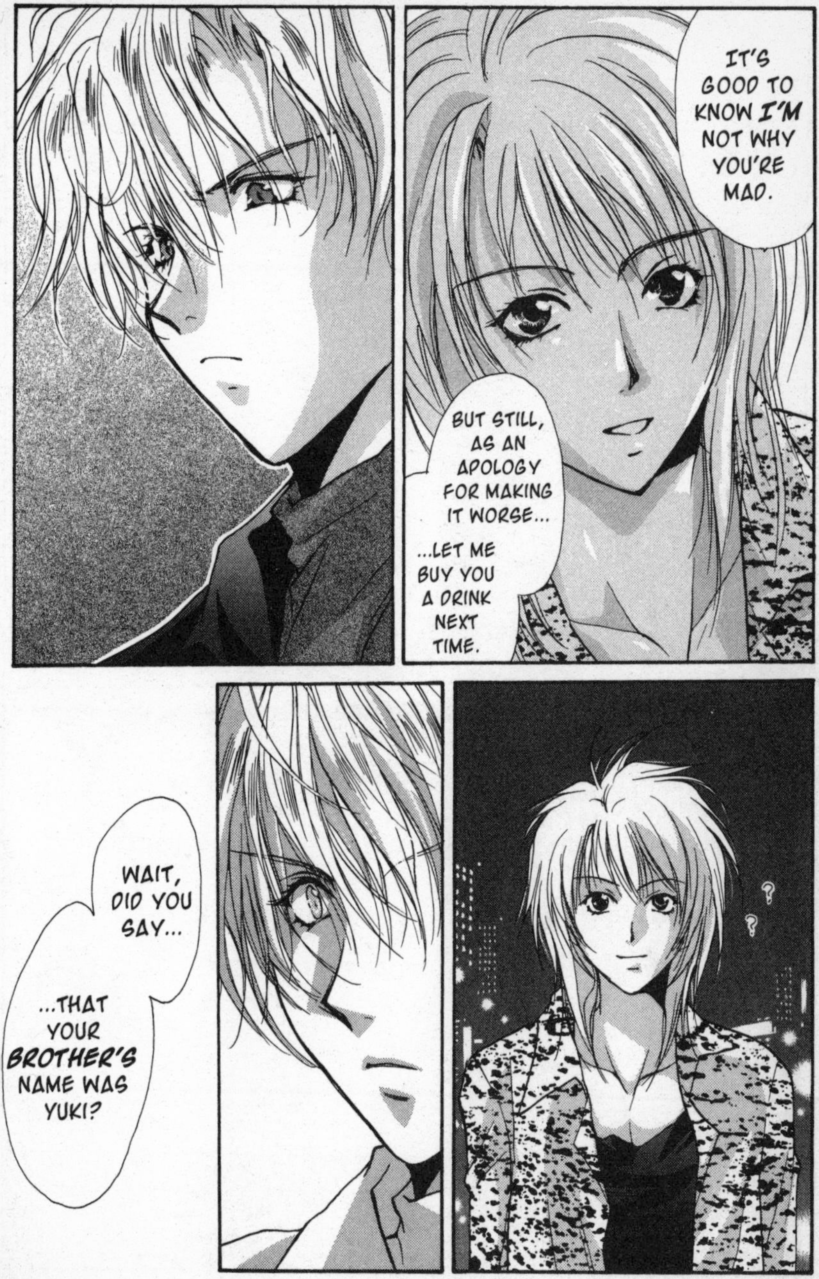
IT'S GOOD TO KNOW *I'M* NOT WHY YOU'RE MAD.
BUT STILL, AS AN APOLOGY FOR MAKING IT WORSE...
...LET ME BUY YOU A DRINK NEXT TIME.
WAIT, DID YOU SAY...
...THAT YOUR **BROTHER'S** NAME WAS YUKI?

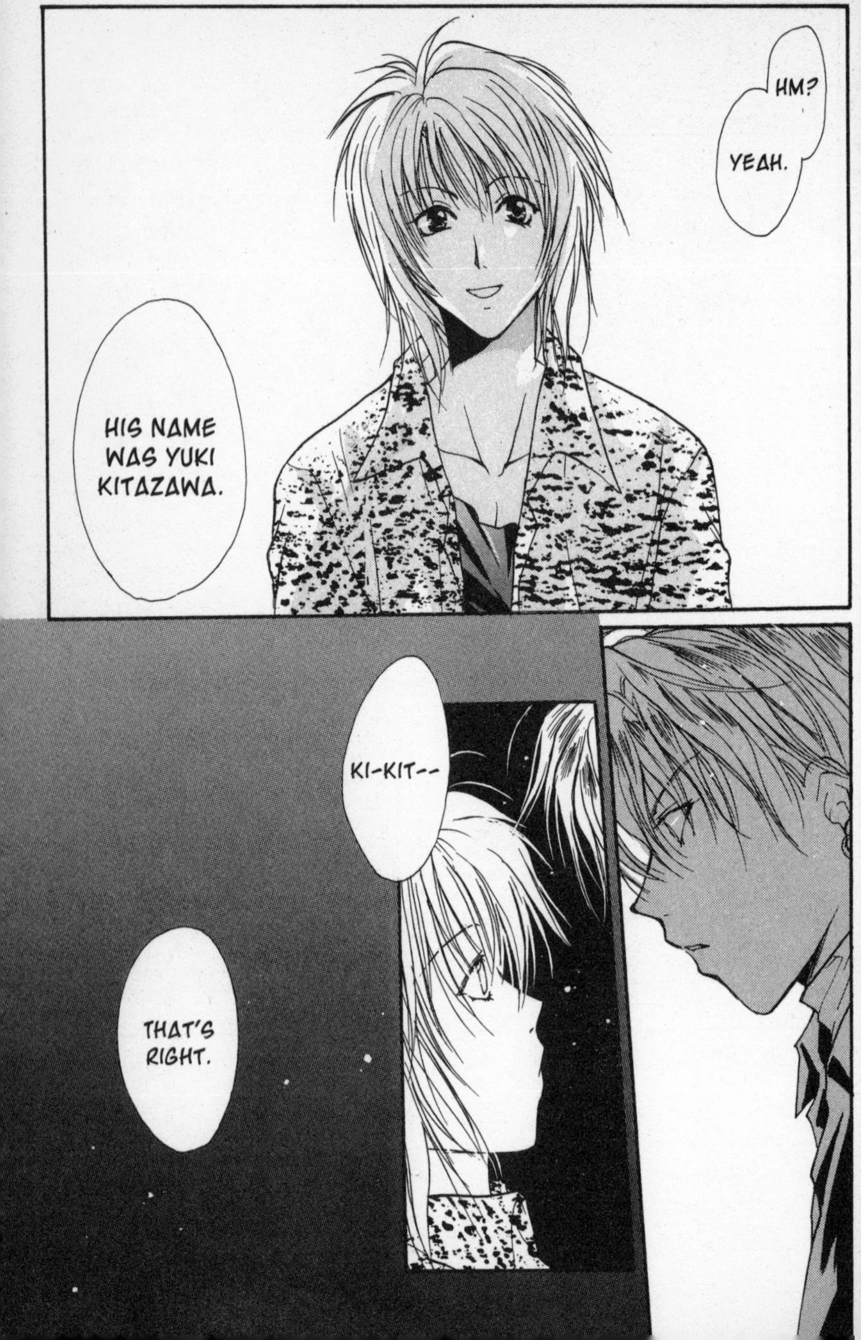
HM?
YEAH.
HIS NAME WAS YUKI KITAZAWA.
KI-KIT--
THAT'S RIGHT.

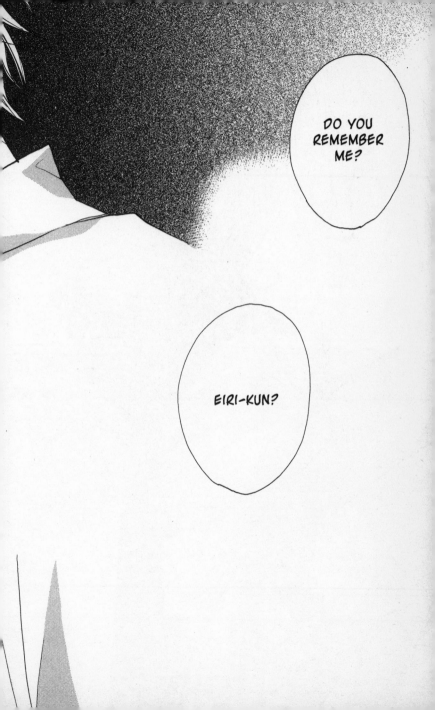

DO YOU REMEMBER ME?

EIRI-KUN?

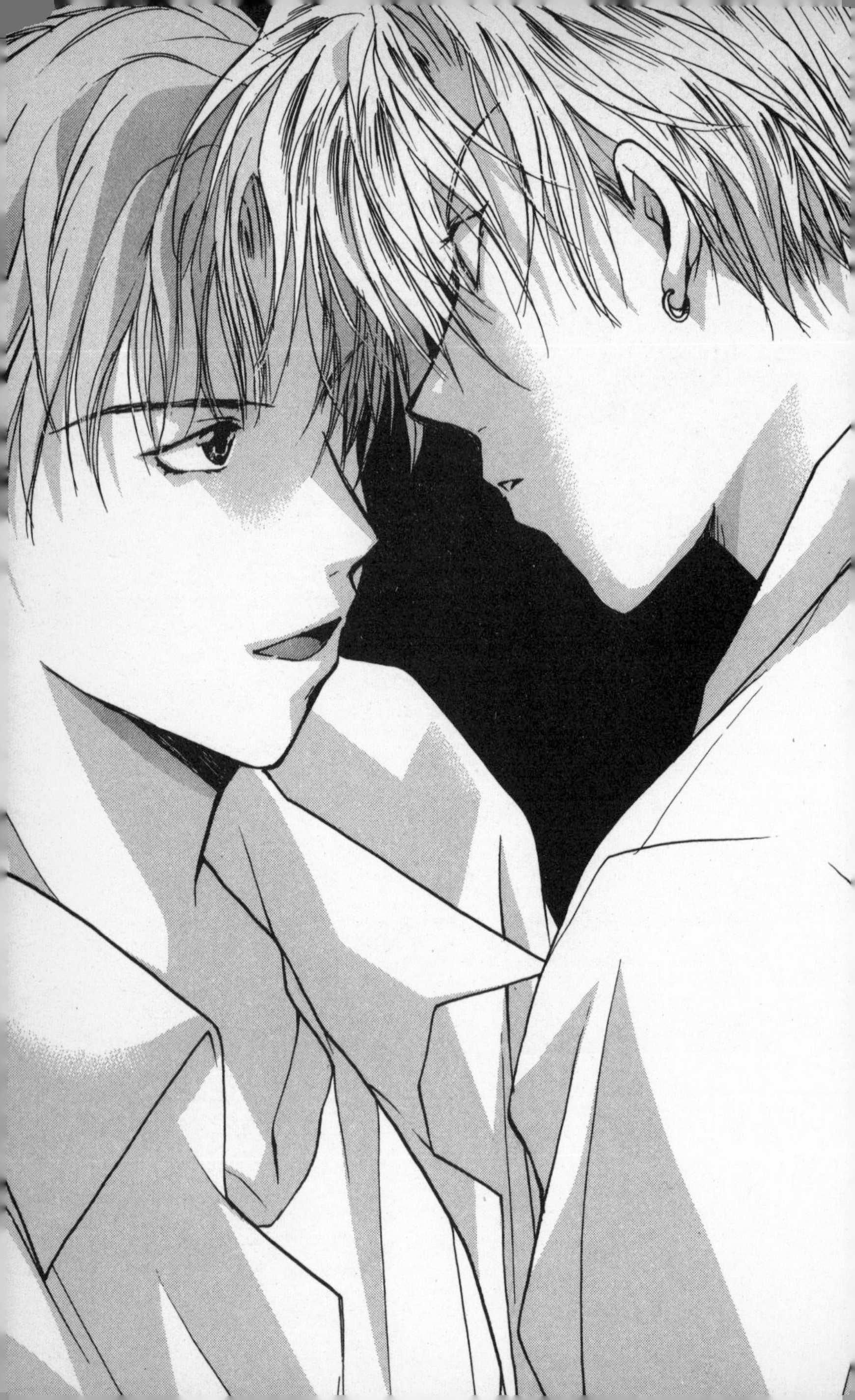

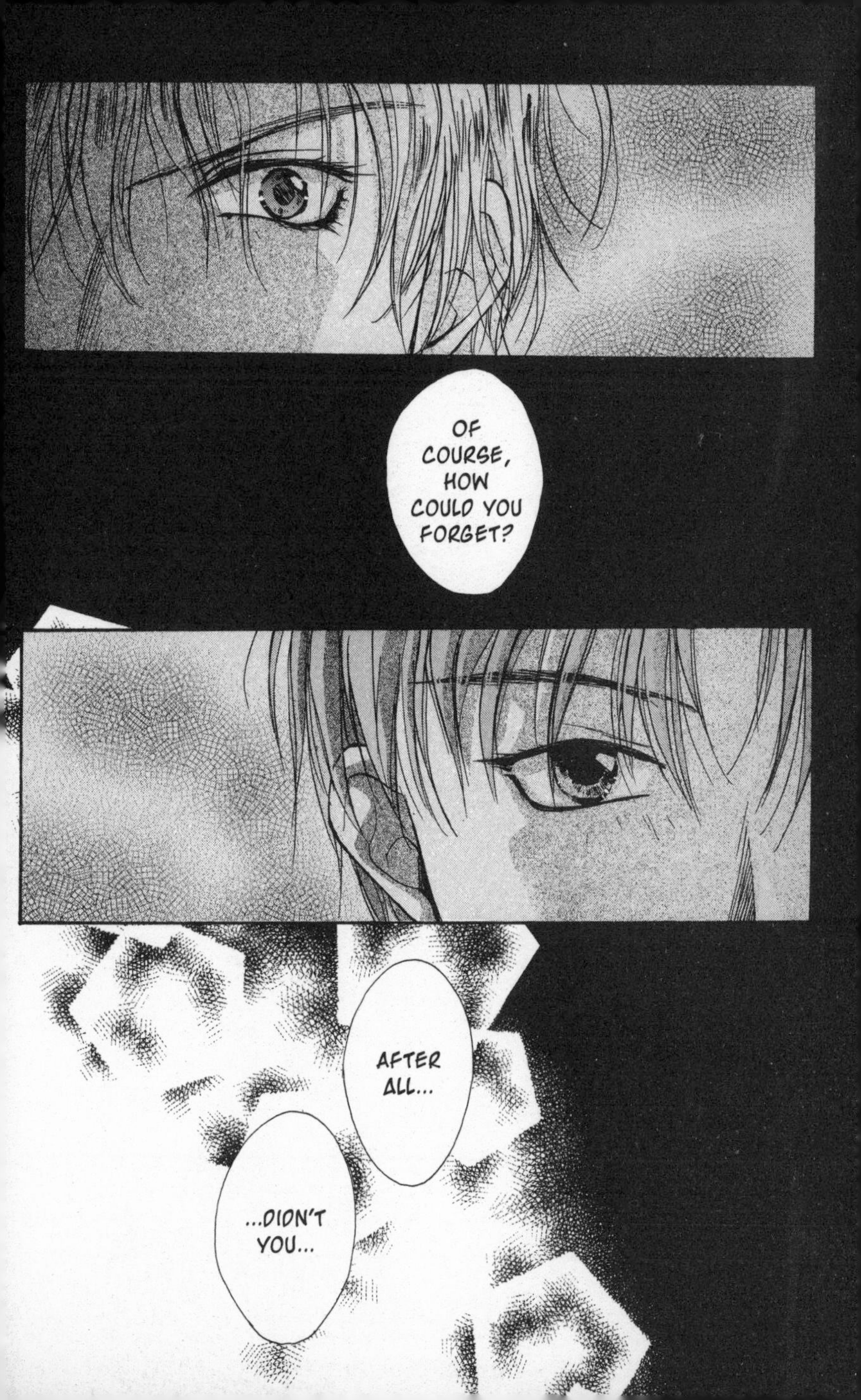
OF COURSE, HOW COULD YOU FORGET?
AFTER ALL...
...DIDN'T YOU...

...LOVE ME ONCE UPON A TIME?
track38▶END

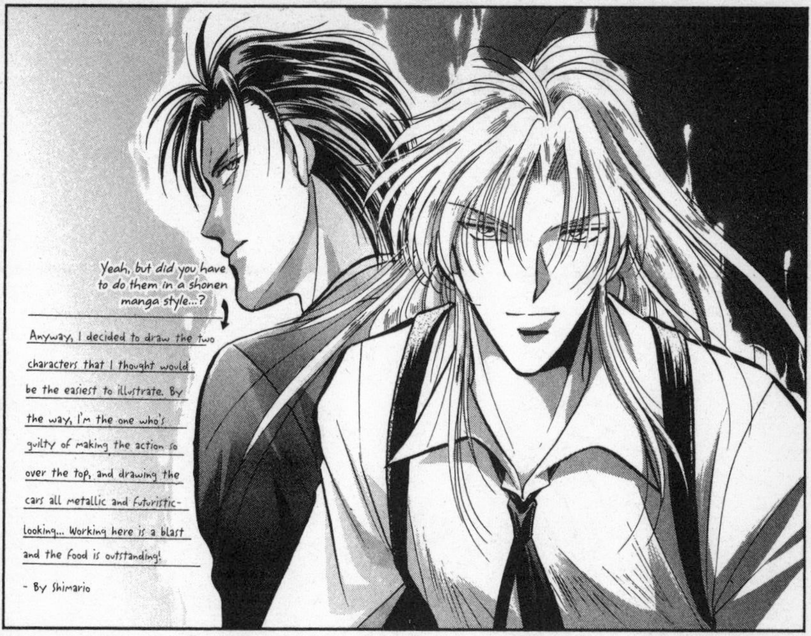
Yeah, but did you have to do them in a shonen manga style...?
Anyway, I decided to draw the two characters that I thought would be the easiest to illustrate. By the way, I'm the one who's guilty of making the action so over the top, and drawing the cars all metallic and futuristic-looking... Working here is a blast and the food is outstanding!
- By Shimario

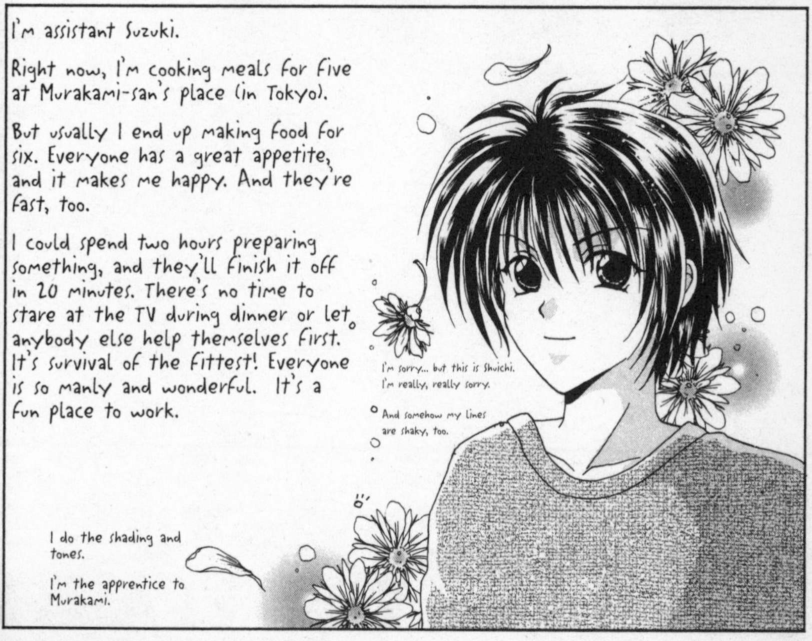
I'm assistant Suzuki.
Right now, I'm cooking meals for five at Murakami-san's place (in Tokyo).
But usually I end up making food for six. Everyone has a great appetite, and it makes me happy. And they're fast, too.
I could spend two hours preparing something, and they'll finish it off in 20 minutes. There's no time to stare at the TV during dinner or let anybody else help themselves first. It's survival of the fittest! Everyone is so manly and wonderful. It's a fun place to work.
I'm sorry... but this is Shuichi. I'm really, really sorry.
And somehow my lines are shaky, too.
I do the shading and tones.
I'm the apprentice to Murakami.

Gravitation

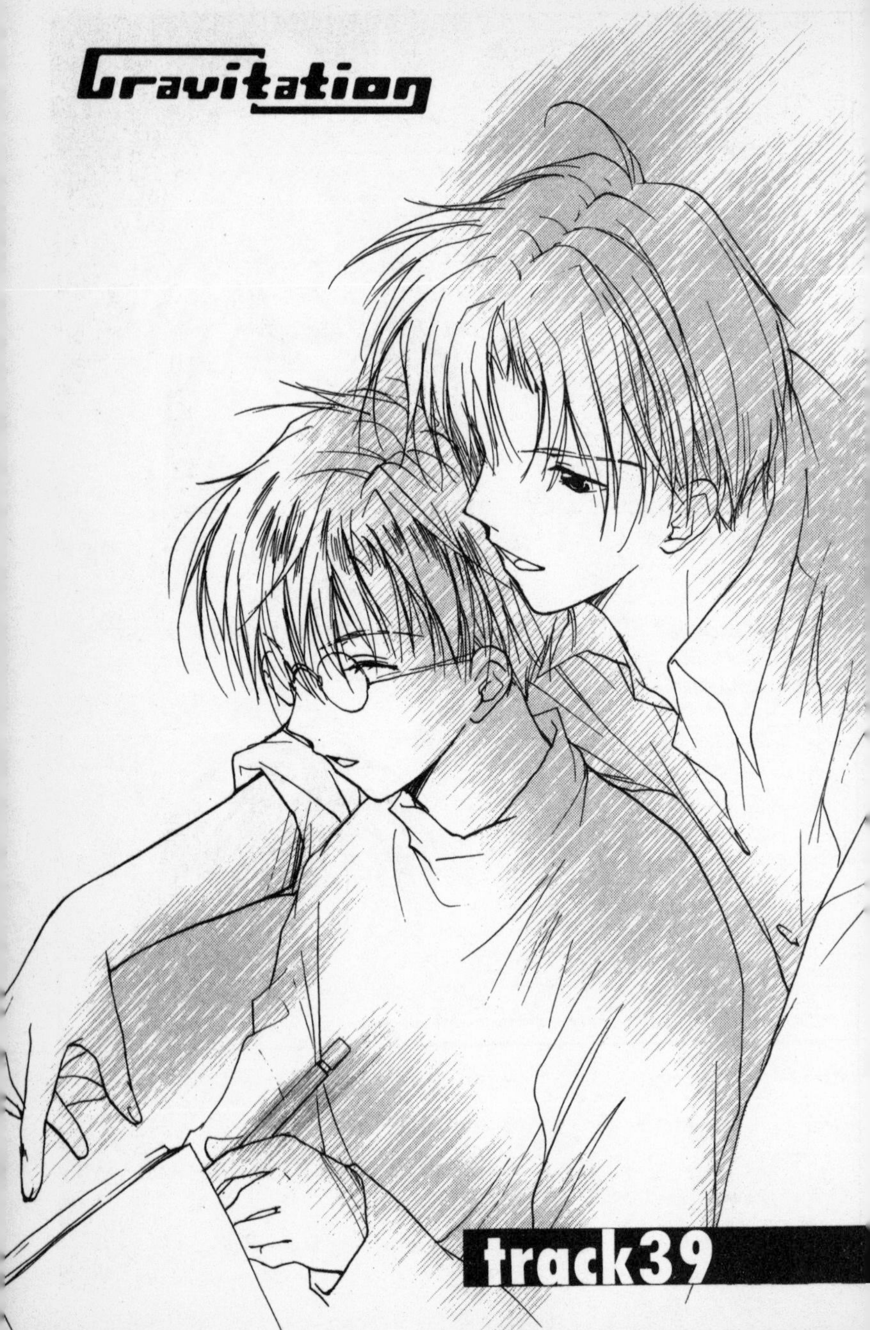

track 39

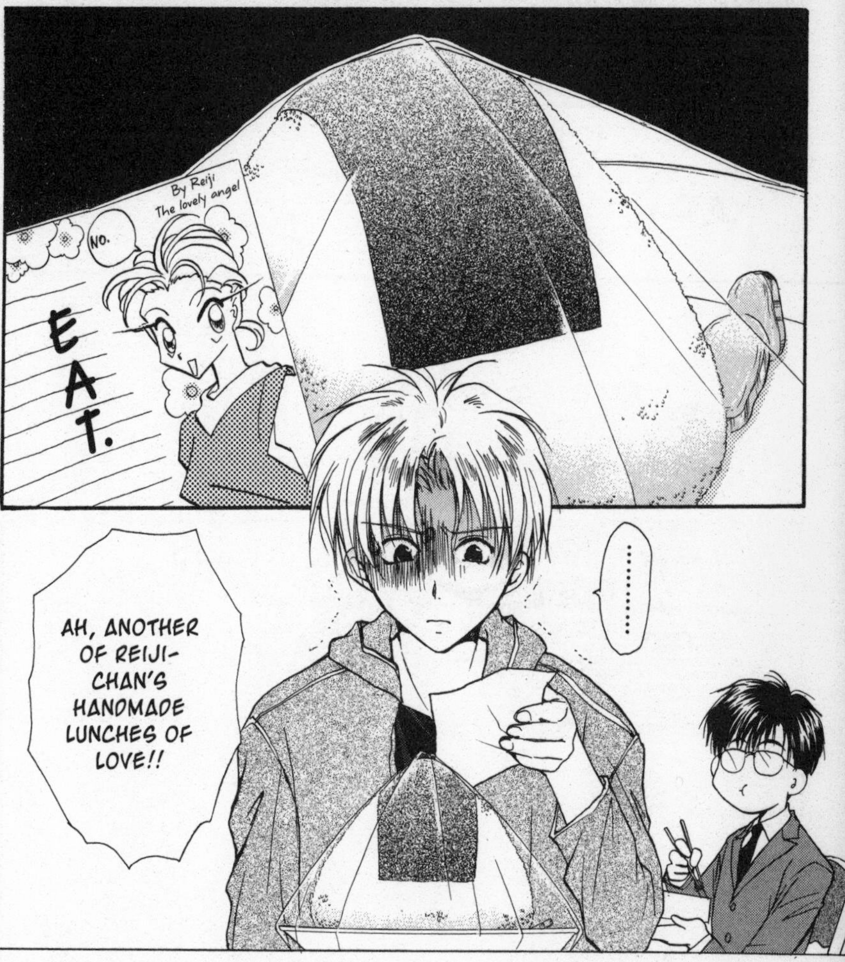
By Reiji
The lovely angel
NO.
EAT.
……
AH, ANOTHER OF REIJI-CHAN'S HANDMADE LUNCHES OF LOVE!!

ABOUT GRAVITATION TRACK 39

With each episode, Reiji begins to show more and more of her true self. I'm sure you sharper readers out there have already caught on to the hints hidden in the side items contained in the letterheads that Reiji uses!!

That's right. It's just as you thought. I intend on dropping more clues in further episodes as well, so keep on reading.

Personally, I don't know of a better-matched couple than Reiji and Shuichi, but we'll have to see how things turn out between them.

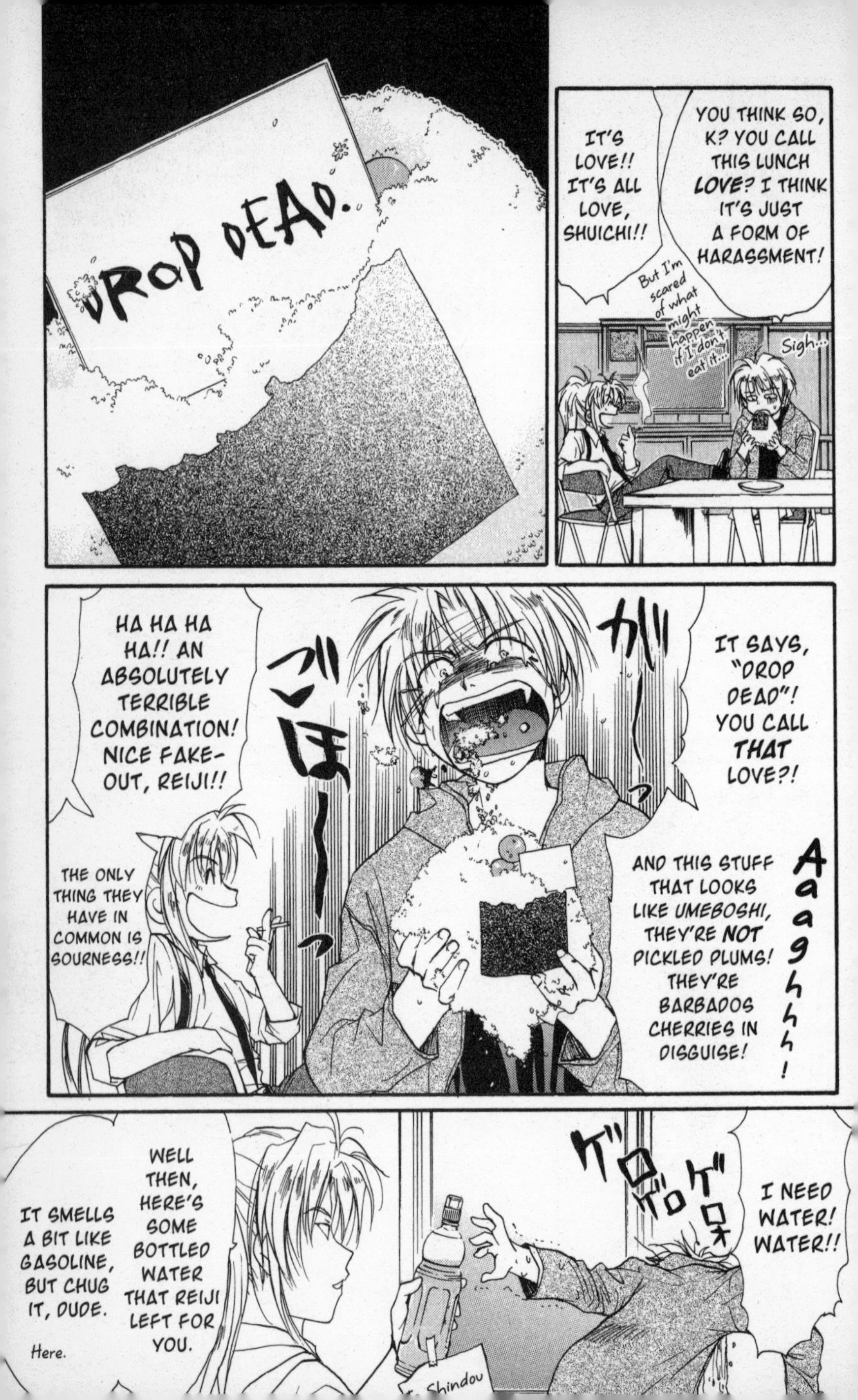
YOU THINK SO, K? YOU CALL THIS LUNCH *LOVE*? I THINK IT'S JUST A FORM OF HARASSMENT!
IT'S LOVE!! IT'S ALL LOVE, SHUICHI!!
Sigh...
But I'm scared of what might happen if I don't eat it...
DROP DEAD.
IT SAYS, "DROP DEAD"! YOU CALL **THAT** LOVE?!
ガリーっ
AND THIS STUFF THAT LOOKS LIKE UMEBOSHI, THEY'RE **NOT** PICKLED PLUMS! THEY'RE BARBADOS CHERRIES IN DISGUISE!
Aaaghhhh!
ごほーっ
HA HA HA HA!! AN ABSOLUTELY TERRIBLE COMBINATION! NICE FAKE-OUT, REIJI!!
THE ONLY THING THEY HAVE IN COMMON IS SOURNESS!!
I NEED WATER! WATER!!
ゲロゲロゲロ
WELL THEN, HERE'S SOME BOTTLED WATER THAT REIJI LEFT FOR YOU.
IT SMELLS A BIT LIKE GASOLINE, BUT CHUG IT, DUDE.
Here.
Shindou

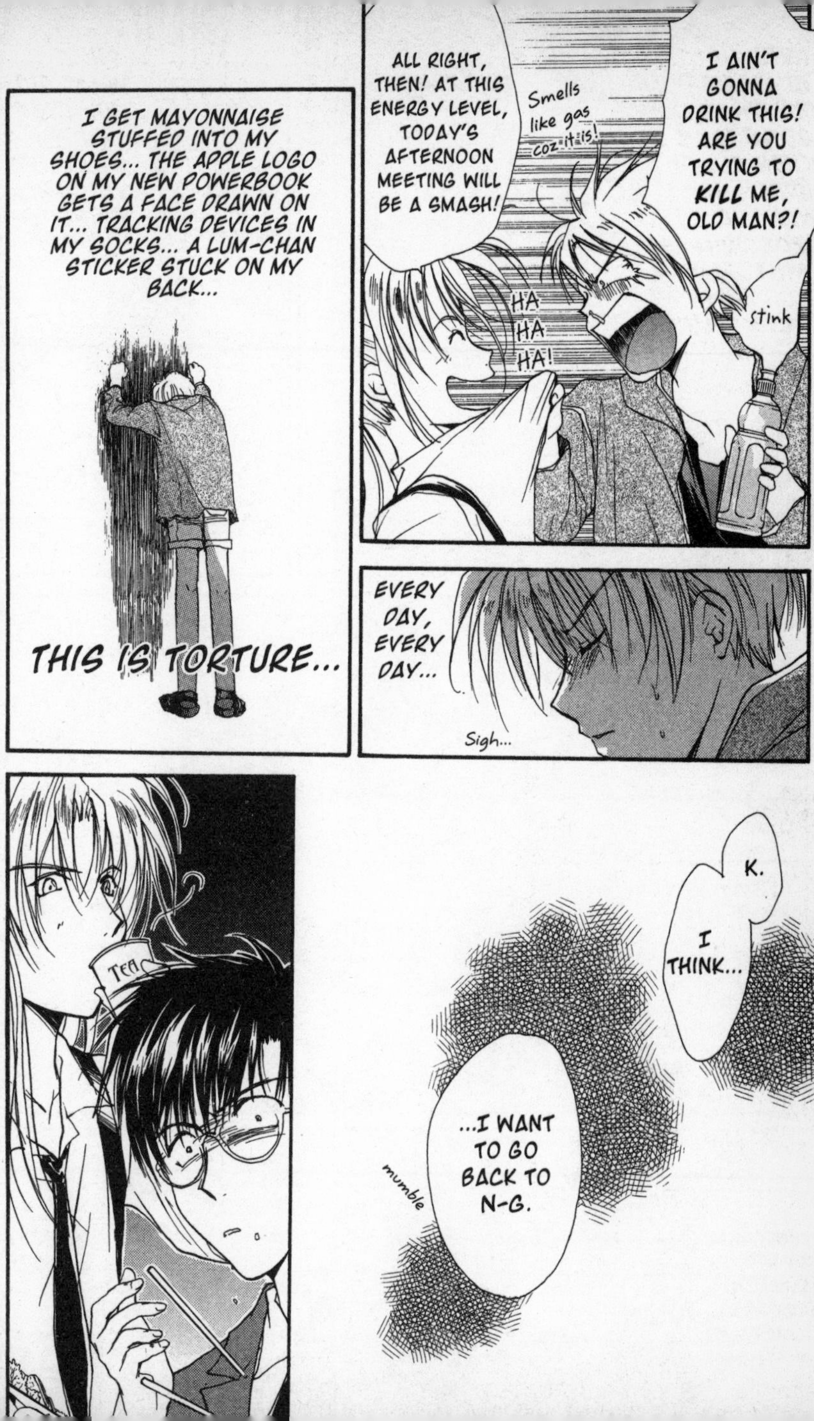
I AIN'T GONNA DRINK THIS! ARE YOU TRYING TO **KILL** ME, OLD MAN?!
ALL RIGHT, THEN! AT THIS ENERGY LEVEL, TODAY'S AFTERNOON MEETING WILL BE A SMASH!
Smells like gas coz it is!
stink
HA HA HA!
EVERY DAY, EVERY DAY...
Sigh...
I GET MAYONNAISE STUFFED INTO MY SHOES... THE APPLE LOGO ON MY NEW POWERBOOK GETS A FACE DRAWN ON IT... TRACKING DEVICES IN MY SOCKS... A LUM-CHAN STICKER STUCK ON MY BACK...
THIS IS TORTURE...
K.
I THINK...
...I WANT TO GO BACK TO N-G.
mumble
TEA

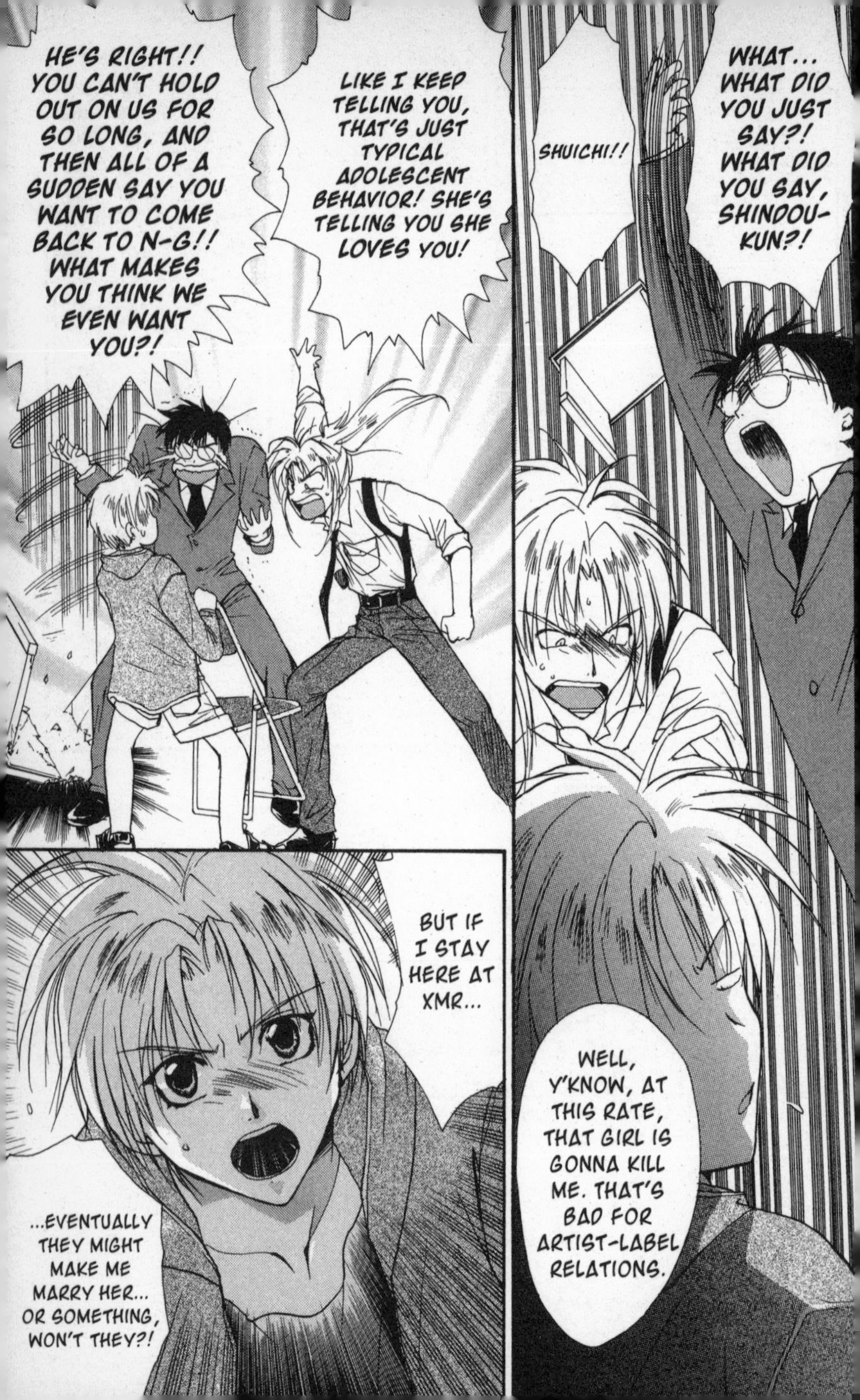
WHAT... WHAT DID YOU JUST SAY?! WHAT DID YOU SAY, SHINDOU-KUN?!
SHUICHI!!
WELL, Y'KNOW, AT THIS RATE, THAT GIRL IS GONNA KILL ME. THAT'S BAD FOR ARTIST-LABEL RELATIONS.
LIKE I KEEP TELLING YOU, THAT'S JUST TYPICAL ADOLESCENT BEHAVIOR! SHE'S TELLING YOU SHE LOVES YOU!
HE'S RIGHT!! YOU CAN'T HOLD OUT ON US FOR SO LONG, AND THEN ALL OF A SUDDEN SAY YOU WANT TO COME BACK TO N-G!! WHAT MAKES YOU THINK WE EVEN WANT YOU?!
BUT IF I STAY HERE AT XMR...
...EVENTUALLY THEY MIGHT MAKE ME MARRY HER... OR SOMETHING, WON'T THEY?!

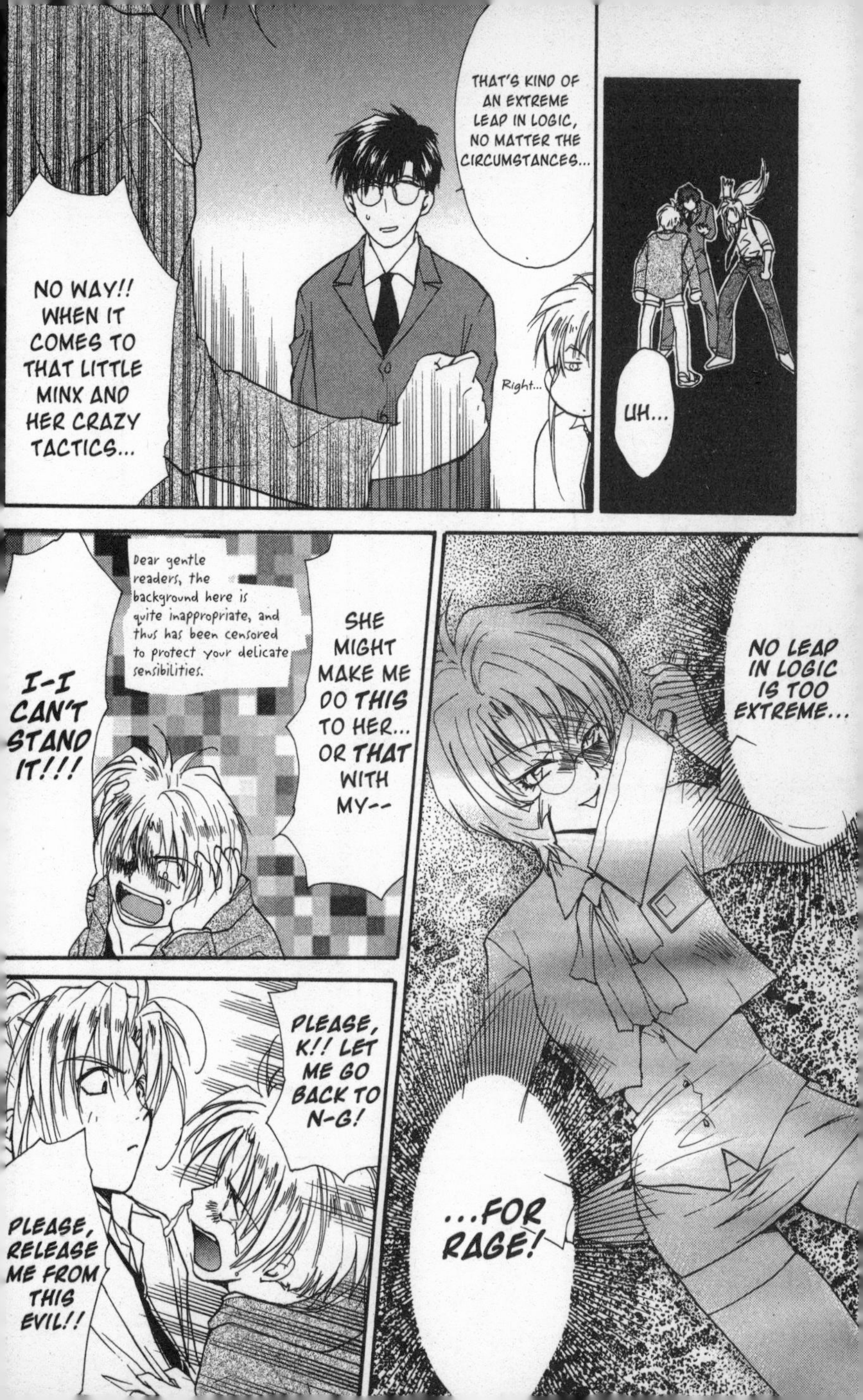
UH...
THAT'S KIND OF AN EXTREME LEAP IN LOGIC, NO MATTER THE CIRCUMSTANCES...
Right...
NO WAY!! WHEN IT COMES TO THAT LITTLE MINX AND HER CRAZY TACTICS...
NO LEAP IN LOGIC IS TOO EXTREME...
...FOR RAGE!
SHE MIGHT MAKE ME DO THIS TO HER... OR THAT WITH MY--
Dear gentle readers, the background here is quite inappropriate, and thus has been censored to protect your delicate sensibilities.
I-I CAN'T STAND IT!!!
PLEASE, K!! LET ME GO BACK TO N-G!
PLEASE, RELEASE ME FROM THIS EVIL!!

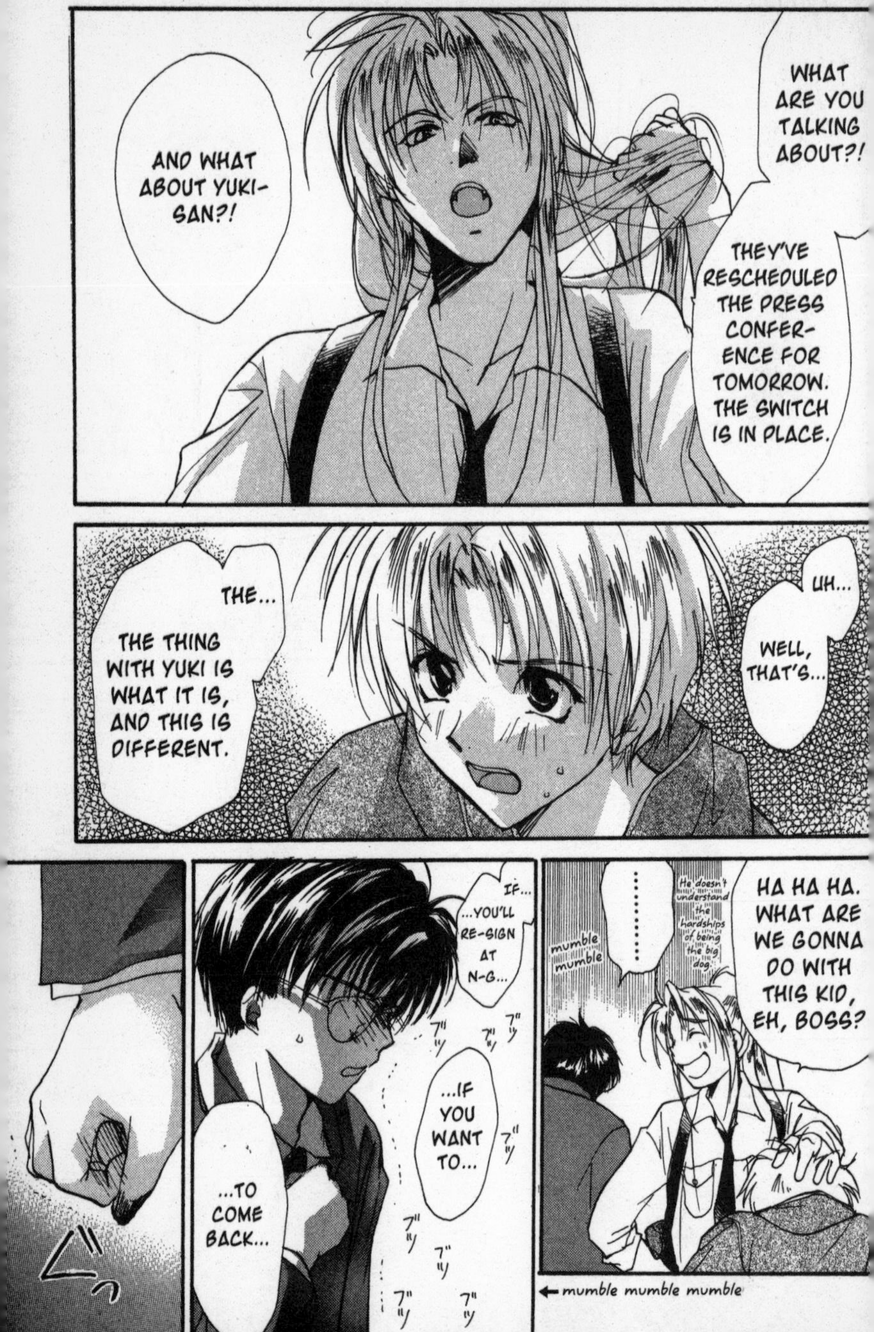
WHAT ARE YOU TALKING ABOUT?!
THEY'VE RESCHEDULED THE PRESS CONFER-ENCE FOR TOMORROW. THE SWITCH IS IN PLACE.
AND WHAT ABOUT YUKI-SAN?!
UH...
WELL, THAT'S...
THE...
THE THING WITH YUKI IS WHAT IT IS, AND THIS IS DIFFERENT.
HA HA HA. WHAT ARE WE GONNA DO WITH THIS KID, EH, BOSS?
He doesn't understand the hardships of being the big dog.
......
mumble mumble
IF...
...YOU'LL RE-SIGN AT N-G...
...IF YOU WANT TO...
...TO COME BACK...
← mumble mumble mumble
ぐっ

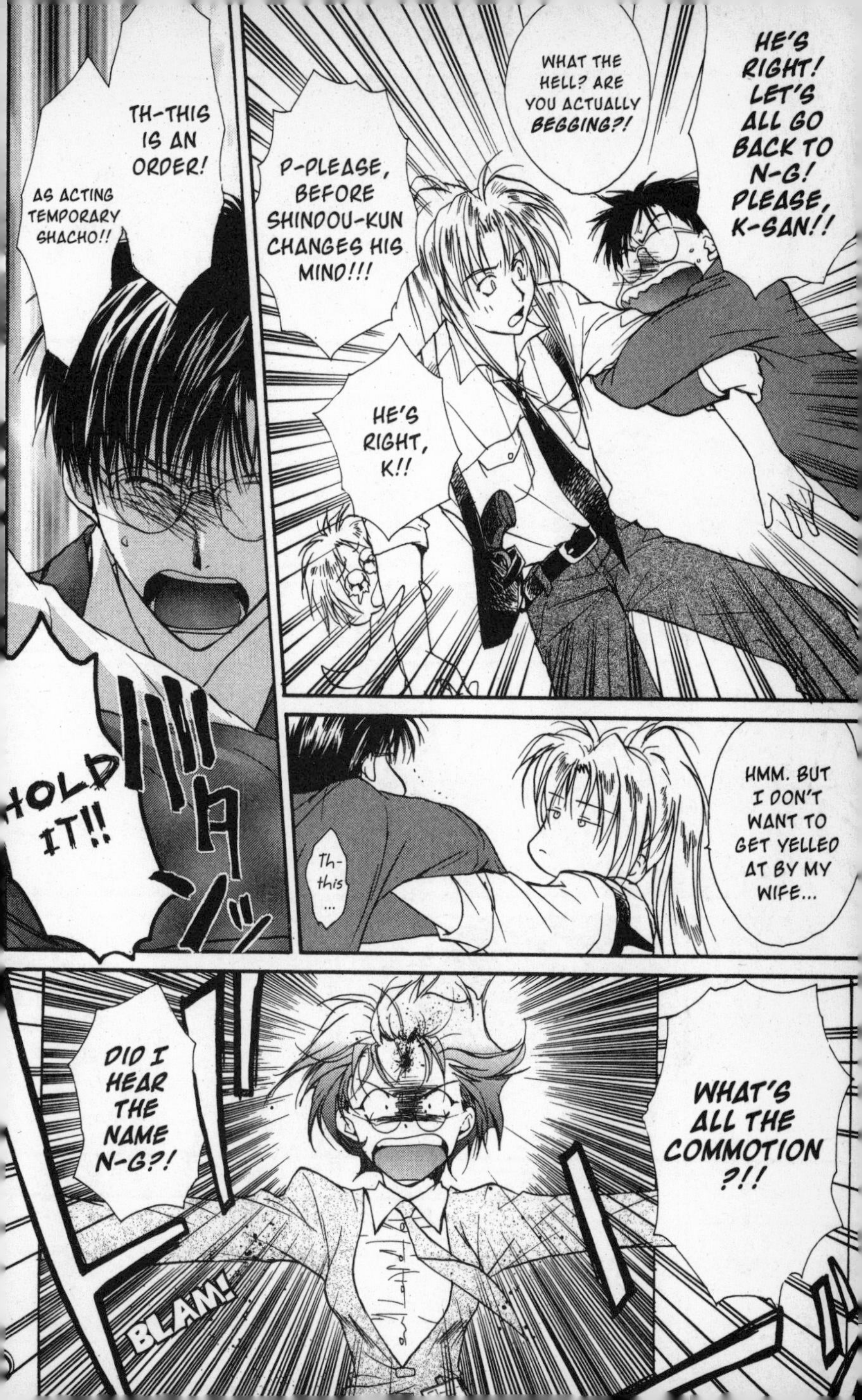

HE'S RIGHT! LET'S ALL GO BACK TO N-G! PLEASE, K-SAN!!
WHAT THE HELL? ARE YOU ACTUALLY BEGGING?!
P-PLEASE, BEFORE SHINDOU-KUN CHANGES HIS MIND!!!
HE'S RIGHT, K!!
HMM. BUT I DON'T WANT TO GET YELLED AT BY MY WIFE...
Th-this ...
TH-THIS IS AN ORDER!
AS ACTING TEMPORARY SHACHO!!
HOLD IT!!
WHAT'S ALL THE COMMOTION ?!!
DID I HEAR THE NAME N-G?!
BLAM!

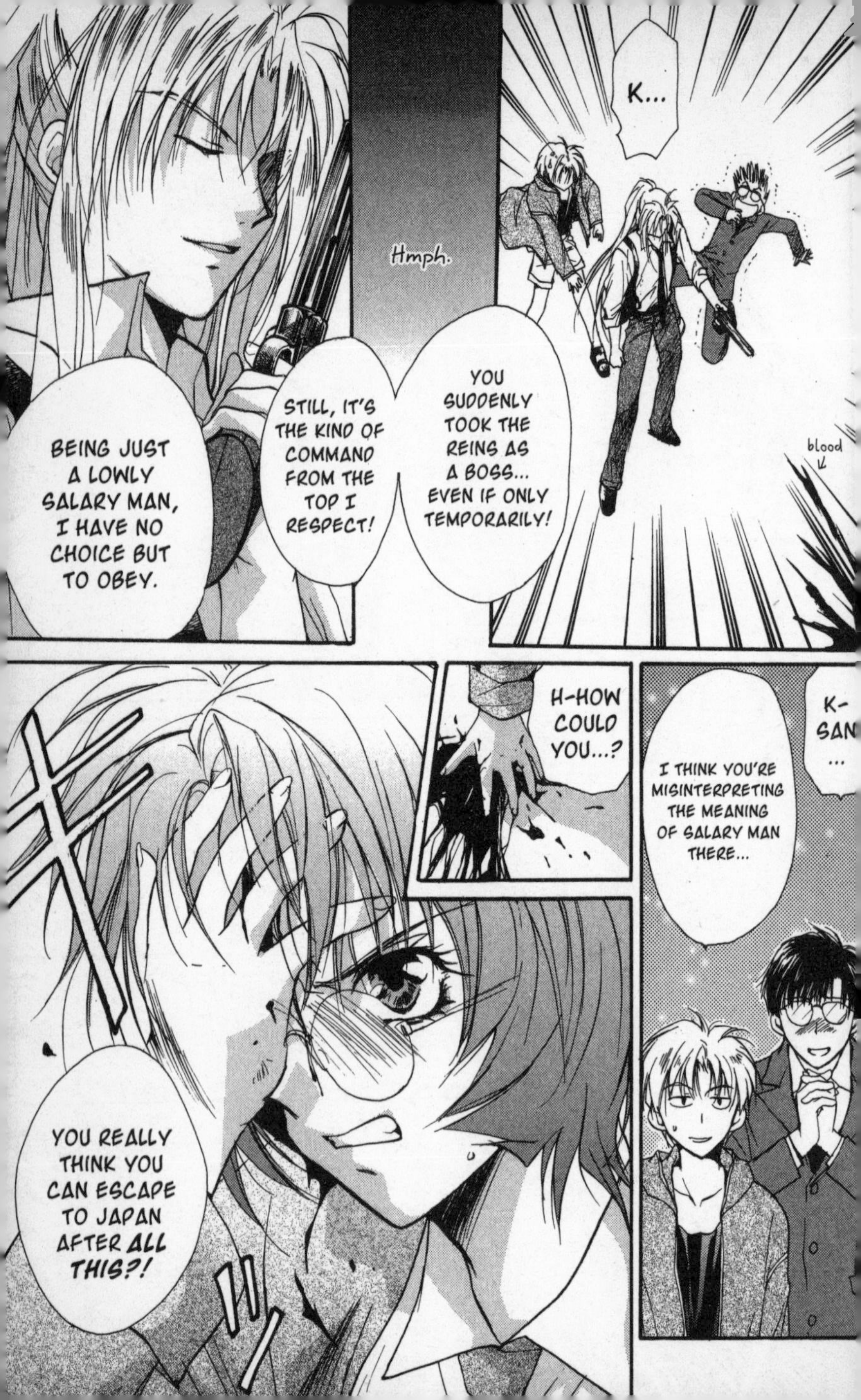
K...
blood
Hmph.
YOU SUDDENLY TOOK THE REINS AS A BOSS... EVEN IF ONLY TEMPORARILY!
STILL, IT'S THE KIND OF COMMAND FROM THE TOP I RESPECT!
BEING JUST A LOWLY SALARY MAN, I HAVE NO CHOICE BUT TO OBEY.
K-SAN...
I THINK YOU'RE MISINTERPRETING THE MEANING OF SALARY MAN THERE...
H-HOW COULD YOU...?
YOU REALLY THINK YOU CAN ESCAPE TO JAPAN AFTER **ALL THIS?!**

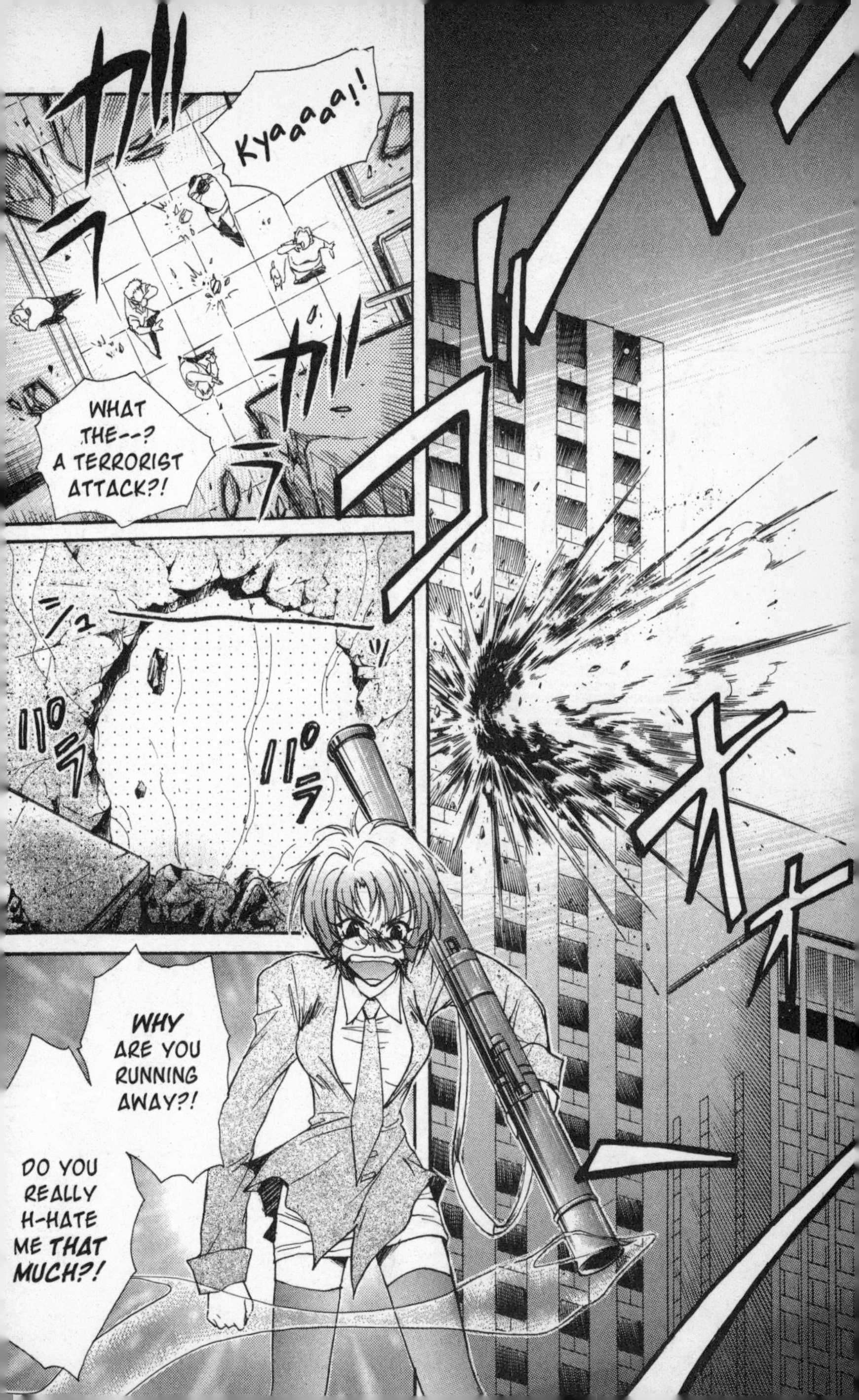
Kyaaaaa!!
WHAT THE--? A TERRORIST ATTACK?!
WHY ARE YOU RUNNING AWAY?!
DO YOU REALLY H-HATE ME THAT MUCH?!

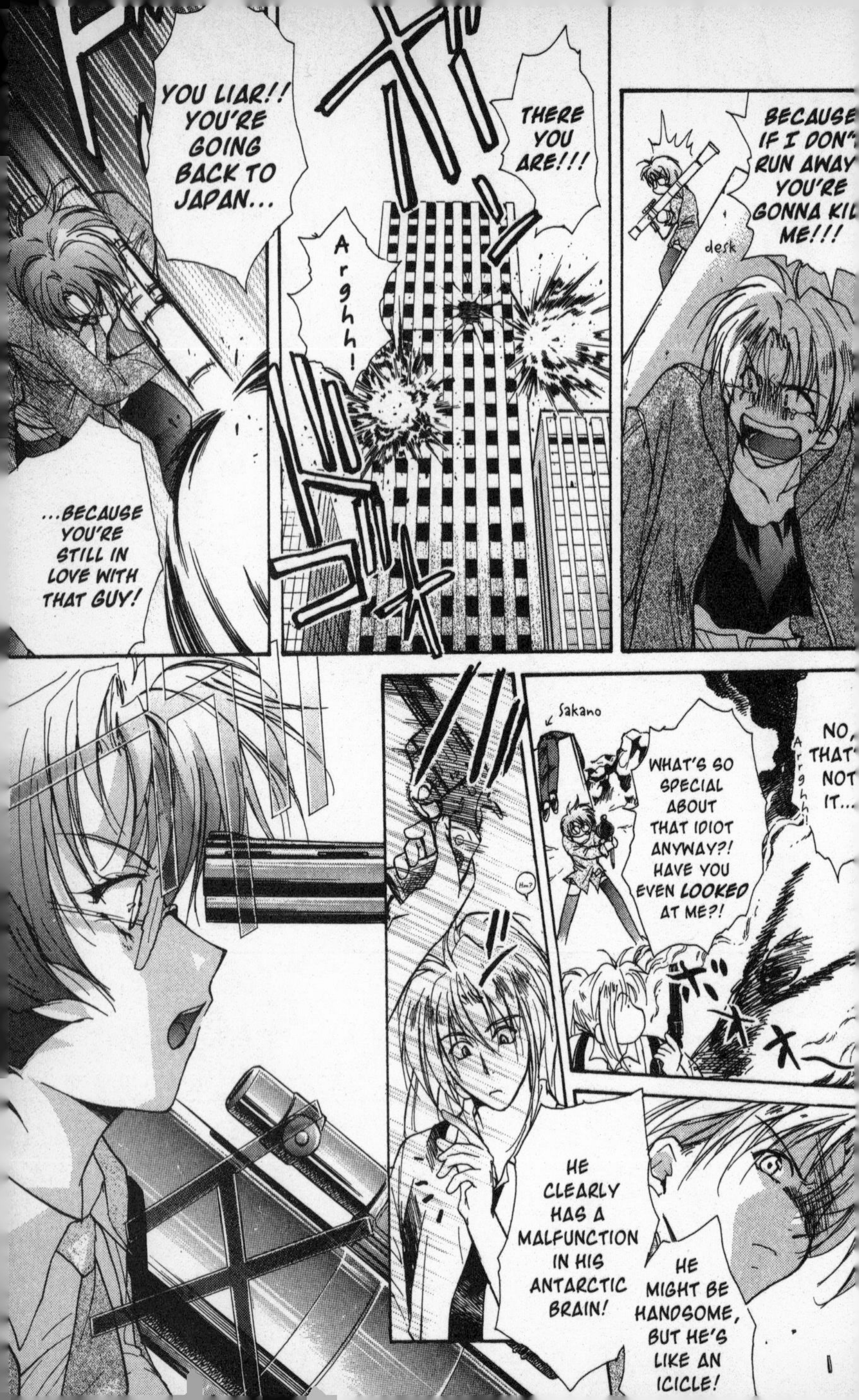
BECAUSE IF I DON'T RUN AWAY YOU'RE GONNA KIL ME!!!
desk
THERE YOU ARE!!!
Arghh!
YOU LIAR!! YOU'RE GOING BACK TO JAPAN...
...BECAUSE YOU'RE STILL IN LOVE WITH THAT GUY!
NO, THAT' NOT IT...
Arrghh!
WHAT'S SO SPECIAL ABOUT THAT IDIOT ANYWAY?! HAVE YOU EVEN LOOKED AT ME?!
Sakano
Hm?
HE MIGHT BE HANDSOME, BUT HE'S LIKE AN ICICLE!
HE CLEARLY HAS A MALFUNCTION IN HIS ANTARCTIC BRAIN!

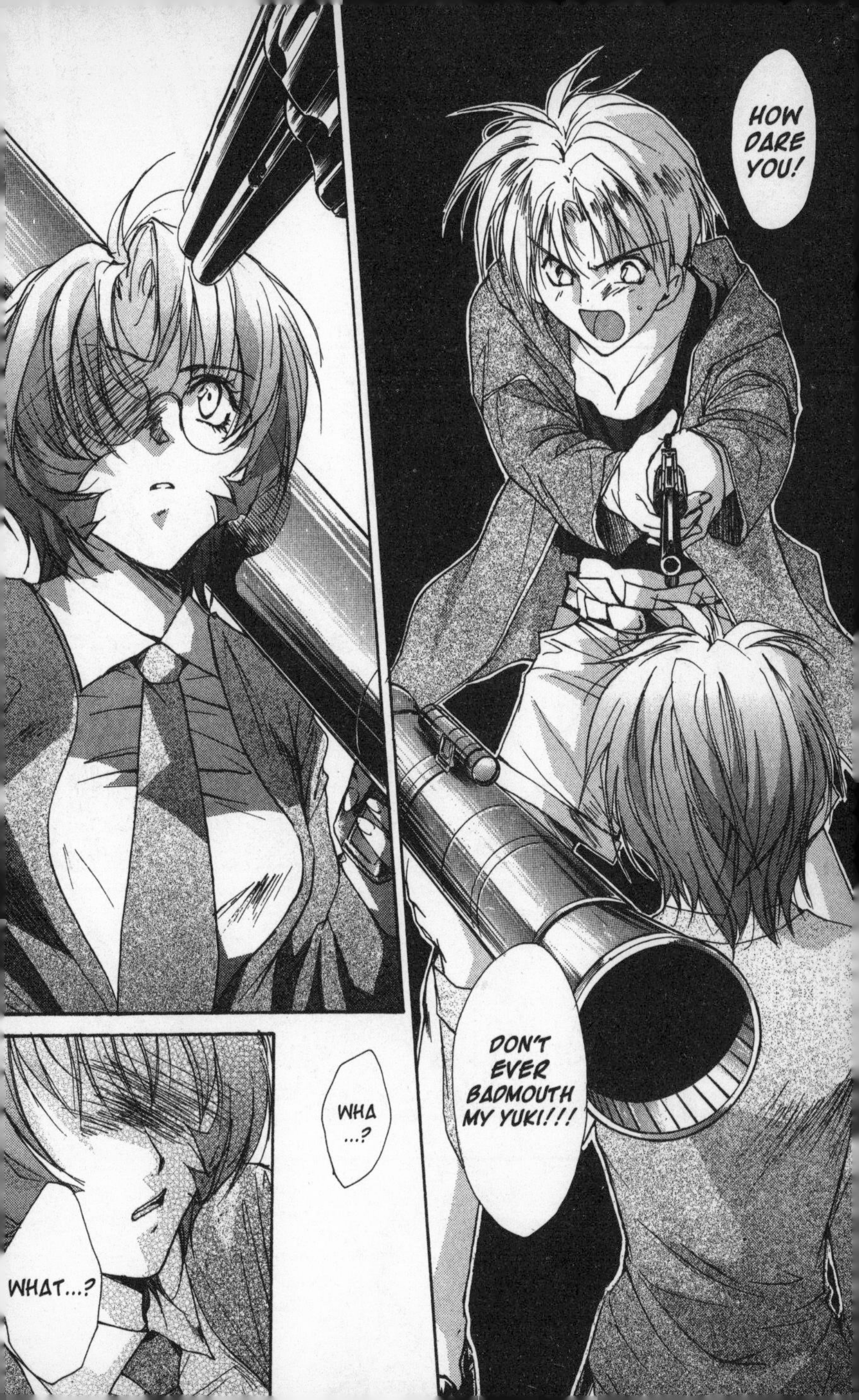

HOW DARE YOU!
DON'T EVER BADMOUTH MY YUKI!!!
WHA ...?
WHAT...?

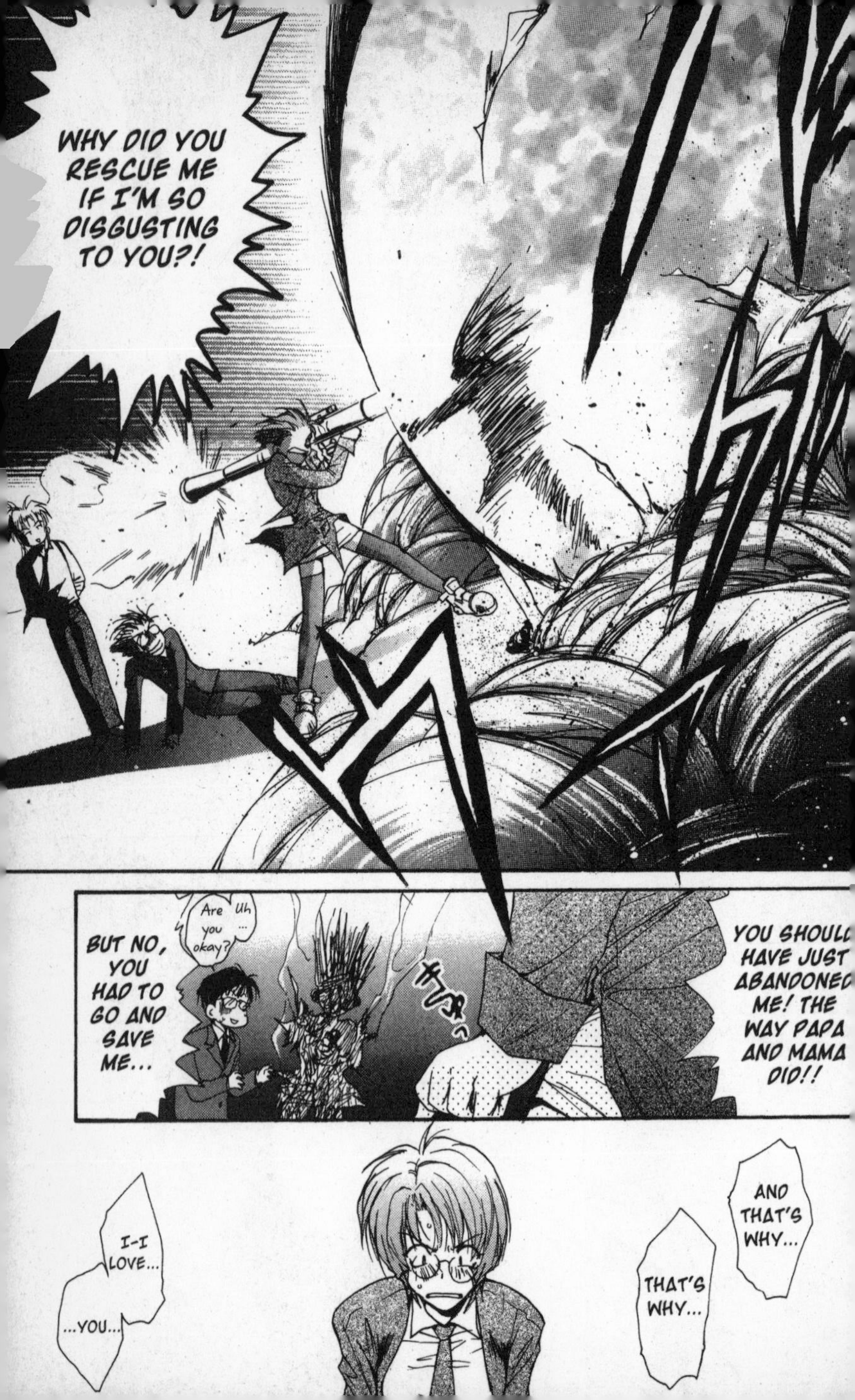
WHY DID YOU RESCUE ME IF I'M SO DISGUSTING TO YOU?!
YOU SHOUL HAVE JUST ABANDONE ME! THE WAY PAPA AND MAMA DID!!
Uh ...
Are you okay?
BUT NO, YOU HAD TO GO AND SAVE ME...
AND THAT'S WHY...
THAT'S WHY...
I-I LOVE...
...YOU...

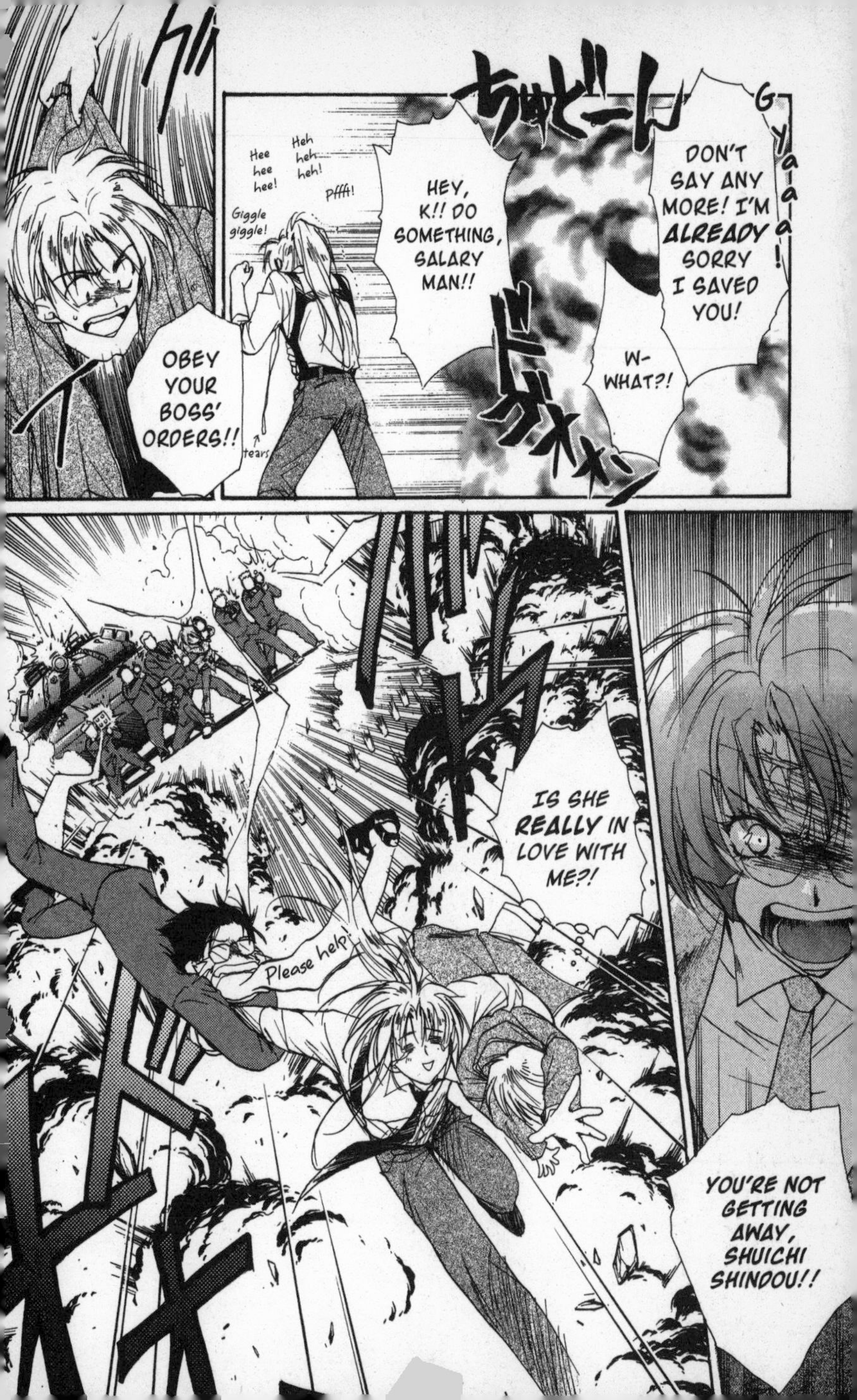

ちゅどーん
Gyaaaa!
DON'T SAY ANY MORE! I'M **ALREADY** SORRY I SAVED YOU!
W-WHAT?!
HEY, K!! DO SOMETHING, SALARY MAN!!
Pffft!
Heh heh heh!
Hee hee hee!
Giggle giggle!
tears
OBEY YOUR BOSS' ORDERS!!
YOU'RE NOT GETTING AWAY, SHUICHI SHINDOU!!
IS SHE **REALLY** IN LOVE WITH ME?!
Please help

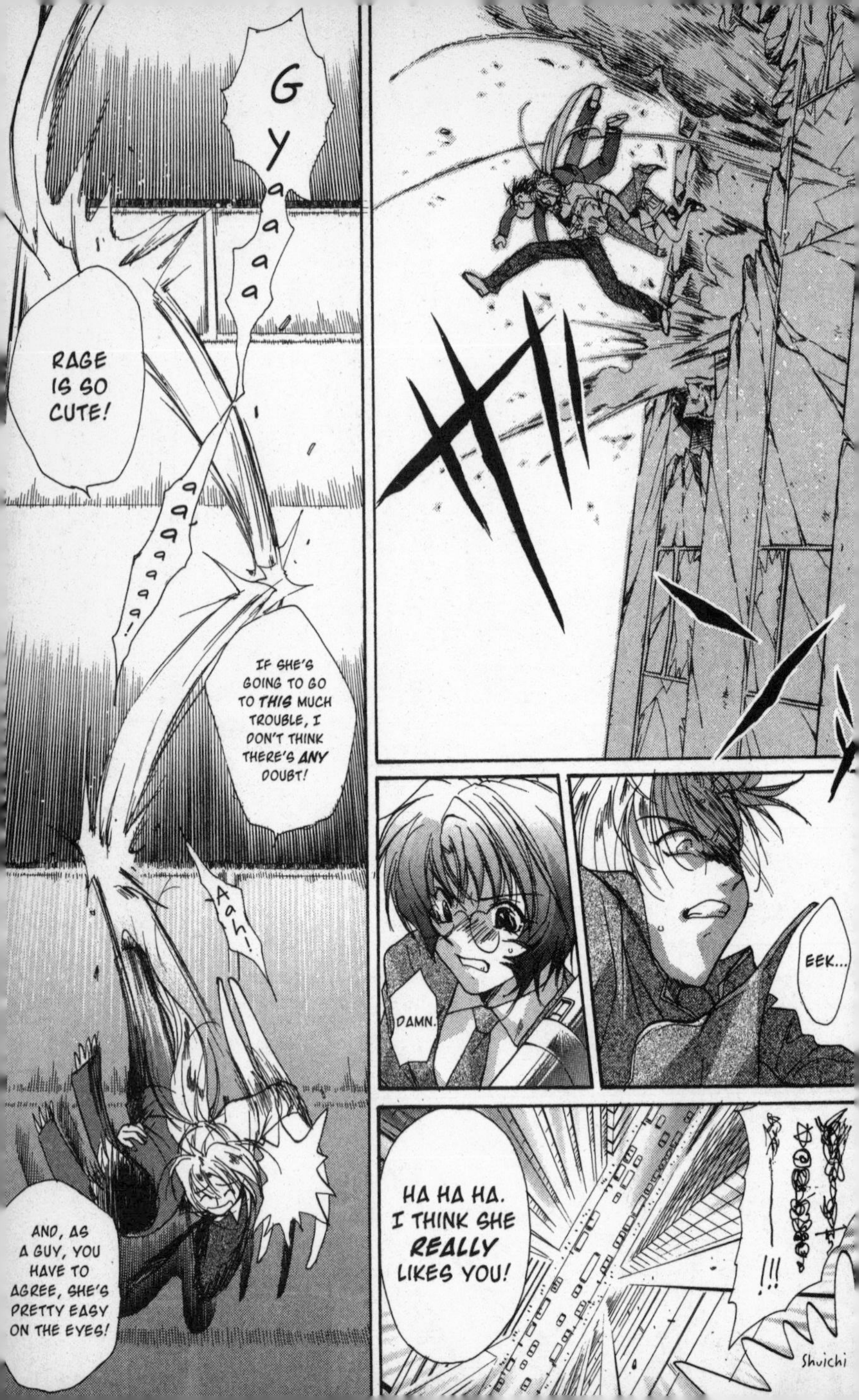
EEK...
DAMN.
!!
Shuichi
HA HA HA. I THINK SHE ***REALLY*** LIKES YOU!
Gyaaaa
RAGE IS SO CUTE!
aaaaaaaaa!
IF SHE'S GOING TO GO TO ***THIS*** MUCH TROUBLE, I DON'T THINK THERE'S ***ANY*** DOUBT!
Aah!
AND, AS A GUY, YOU HAVE TO AGREE, SHE'S PRETTY EASY ON THE EYES!

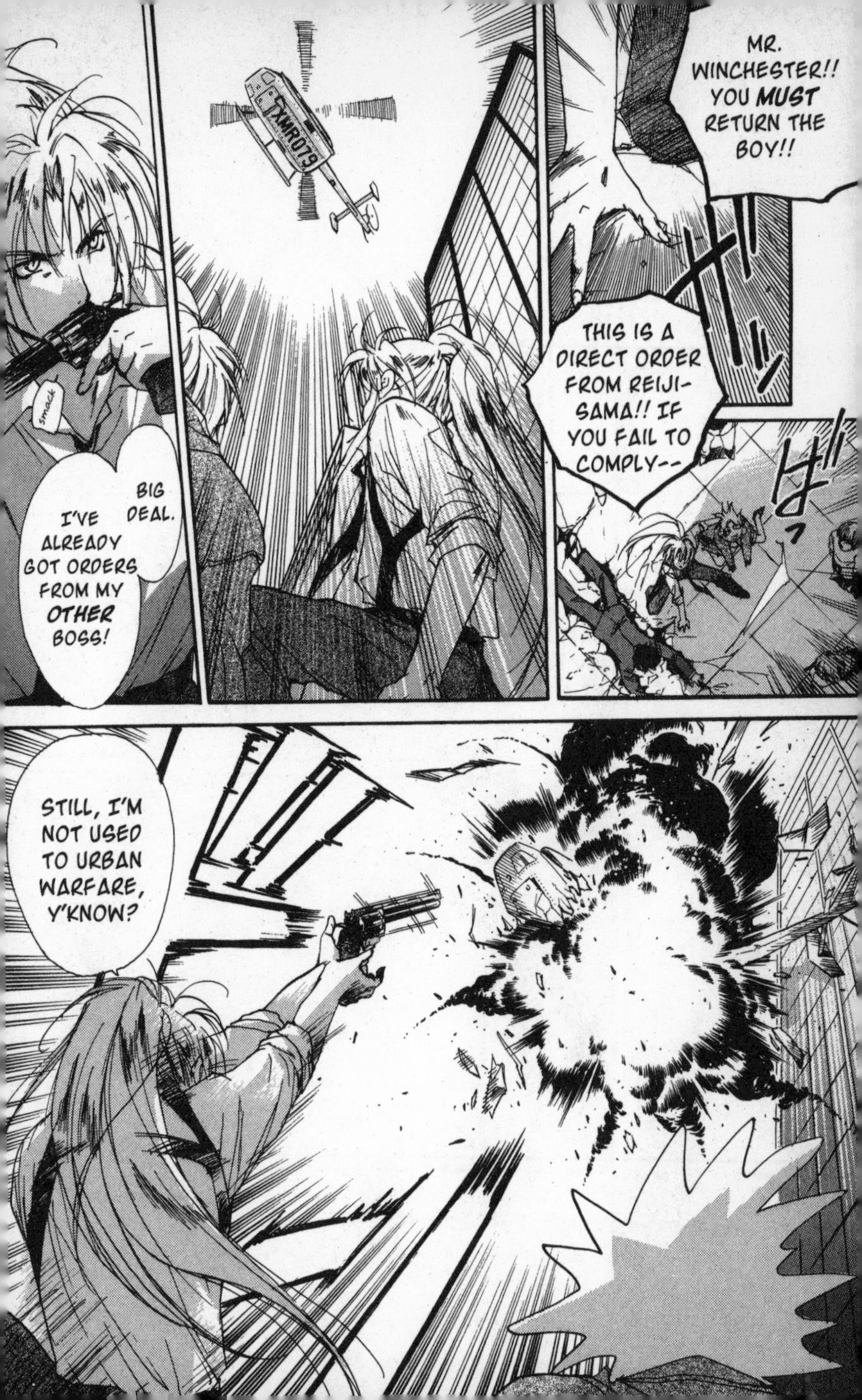
MR. WINCHESTER!! YOU MUST RETURN THE BOY!!
THIS IS A DIRECT ORDER FROM REIJI-SAMA!! IF YOU FAIL TO COMPLY--
ばっ
XMR079
smack
BIG DEAL. I'VE ALREADY GOT ORDERS FROM MY OTHER BOSS!
STILL, I'M NOT USED TO URBAN WARFARE, Y'KNOW?

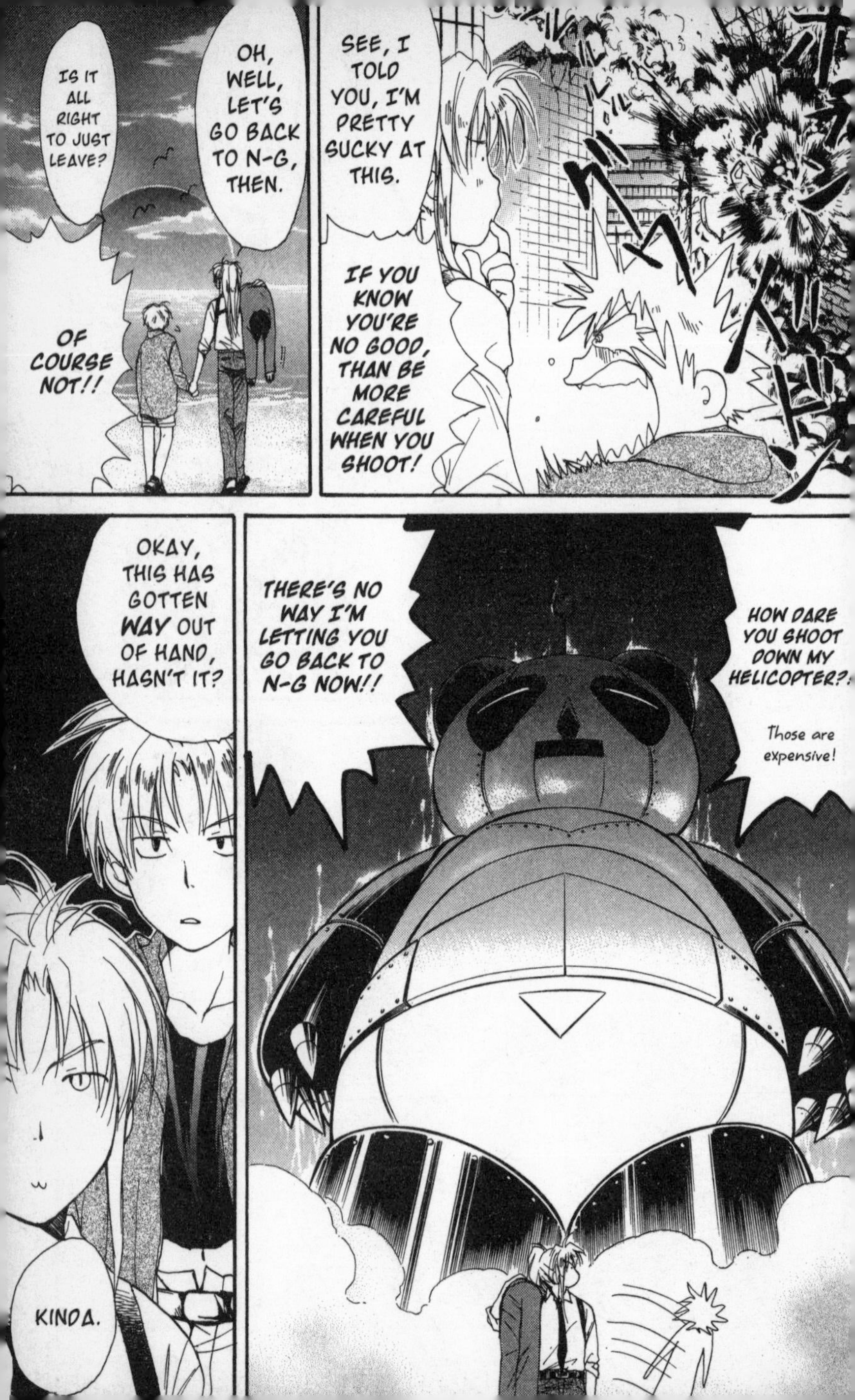
SEE, I TOLD YOU, I'M PRETTY SUCKY AT THIS.
IF YOU KNOW YOU'RE NO GOOD, THAN BE MORE CAREFUL WHEN YOU SHOOT!
OH, WELL, LET'S GO BACK TO N-G, THEN.
IS IT ALL RIGHT TO JUST LEAVE?
OF COURSE NOT!!
HOW DARE YOU SHOOT DOWN MY HELICOPTER?!
Those are expensive!
THERE'S NO WAY I'M LETTING YOU GO BACK TO N-G NOW!!
OKAY, THIS HAS GOTTEN WAY OUT OF HAND, HASN'T IT?
KINDA.

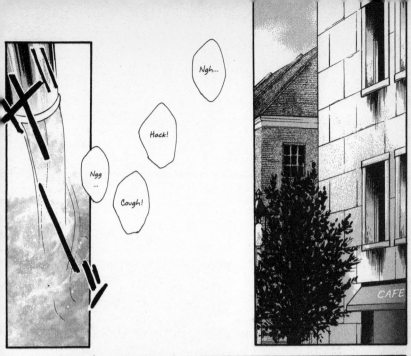

Ngh...

Hack!

Ngg
...

Cough!

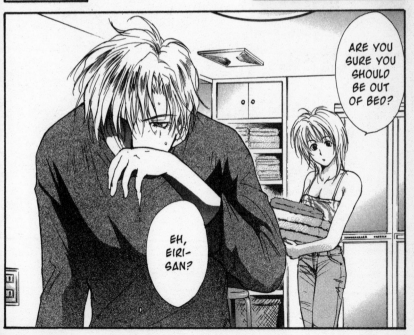

ARE YOU SURE YOU SHOULD BE OUT OF BED?

EH, EIRI-SAN?

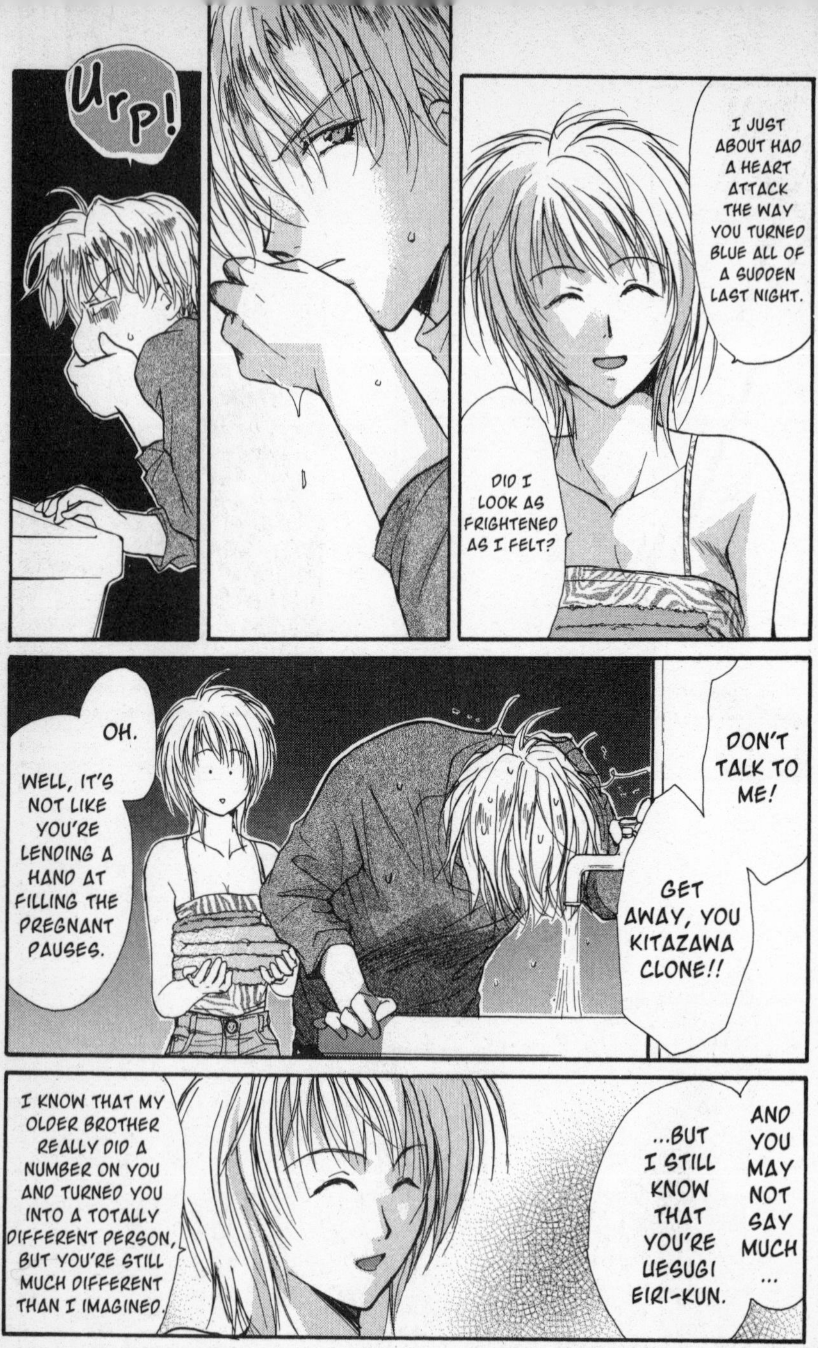
I JUST ABOUT HAD A HEART ATTACK THE WAY YOU TURNED BLUE ALL OF A SUDDEN LAST NIGHT.
DID I LOOK AS FRIGHTENED AS I FELT?
Urp!
DON'T TALK TO ME!
GET AWAY, YOU KITAZAWA CLONE!!
OH.
WELL, IT'S NOT LIKE YOU'RE LENDING A HAND AT FILLING THE PREGNANT PAUSES.
AND YOU MAY NOT SAY MUCH ...
...BUT I STILL KNOW THAT YOU'RE UESUGI EIRI-KUN.
I KNOW THAT MY OLDER BROTHER REALLY DID A NUMBER ON YOU AND TURNED YOU INTO A TOTALLY DIFFERENT PERSON, BUT YOU'RE STILL MUCH DIFFERENT THAN I IMAGINED.

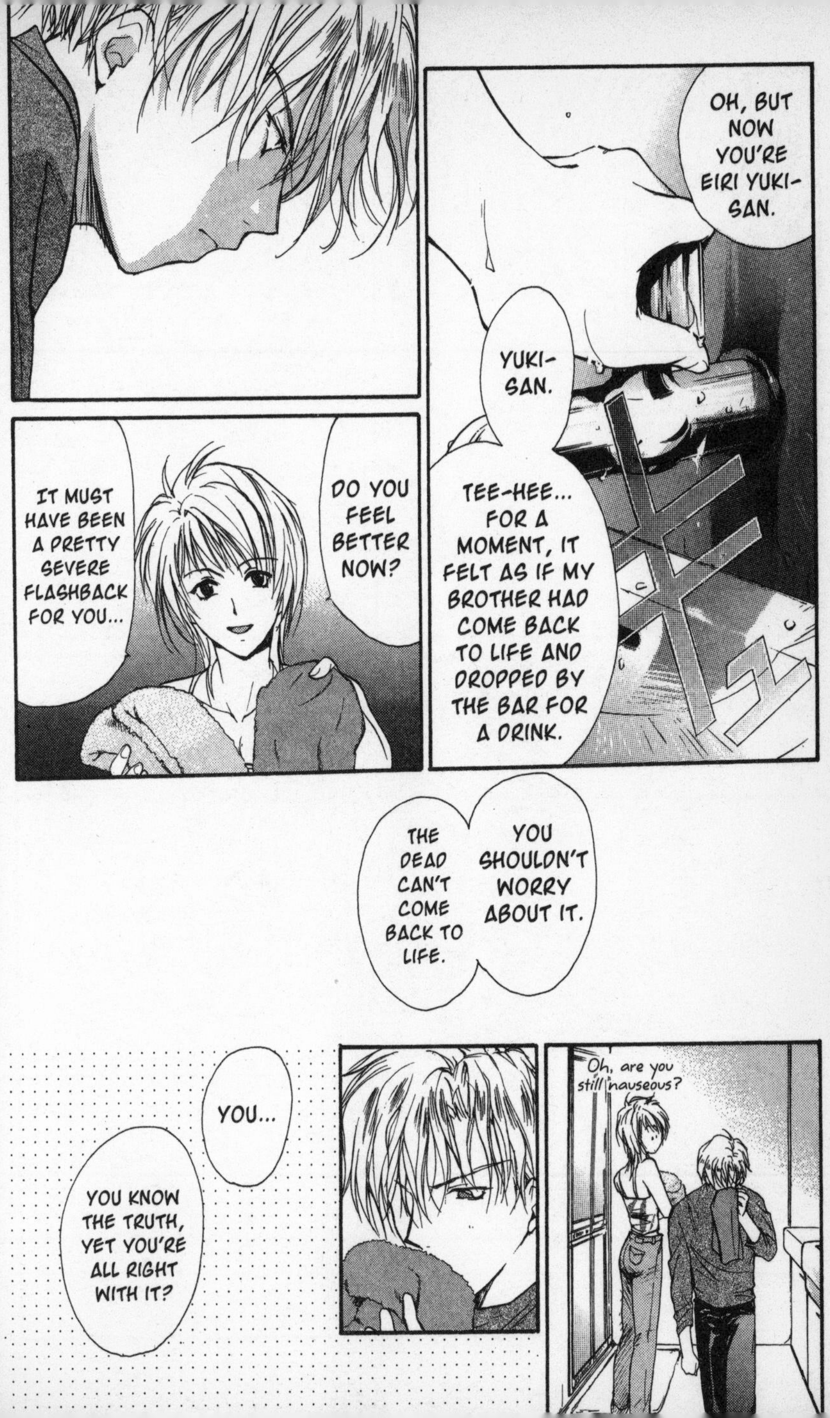
OH, BUT NOW YOU'RE EIRI YUKI-SAN.
YUKI-SAN.
TEE-HEE... FOR A MOMENT, IT FELT AS IF MY BROTHER HAD COME BACK TO LIFE AND DROPPED BY THE BAR FOR A DRINK.
DO YOU FEEL BETTER NOW?
IT MUST HAVE BEEN A PRETTY SEVERE FLASHBACK FOR YOU...
YOU SHOULDN'T WORRY ABOUT IT.
THE DEAD CAN'T COME BACK TO LIFE.
Oh, are you still nauseous?
YOU...
YOU KNOW THE TRUTH, YET YOU'RE ALL RIGHT WITH IT?

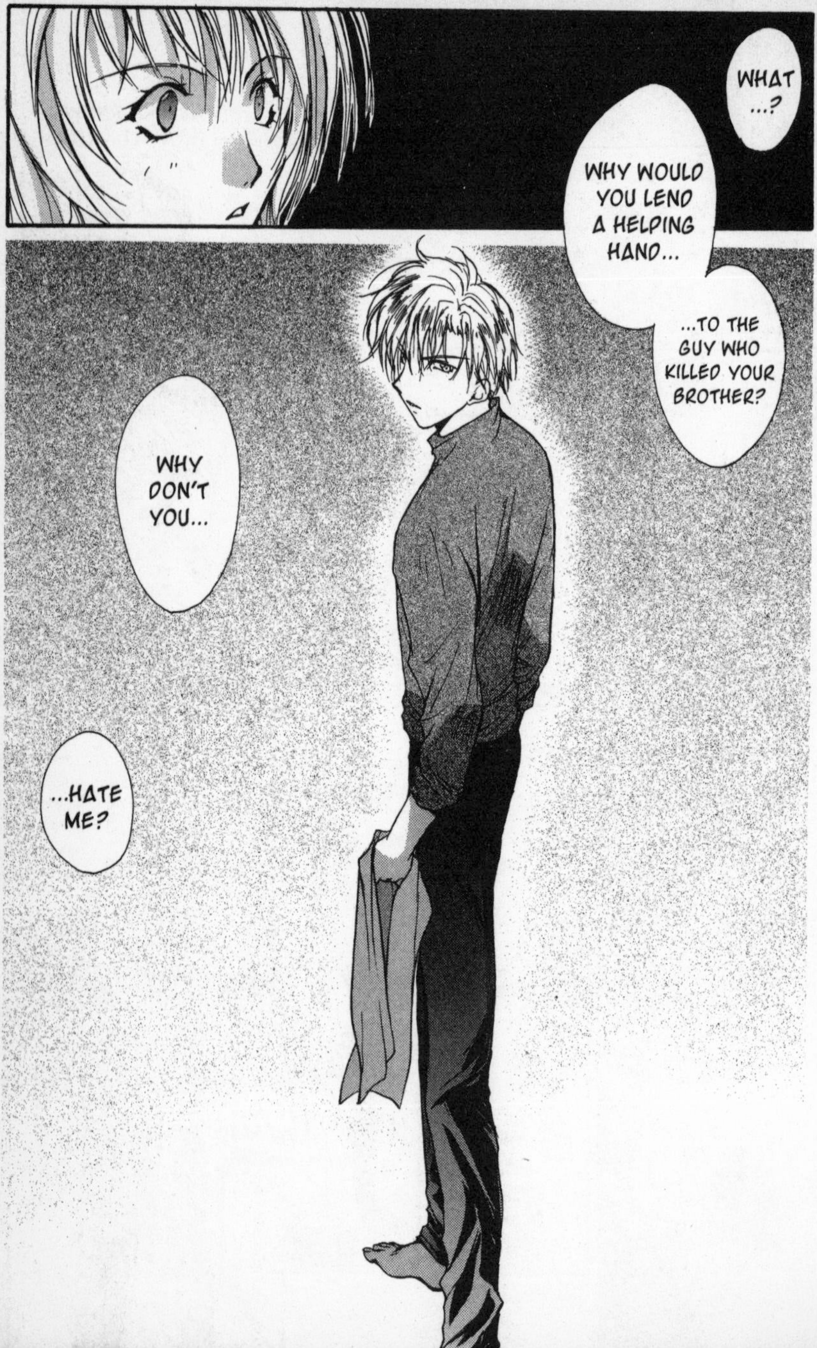
WHAT ...?
WHY WOULD YOU LEND A HELPING HAND...
...TO THE GUY WHO KILLED YOUR BROTHER?
WHY DON'T YOU...
...HATE ME?

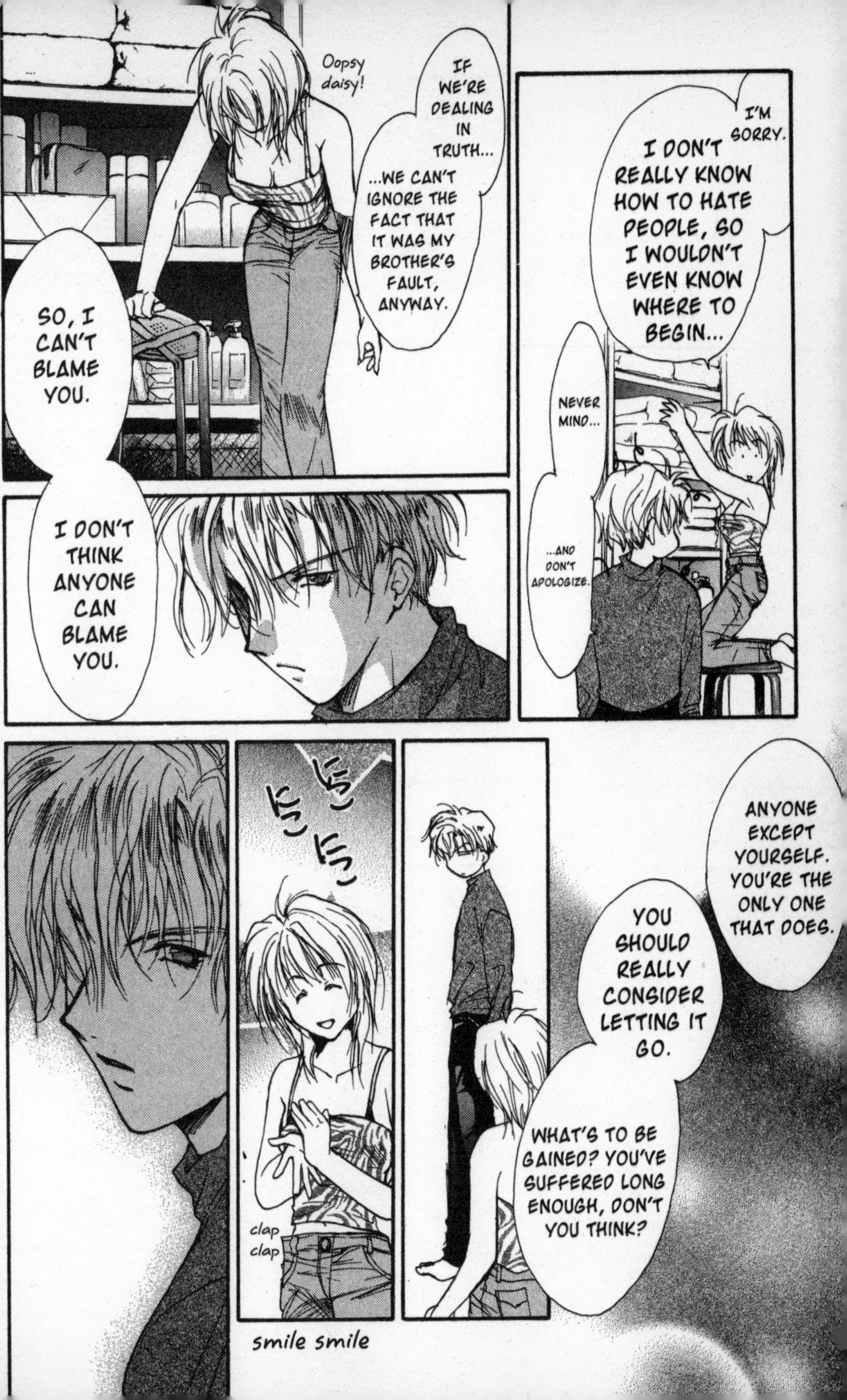

I'M SORRY.
I DON'T REALLY KNOW HOW TO HATE PEOPLE, SO I WOULDN'T EVEN KNOW WHERE TO BEGIN...
NEVER MIND...
...AND DON'T APOLOGIZE.
Oopsy daisy!
IF WE'RE DEALING IN TRUTH...
...WE CAN'T IGNORE THE FACT THAT IT WAS MY BROTHER'S FAULT, ANYWAY.
...
SO, I CAN'T BLAME YOU.
I DON'T THINK ANYONE CAN BLAME YOU.
ANYONE EXCEPT YOURSELF. YOU'RE THE ONLY ONE THAT DOES.
YOU SHOULD REALLY CONSIDER LETTING IT GO.
WHAT'S TO BE GAINED? YOU'VE SUFFERED LONG ENOUGH, DON'T YOU THINK?
clap clap
smile smile

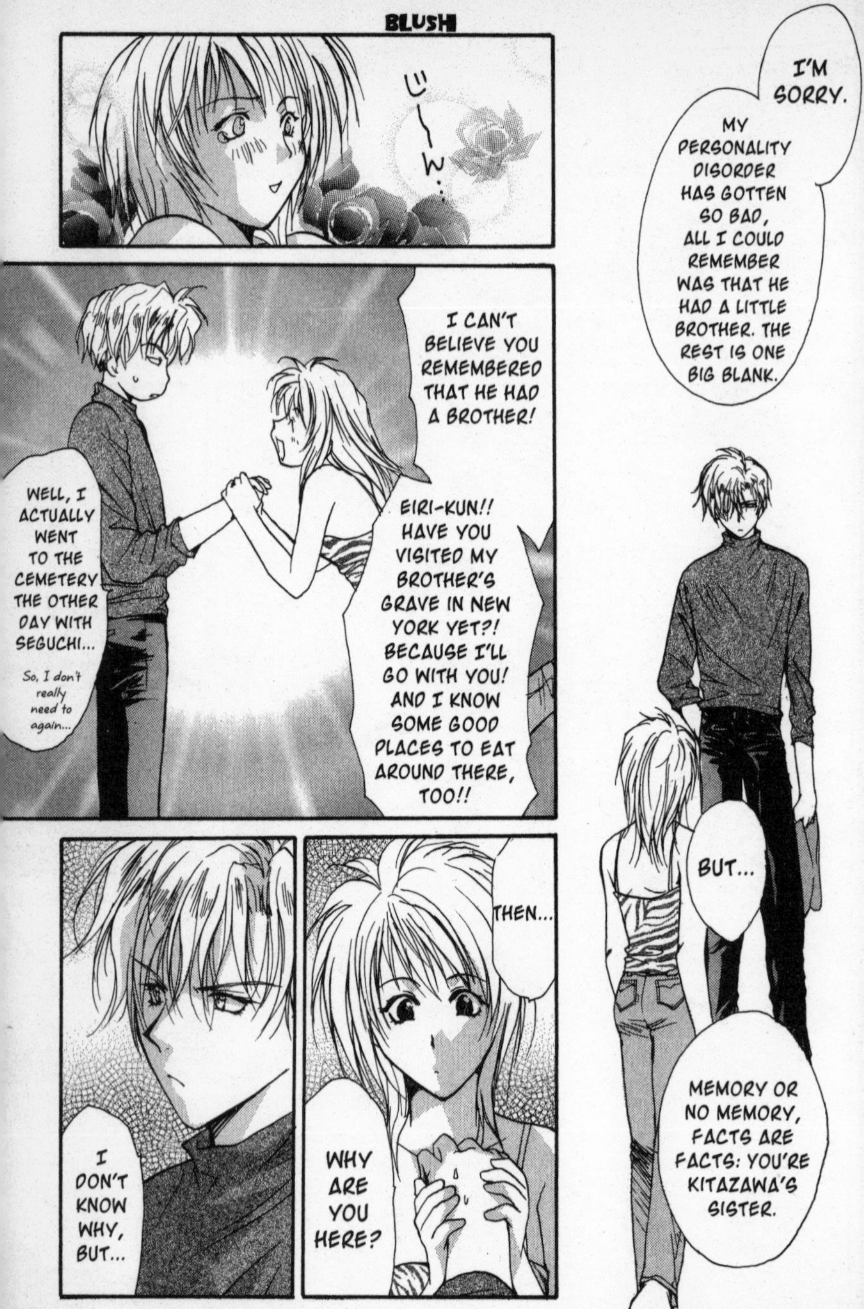
I'M SORRY.
MY PERSONALITY DISORDER HAS GOTTEN SO BAD, ALL I COULD REMEMBER WAS THAT HE HAD A LITTLE BROTHER. THE REST IS ONE BIG BLANK.
BUT...
MEMORY OR NO MEMORY, FACTS ARE FACTS: YOU'RE KITAZAWA'S SISTER.
BLUSH
じ〜ん...
I CAN'T BELIEVE YOU REMEMBERED THAT HE HAD A BROTHER!
EIRI-KUN!! HAVE YOU VISITED MY BROTHER'S GRAVE IN NEW YORK YET?! BECAUSE I'LL GO WITH YOU! AND I KNOW SOME GOOD PLACES TO EAT AROUND THERE, TOO!!
WELL, I ACTUALLY WENT TO THE CEMETERY THE OTHER DAY WITH SEGUCHI...
So, I don't really need to again...
THEN...
WHY ARE YOU HERE?
I DON'T KNOW WHY, BUT...

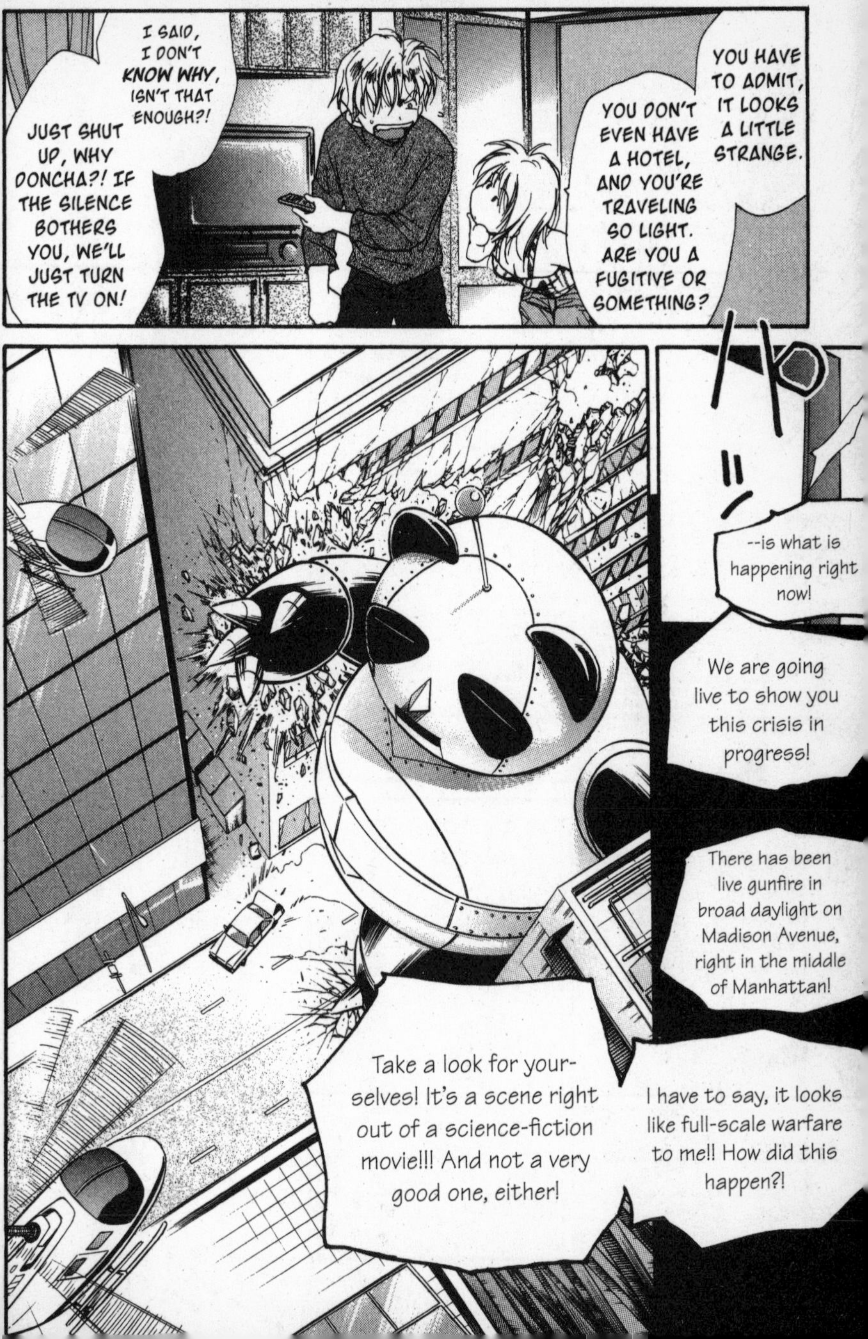
YOU HAVE TO ADMIT, IT LOOKS A LITTLE STRANGE.
YOU DON'T EVEN HAVE A HOTEL, AND YOU'RE TRAVELING SO LIGHT. ARE YOU A FUGITIVE OR SOMETHING?
I SAID, I DON'T KNOW WHY, ISN'T THAT ENOUGH?!
JUST SHUT UP, WHY DONCHA?! IF THE SILENCE BOTHERS YOU, WE'LL JUST TURN THE TV ON!
--is what is happening right now!
We are going live to show you this crisis in progress!
There has been live gunfire in broad daylight on Madison Avenue, right in the middle of Manhattan!
I have to say, it looks like full-scale warfare to me!! How did this happen?!
Take a look for your-selves! It's a scene right out of a science-fiction movie!!! And not a very good one, either!

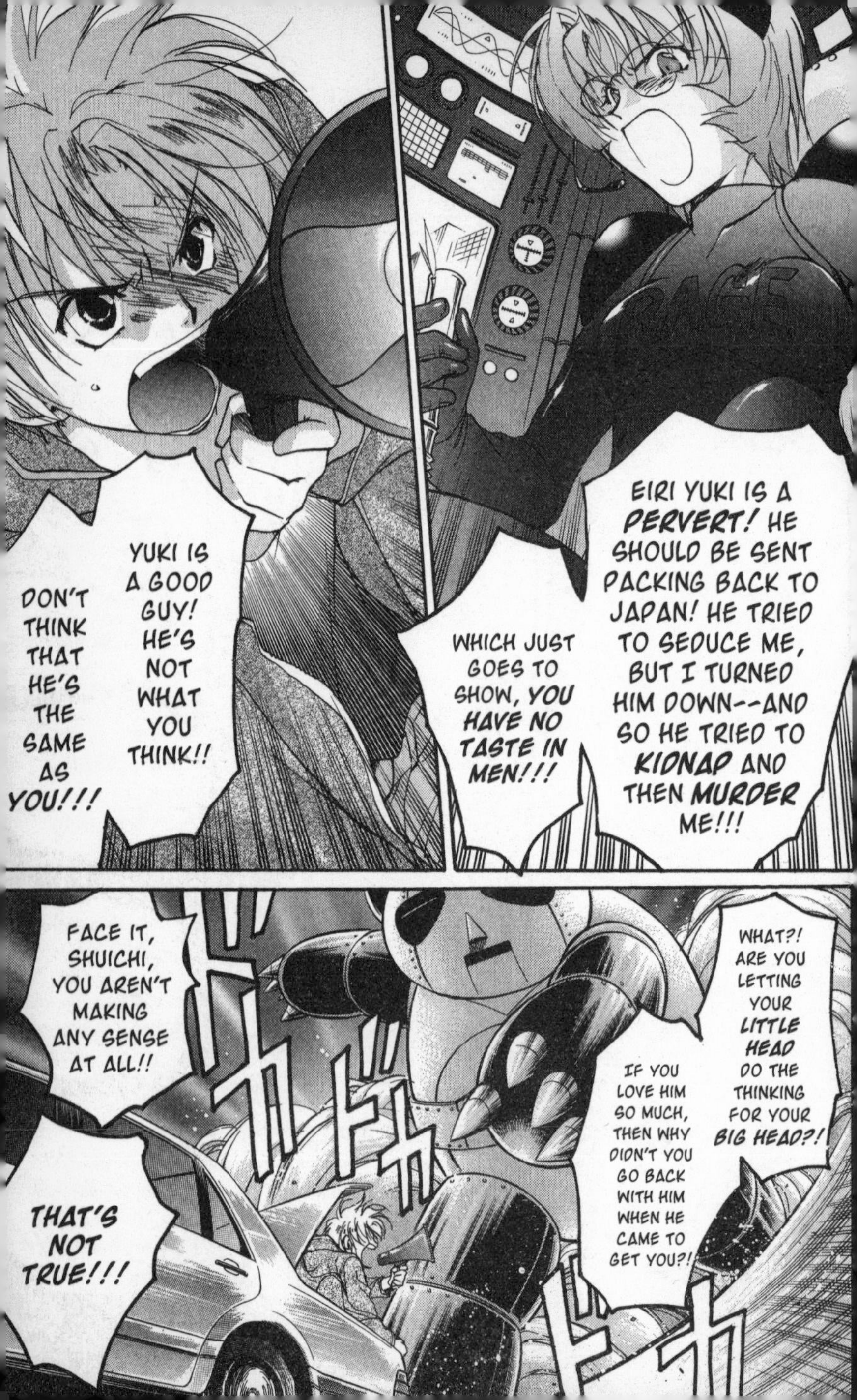
EIRI YUKI IS A PERVERT! HE SHOULD BE SENT PACKING BACK TO JAPAN! HE TRIED TO SEDUCE ME, BUT I TURNED HIM DOWN--AND SO HE TRIED TO KIDNAP AND THEN MURDER ME!!!
WHICH JUST GOES TO SHOW, YOU HAVE NO TASTE IN MEN!!!
YUKI IS A GOOD GUY! HE'S NOT WHAT YOU THINK!!
DON'T THINK THAT HE'S THE SAME AS YOU!!!
WHAT?! ARE YOU LETTING YOUR LITTLE HEAD DO THE THINKING FOR YOUR BIG HEAD?!
IF YOU LOVE HIM SO MUCH, THEN WHY DIDN'T YOU GO BACK WITH HIM WHEN HE CAME TO GET YOU?!
FACE IT, SHUICHI, YOU AREN'T MAKING ANY SENSE AT ALL!!
THAT'S NOT TRUE!!!

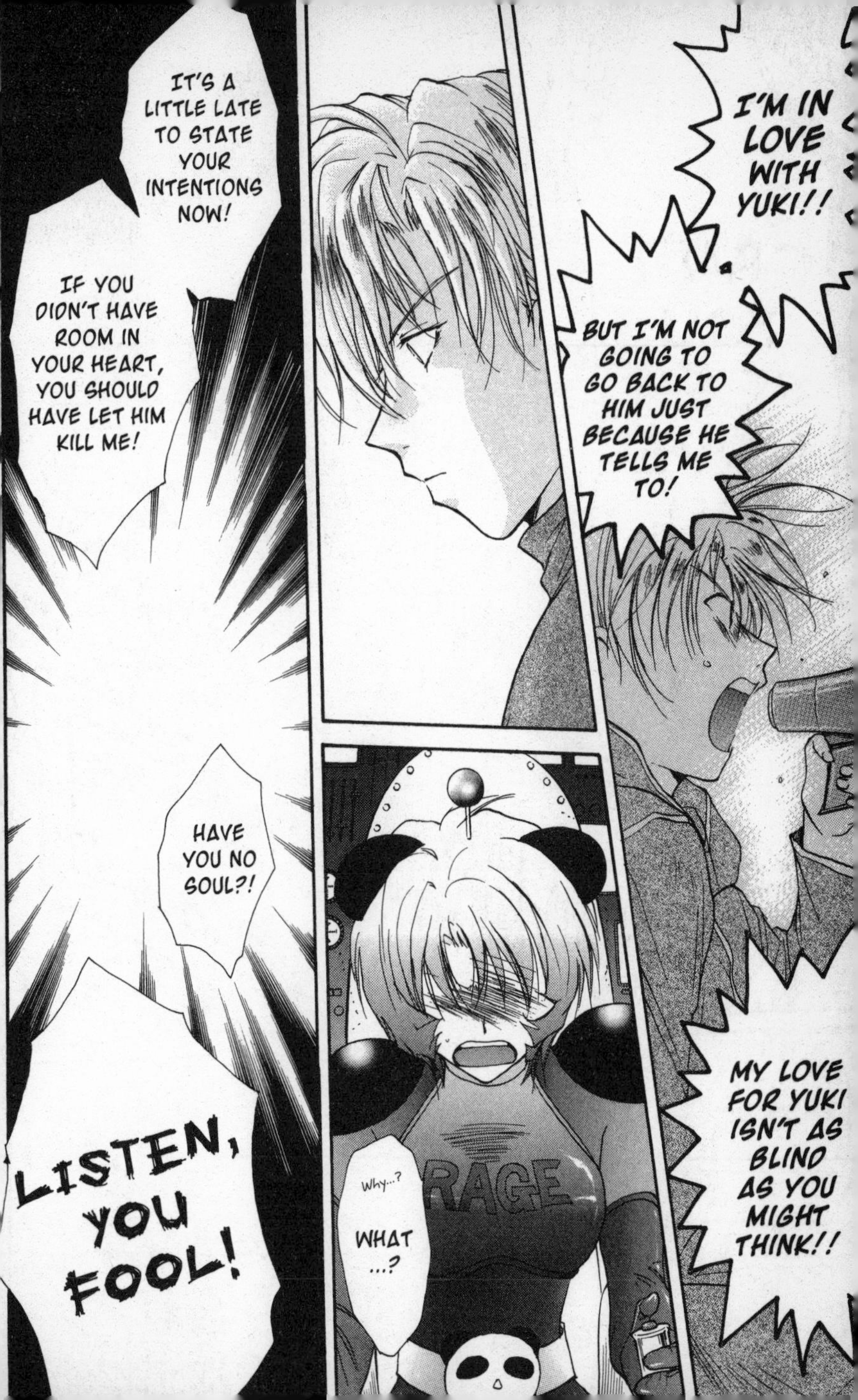
I'M IN LOVE WITH YUKI!!
BUT I'M NOT GOING TO GO BACK TO HIM JUST BECAUSE HE TELLS ME TO!
MY LOVE FOR YUKI ISN'T AS BLIND AS YOU MIGHT THINK!!
WHAT ...?
Why...?
IT'S A LITTLE LATE TO STATE YOUR INTENTIONS NOW!
IF YOU DIDN'T HAVE ROOM IN YOUR HEART, YOU SHOULD HAVE LET HIM KILL ME!
HAVE YOU NO SOUL?!
LISTEN, YOU FOOL!

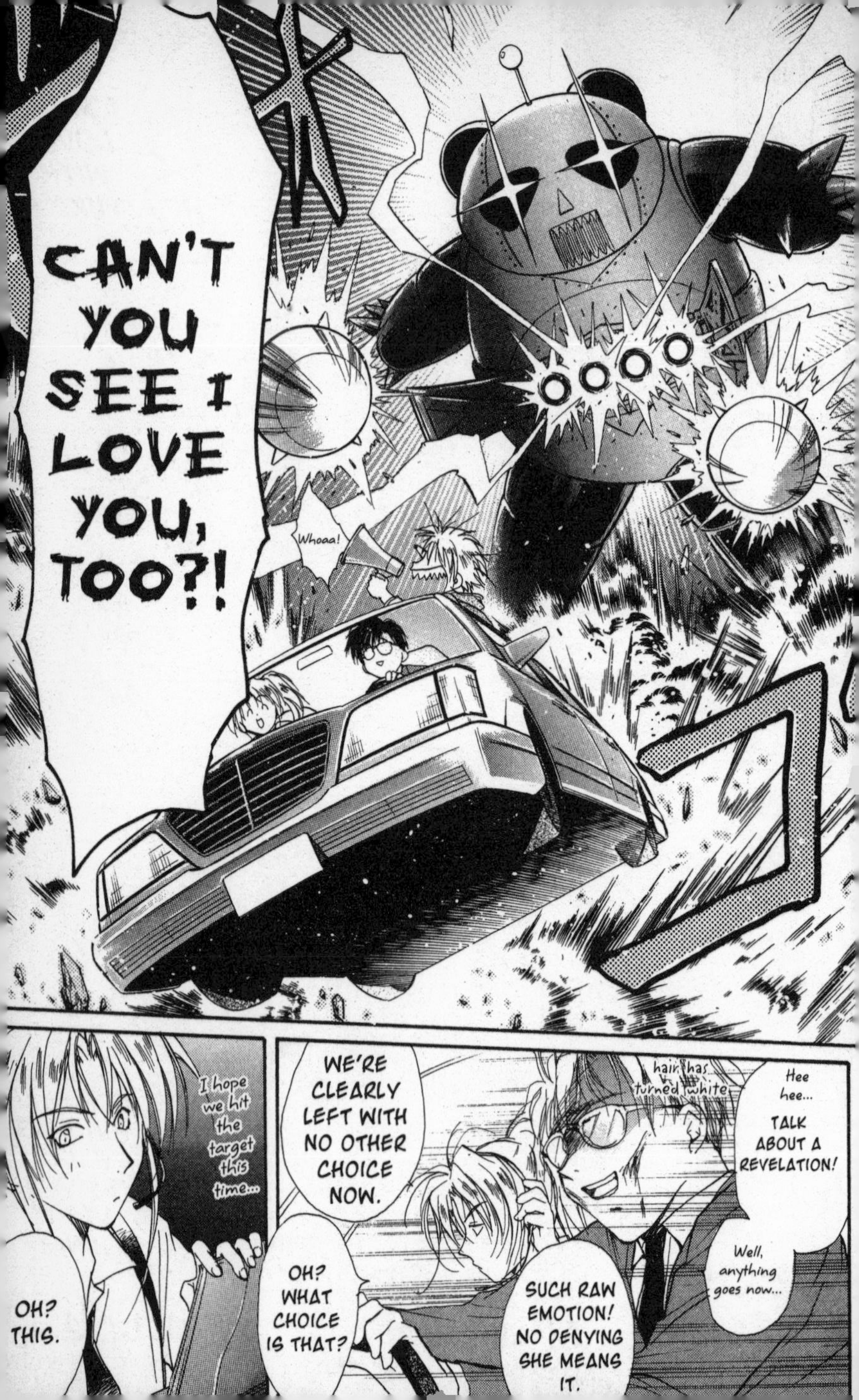
CAN'T YOU SEE I LOVE YOU, TOO?!
Whoaa!
hair has turned white
Hee hee... TALK ABOUT A REVELATION!
WE'RE CLEARLY LEFT WITH NO OTHER CHOICE NOW.
Well, anything goes now...
SUCH RAW EMOTION! NO DENYING SHE MEANS IT.
OH? WHAT CHOICE IS THAT?
I hope we hit the target this time...
OH? THIS.

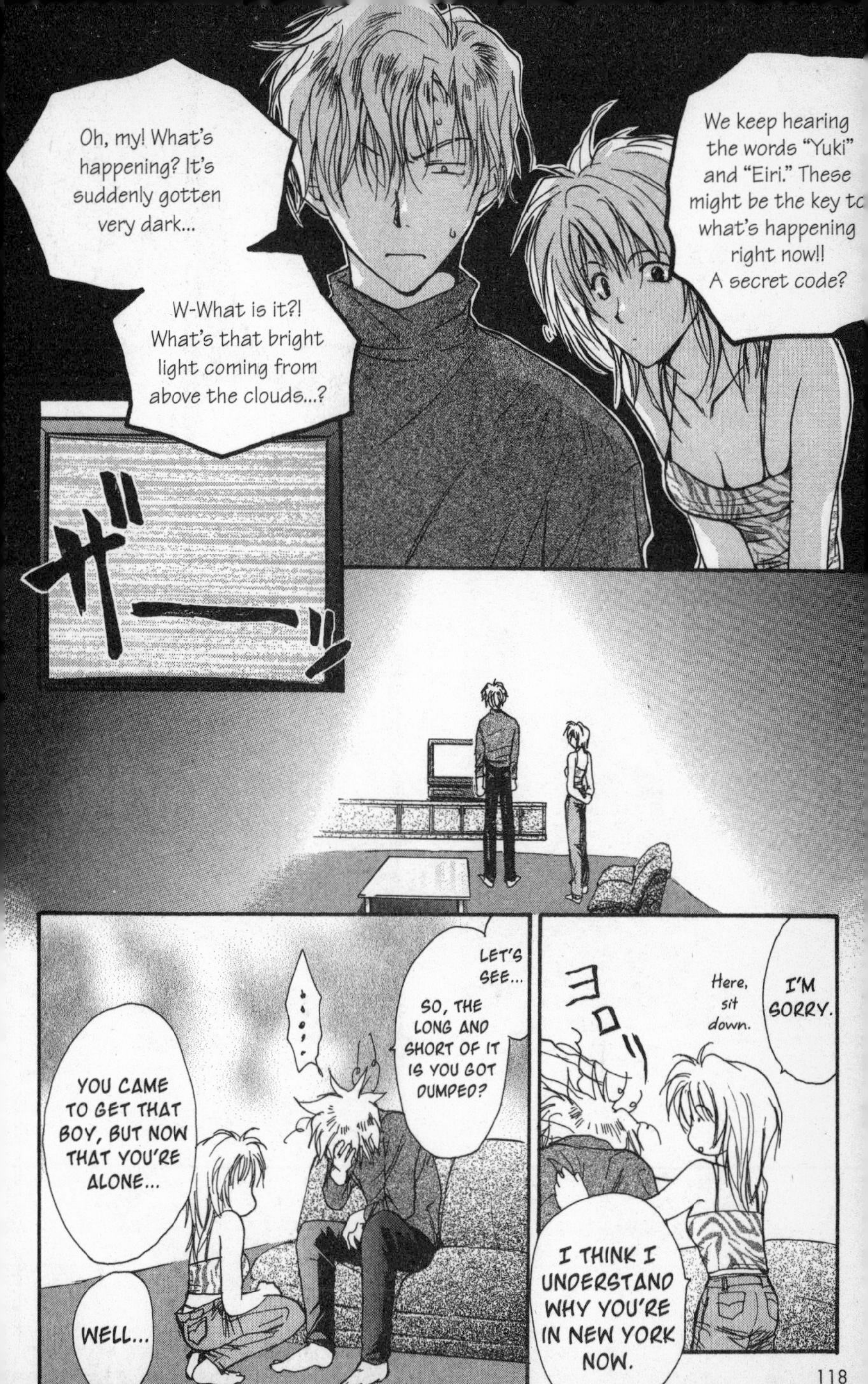

We keep hearing the words "Yuki" and "Eiri." These might be the key tc what's happening right now!! A secret code?
Oh, my! What's happening? It's suddenly gotten very dark...
W-What is it?! What's that bright light coming from above the clouds...?
ザーッ
I'M SORRY.
Here, sit down.
ヨロッ
I THINK I UNDERSTAND WHY YOU'RE IN NEW YORK NOW.
LET'S SEE...
SO, THE LONG AND SHORT OF IT IS YOU GOT DUMPED?
......
YOU CAME TO GET THAT BOY, BUT NOW THAT YOU'RE ALONE...
WELL...

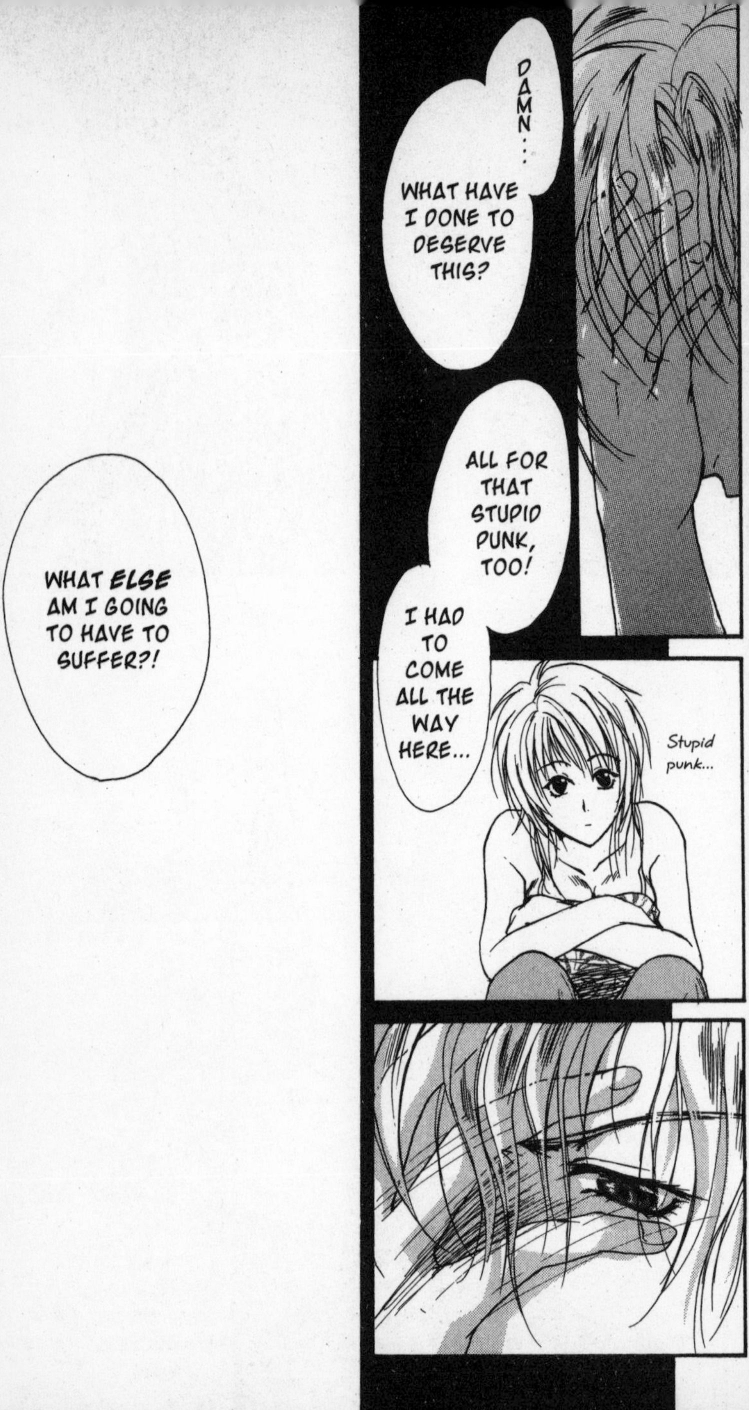
DAMN...
WHAT HAVE I DONE TO DESERVE THIS?
ALL FOR THAT STUPID PUNK, TOO!
I HAD TO COME ALL THE WAY HERE...
Stupid punk...
WHAT ELSE AM I GOING TO HAVE TO SUFFER?!

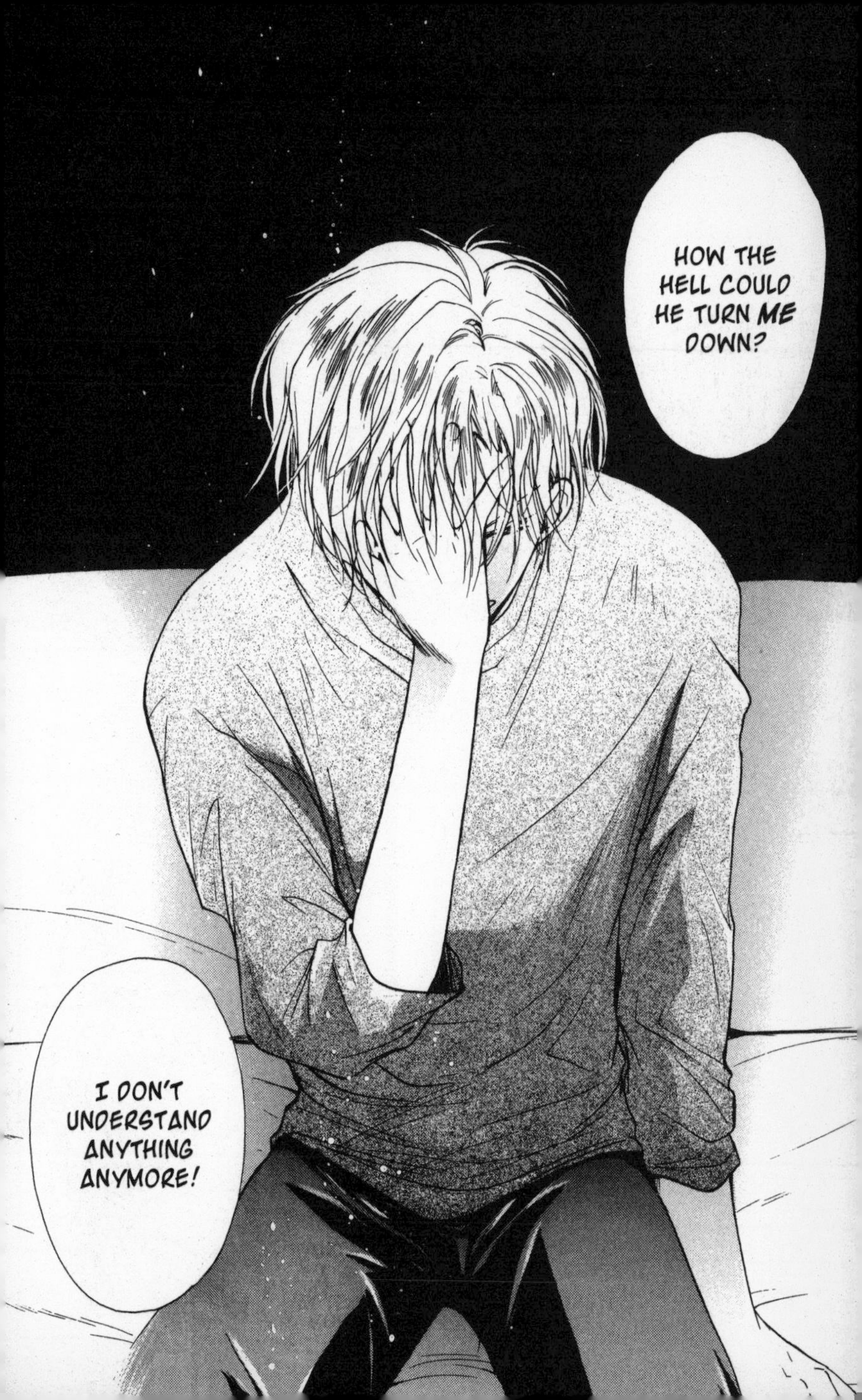
HOW THE HELL COULD HE TURN ME DOWN?
I DON'T UNDERSTAND ANYTHING ANYMORE!

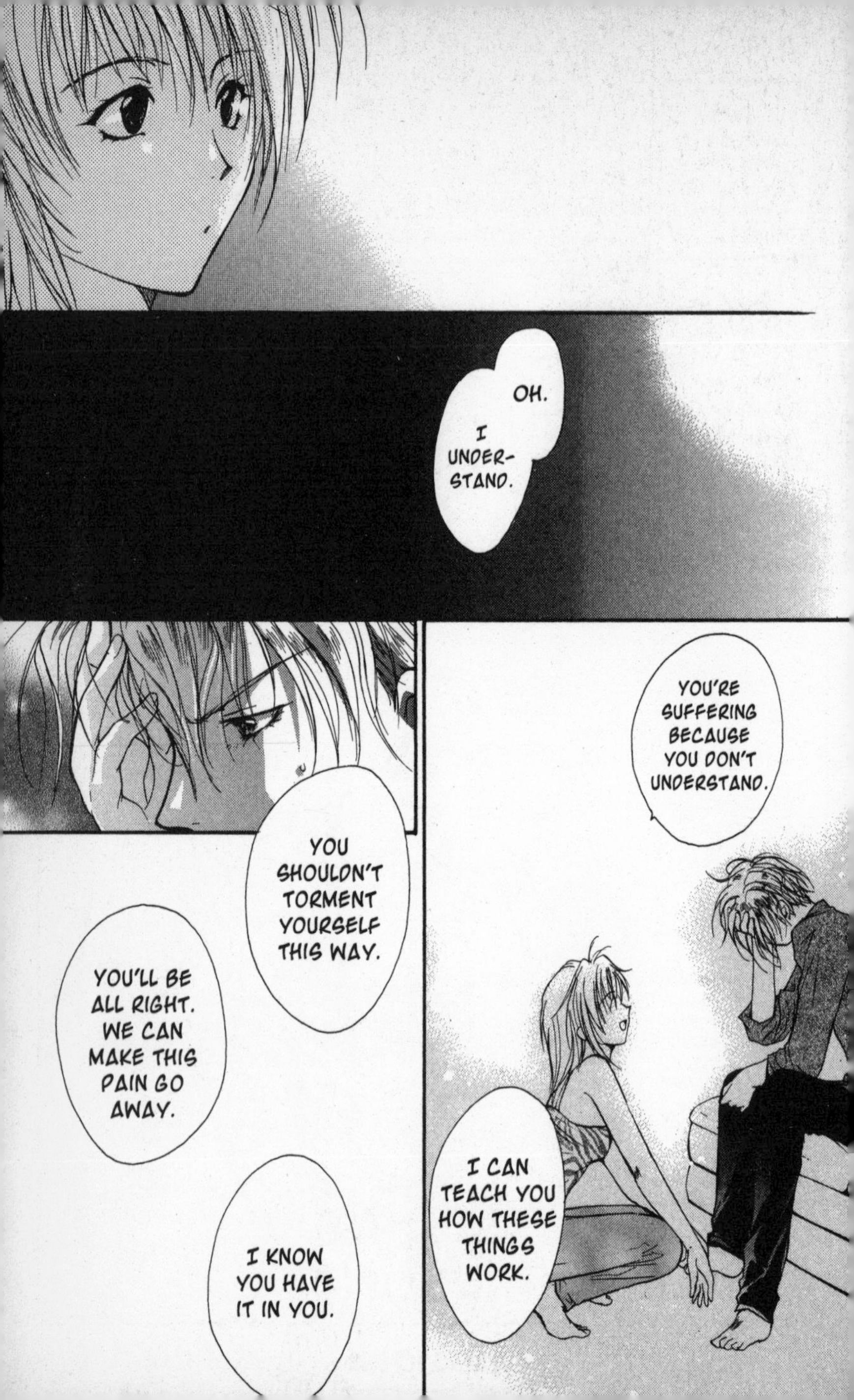
OH. I UNDERSTAND.
YOU'RE SUFFERING BECAUSE YOU DON'T UNDERSTAND.
I CAN TEACH YOU HOW THESE THINGS WORK.
YOU SHOULDN'T TORMENT YOURSELF THIS WAY.
YOU'LL BE ALL RIGHT. WE CAN MAKE THIS PAIN GO AWAY.
I KNOW YOU HAVE IT IN YOU.

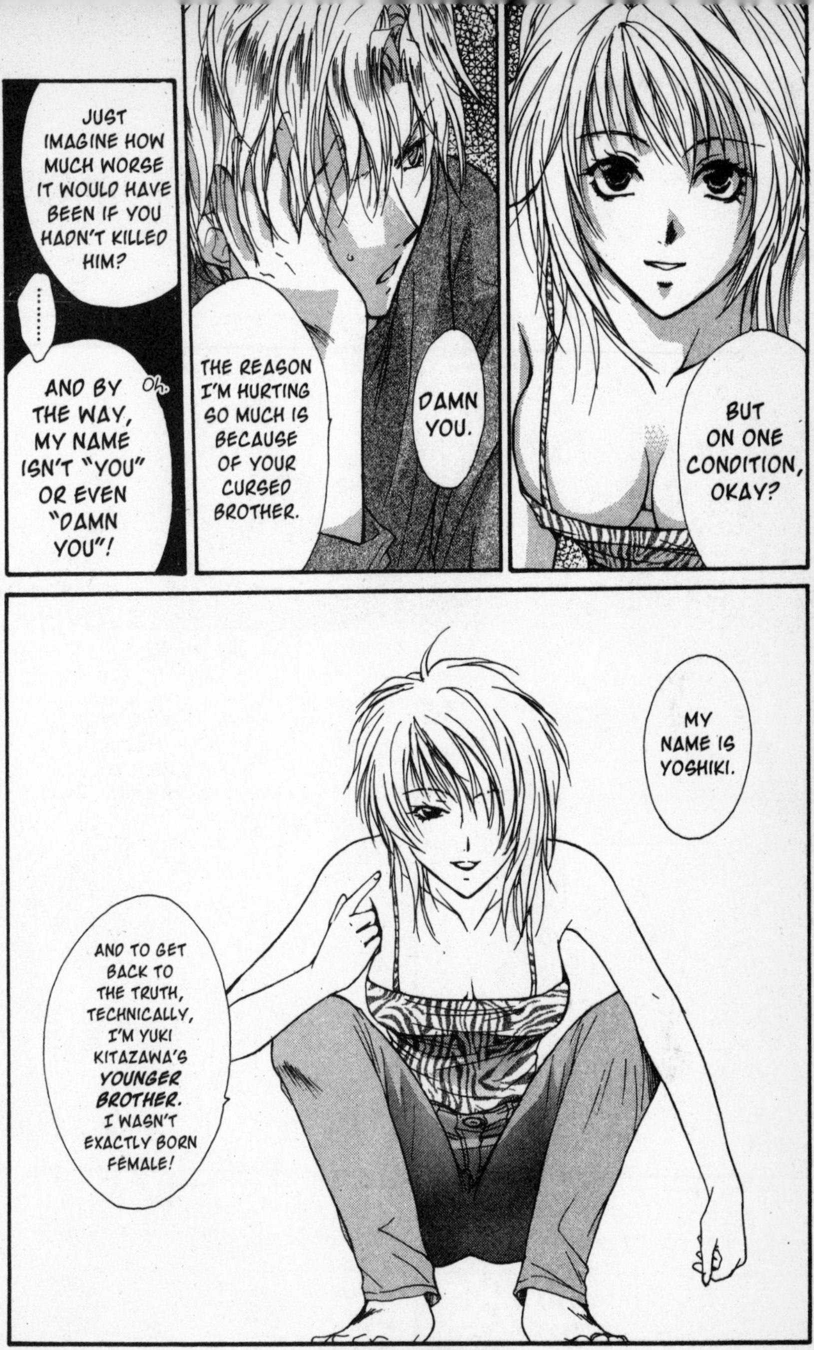
BUT ON ONE CONDITION, OKAY?
DAMN YOU.
THE REASON I'M HURTING SO MUCH IS BECAUSE OF YOUR CURSED BROTHER.
JUST IMAGINE HOW MUCH WORSE IT WOULD HAVE BEEN IF YOU HADN'T KILLED HIM?
......
Oh.
AND BY THE WAY, MY NAME ISN'T "YOU" OR EVEN "DAMN YOU"!
MY NAME IS YOSHIKI.
AND TO GET BACK TO THE TRUTH, TECHNICALLY, I'M YUKI KITAZAWA'S ***YOUNGER BROTHER.*** I WASN'T EXACTLY BORN FEMALE!

track39 ▶ END

Gravitation

track40

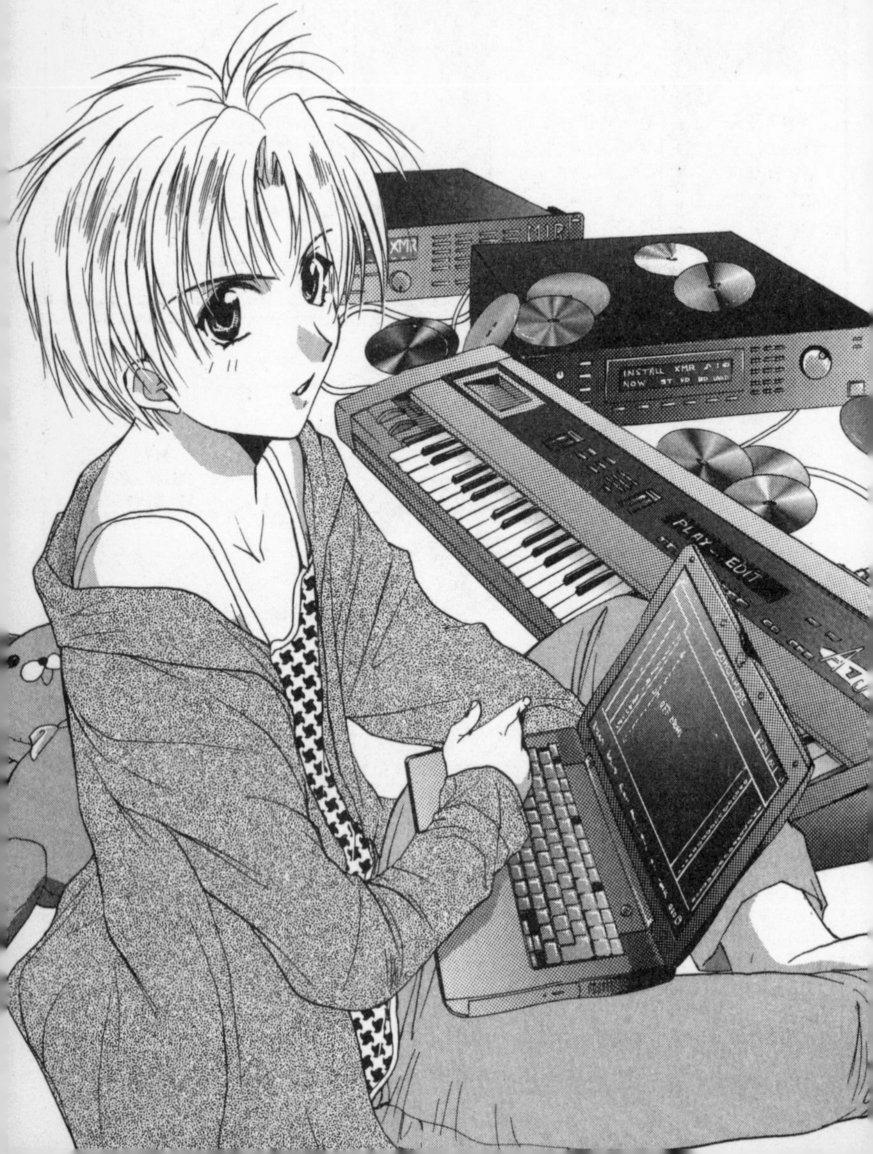
XMR
INSTALL XMR
NOW
PLAY EDIT

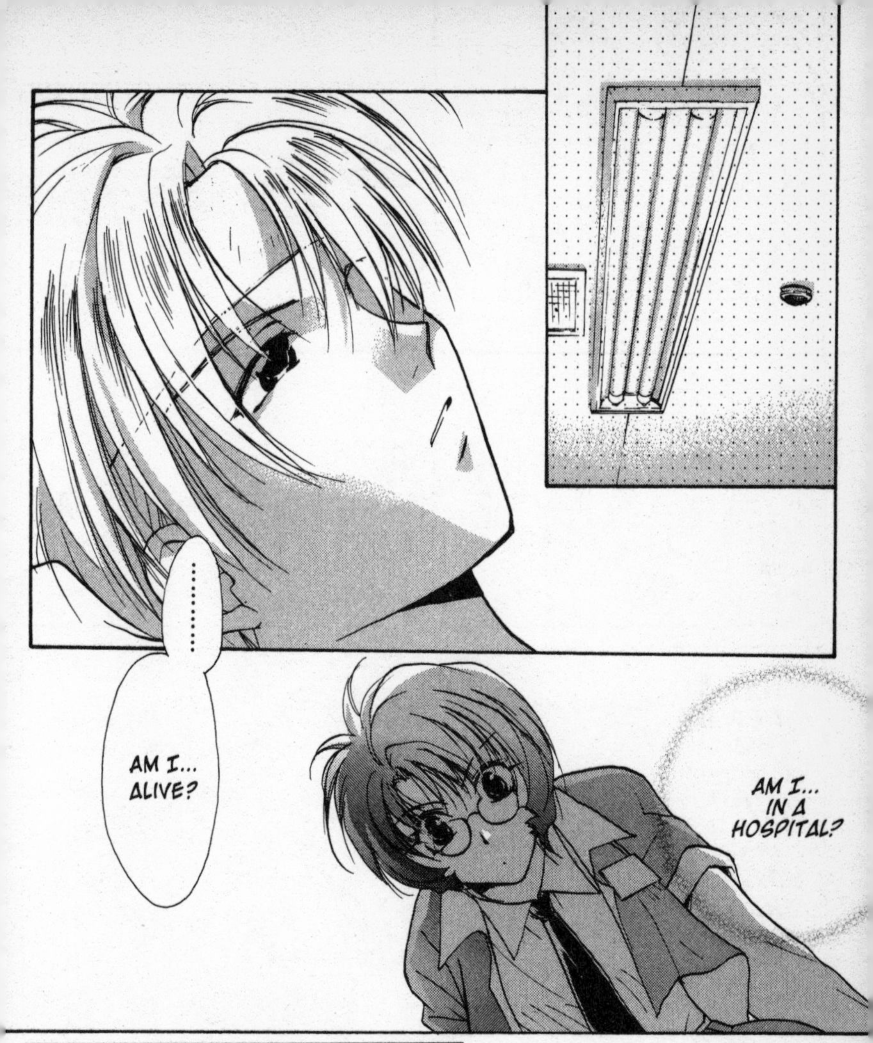
......
AM I... IN A HOSPITAL?
AM I... ALIVE?

ABOUT GRAVITATION TRACK 40

Track 40!! We've made it to episode 40!! Reiji's fashion sense has already gone over the edge, beyond bad taste. It hurts. I've gotten a lot of positive feedback on Reiji's panda of love, which is either good or bad news, I don't know. I would like to take the credit, but actually, my version of the panda...

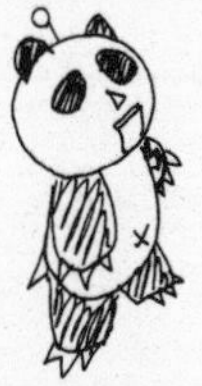

...is this.

I couldn't even approximate the grace and power of a real panda. Anyway, that's just a back story to this manga. So, how do you like Eiri's new 'do? I think it looks good on him, but...

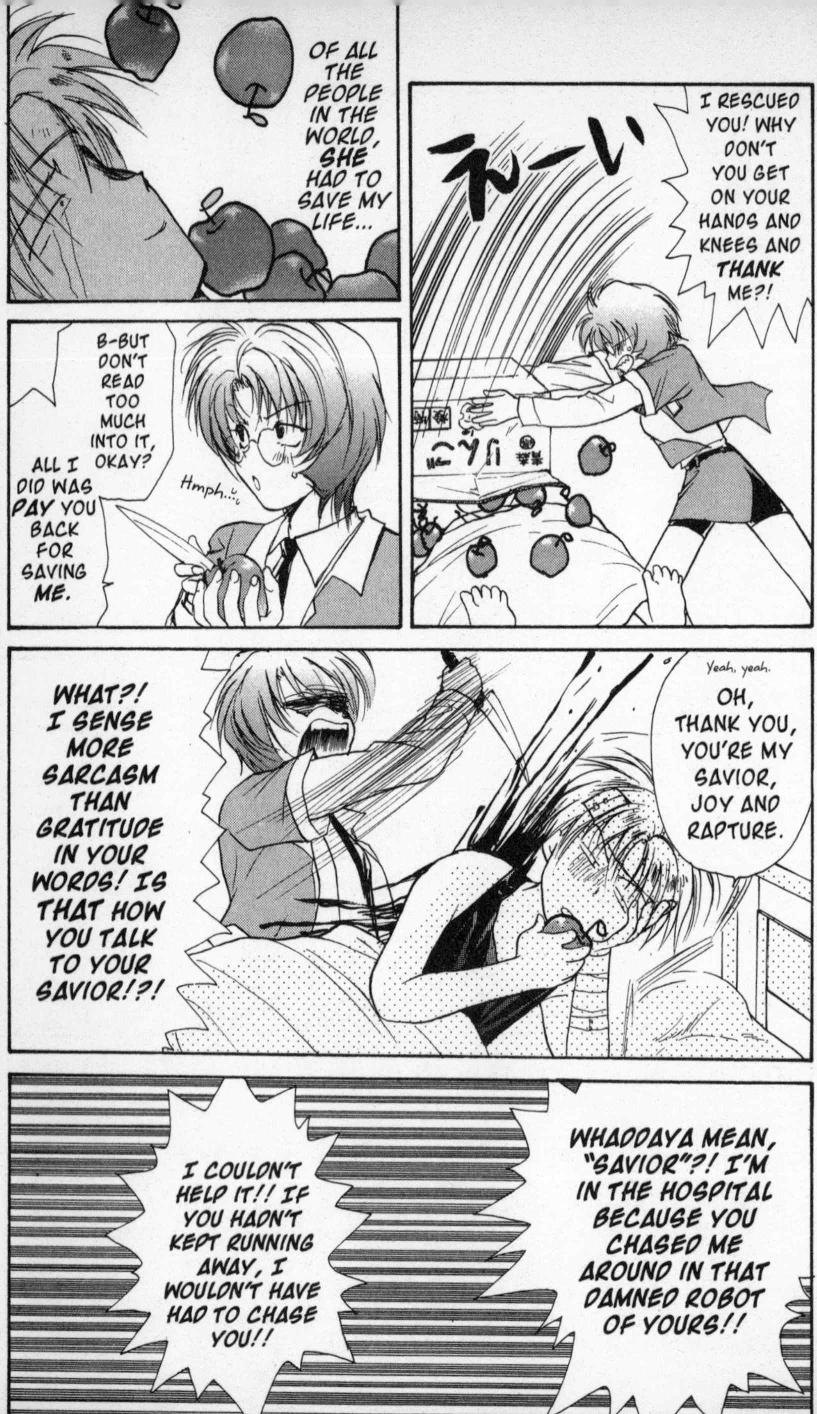
OF ALL THE PEOPLE IN THE WORLD, SHE HAD TO SAVE MY LIFE...
B-BUT DON'T READ TOO MUCH INTO IT, OKAY?
ALL I DID WAS PAY YOU BACK FOR SAVING ME.
Hmph...
えーい
I RESCUED YOU! WHY DON'T YOU GET ON YOUR HANDS AND KNEES AND THANK ME?!
Yeah, yeah.
OH, THANK YOU, YOU'RE MY SAVIOR, JOY AND RAPTURE.
WHAT?! I SENSE MORE SARCASM THAN GRATITUDE IN YOUR WORDS! IS THAT HOW YOU TALK TO YOUR SAVIOR!?!
WHADDAYA MEAN, "SAVIOR"?! I'M IN THE HOSPITAL BECAUSE YOU CHASED ME AROUND IN THAT DAMNED ROBOT OF YOURS!!
I COULDN'T HELP IT!! IF YOU HADN'T KEPT RUNNING AWAY, I WOULDN'T HAVE HAD TO CHASE YOU!!

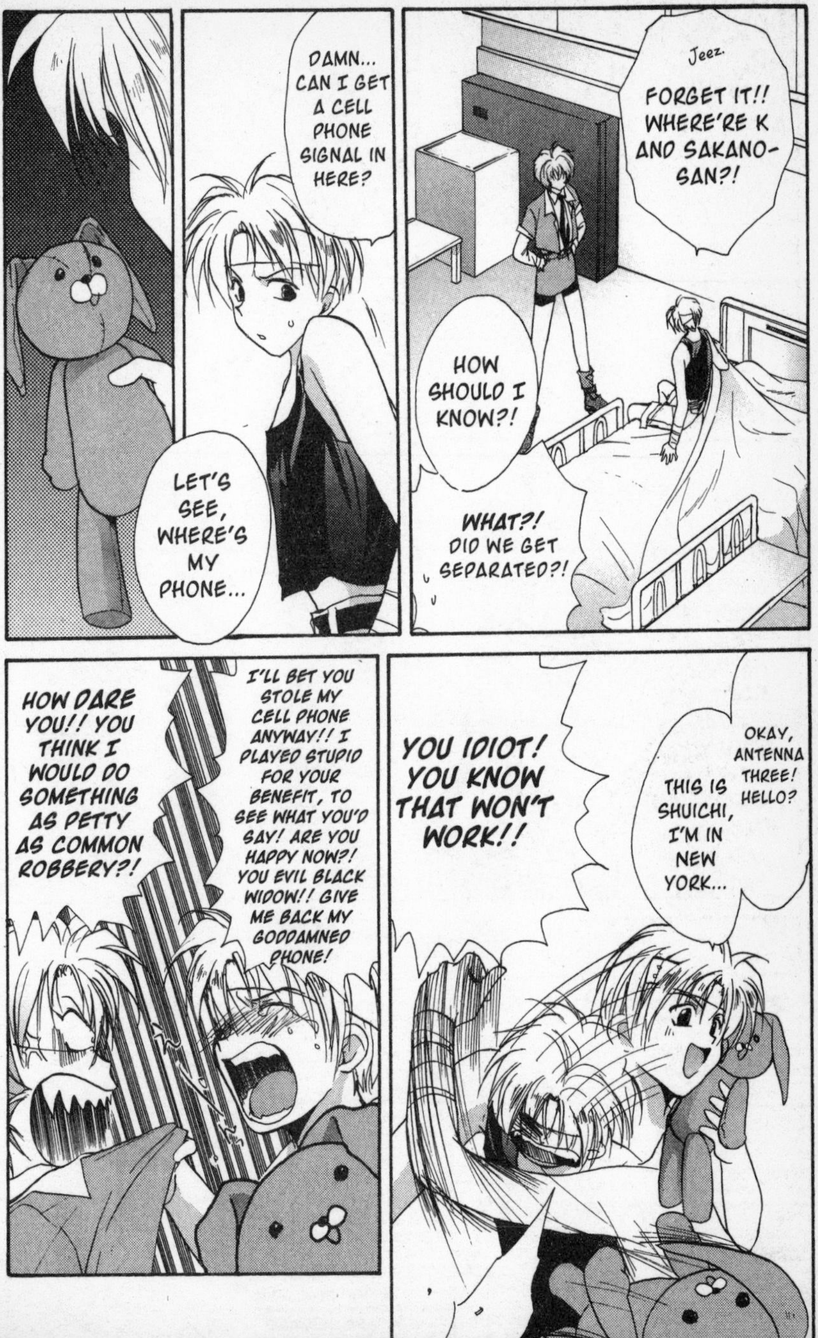

Jeez.
FORGET IT!! WHERE'RE K AND SAKANO-SAN?!
HOW SHOULD I KNOW?!
WHAT?! DID WE GET SEPARATED?!
DAMN... CAN I GET A CELL PHONE SIGNAL IN HERE?
LET'S SEE, WHERE'S MY PHONE...
OKAY, ANTENNA THREE! HELLO?
THIS IS SHUICHI, I'M IN NEW YORK...
YOU IDIOT! YOU KNOW THAT WON'T WORK!!
I'LL BET YOU STOLE MY CELL PHONE ANYWAY!! I PLAYED STUPID FOR YOUR BENEFIT, TO SEE WHAT YOU'D SAY! ARE YOU HAPPY NOW?! YOU EVIL BLACK WIDOW!! GIVE ME BACK MY GODDAMNED PHONE!
HOW DARE YOU!! YOU THINK I WOULD DO SOMETHING AS PETTY AS COMMON ROBBERY?!

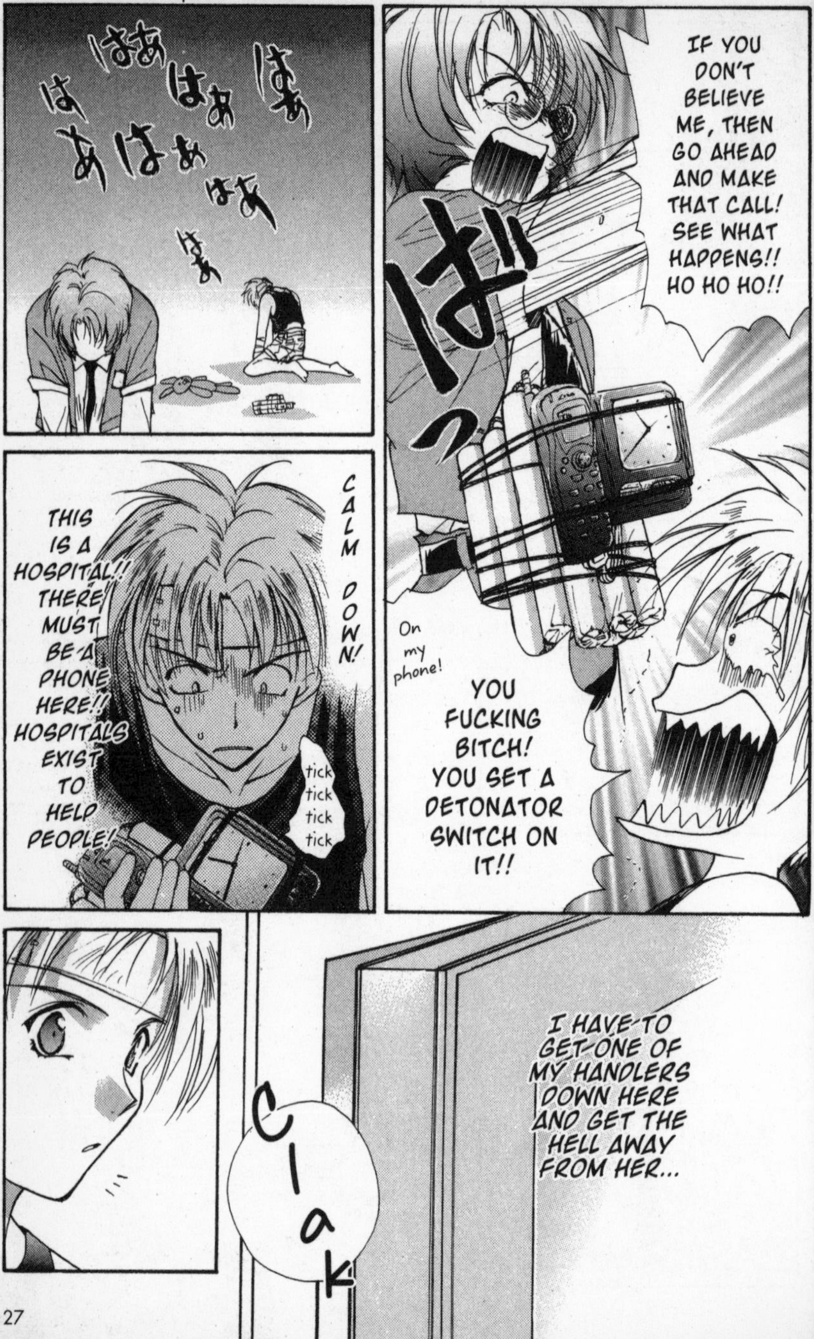
ばっ
IF YOU DON'T BELIEVE ME, THEN GO AHEAD AND MAKE THAT CALL! SEE WHAT HAPPENS!! HO HO HO!!
On my phone!
YOU FUCKING BITCH! YOU SET A DETONATOR SWITCH ON IT!!
huff huff pant wheeze
CALM DOWN!
THIS IS A HOSPITAL!! THERE MUST BE A PHONE HERE!! HOSPITALS EXIST TO HELP PEOPLE!
tick tick tick tick
I HAVE TO GET ONE OF MY HANDLERS DOWN HERE AND GET THE HELL AWAY FROM HER...
Clak

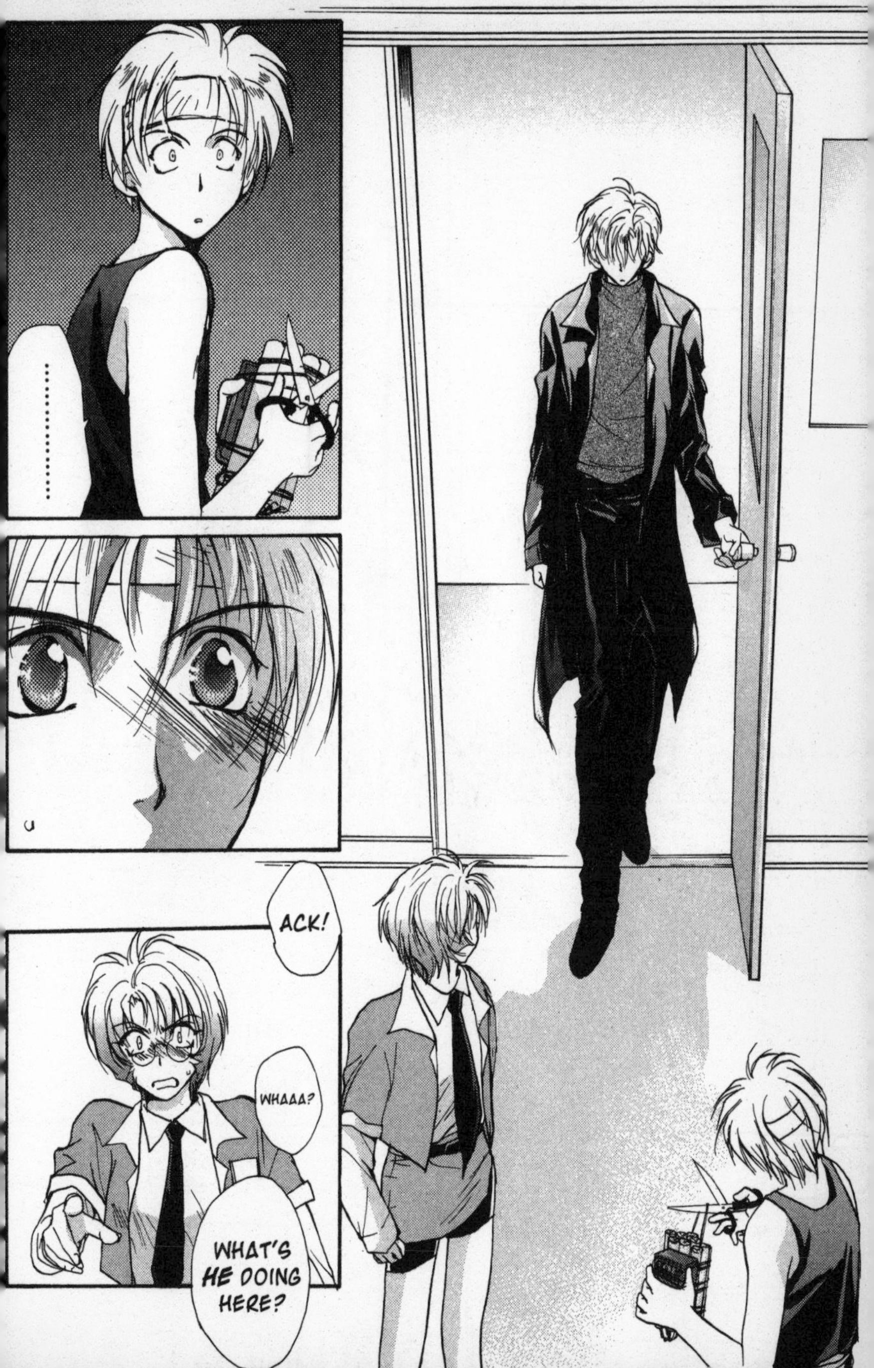
ACK!
......
WHAAA?
WHAT'S HE DOING HERE?

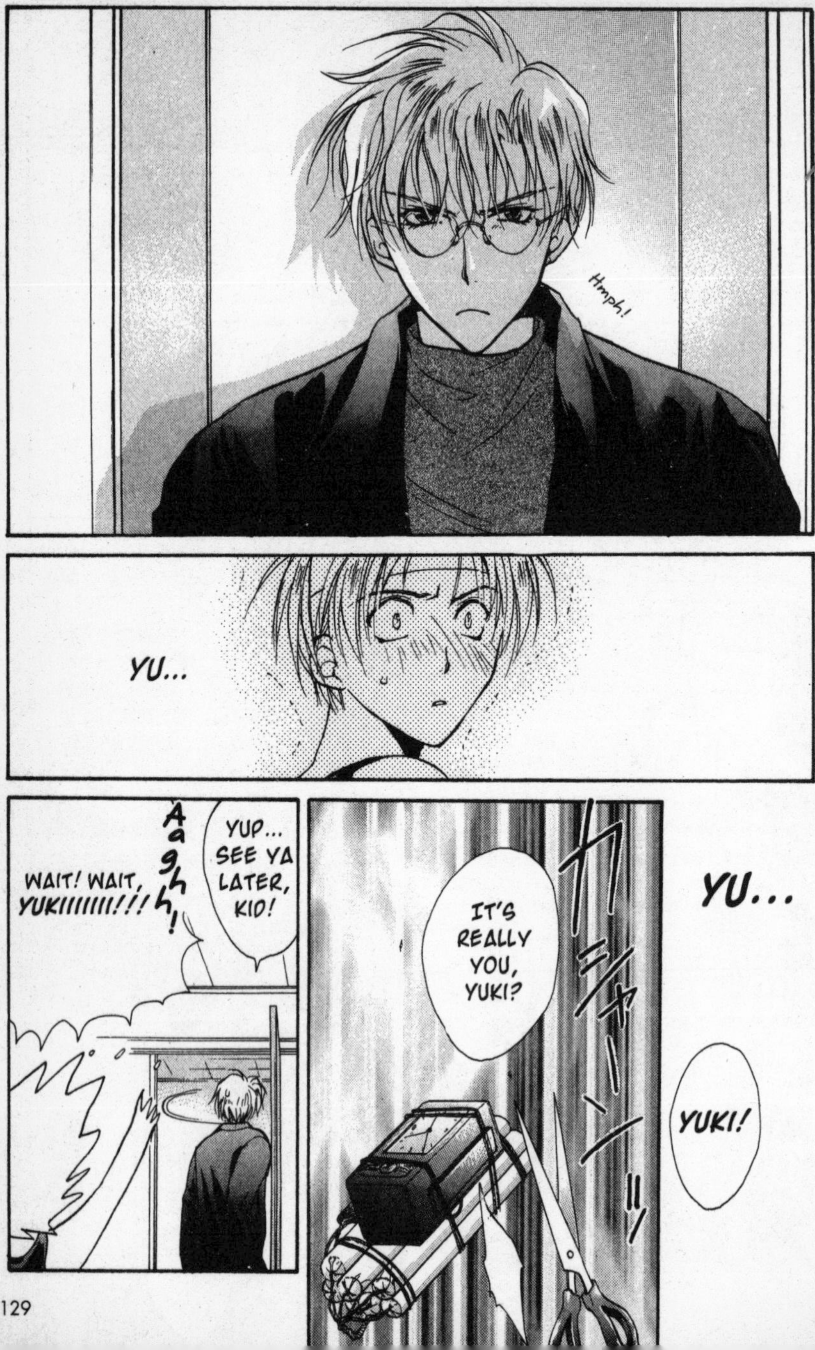
Hmph!
YU...
YU...
YUKI!
IT'S REALLY YOU, YUKI?
YUP... SEE YA LATER, KID!
Aaghh!
WAIT! WAIT, YUKIIIIIIII!!!

dog↓ ↓Tohma is my life

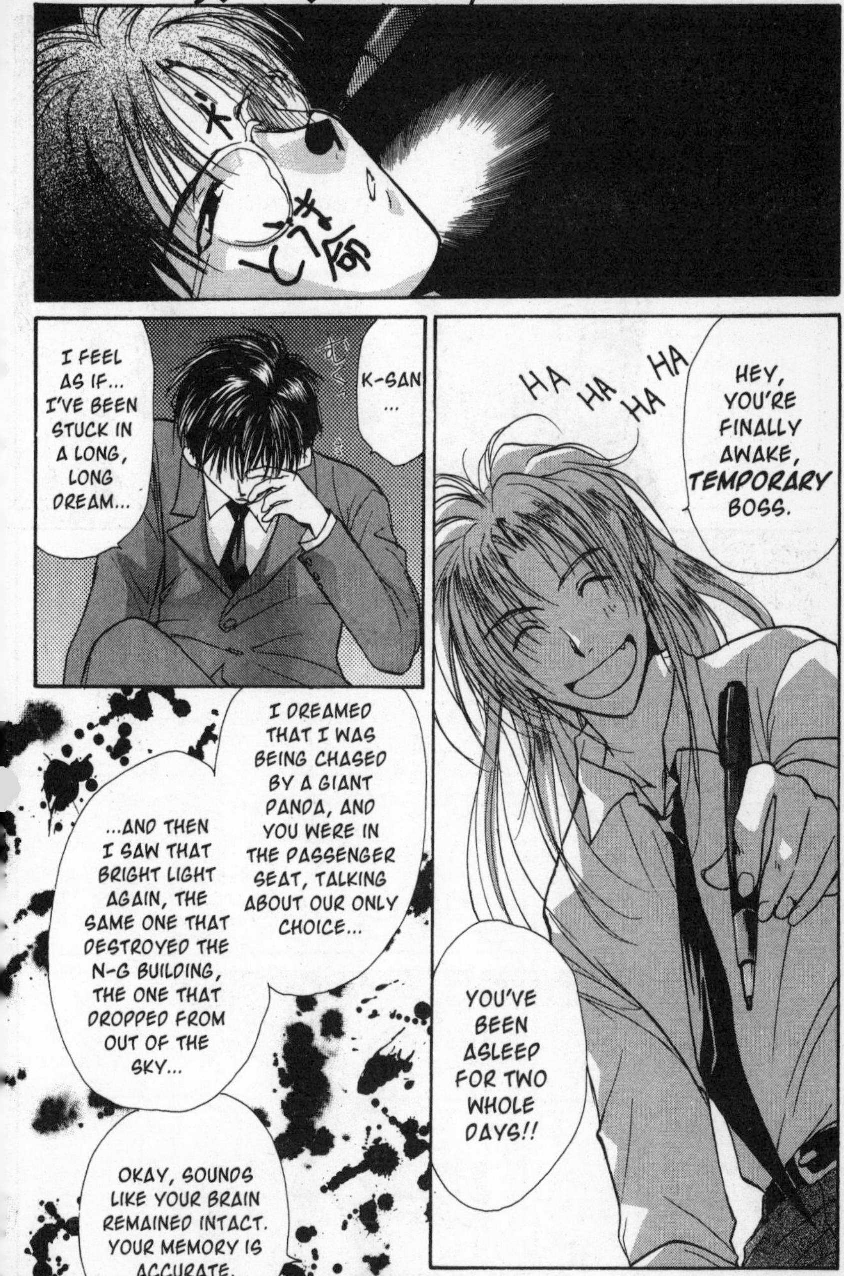
HA HA HA HA
HEY, YOU'RE FINALLY AWAKE, TEMPORARY BOSS.
YOU'VE BEEN ASLEEP FOR TWO WHOLE DAYS!!
K-SAN ...
I FEEL AS IF... I'VE BEEN STUCK IN A LONG, LONG DREAM...
I DREAMED THAT I WAS BEING CHASED BY A GIANT PANDA, AND YOU WERE IN THE PASSENGER SEAT, TALKING ABOUT OUR ONLY CHOICE...
...AND THEN I SAW THAT BRIGHT LIGHT AGAIN, THE SAME ONE THAT DESTROYED THE N-G BUILDING, THE ONE THAT DROPPED FROM OUT OF THE SKY...
OKAY, SOUNDS LIKE YOUR BRAIN REMAINED INTACT. YOUR MEMORY IS ACCURATE.

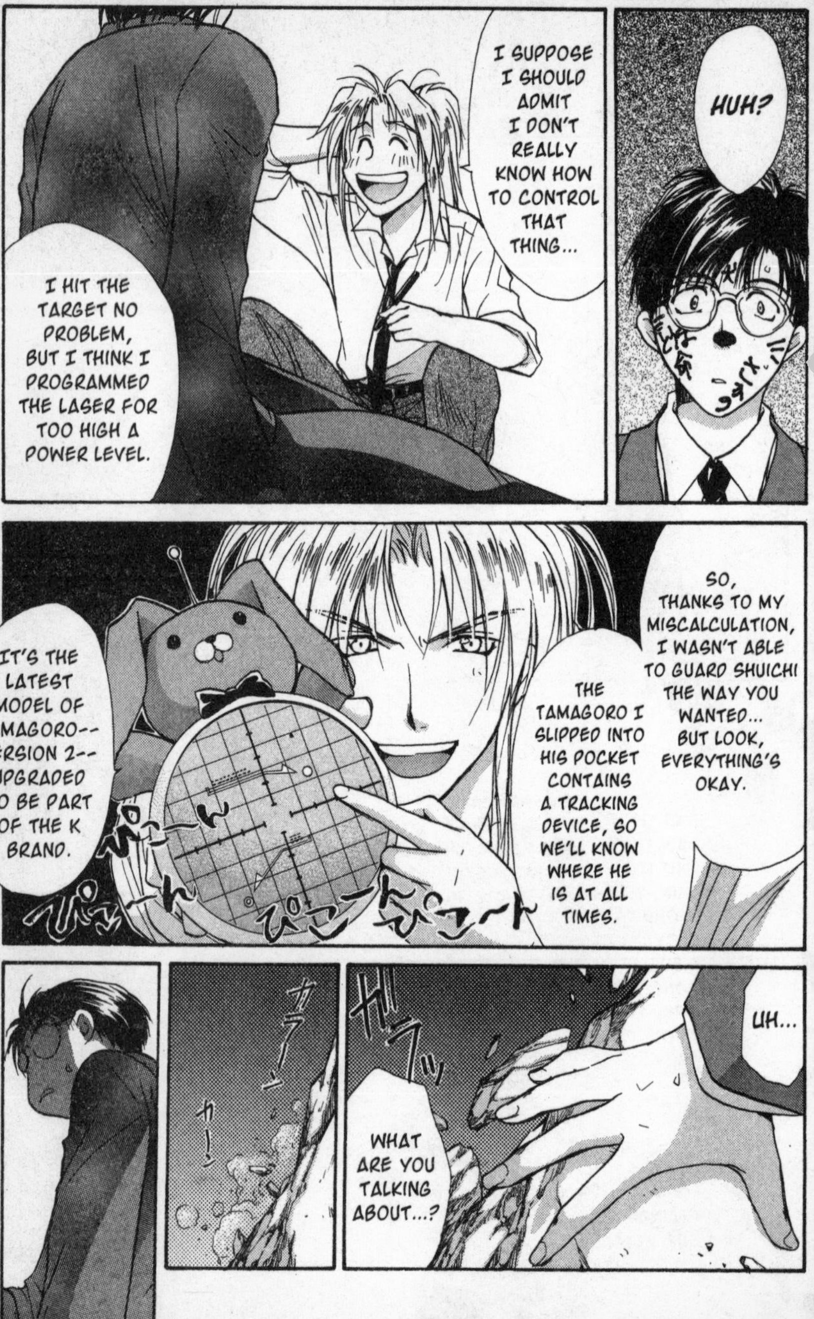
HUH?
I SUPPOSE I SHOULD ADMIT I DON'T REALLY KNOW HOW TO CONTROL THAT THING...
I HIT THE TARGET NO PROBLEM, BUT I THINK I PROGRAMMED THE LASER FOR TOO HIGH A POWER LEVEL.
SO, THANKS TO MY MISCALCULATION, I WASN'T ABLE TO GUARD SHUICHI THE WAY YOU WANTED... BUT LOOK, EVERYTHING'S OKAY.
THE TAMAGORO I SLIPPED INTO HIS POCKET CONTAINS A TRACKING DEVICE, SO WE'LL KNOW WHERE HE IS AT ALL TIMES.
IT'S THE LATEST MODEL OF TAMAGORO--VERSION 2--UPGRADED TO BE PART OF THE K BRAND.
UH...
WHAT ARE YOU TALKING ABOUT...?

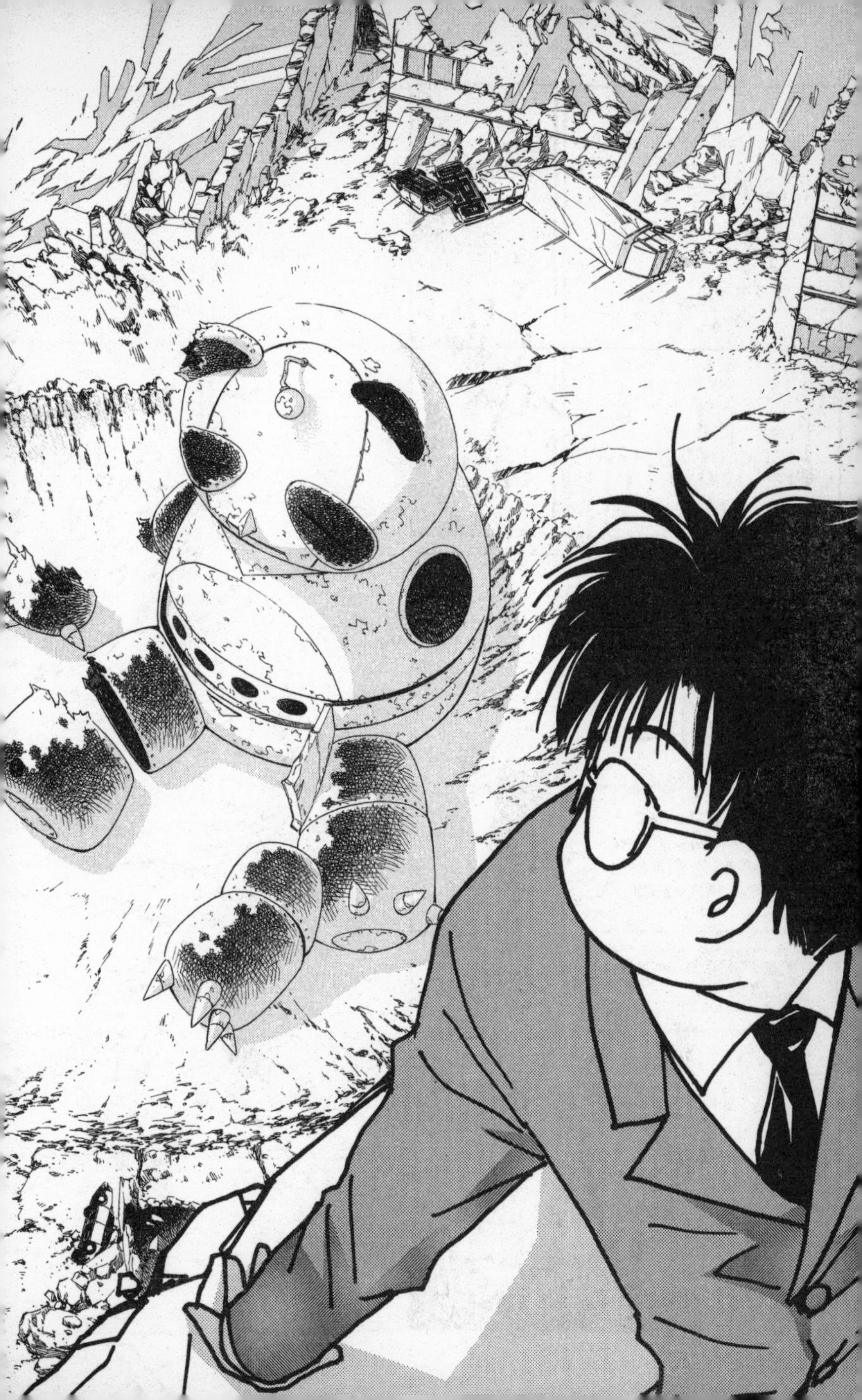

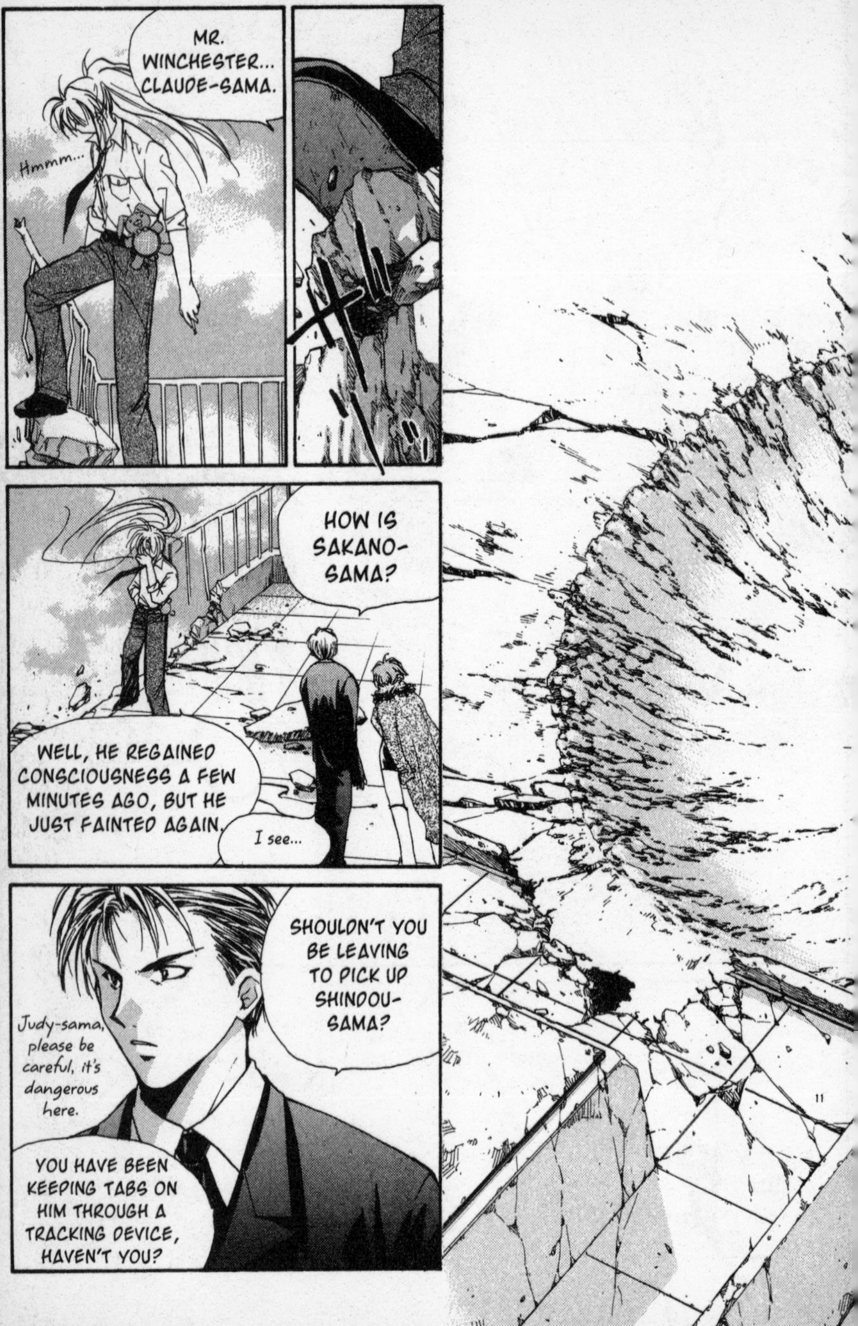
MR. WINCHESTER... CLAUDE-SAMA.
Hmmm...
HOW IS SAKANO-SAMA?
WELL, HE REGAINED CONSCIOUSNESS A FEW MINUTES AGO, BUT HE JUST FAINTED AGAIN.
I see...
SHOULDN'T YOU BE LEAVING TO PICK UP SHINDOU-SAMA?
Judy-sama, please be careful, it's dangerous here.
YOU HAVE BEEN KEEPING TABS ON HIM THROUGH A TRACKING DEVICE, HAVEN'T YOU?

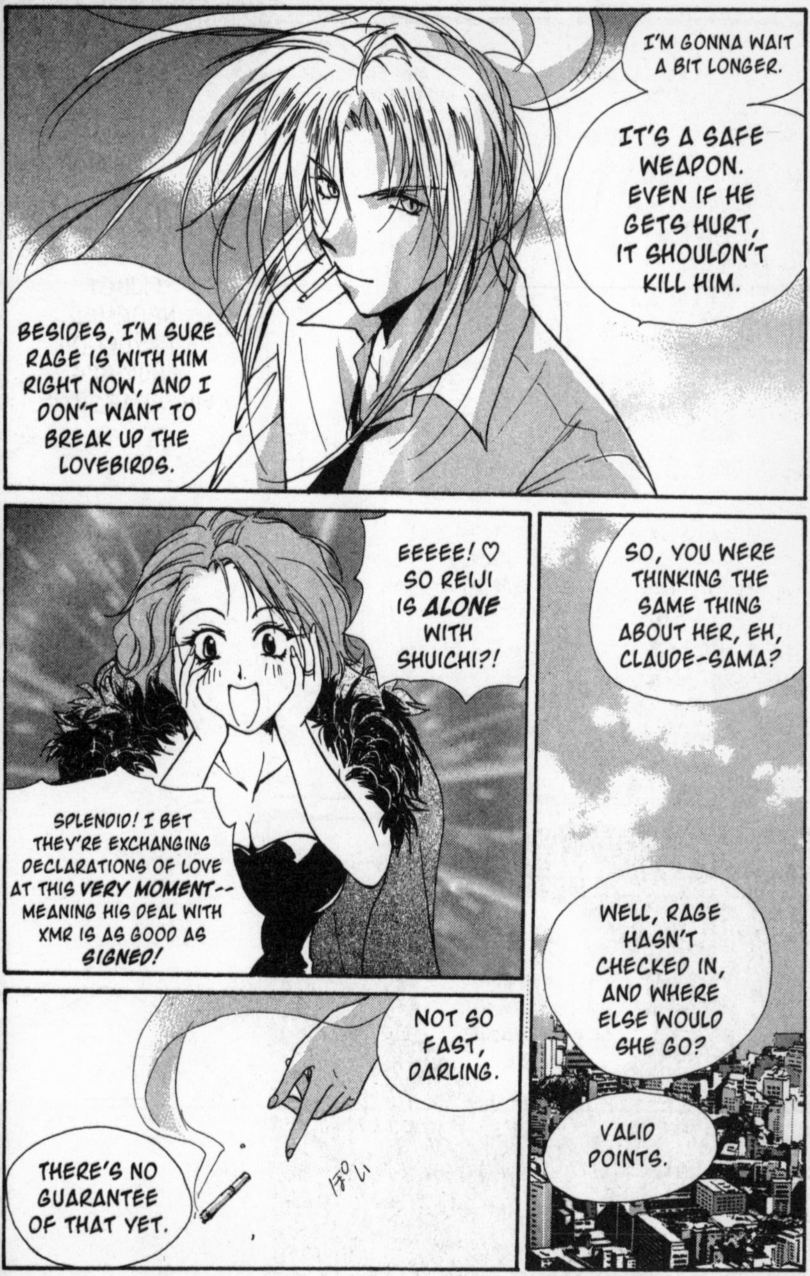
I'M GONNA WAIT A BIT LONGER.
IT'S A SAFE WEAPON. EVEN IF HE GETS HURT, IT SHOULDN'T KILL HIM.
BESIDES, I'M SURE RAGE IS WITH HIM RIGHT NOW, AND I DON'T WANT TO BREAK UP THE LOVEBIRDS.
SO, YOU WERE THINKING THE SAME THING ABOUT HER, EH, CLAUDE-SAMA?
WELL, RAGE HASN'T CHECKED IN, AND WHERE ELSE WOULD SHE GO?
VALID POINTS.
EEEEE! ♡ SO REIJI IS *ALONE* WITH SHUICHI?!
SPLENDID! I BET THEY'RE EXCHANGING DECLARATIONS OF LOVE AT THIS *VERY MOMENT*-- MEANING HIS DEAL WITH XMR IS AS GOOD AS *SIGNED!*
NOT SO FAST, DARLING.
ぽい
THERE'S NO GUARANTEE OF THAT YET.

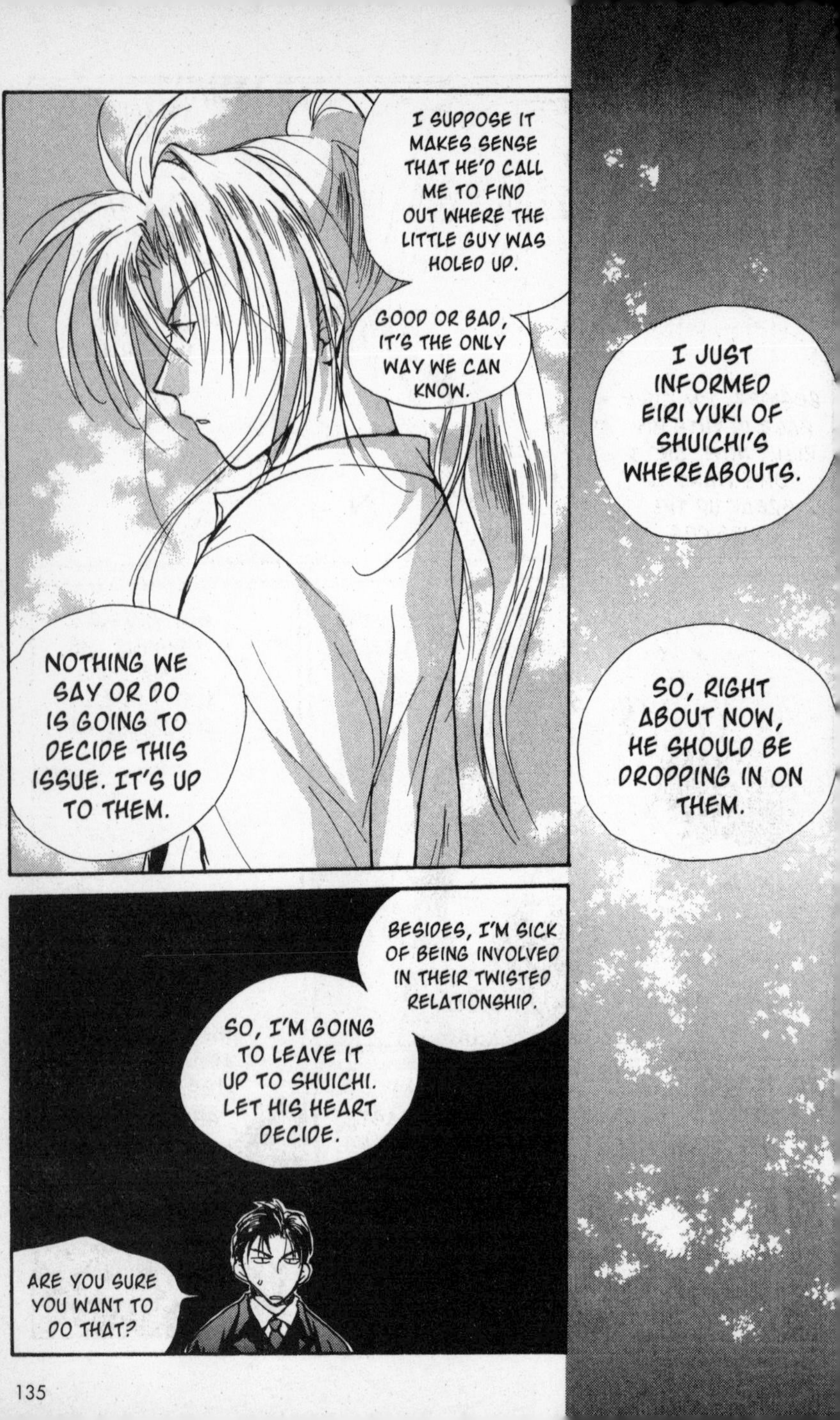
I JUST INFORMED EIRI YUKI OF SHUICHI'S WHEREABOUTS.
SO, RIGHT ABOUT NOW, HE SHOULD BE DROPPING IN ON THEM.
I SUPPOSE IT MAKES SENSE THAT HE'D CALL ME TO FIND OUT WHERE THE LITTLE GUY WAS HOLED UP.
GOOD OR BAD, IT'S THE ONLY WAY WE CAN KNOW.
NOTHING WE SAY OR DO IS GOING TO DECIDE THIS ISSUE. IT'S UP TO THEM.
BESIDES, I'M SICK OF BEING INVOLVED IN THEIR TWISTED RELATIONSHIP.
SO, I'M GOING TO LEAVE IT UP TO SHUICHI. LET HIS HEART DECIDE.
ARE YOU SURE YOU WANT TO DO THAT?

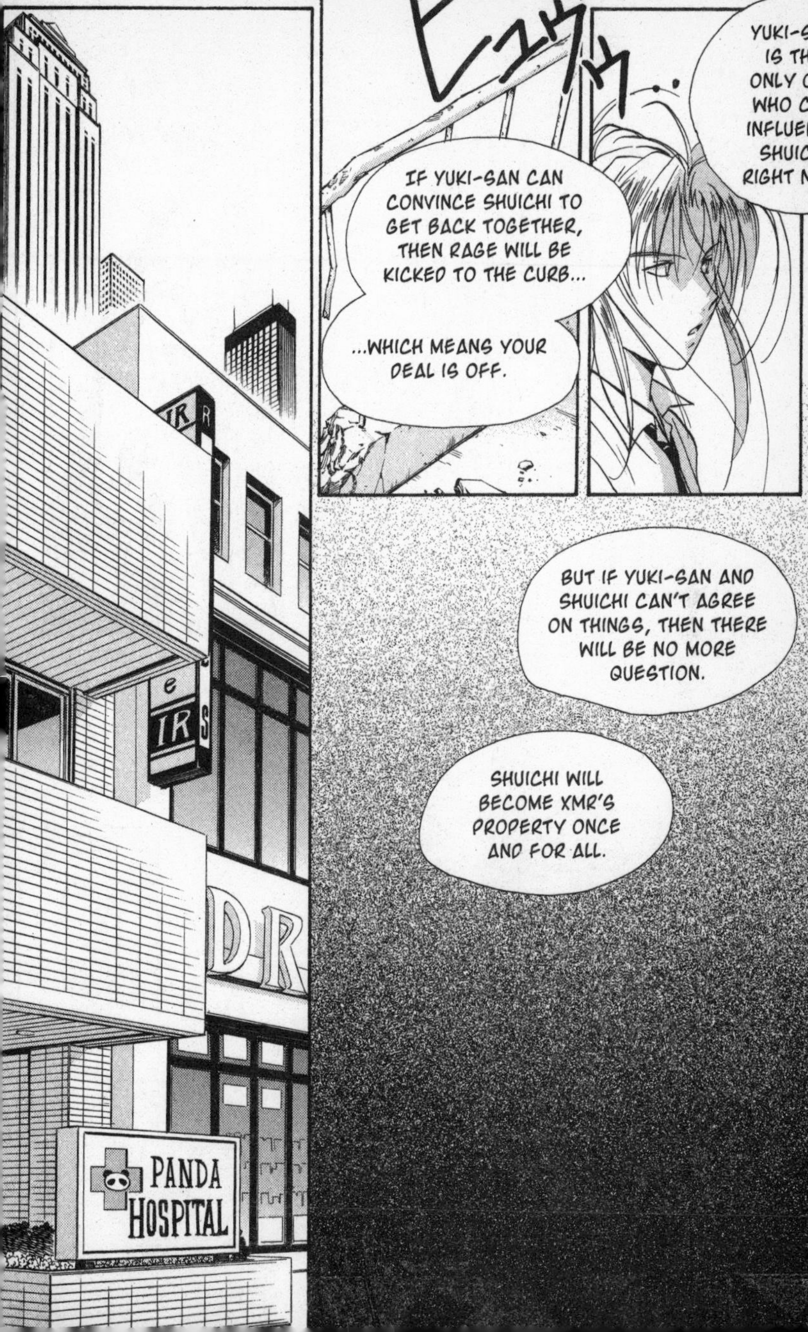

ヒュウゥ
YUKI-SAN IS THE ONLY ONE WHO CAN INFLUENCE SHUICHI RIGHT NOW.
IF YUKI-SAN CAN CONVINCE SHUICHI TO GET BACK TOGETHER, THEN RAGE WILL BE KICKED TO THE CURB...
...WHICH MEANS YOUR DEAL IS OFF.
BUT IF YUKI-SAN AND SHUICHI CAN'T AGREE ON THINGS, THEN THERE WILL BE NO MORE QUESTION.
SHUICHI WILL BECOME XMR'S PROPERTY ONCE AND FOR ALL.
PANDA HOSPITAL

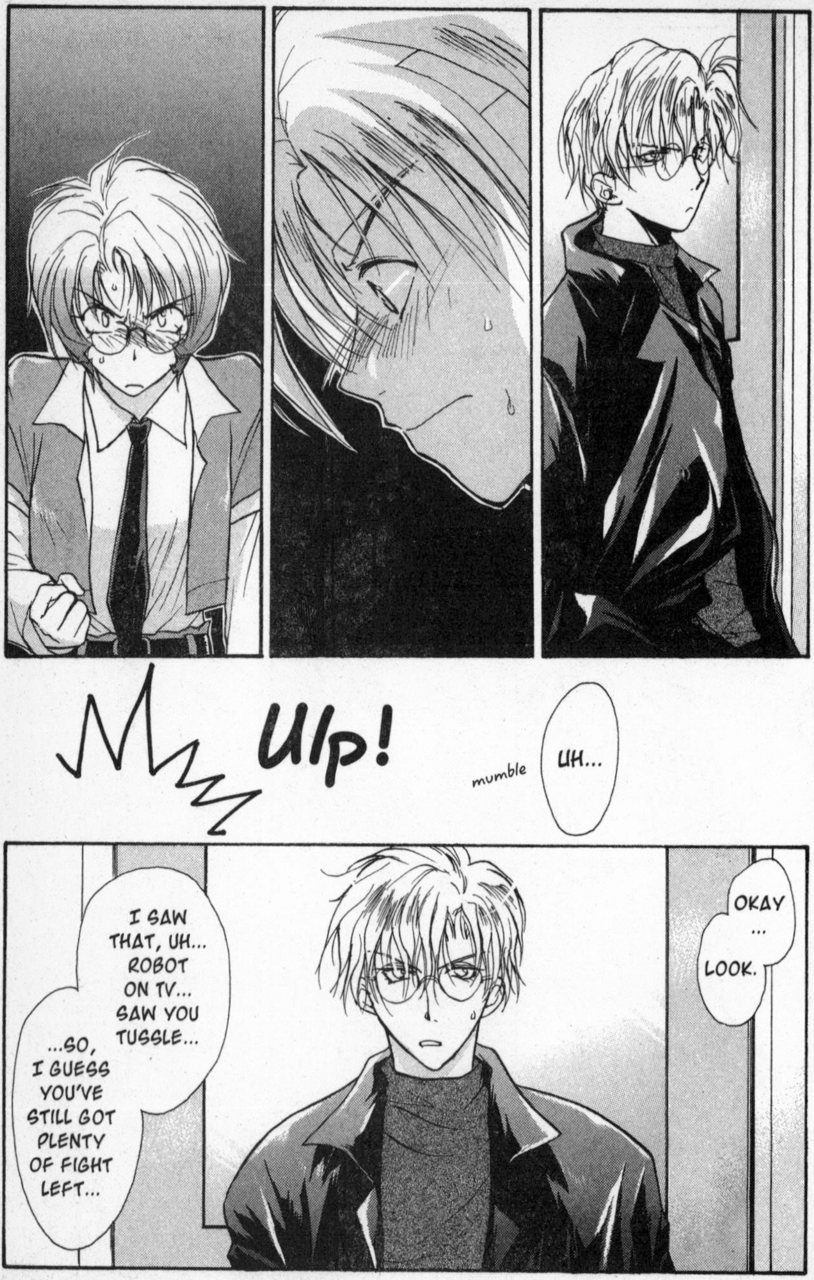
UH...
mumble
Ulp!
OKAY ... LOOK.
I SAW THAT, UH... ROBOT ON TV... SAW YOU TUSSLE...
...SO, I GUESS YOU'VE STILL GOT PLENTY OF FIGHT LEFT...

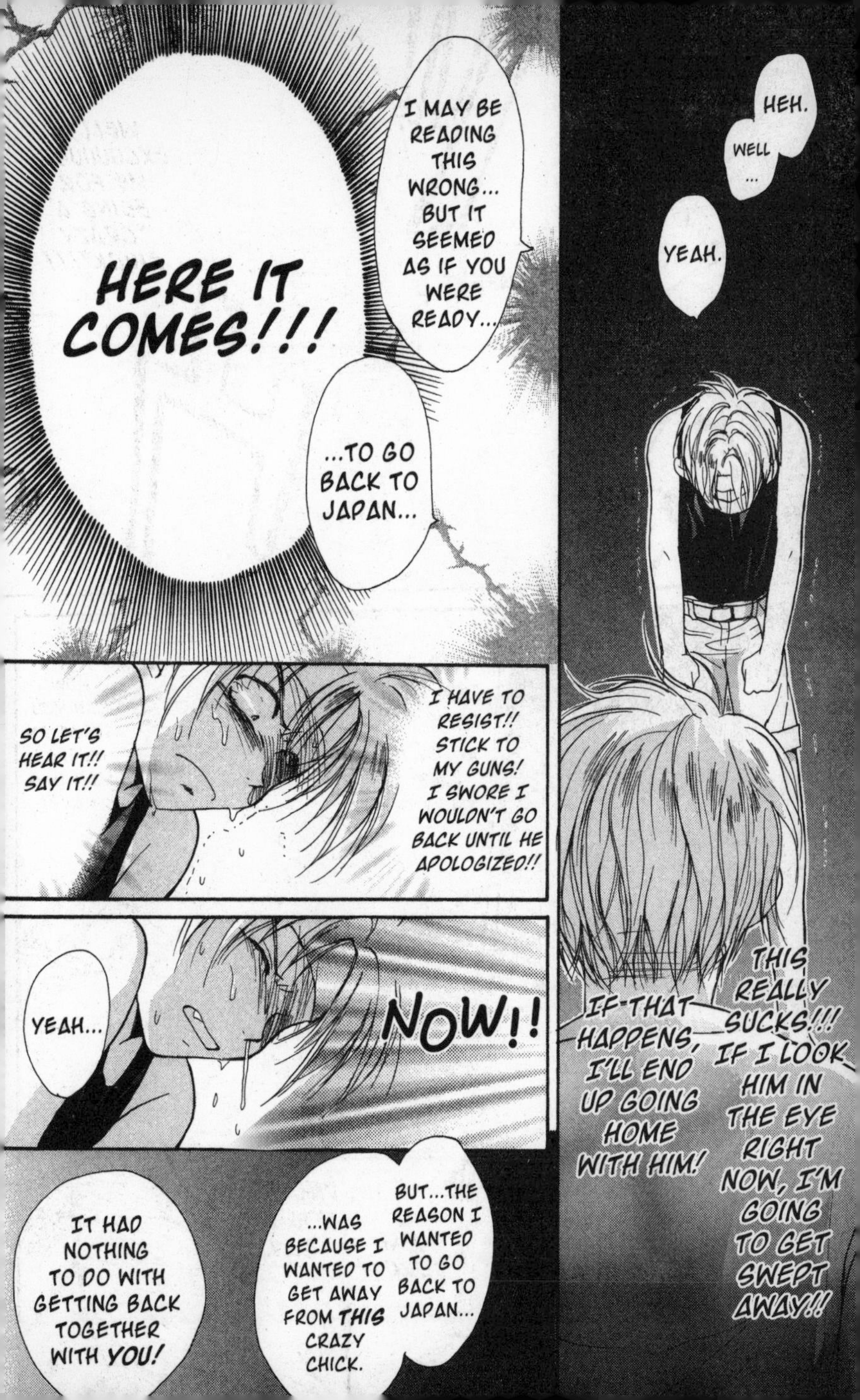
HEH.
WELL...
YEAH.
THIS REALLY SUCKS!!! IF I LOOK HIM IN THE EYE RIGHT NOW, I'M GOING TO GET SWEPT AWAY!!
IF THAT HAPPENS, I'LL END UP GOING HOME WITH HIM!
I MAY BE READING THIS WRONG... BUT IT SEEMED AS IF YOU WERE READY...
HERE IT COMES!!!
...TO GO BACK TO JAPAN...
I HAVE TO RESIST!! STICK TO MY GUNS! I SWORE I WOULDN'T GO BACK UNTIL HE APOLOGIZED!!
SO LET'S HEAR IT!! SAY IT!!
NOW!!
YEAH...
BUT...THE REASON I WANTED TO GO BACK TO JAPAN...
...WAS BECAUSE I WANTED TO GET AWAY FROM THIS CRAZY CHICK.
IT HAD NOTHING TO DO WITH GETTING BACK TOGETHER WITH YOU!

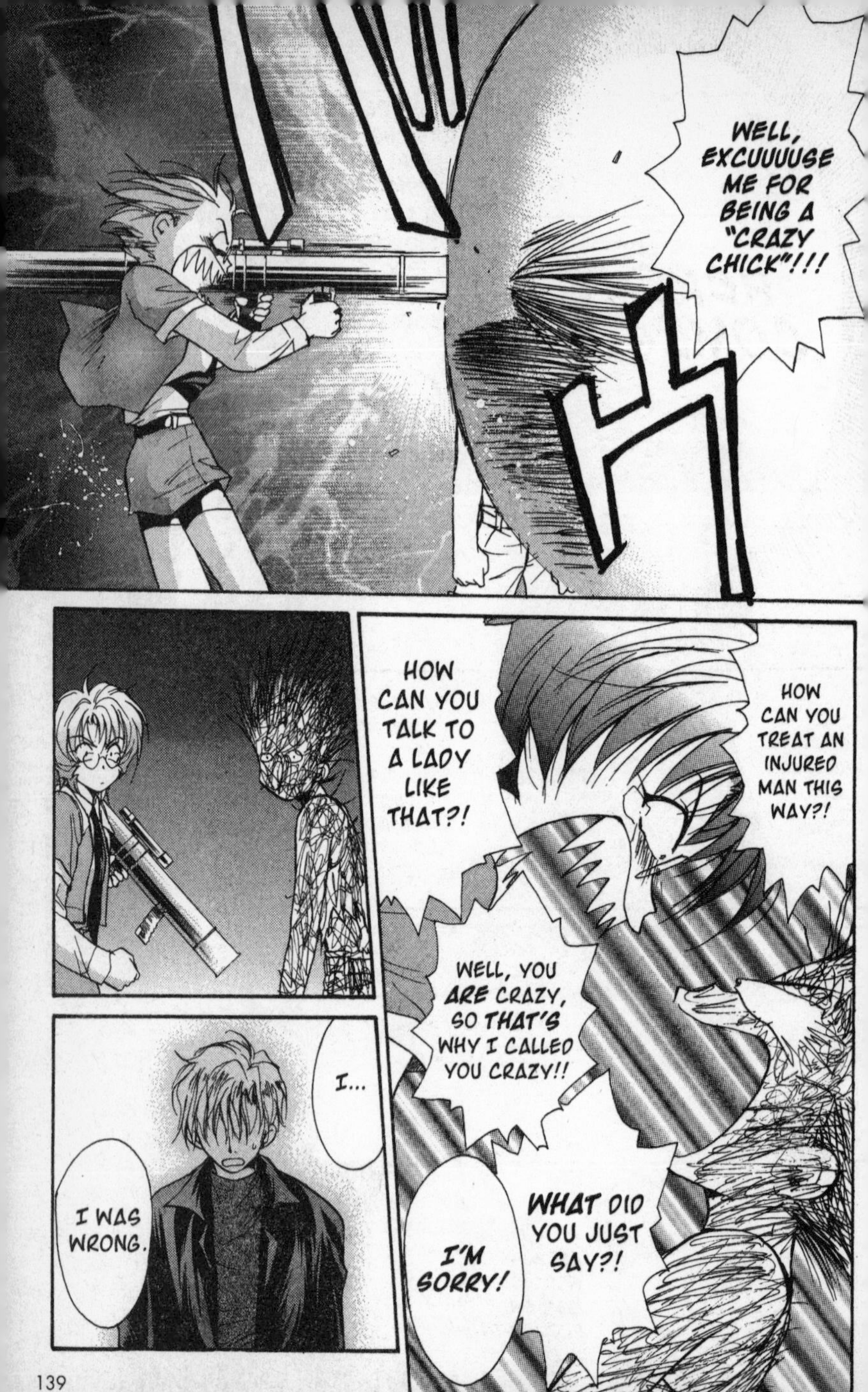
WELL, EXCUUUUSE ME FOR BEING A "CRAZY CHICK"!!!
HOW CAN YOU TREAT AN INJURED MAN THIS WAY?!
HOW CAN YOU TALK TO A LADY LIKE THAT?!
WELL, YOU **ARE** CRAZY, SO **THAT'S** WHY I CALLED YOU CRAZY!!
WHAT DID YOU JUST SAY?!
I'M SORRY!
I...
I WAS WRONG.

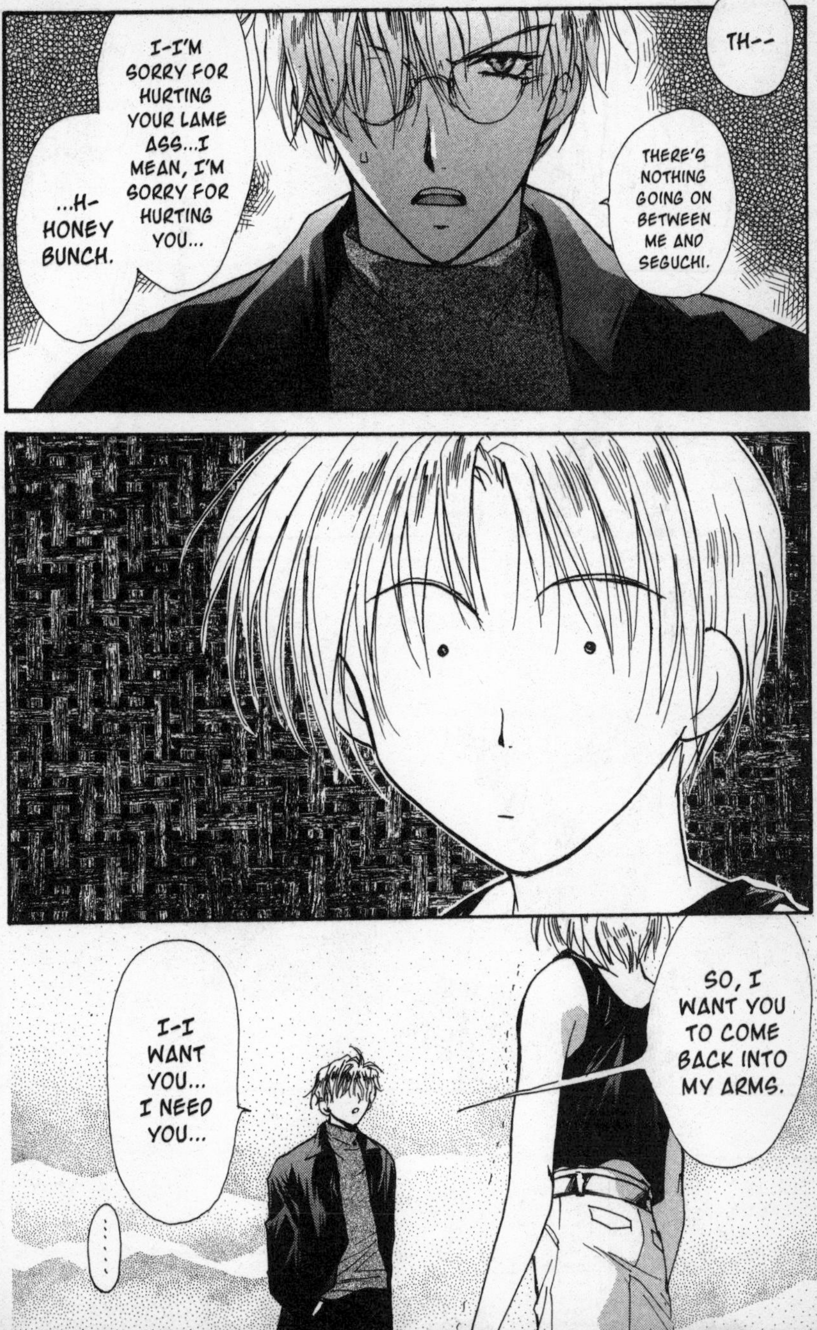
TH--
THERE'S NOTHING GOING ON BETWEEN ME AND SEGUCHI.
I-I'M SORRY FOR HURTING YOUR LAME ASS...I MEAN, I'M SORRY FOR HURTING YOU...
...H-HONEY BUNCH.
SO, I WANT YOU TO COME BACK INTO MY ARMS.
I-I WANT YOU... I NEED YOU...
......

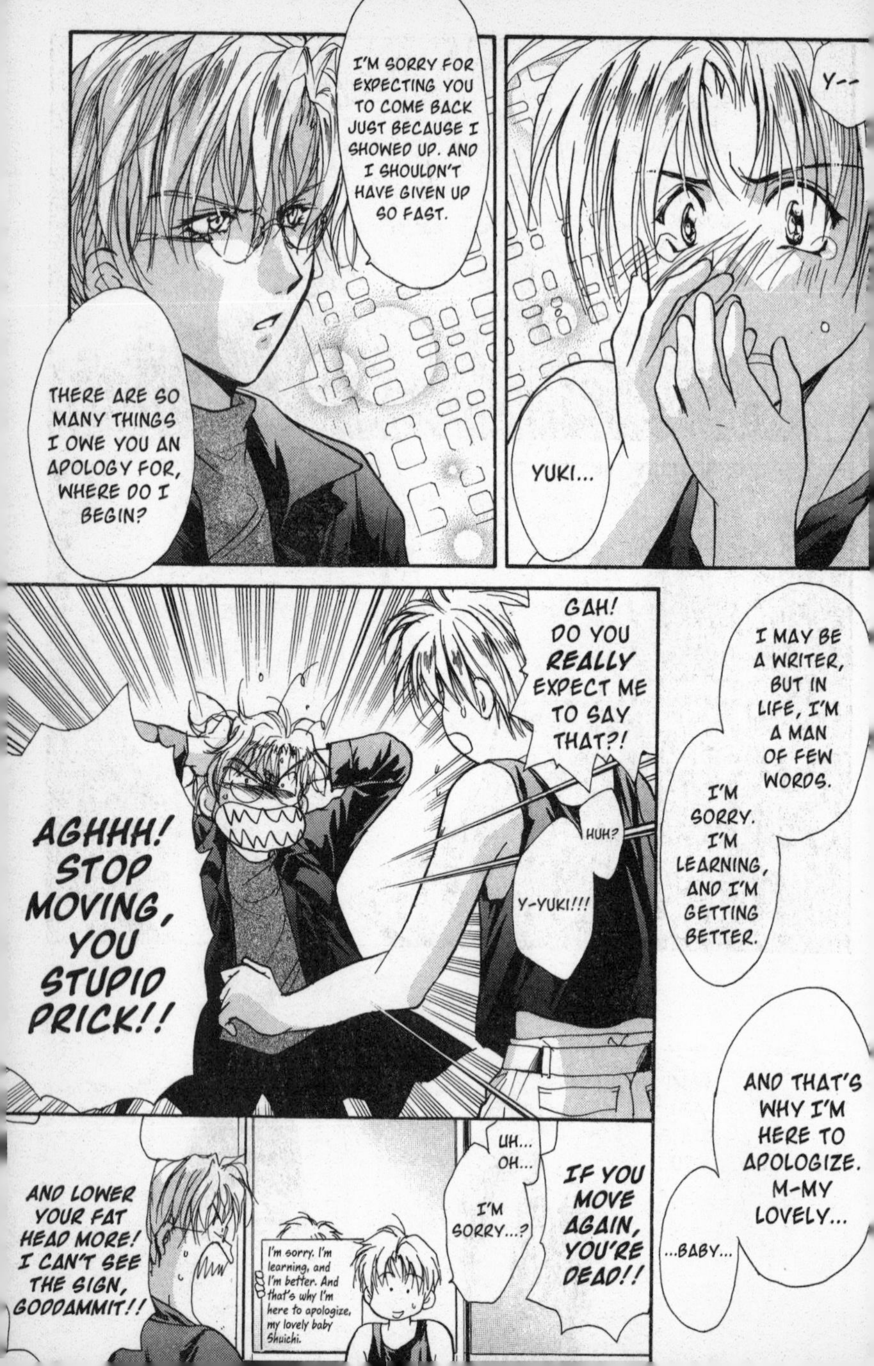
Y--
YUKI...
I'M SORRY FOR EXPECTING YOU TO COME BACK JUST BECAUSE I SHOWED UP. AND I SHOULDN'T HAVE GIVEN UP SO FAST.
THERE ARE SO MANY THINGS I OWE YOU AN APOLOGY FOR, WHERE DO I BEGIN?
I MAY BE A WRITER, BUT IN LIFE, I'M A MAN OF FEW WORDS.
I'M SORRY. I'M LEARNING, AND I'M GETTING BETTER.
GAH! DO YOU REALLY EXPECT ME TO SAY THAT?!
HUH?
Y-YUKI!!!
AGHHH! STOP MOVING, YOU STUPID PRICK!!
AND THAT'S WHY I'M HERE TO APOLOGIZE. M-MY LOVELY...
...BABY...
IF YOU MOVE AGAIN, YOU'RE DEAD!!
UH... OH...
I'M SORRY...?
I'm sorry. I'm learning, and I'm better. And that's why I'm here to apologize, my lovely baby Shuichi.
AND LOWER YOUR FAT HEAD MORE! I CAN'T SEE THE SIGN, GODDAMMIT!!

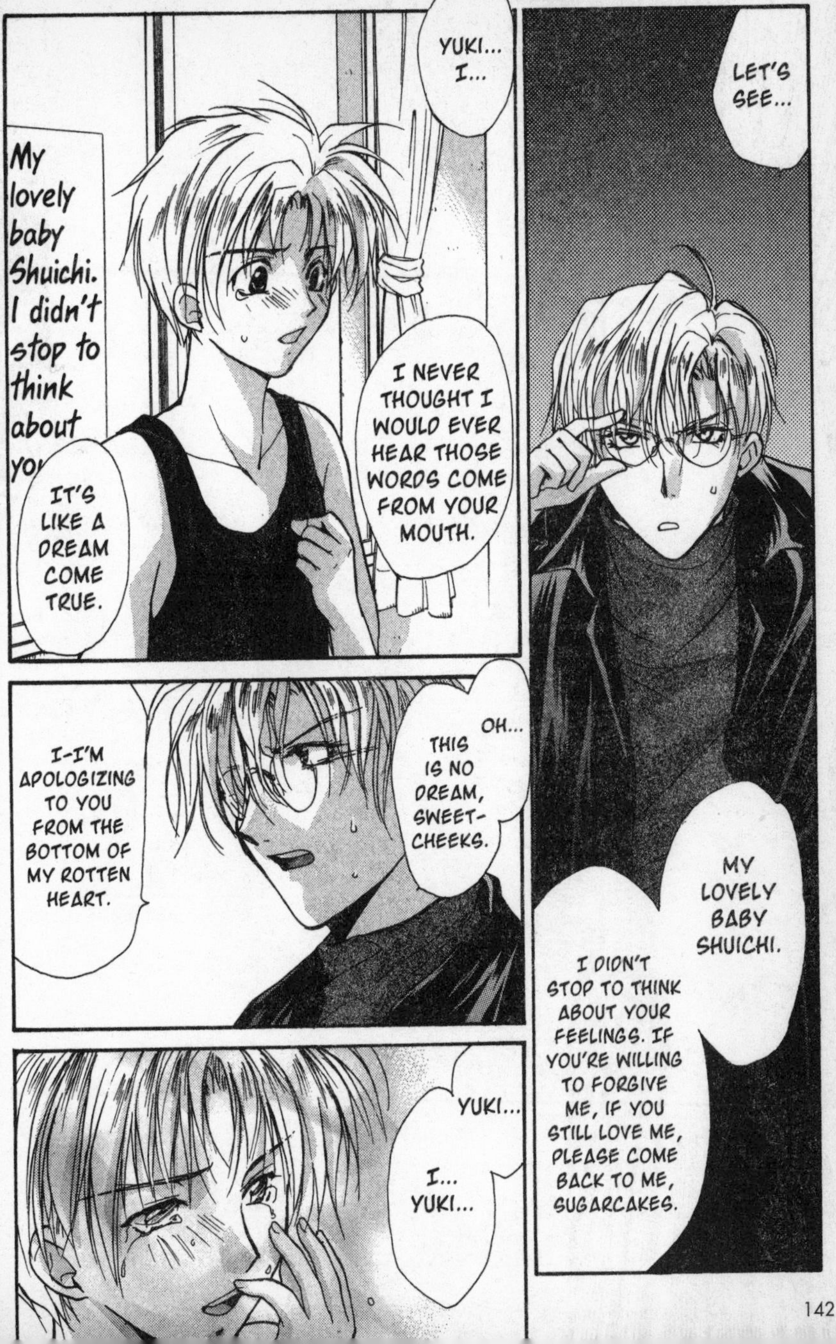
LET'S SEE...
MY LOVELY BABY SHUICHI.
I DIDN'T STOP TO THINK ABOUT YOUR FEELINGS. IF YOU'RE WILLING TO FORGIVE ME, IF YOU STILL LOVE ME, PLEASE COME BACK TO ME, SUGARCAKES.
YUKI... I...
I NEVER THOUGHT I WOULD EVER HEAR THOSE WORDS COME FROM YOUR MOUTH.
My lovely baby Shuichi. I didn't stop to think about
IT'S LIKE A DREAM COME TRUE.
OH... THIS IS NO DREAM, SWEET-CHEEKS.
I-I'M APOLOGIZING TO YOU FROM THE BOTTOM OF MY ROTTEN HEART.
YUKI...
I... YUKI...

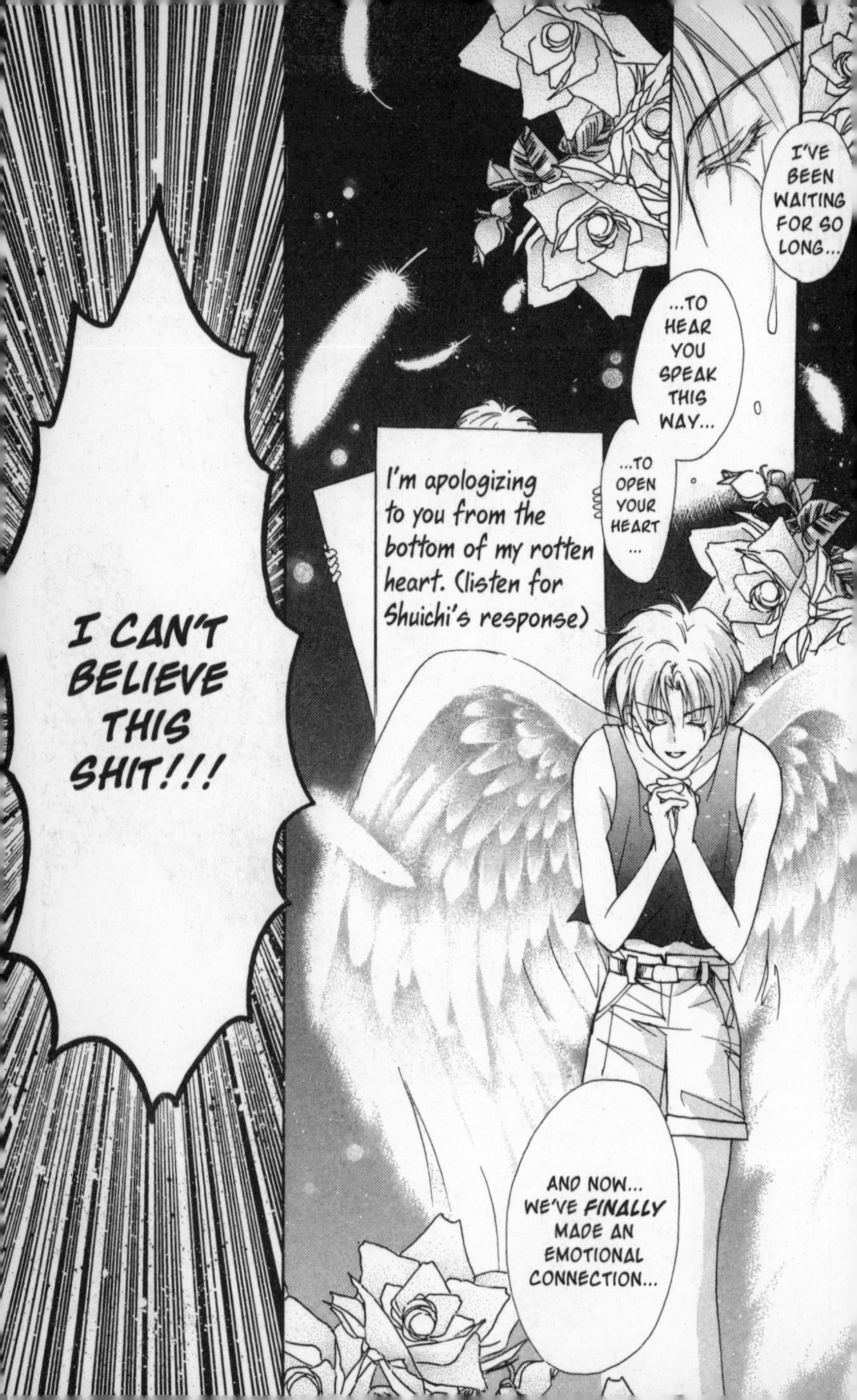
I'VE BEEN WAITING FOR SO LONG...
...TO HEAR YOU SPEAK THIS WAY...
...TO OPEN YOUR HEART...
I'm apologizing to you from the bottom of my rotten heart. (listen for Shuichi's response)
AND NOW... WE'VE FINALLY MADE AN EMOTIONAL CONNECTION...
I CAN'T BELIEVE THIS SHIT!!!

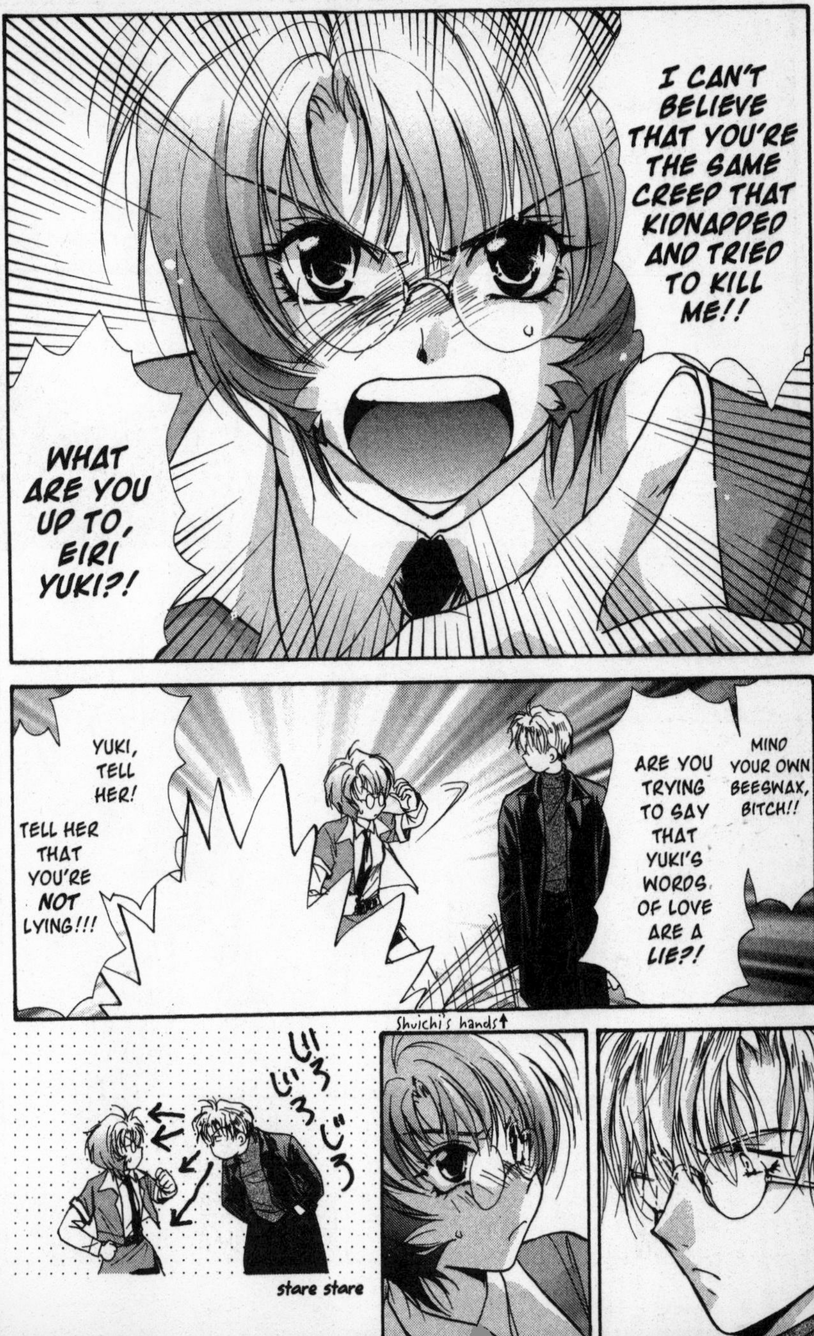
I CAN'T BELIEVE THAT YOU'RE THE SAME CREEP THAT KIDNAPPED AND TRIED TO KILL ME!!
WHAT ARE YOU UP TO, EIRI YUKI?!
MIND YOUR OWN BEESWAX, BITCH!!
ARE YOU TRYING TO SAY THAT YUKI'S WORDS OF LOVE ARE A LIE?!
YUKI, TELL HER!
TELL HER THAT YOU'RE **NOT** LYING!!!
Shuichi's hands↑
じろじろ
じろじろ
stare stare

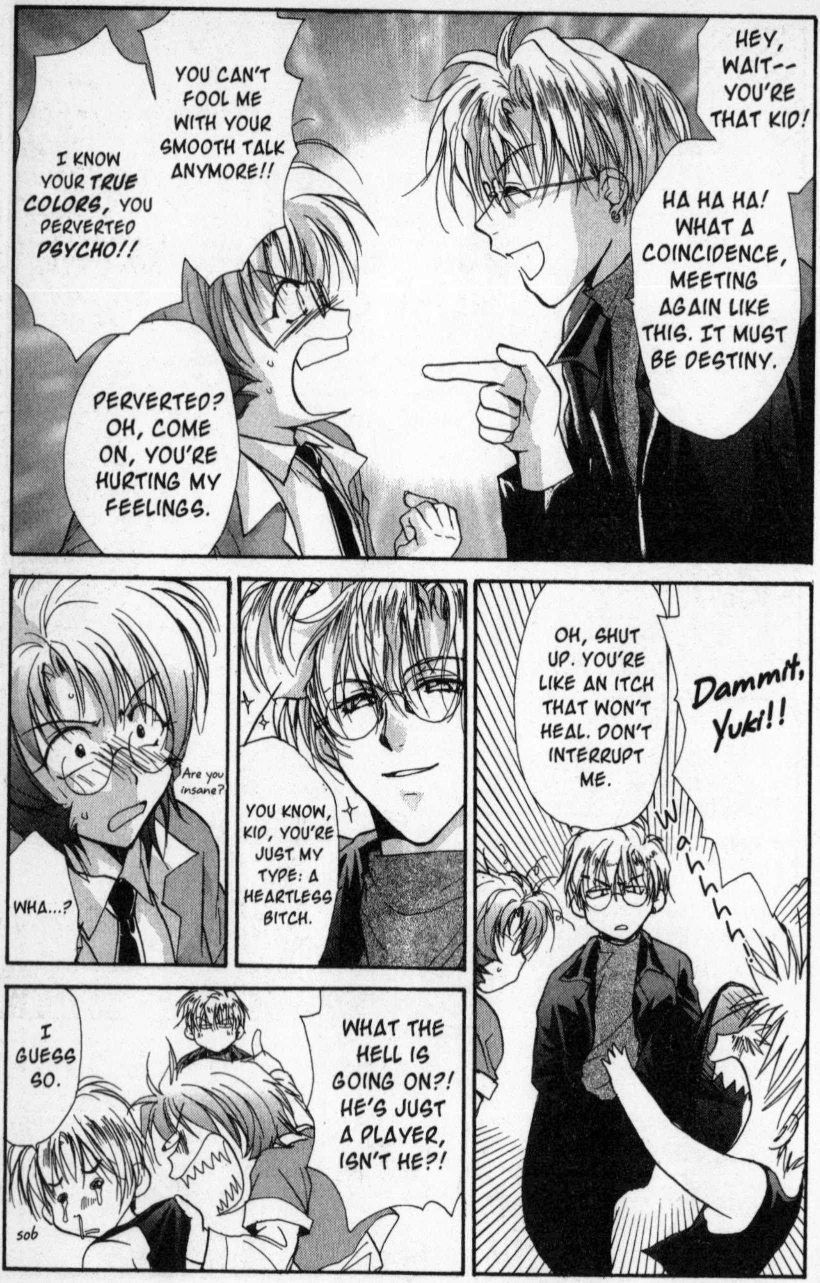
HEY, WAIT-- YOU'RE THAT KID!
HA HA HA! WHAT A COINCIDENCE, MEETING AGAIN LIKE THIS. IT MUST BE DESTINY.
YOU CAN'T FOOL ME WITH YOUR SMOOTH TALK ANYMORE!!
I KNOW YOUR TRUE COLORS, YOU PERVERTED PSYCHO!!
PERVERTED? OH, COME ON, YOU'RE HURTING MY FEELINGS.
OH, SHUT UP. YOU'RE LIKE AN ITCH THAT WON'T HEAL. DON'T INTERRUPT ME.
Dammit, Yuki!!
Wahhhh...
YOU KNOW, KID, YOU'RE JUST MY TYPE: A HEARTLESS BITCH.
Are you insane?
WHA...?
WHAT THE HELL IS GOING ON?! HE'S JUST A PLAYER, ISN'T HE?!
I GUESS SO.
sob

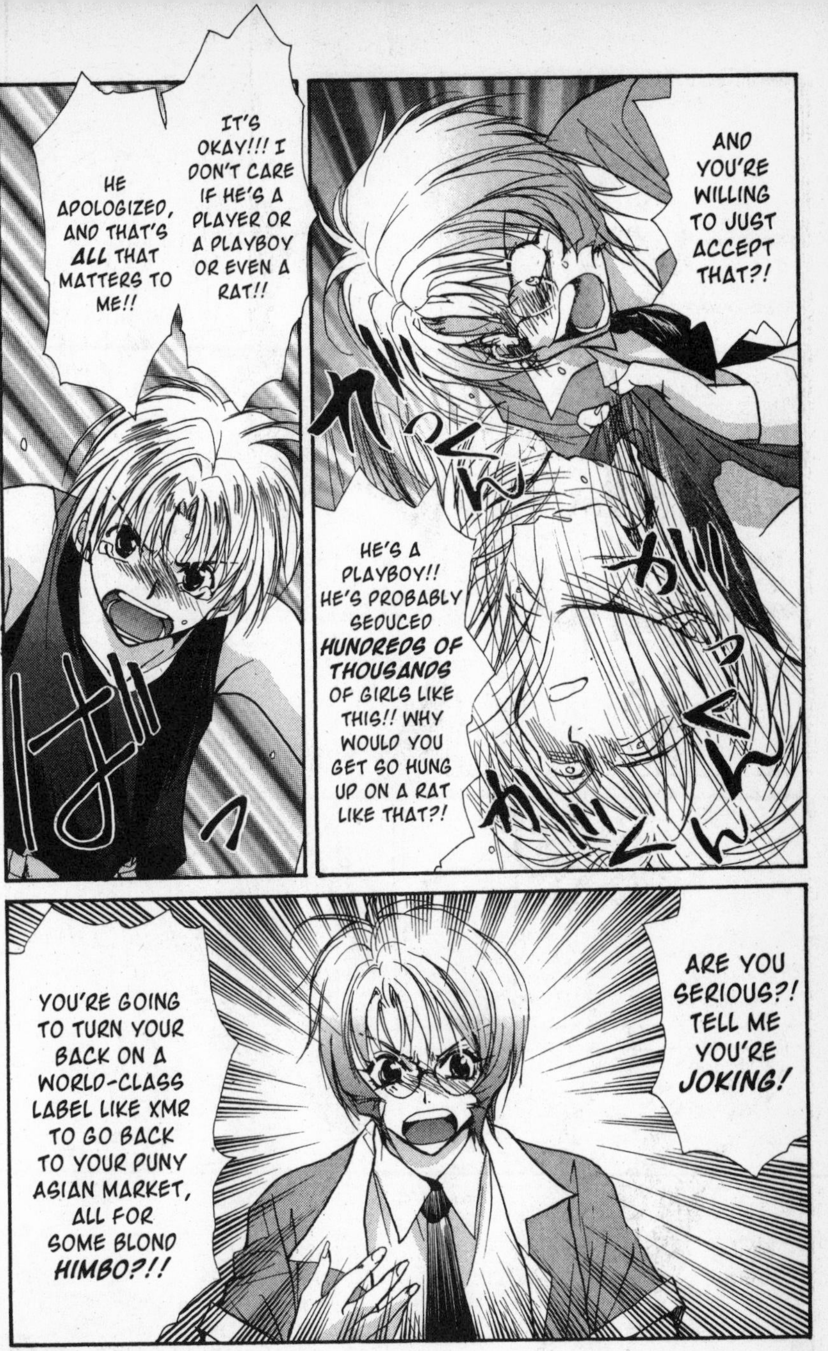
AND YOU'RE WILLING TO JUST ACCEPT THAT?!
HE'S A PLAYBOY!! HE'S PROBABLY SEDUCED **HUNDREDS OF THOUSANDS** OF GIRLS LIKE THIS!! WHY WOULD YOU GET SO HUNG UP ON A RAT LIKE THAT?!
IT'S OKAY!!! I DON'T CARE IF HE'S A PLAYER OR A PLAYBOY OR EVEN A RAT!!
HE APOLOGIZED, AND THAT'S ***ALL*** THAT MATTERS TO ME!!
ARE YOU SERIOUS?! TELL ME YOU'RE ***JOKING!***
YOU'RE GOING TO TURN YOUR BACK ON A WORLD-CLASS LABEL LIKE XMR TO GO BACK TO YOUR PUNY ASIAN MARKET, ALL FOR SOME BLOND ***HIMBO?!!***

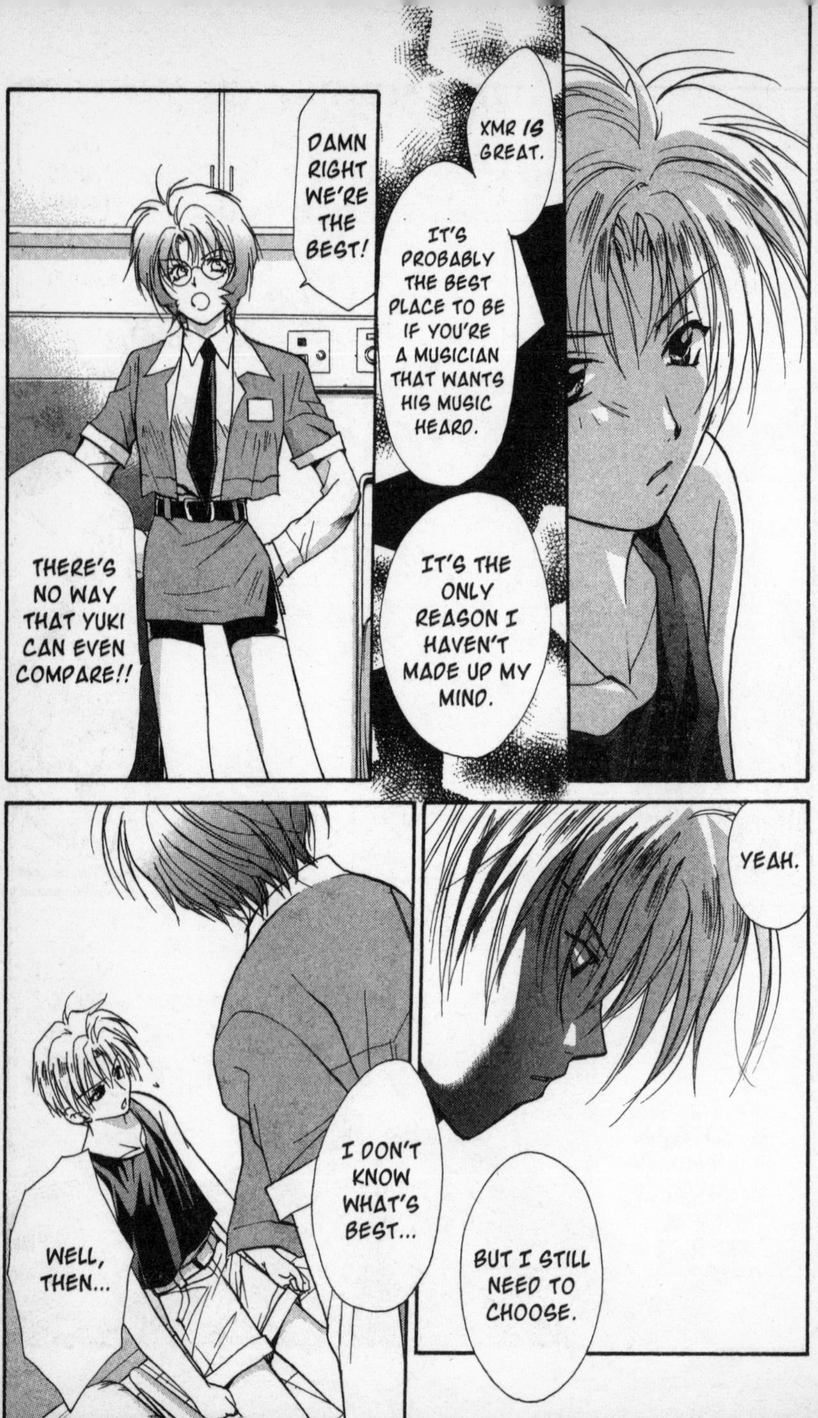
XMR IS GREAT.
IT'S PROBABLY THE BEST PLACE TO BE IF YOU'RE A MUSICIAN THAT WANTS HIS MUSIC HEARD.
IT'S THE ONLY REASON I HAVEN'T MADE UP MY MIND.
DAMN RIGHT WE'RE THE BEST!
THERE'S NO WAY THAT YUKI CAN EVEN COMPARE!!
YEAH.
I DON'T KNOW WHAT'S BEST...
BUT I STILL NEED TO CHOOSE.
WELL, THEN...

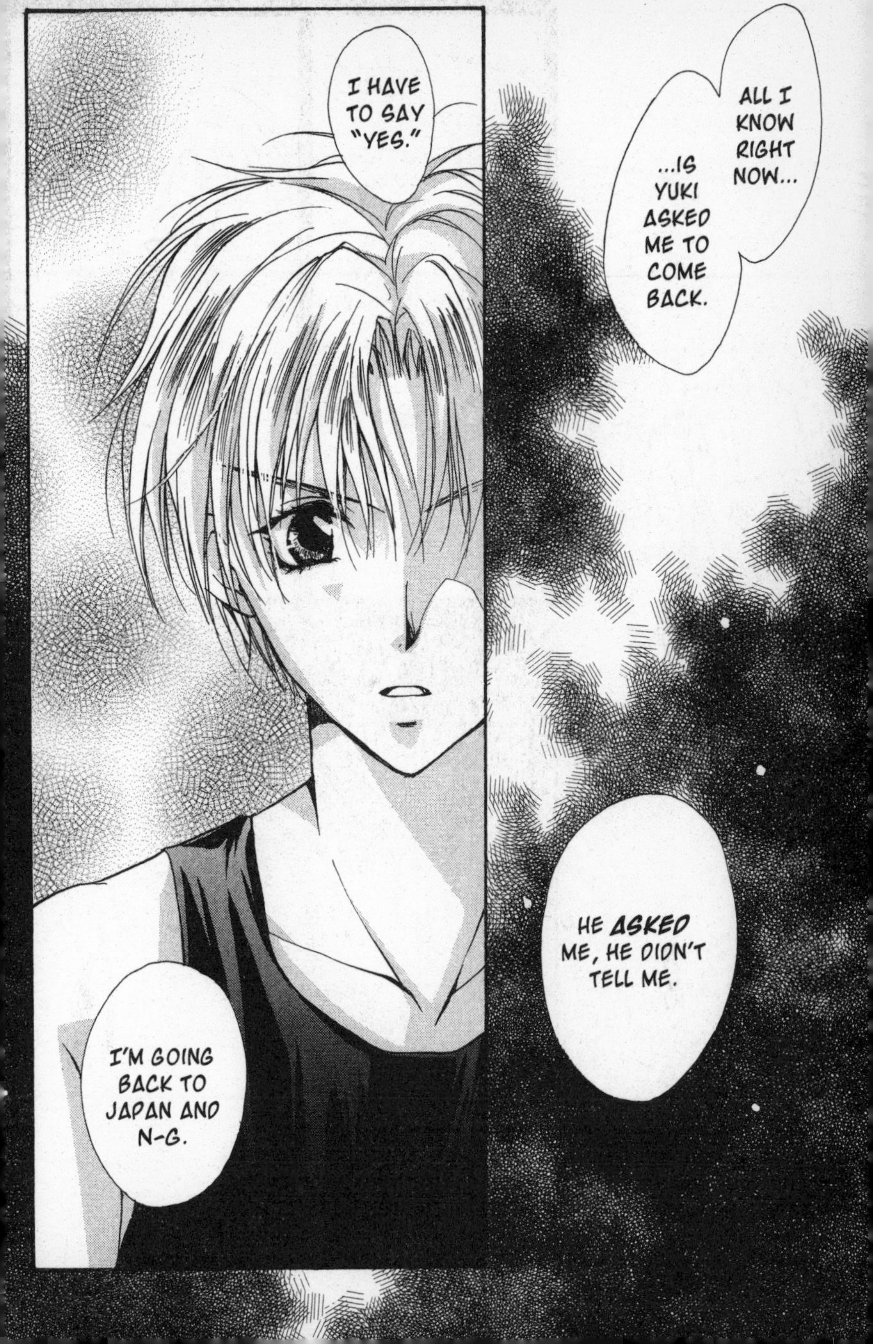
ALL I KNOW RIGHT NOW...
...IS YUKI ASKED ME TO COME BACK.
I HAVE TO SAY "YES."
HE *ASKED* ME, HE DIDN'T TELL ME.
I'M GOING BACK TO JAPAN AND N-G.

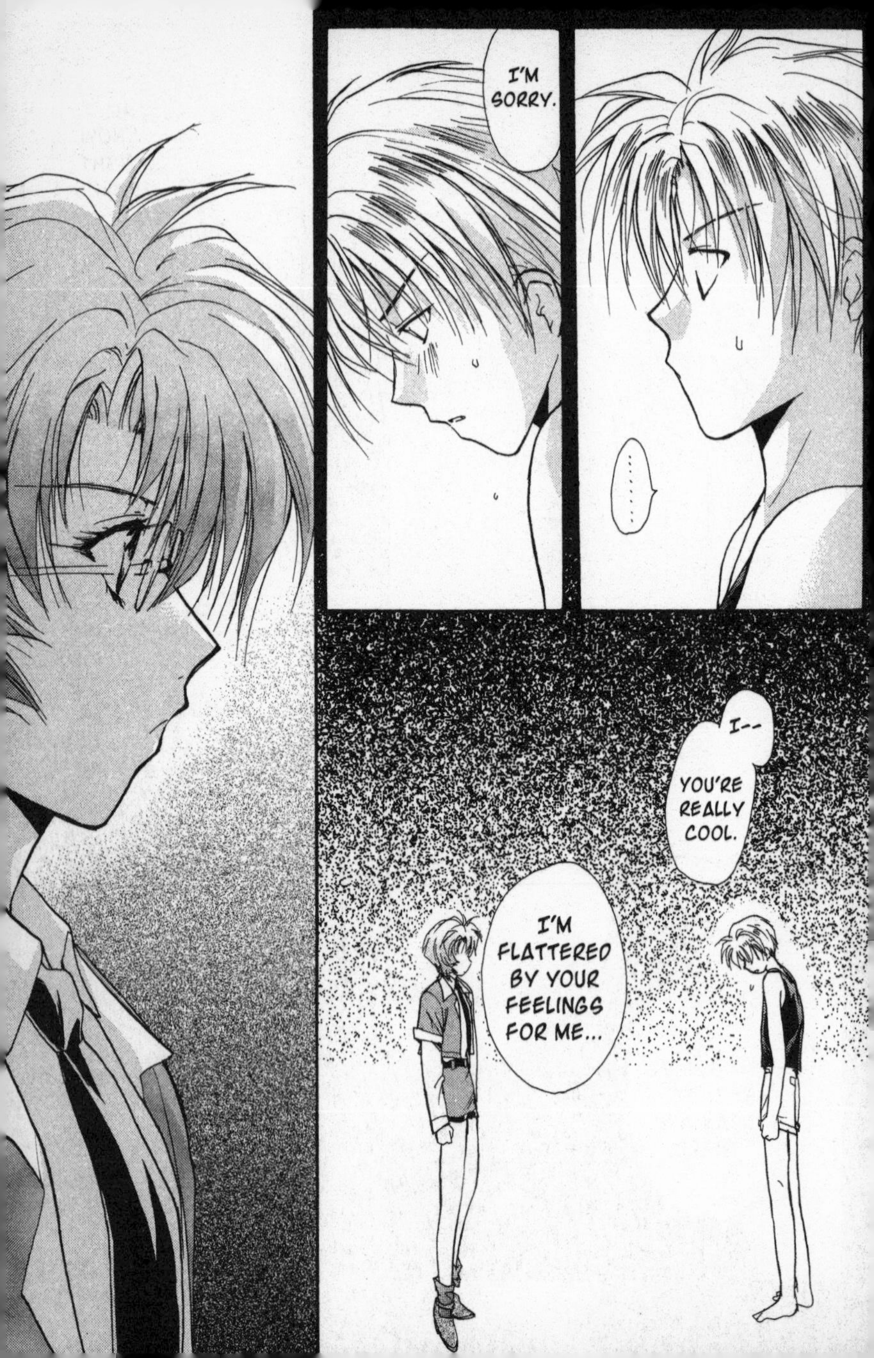
......
I'M SORRY.
I--
YOU'RE REALLY COOL.
I'M FLATTERED BY YOUR FEELINGS FOR ME...

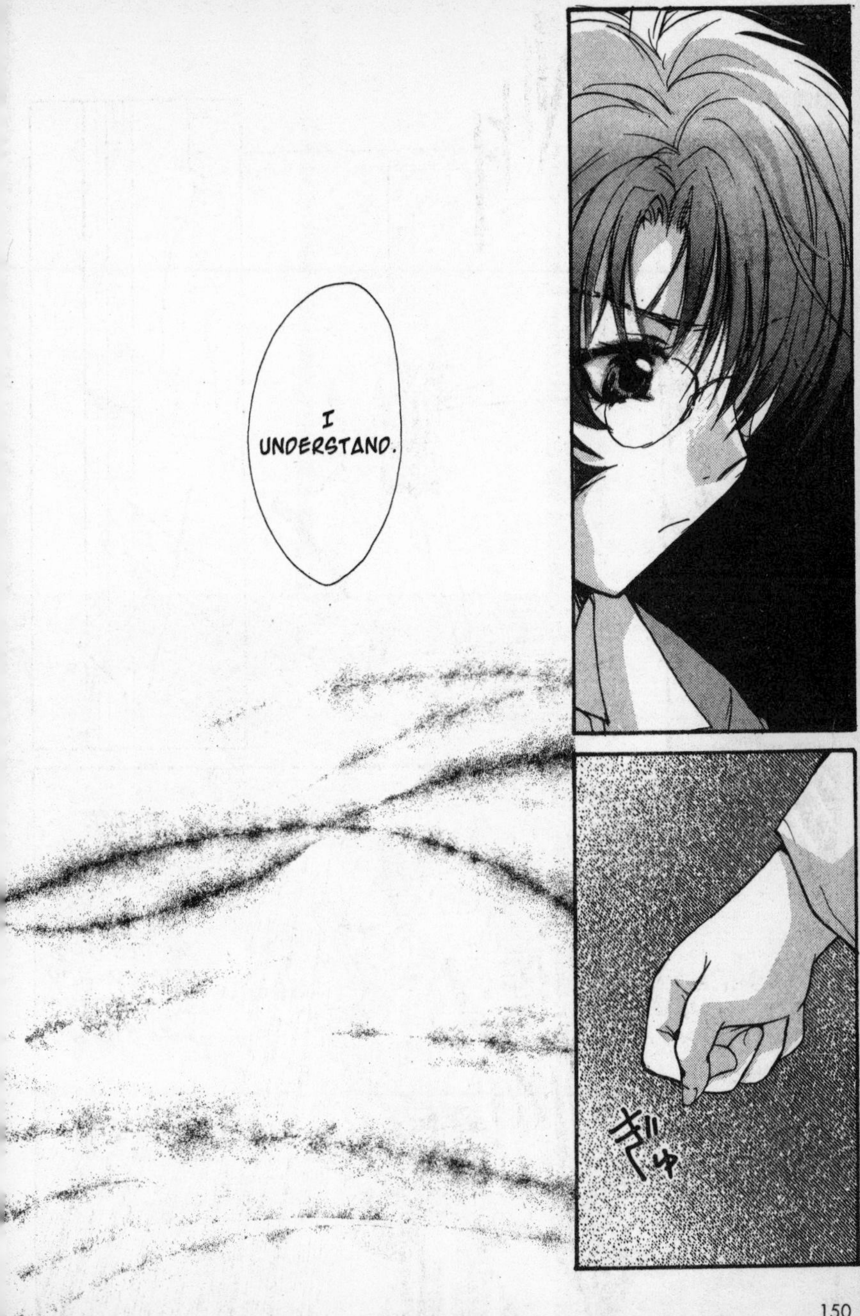
I UNDERSTAND.
ぎゅ

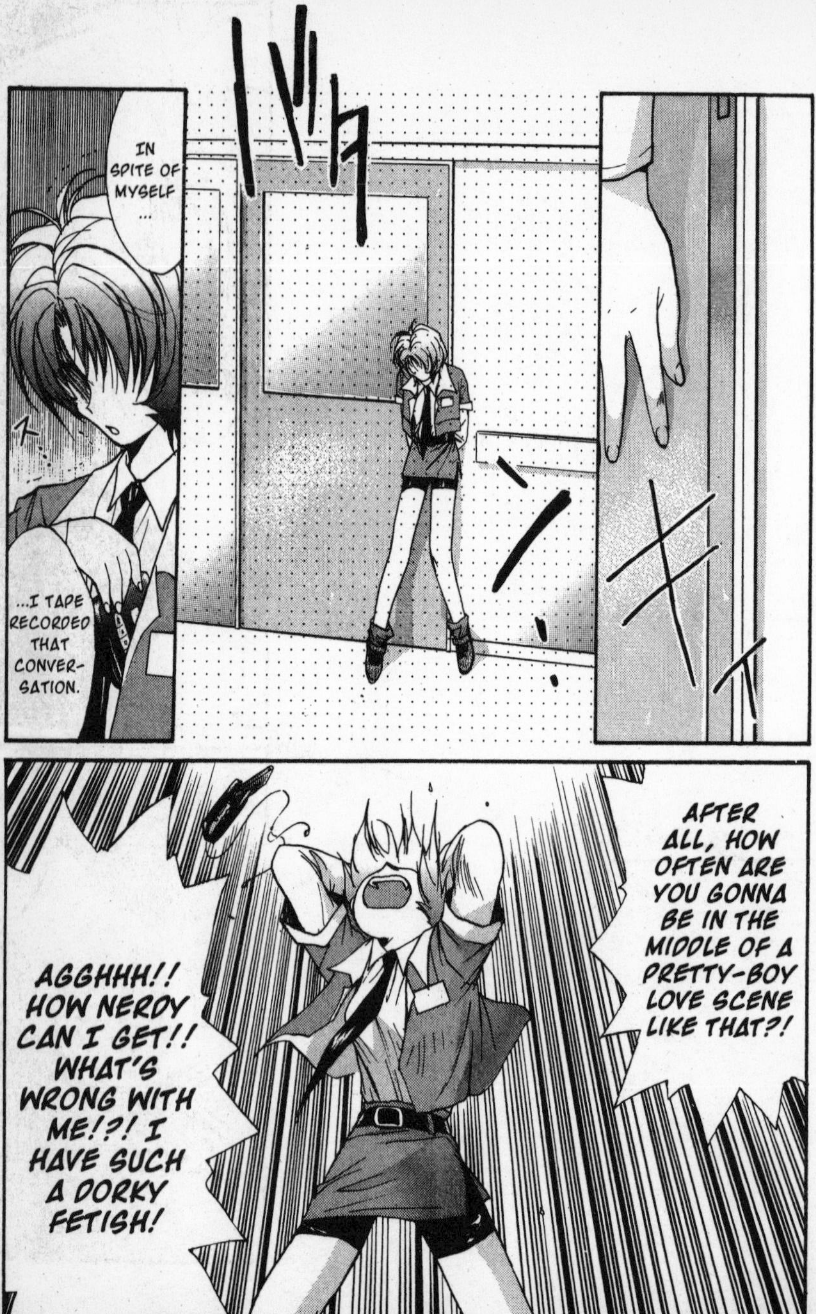
IN SPITE OF MYSELF ...
...I TAPE RECORDED THAT CONVERSATION.
AFTER ALL, HOW OFTEN ARE YOU GONNA BE IN THE MIDDLE OF A PRETTY-BOY LOVE SCENE LIKE THAT?!
AGGHHH!! HOW NERDY CAN I GET!! WHAT'S WRONG WITH ME!?! I HAVE SUCH A DORKY FETISH!

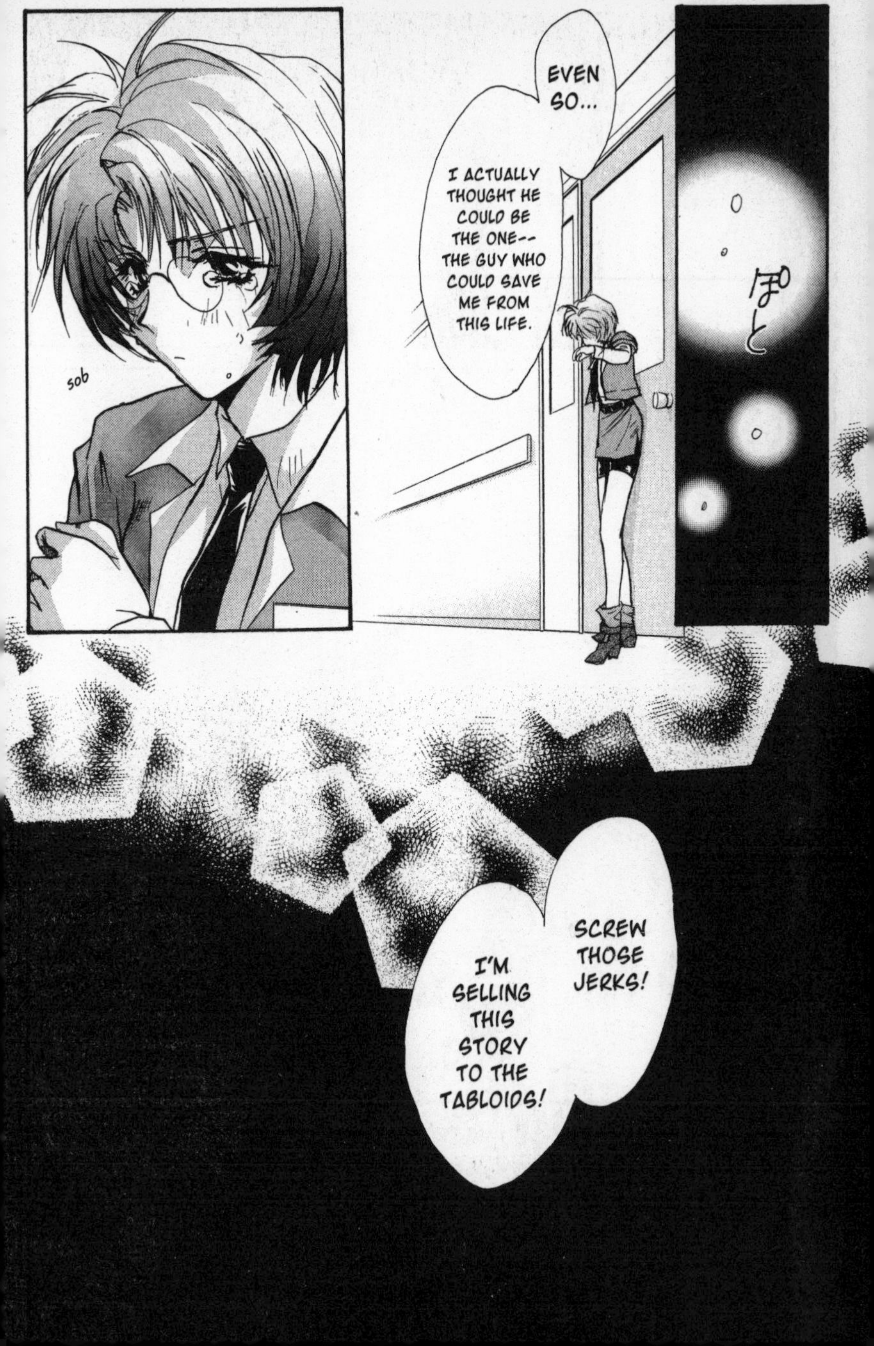
ぽと
EVEN SO...
I ACTUALLY THOUGHT HE COULD BE THE ONE-- THE GUY WHO COULD SAVE ME FROM THIS LIFE.
sob
SCREW THOSE JERKS!
I'M SELLING THIS STORY TO THE TABLOIDS!

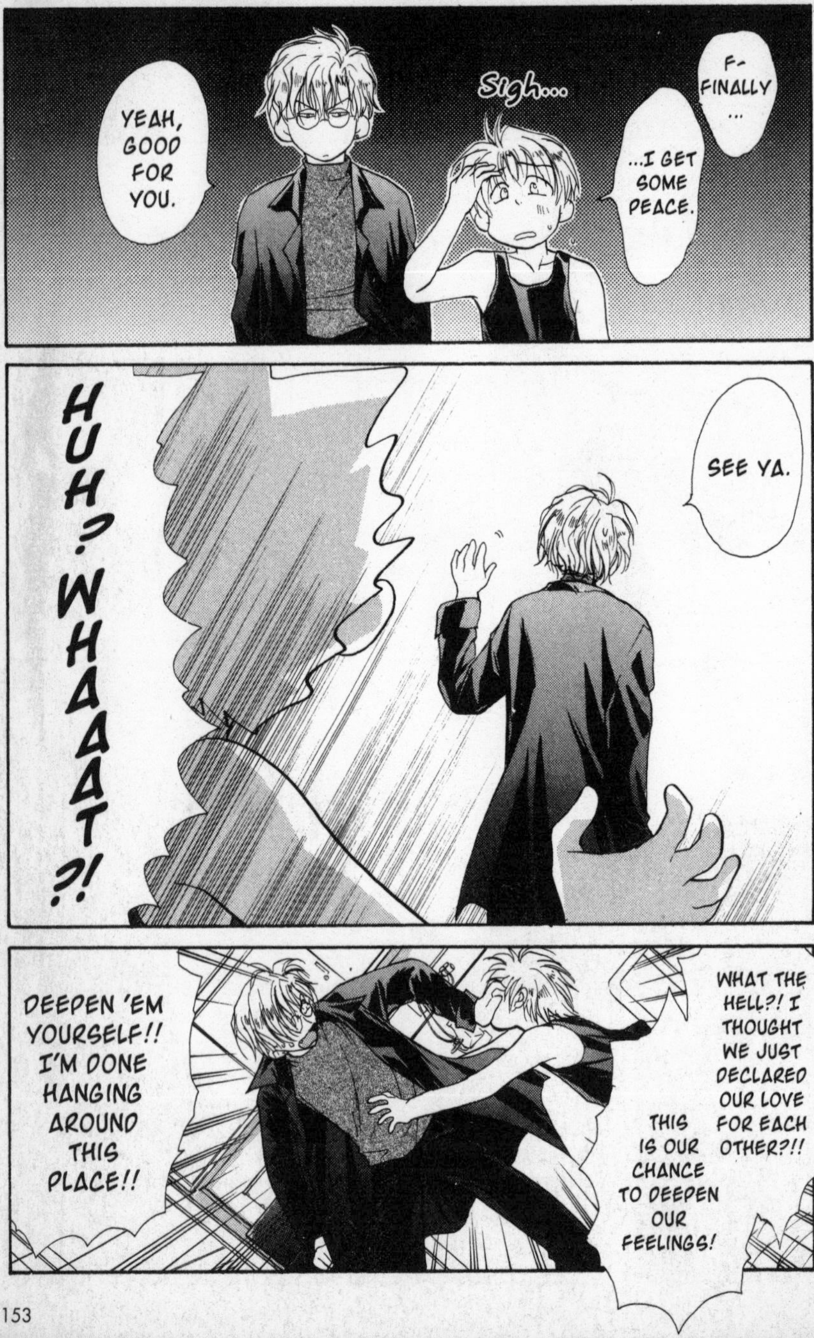
F-FINALLY...
...I GET SOME PEACE.
Sigh...
YEAH, GOOD FOR YOU.
SEE YA.
HUH?! WHAAAT?!
WHAT THE HELL?! I THOUGHT WE JUST DECLARED OUR LOVE FOR EACH OTHER?!!
THIS IS OUR CHANCE TO DEEPEN OUR FEELINGS!
DEEPEN 'EM YOURSELF!! I'M DONE HANGING AROUND THIS PLACE!!

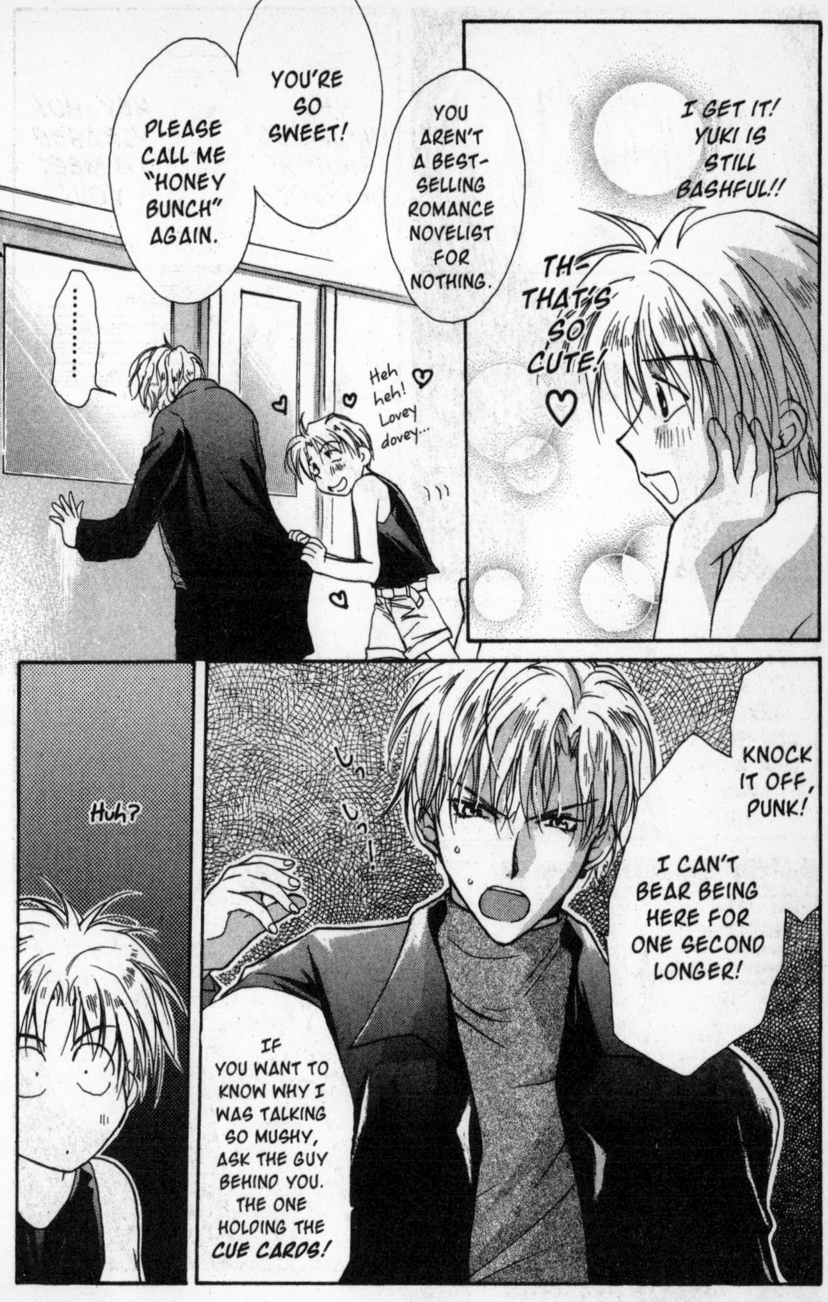
I GET IT! YUKI IS STILL BASHFUL!!
TH-THAT'S SO CUTE!
YOU AREN'T A BEST-SELLING ROMANCE NOVELIST FOR NOTHING.
YOU'RE SO SWEET!
PLEASE CALL ME "HONEY BUNCH" AGAIN.
Heh heh! Lovey dovey...
......
KNOCK IT OFF, PUNK!
I CAN'T BEAR BEING HERE FOR ONE SECOND LONGER!
IF YOU WANT TO KNOW WHY I WAS TALKING SO MUSHY, ASK THE GUY BEHIND YOU. THE ONE HOLDING THE CUE CARDS!
Huh?

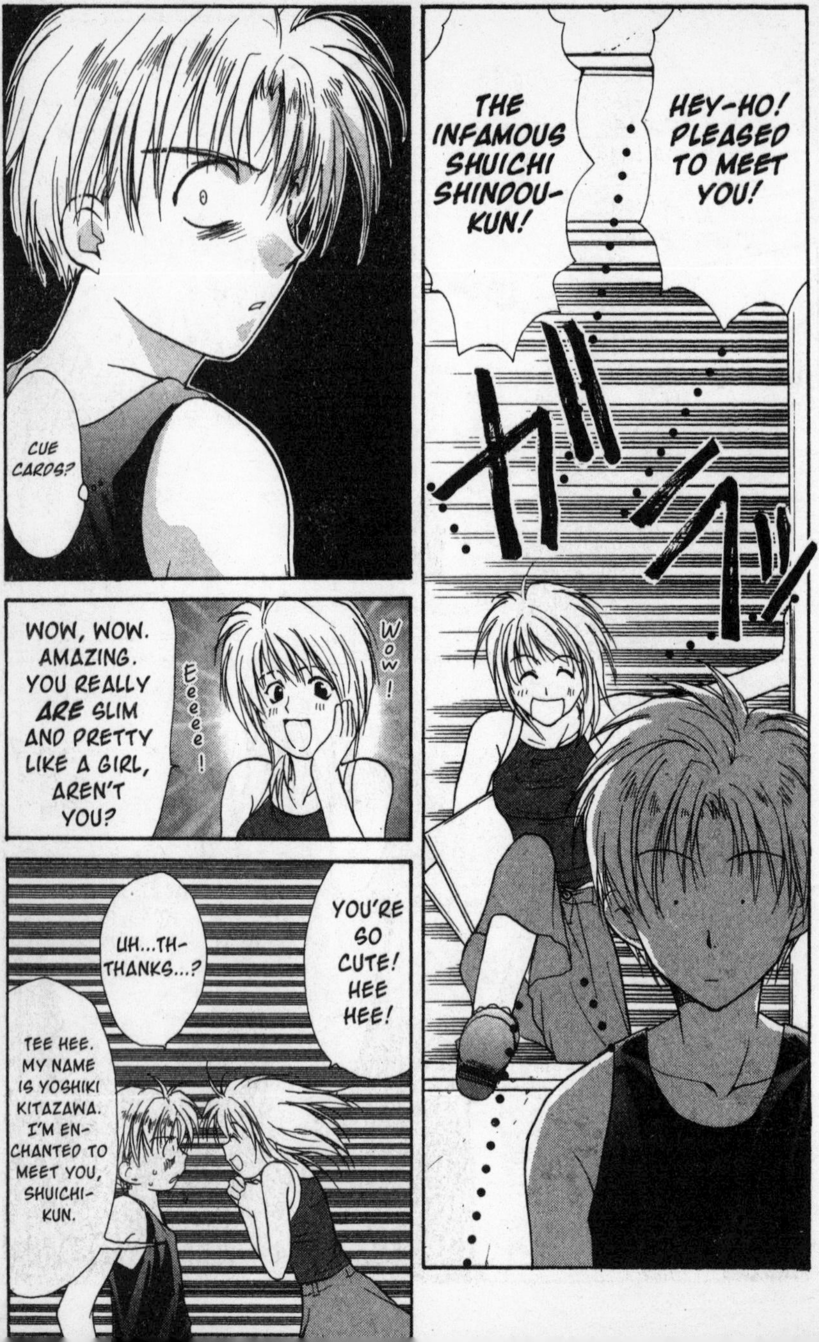
HEY-HO! PLEASED TO MEET YOU!
THE INFAMOUS SHUICHI SHINDOU-KUN!
CUE CARDS?
WOW, WOW. AMAZING. YOU REALLY ARE SLIM AND PRETTY LIKE A GIRL, AREN'T YOU?
Wow!
Eeeee!
YOU'RE SO CUTE! HEE HEE!
UH...TH-THANKS...?
TEE HEE. MY NAME IS YOSHIKI KITAZAWA. I'M EN-CHANTED TO MEET YOU, SHUICHI-KUN.

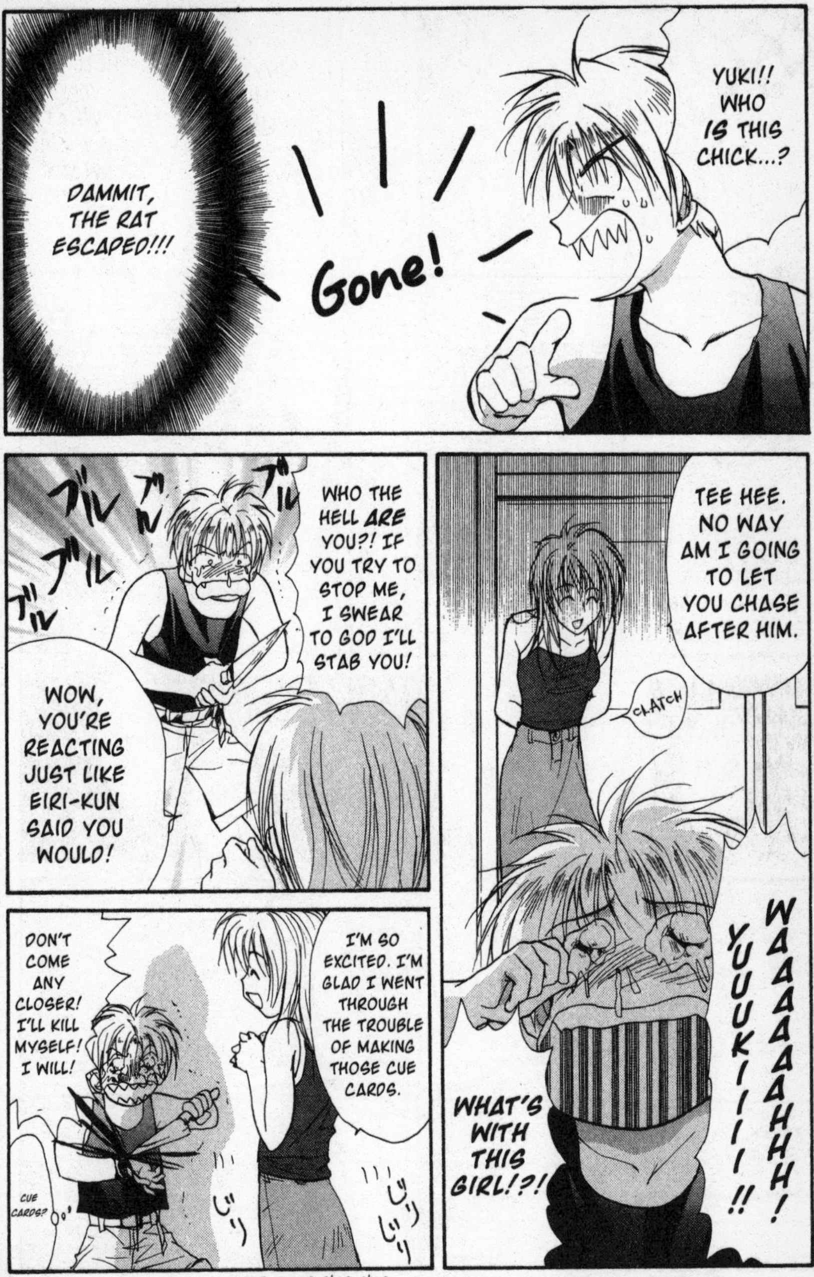
YUKI!! WHO IS THIS CHICK...?
Gone!
DAMMIT, THE RAT ESCAPED!!!
TEE HEE. NO WAY AM I GOING TO LET YOU CHASE AFTER HIM.
CLATCH
WAAAAAAAAHHH! YUUUKIIIII!!
WHAT'S WITH THIS GIRL!?!
ブル
ブル
ブル
ブル
WHO THE HELL ARE YOU?! IF YOU TRY TO STOP ME, I SWEAR TO GOD I'LL STAB YOU!
WOW, YOU'RE REACTING JUST LIKE EIRI-KUN SAID YOU WOULD!
I'M SO EXCITED. I'M GLAD I WENT THROUGH THE TROUBLE OF MAKING THOSE CUE CARDS.
じり じり
DON'T COME ANY CLOSER! I'LL KILL MYSELF! I WILL!
じり
CUE CARDS?

creep creep step step

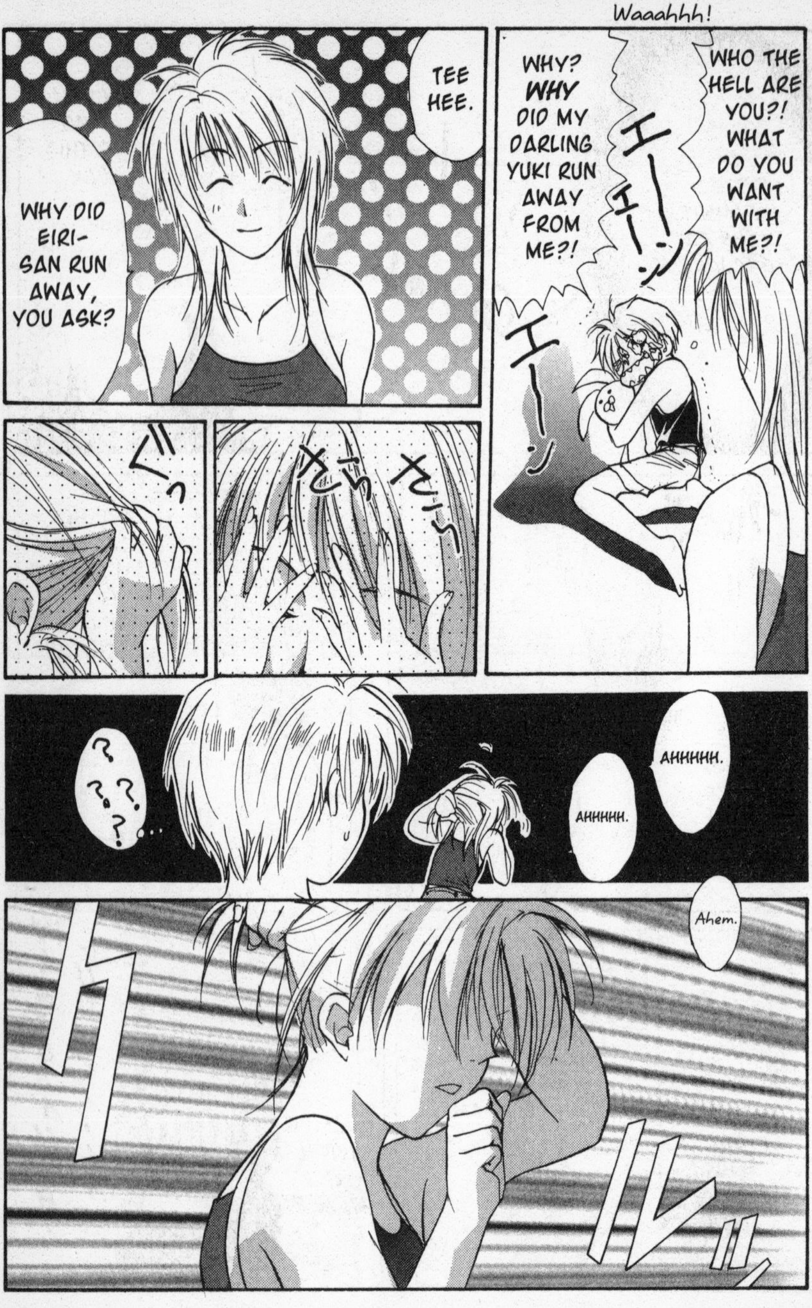
Waaahhh!
WHO THE HELL ARE YOU?! WHAT DO YOU WANT WITH ME?!
WHY? **WHY** DID MY DARLING YUKI RUN AWAY FROM ME?!
エーーン
エーーン
TEE HEE.
WHY DID EIRI-SAN RUN AWAY, YOU ASK?
さら さら
ぐっ
AHHHHH.
AHHHHH.
? ? ? ? ?...
Ahem.

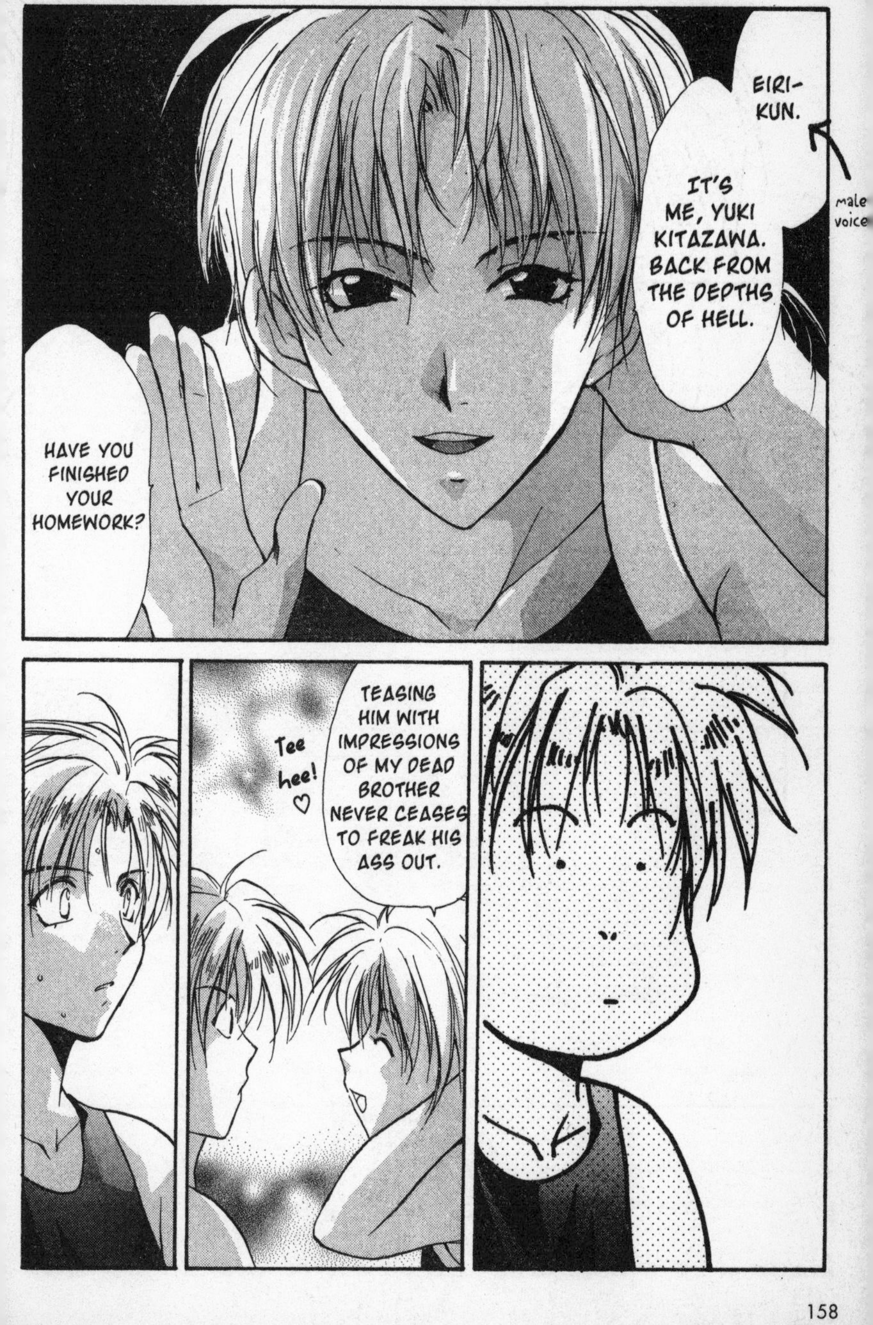
EIRI-KUN.
male voice
IT'S ME, YUKI KITAZAWA. BACK FROM THE DEPTHS OF HELL.
HAVE YOU FINISHED YOUR HOMEWORK?
TEASING HIM WITH IMPRESSIONS OF MY DEAD BROTHER NEVER CEASES TO FREAK HIS ASS OUT.
Tee hee! ♡

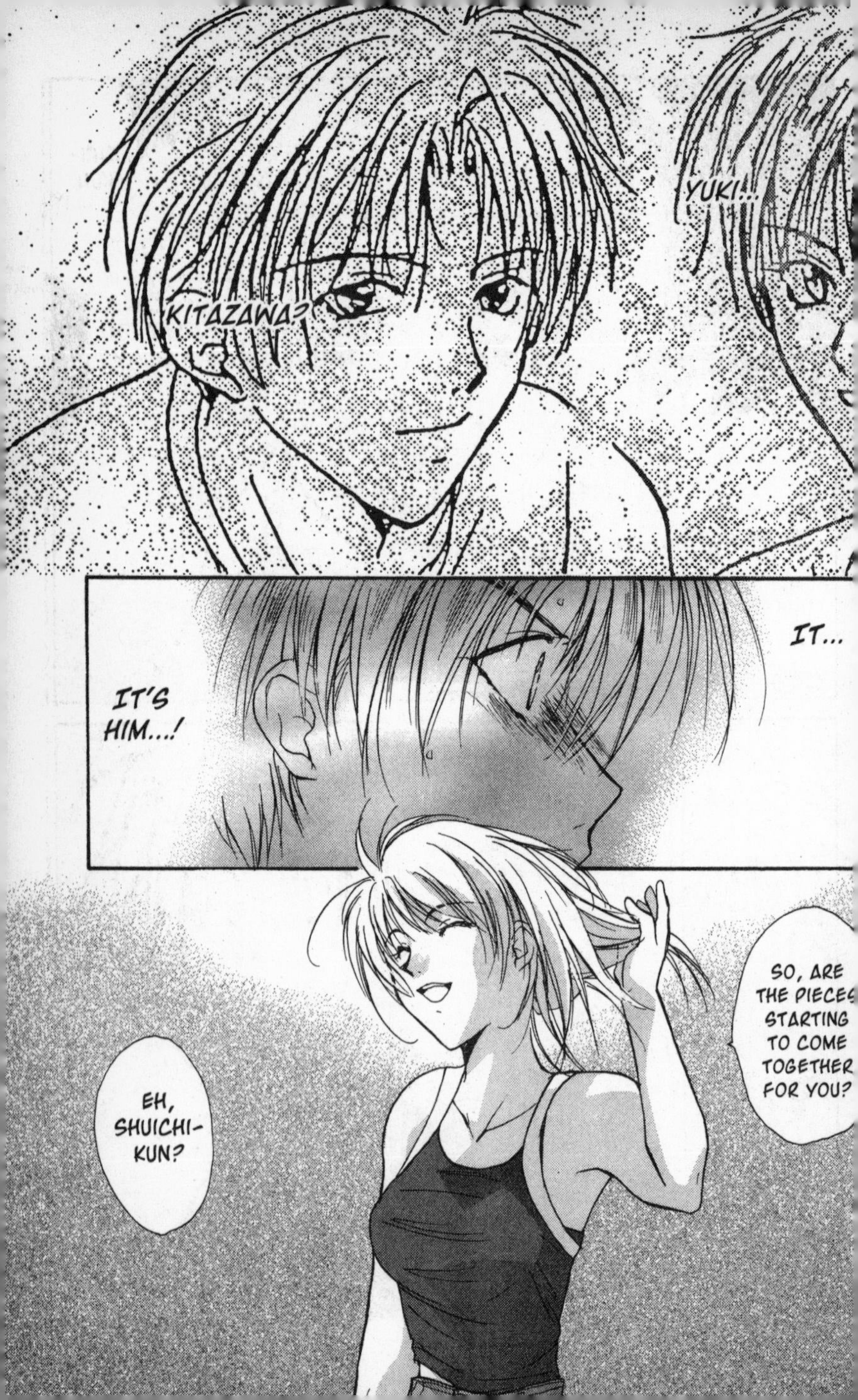
YUKI...
KITAZAWA?
IT...
IT'S HIM...!
SO, ARE THE PIECES STARTING TO COME TOGETHER FOR YOU?
EH, SHUICHI-KUN?

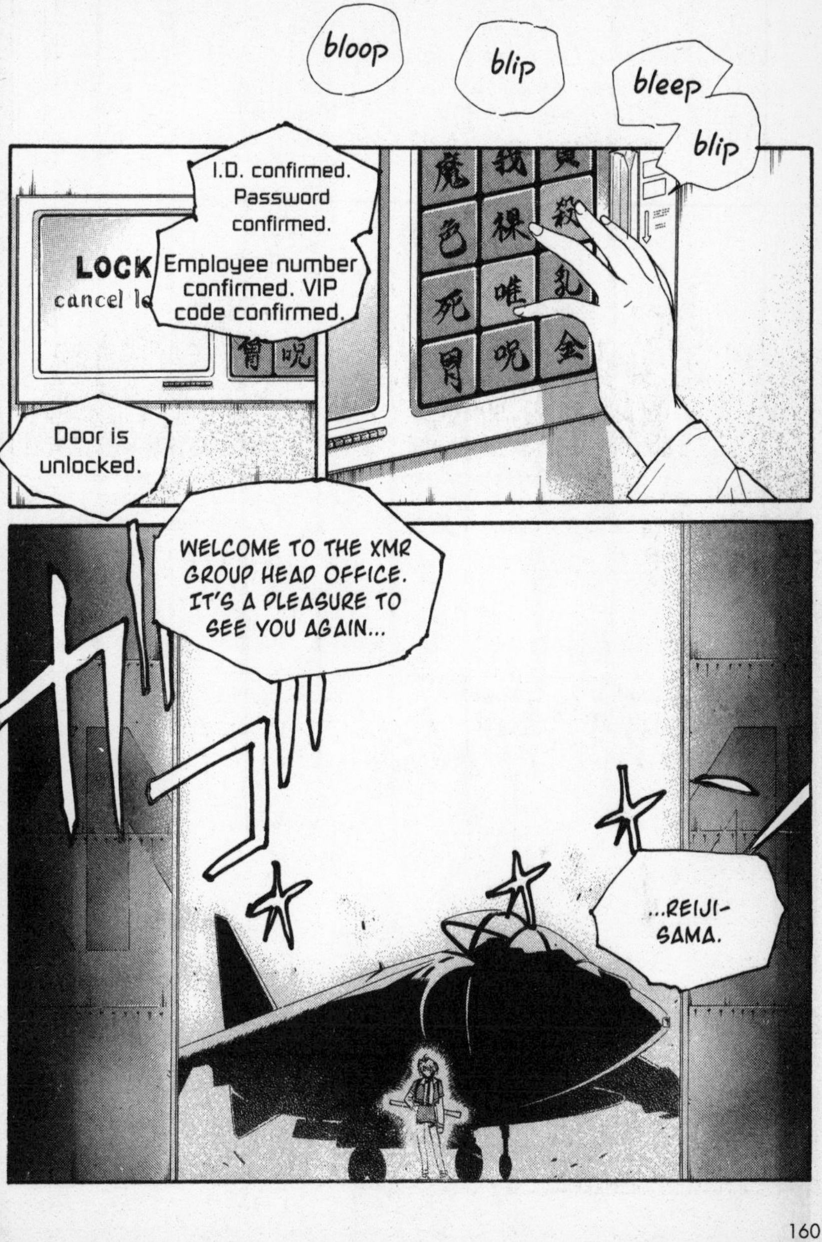
blip
bleep
blip
bloop
I.D. confirmed. Password confirmed.
Employee number confirmed. VIP code confirmed.
LOCK
Door is unlocked.
WELCOME TO THE XMR GROUP HEAD OFFICE. IT'S A PLEASURE TO SEE YOU AGAIN...
...REIJI-SAMA.

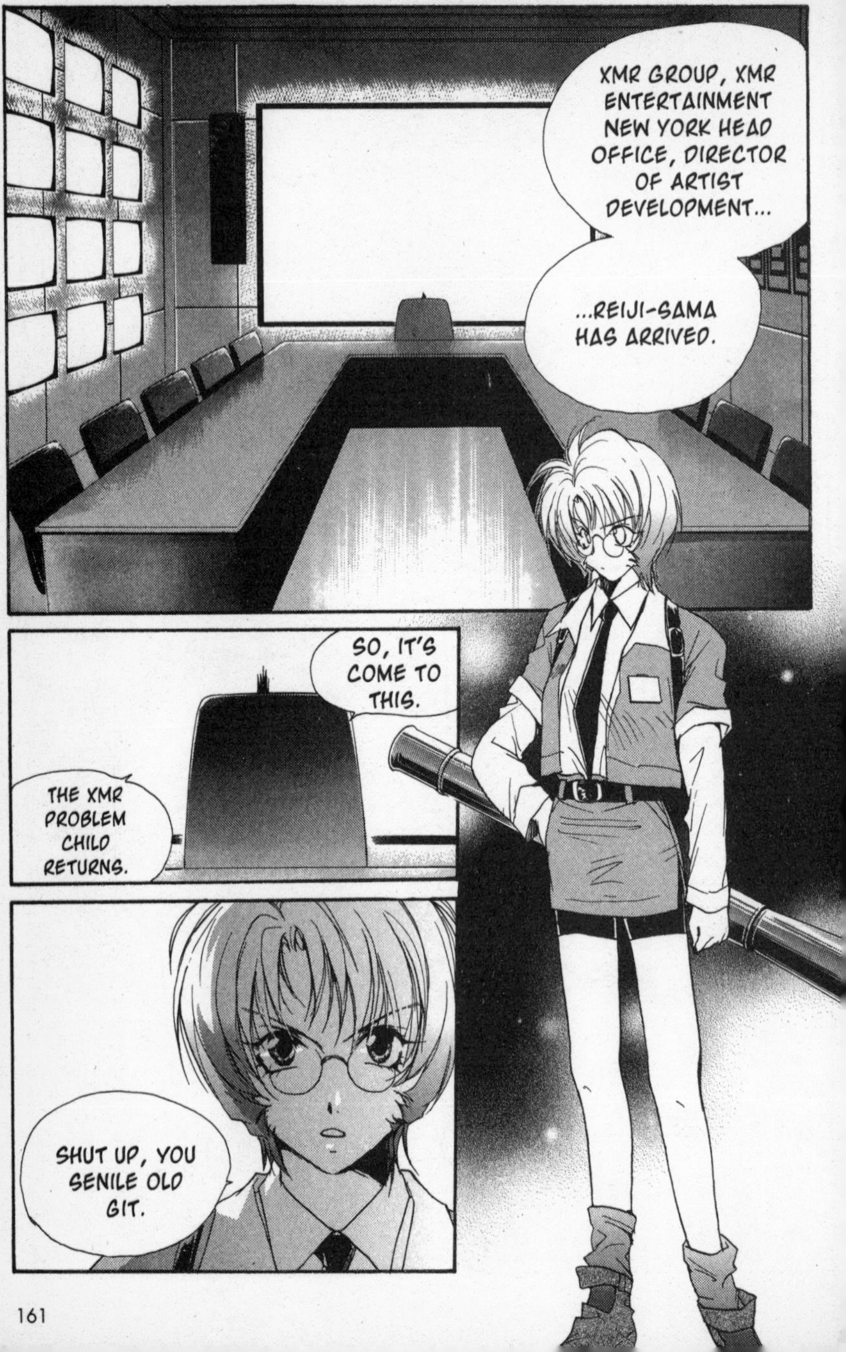
XMR GROUP, XMR ENTERTAINMENT NEW YORK HEAD OFFICE, DIRECTOR OF ARTIST DEVELOPMENT...
...REIJI-SAMA HAS ARRIVED.
SO, IT'S COME TO THIS.
THE XMR PROBLEM CHILD RETURNS.
SHUT UP, YOU SENILE OLD GIT.

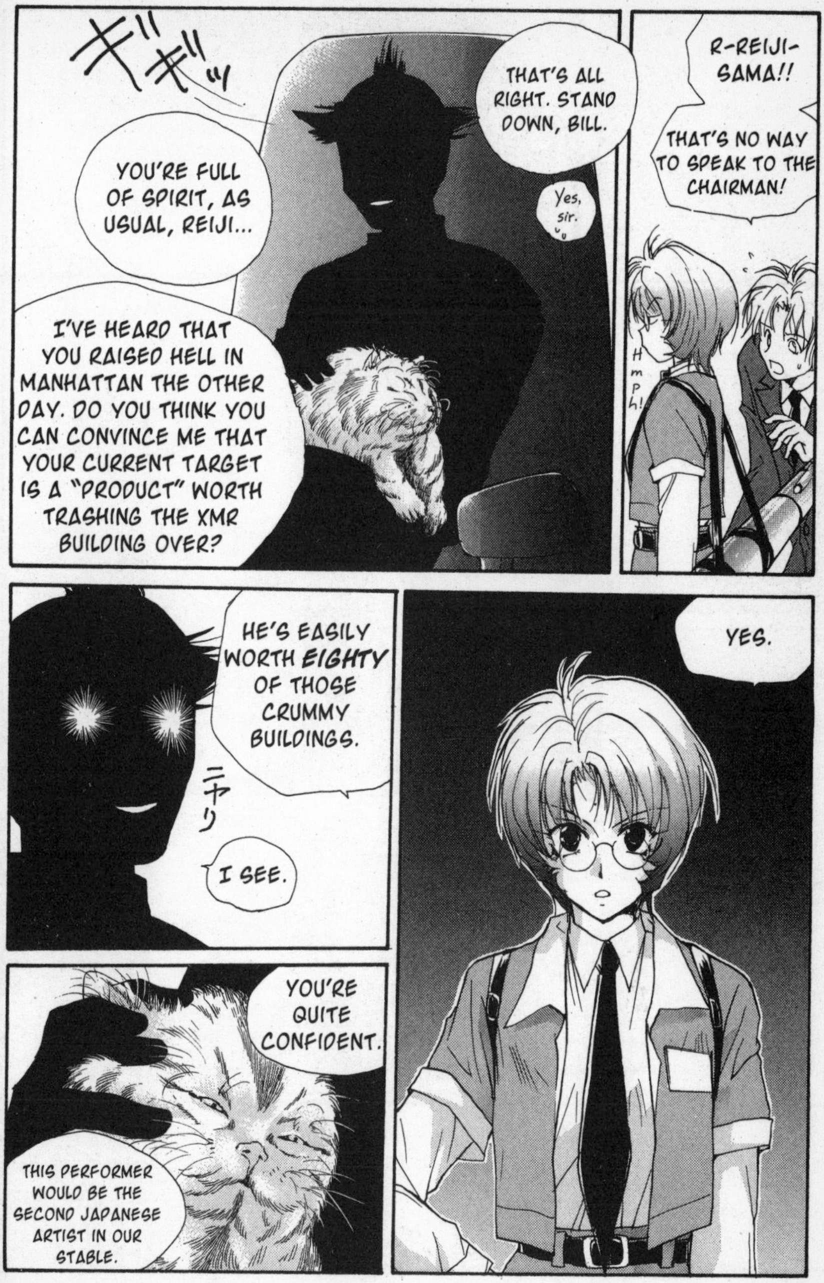
R-REIJI-SAMA!!
THAT'S NO WAY TO SPEAK TO THE CHAIRMAN!
Hmph!
THAT'S ALL RIGHT. STAND DOWN, BILL.
Yes, sir.
ギギッ
YOU'RE FULL OF SPIRIT, AS USUAL, REIJI...
I'VE HEARD THAT YOU RAISED HELL IN MANHATTAN THE OTHER DAY. DO YOU THINK YOU CAN CONVINCE ME THAT YOUR CURRENT TARGET IS A "PRODUCT" WORTH TRASHING THE XMR BUILDING OVER?
YES.
HE'S EASILY WORTH EIGHTY OF THOSE CRUMMY BUILDINGS.
ニヤリ
I SEE.
YOU'RE QUITE CONFIDENT.
THIS PERFORMER WOULD BE THE SECOND JAPANESE ARTIST IN OUR STABLE.

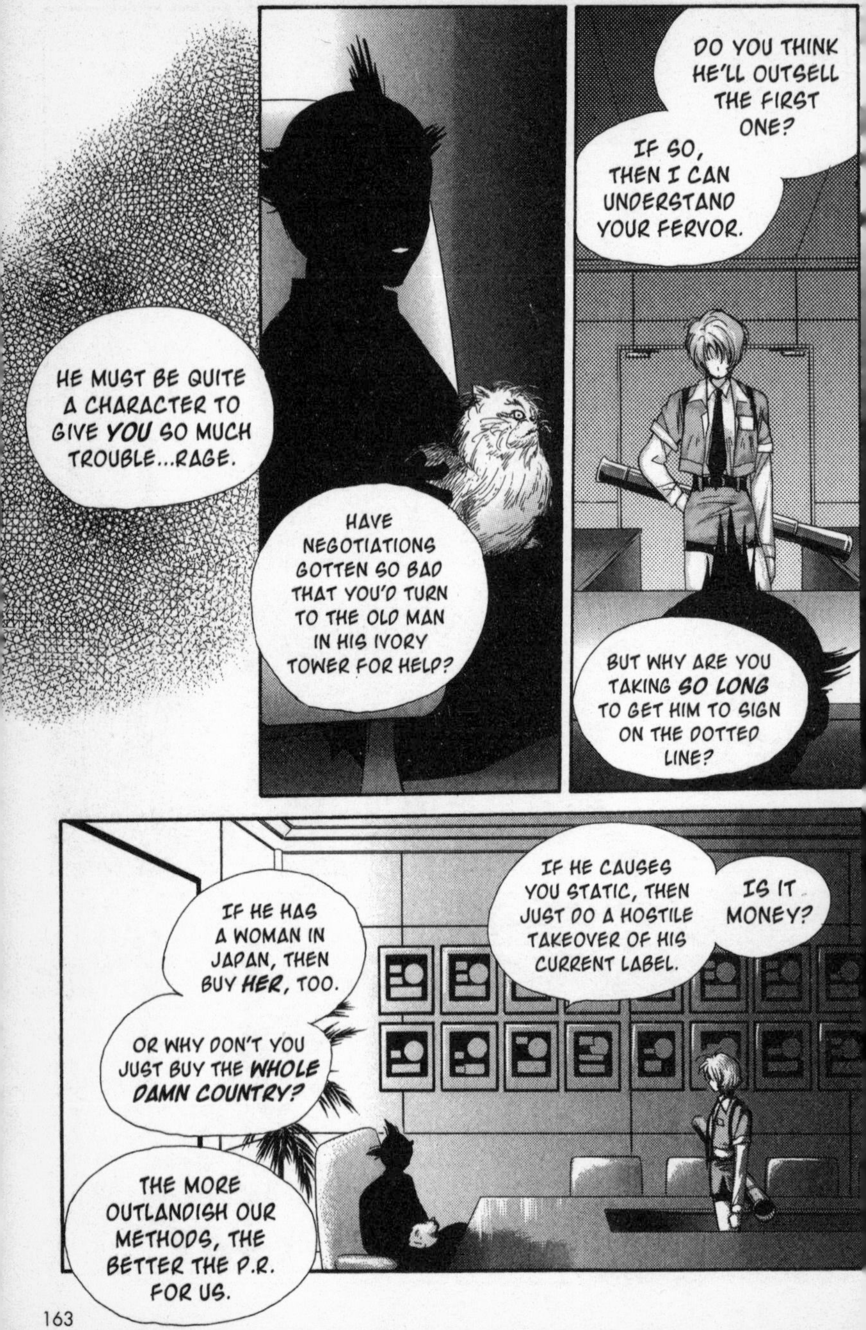
DO YOU THINK HE'LL OUTSELL THE FIRST ONE?
IF SO, THEN I CAN UNDERSTAND YOUR FERVOR.
BUT WHY ARE YOU TAKING **SO LONG** TO GET HIM TO SIGN ON THE DOTTED LINE?
HAVE NEGOTIATIONS GOTTEN SO BAD THAT YOU'D TURN TO THE OLD MAN IN HIS IVORY TOWER FOR HELP?
HE MUST BE QUITE A CHARACTER TO GIVE ***YOU*** SO MUCH TROUBLE...RAGE.
IS IT MONEY?
IF HE CAUSES YOU STATIC, THEN JUST DO A HOSTILE TAKEOVER OF HIS CURRENT LABEL.
IF HE HAS A WOMAN IN JAPAN, THEN BUY ***HER***, TOO.
OR WHY DON'T YOU JUST BUY THE ***WHOLE DAMN COUNTRY?***
THE MORE OUTLANDISH OUR METHODS, THE BETTER THE P.R. FOR US.

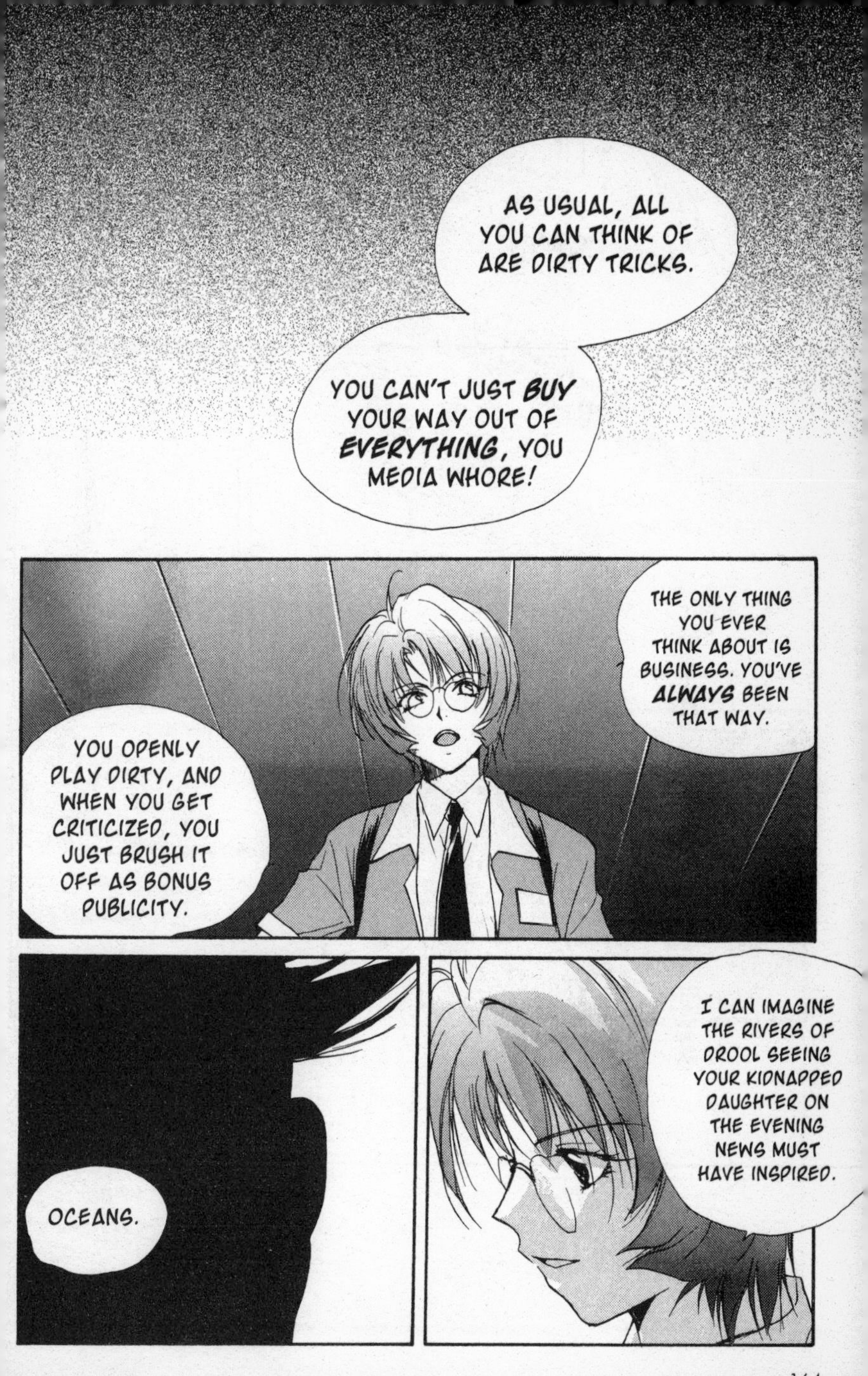
AS USUAL, ALL YOU CAN THINK OF ARE DIRTY TRICKS.
YOU CAN'T JUST **BUY** YOUR WAY OUT OF **EVERYTHING**, YOU MEDIA WHORE!
THE ONLY THING YOU EVER THINK ABOUT IS BUSINESS. YOU'VE **ALWAYS** BEEN THAT WAY.
YOU OPENLY PLAY DIRTY, AND WHEN YOU GET CRITICIZED, YOU JUST BRUSH IT OFF AS BONUS PUBLICITY.
I CAN IMAGINE THE RIVERS OF DROOL SEEING YOUR KIDNAPPED DAUGHTER ON THE EVENING NEWS MUST HAVE INSPIRED.
OCEANS.

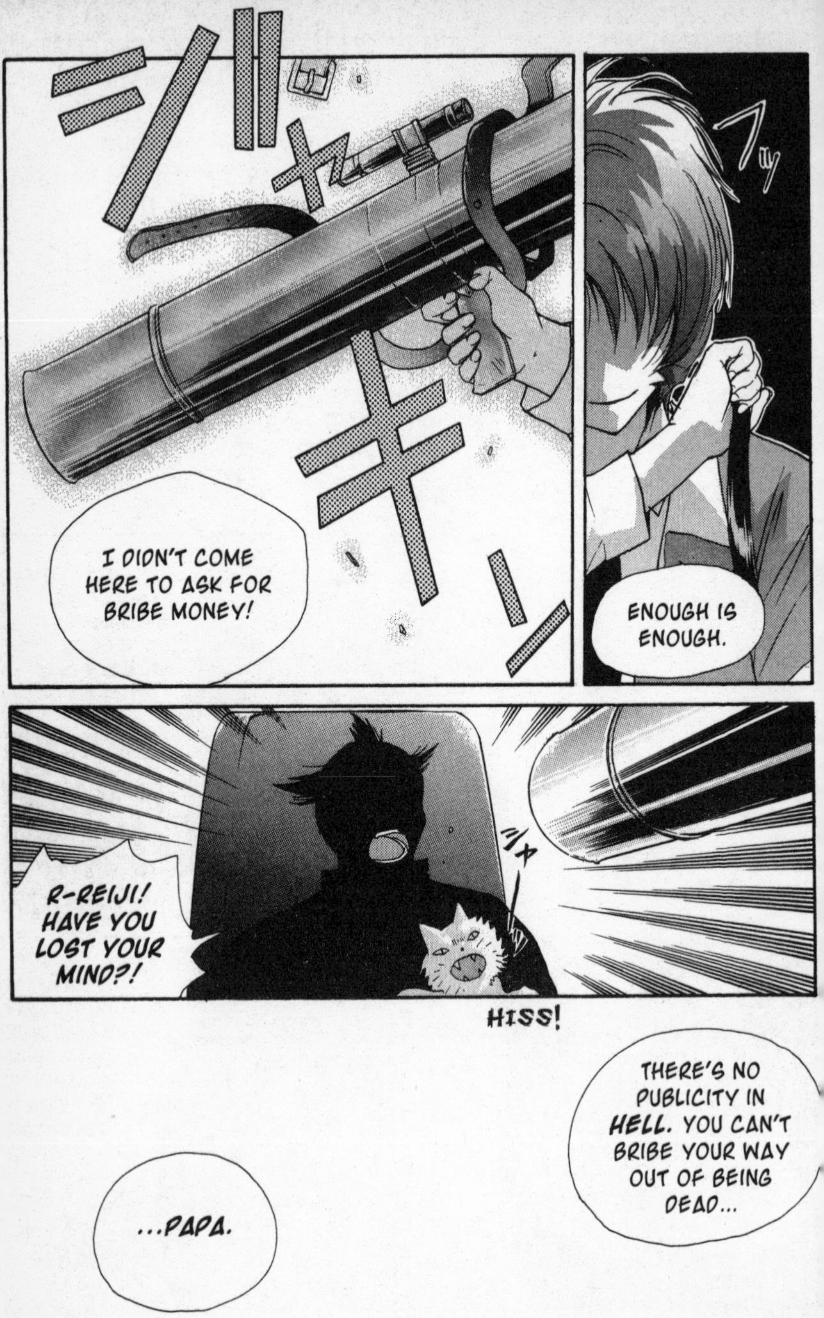
ENOUGH IS ENOUGH.
I DIDN'T COME HERE TO ASK FOR BRIBE MONEY!
R-REIJI! HAVE YOU LOST YOUR MIND?!
HISS!
THERE'S NO PUBLICITY IN **HELL.** YOU CAN'T BRIBE YOUR WAY OUT OF BEING DEAD...
...PAPA.

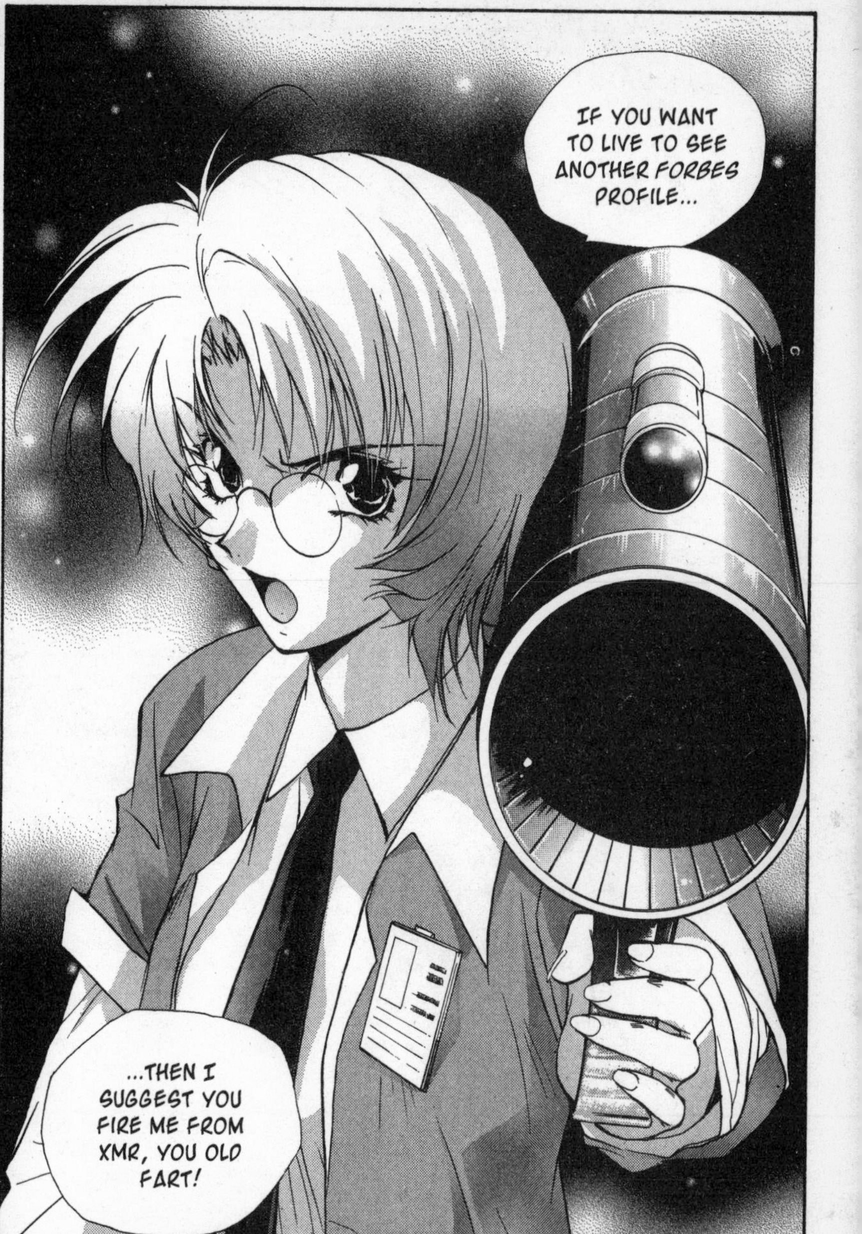
IF YOU WANT TO LIVE TO SEE ANOTHER *FORBES* PROFILE...
...THEN I SUGGEST YOU FIRE ME FROM XMR, YOU OLD FART!

track40▶END

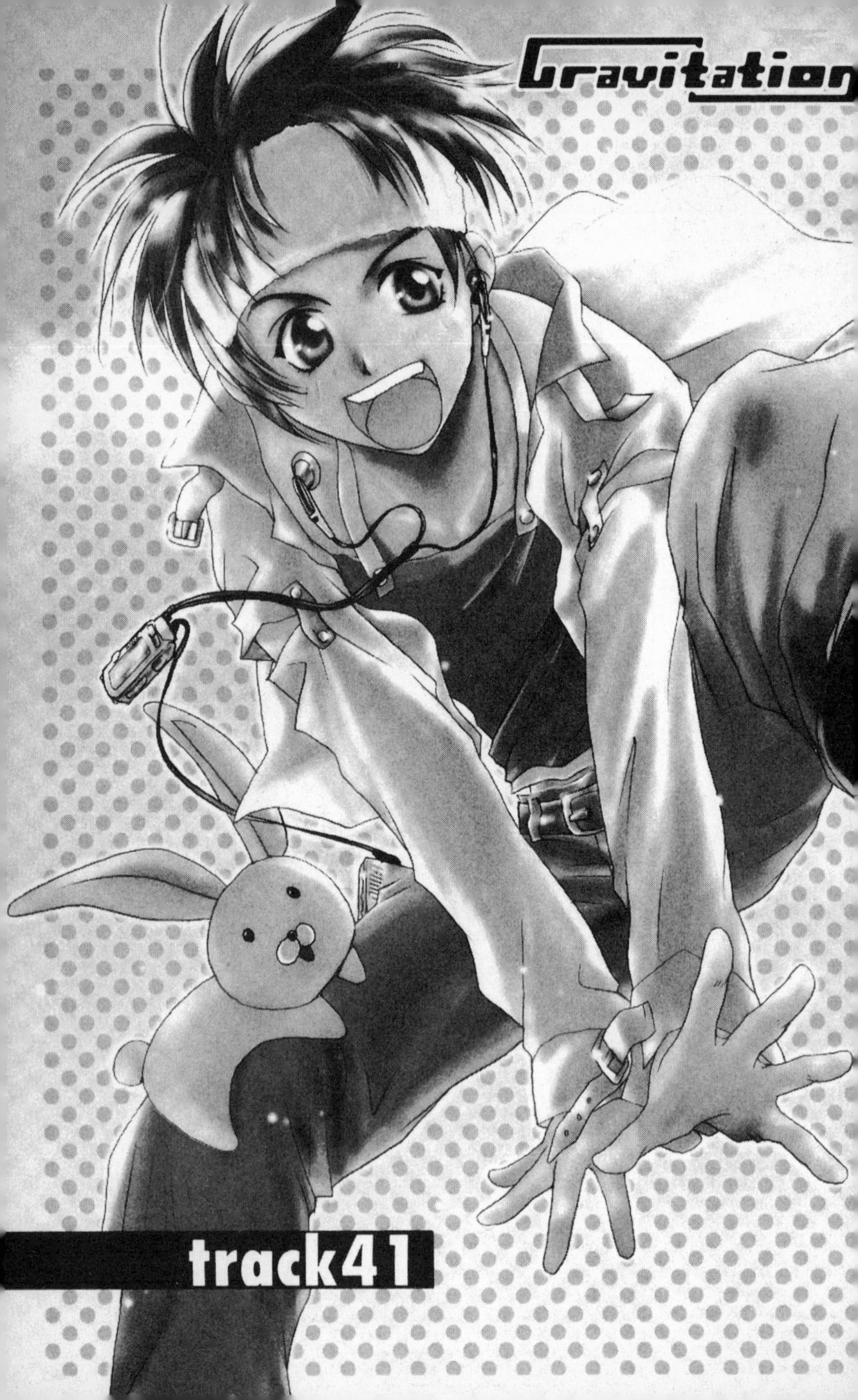
Gravitation
track41

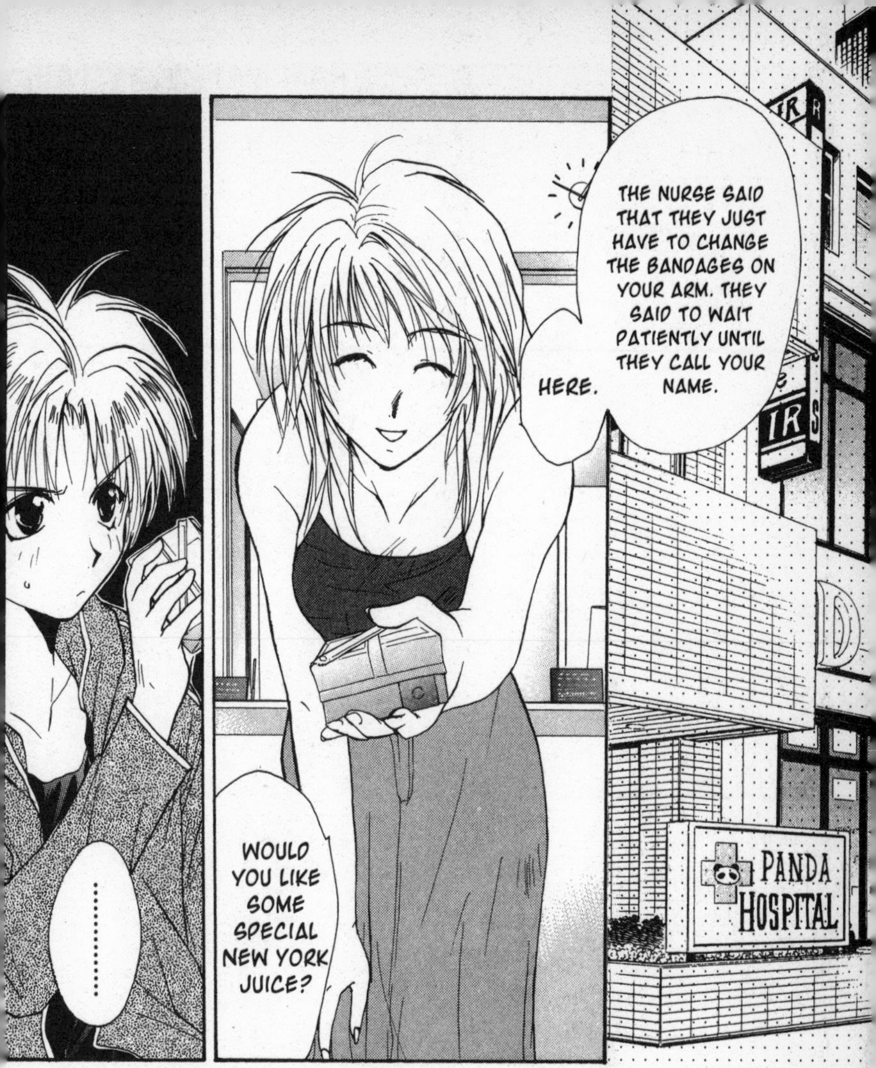
PANDA HOSPITAL
THE NURSE SAID THAT THEY JUST HAVE TO CHANGE THE BANDAGES ON YOUR ARM. THEY SAID TO WAIT PATIENTLY UNTIL THEY CALL YOUR NAME. HERE.
WOULD YOU LIKE SOME SPECIAL NEW YORK JUICE?
......

ABOUT GRAVITATION TRACK 41

The third "**Comments By People Who Just Happened To Be There**" has just been completed. In this episode, we have our trusty assistant to Murakami Maki, assistant Run-chan, and dandy Ucchi-san, along with another dandy, T-san, and even a third, Shimario-san, total number: 49. (Editorial error.) There's no way I would have completed *Gravitation 9* without them. Although, in every issue I keep talking about returning to a beautiful environment, I still haven't gotten back to Japan. I'm stuck in the New York episodes. Whenever I get stuck, I just keep introducing new characters. You have to wonder how I'm going to deal with them all in the end, but I guess I'm just "going my way." Still, I wonder how I'm going to manage this huge cast when it's all winding down...

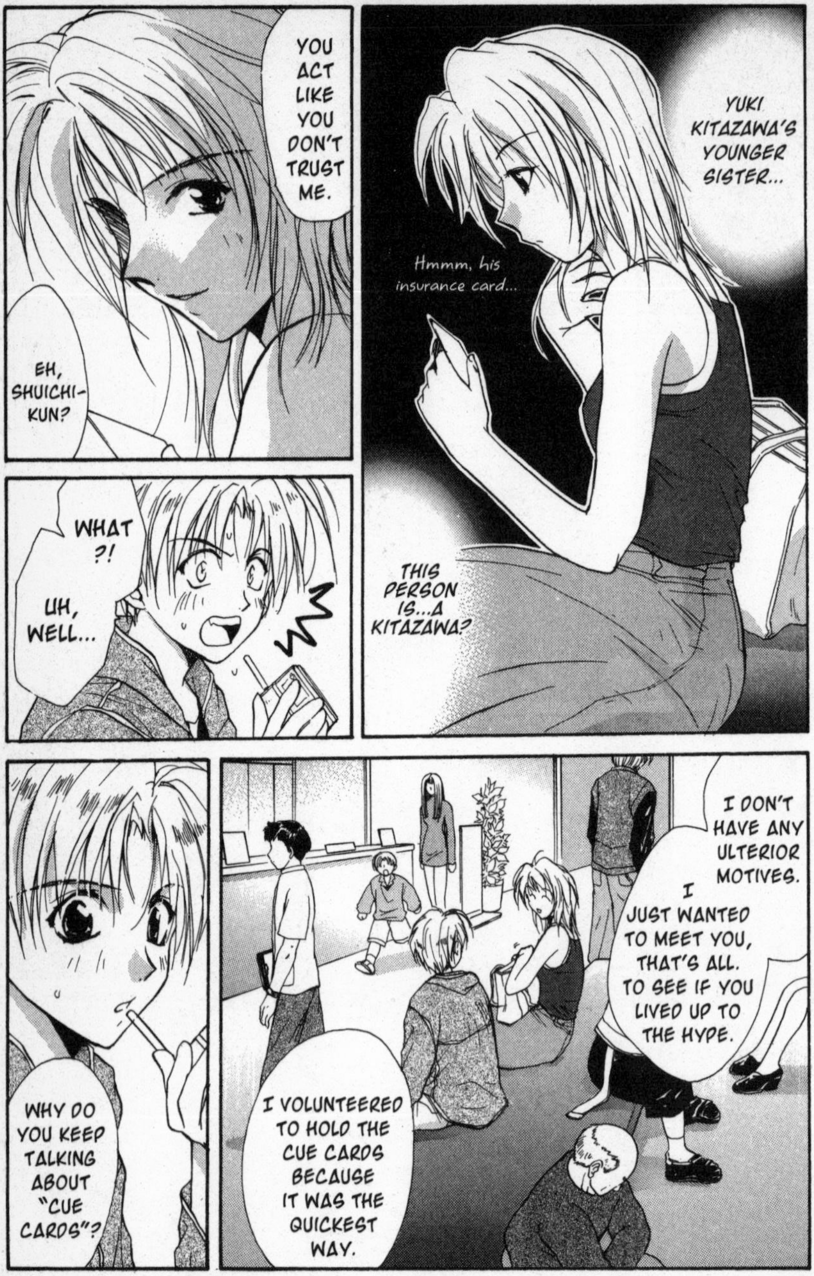
YUKI KITAZAWA'S YOUNGER SISTER...
Hmmm, his insurance card...
THIS PERSON IS...A KITAZAWA?
YOU ACT LIKE YOU DON'T TRUST ME.
EH, SHUICHI-KUN?
WHAT ?!
UH, WELL...
I DON'T HAVE ANY ULTERIOR MOTIVES.
I JUST WANTED TO MEET YOU, THAT'S ALL. TO SEE IF YOU LIVED UP TO THE HYPE.
I VOLUNTEERED TO HOLD THE CUE CARDS BECAUSE IT WAS THE QUICKEST WAY.
WHY DO YOU KEEP TALKING ABOUT "CUE CARDS"?

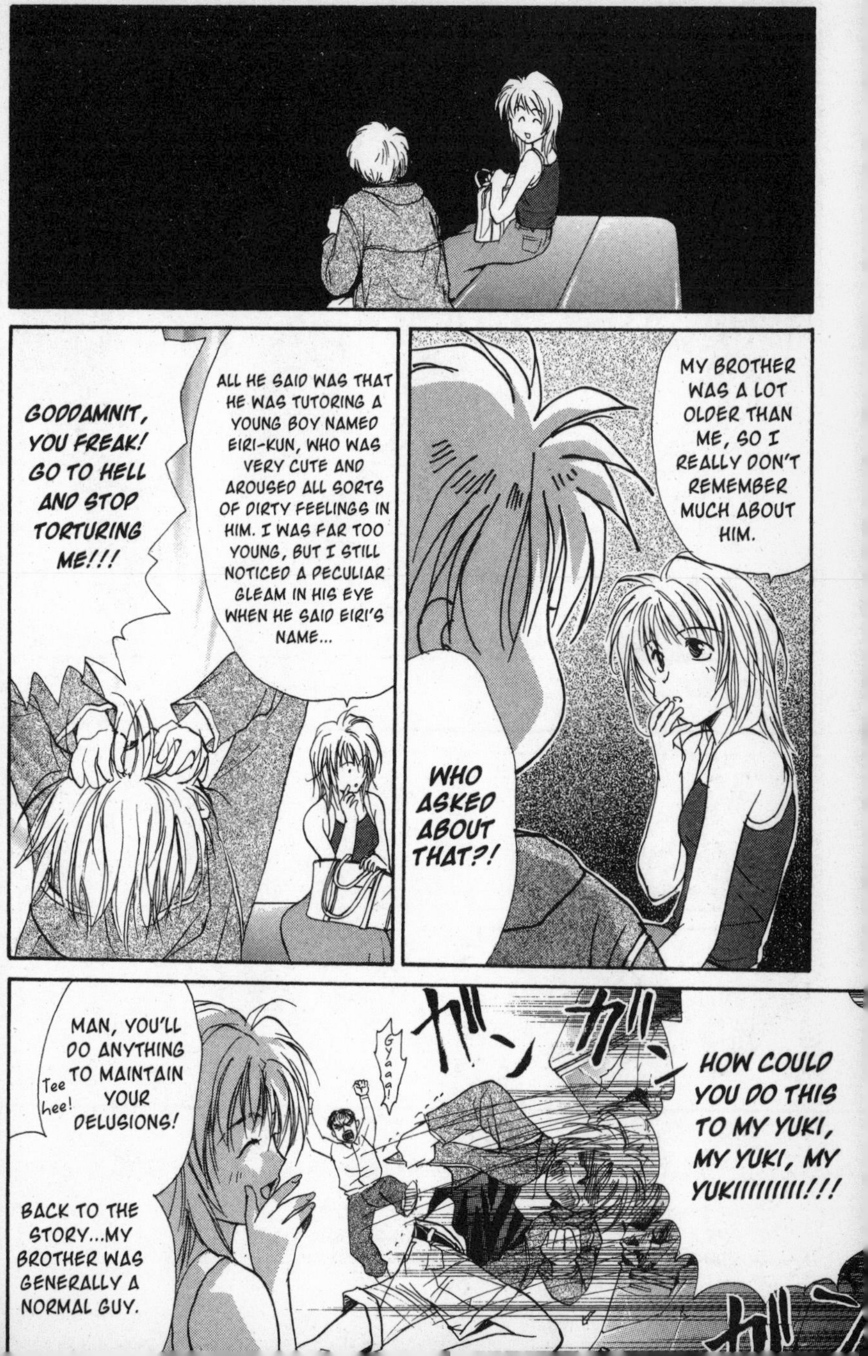
MY BROTHER WAS A LOT OLDER THAN ME, SO I REALLY DON'T REMEMBER MUCH ABOUT HIM.
WHO ASKED ABOUT THAT?!
ALL HE SAID WAS THAT HE WAS TUTORING A YOUNG BOY NAMED EIRI-KUN, WHO WAS VERY CUTE AND AROUSED ALL SORTS OF DIRTY FEELINGS IN HIM. I WAS FAR TOO YOUNG, BUT I STILL NOTICED A PECULIAR GLEAM IN HIS EYE WHEN HE SAID EIRI'S NAME...
GODDAMNIT, YOU FREAK! GO TO HELL AND STOP TORTURING ME!!!
HOW COULD YOU DO THIS TO MY YUKI, MY YUKI, MY YUKIIIIIIIIII!!!
Gyaaa!
MAN, YOU'LL DO ANYTHING TO MAINTAIN YOUR DELUSIONS!
Tee hee!
BACK TO THE STORY...MY BROTHER WAS GENERALLY A NORMAL GUY.

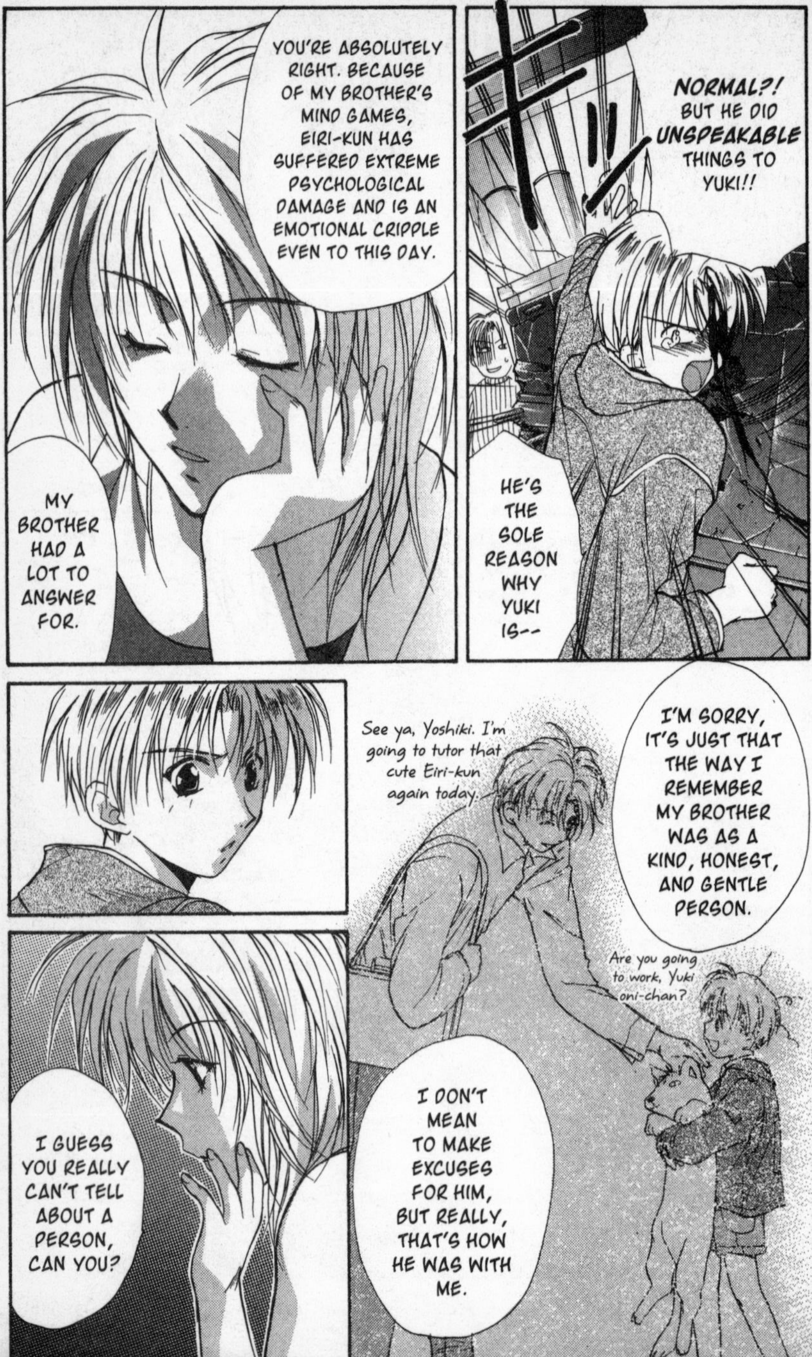
NORMAL?! BUT HE DID UNSPEAKABLE THINGS TO YUKI!!
HE'S THE SOLE REASON WHY YUKI IS--
YOU'RE ABSOLUTELY RIGHT. BECAUSE OF MY BROTHER'S MIND GAMES, EIRI-KUN HAS SUFFERED EXTREME PSYCHOLOGICAL DAMAGE AND IS AN EMOTIONAL CRIPPLE EVEN TO THIS DAY.
MY BROTHER HAD A LOT TO ANSWER FOR.
I'M SORRY, IT'S JUST THAT THE WAY I REMEMBER MY BROTHER WAS AS A KIND, HONEST, AND GENTLE PERSON.
See ya, Yoshiki. I'm going to tutor that cute Eiri-kun again today.
Are you going to work, Yuki oni-chan?
I DON'T MEAN TO MAKE EXCUSES FOR HIM, BUT REALLY, THAT'S HOW HE WAS WITH ME.
I GUESS YOU REALLY CAN'T TELL ABOUT A PERSON, CAN YOU?

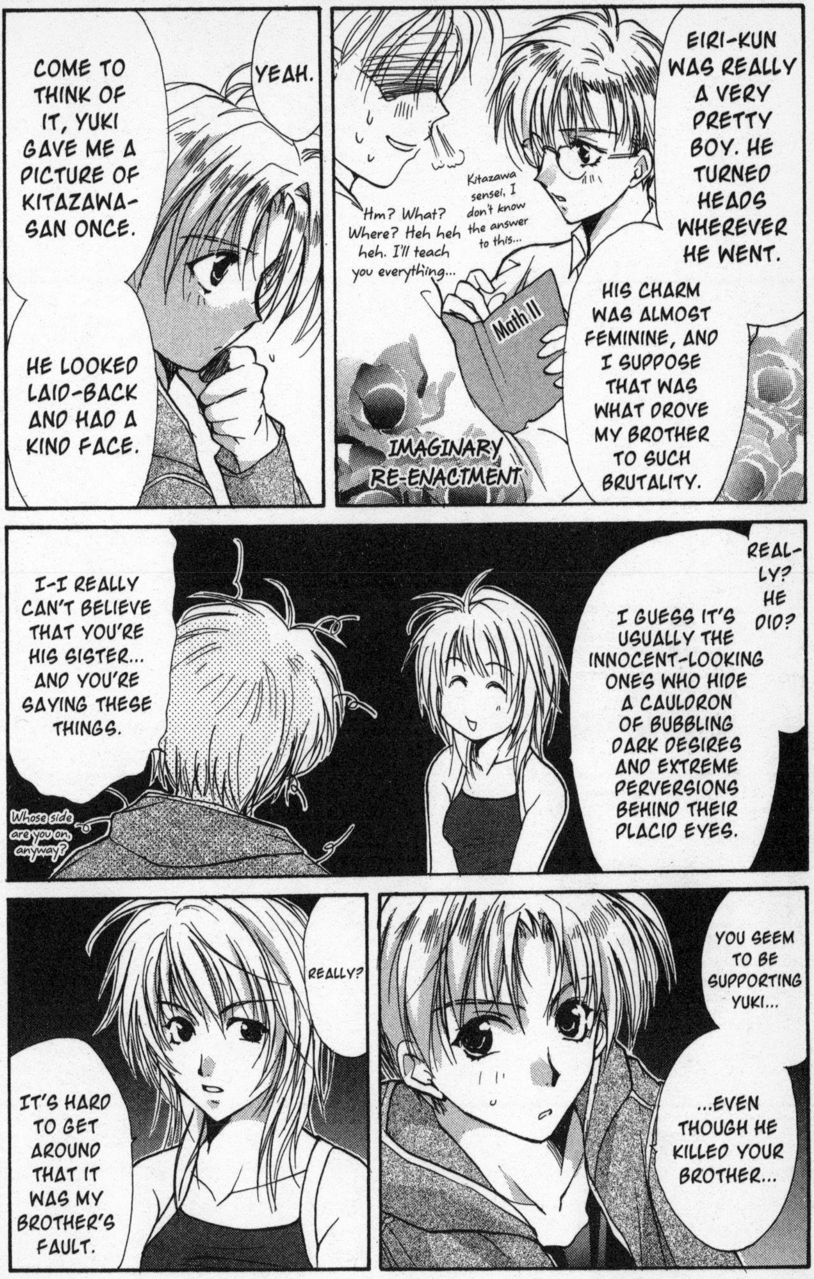
EIRI-KUN WAS REALLY A VERY PRETTY BOY. HE TURNED HEADS WHEREVER HE WENT.
Kitazawa sensei, I don't know the answer to this...
Hm? What? Where? Heh heh heh. I'll teach you everything...
Math II
HIS CHARM WAS ALMOST FEMININE, AND I SUPPOSE THAT WAS WHAT DROVE MY BROTHER TO SUCH BRUTALITY.
IMAGINARY RE-ENACTMENT
YEAH.
COME TO THINK OF IT, YUKI GAVE ME A PICTURE OF KITAZAWA-SAN ONCE.
HE LOOKED LAID-BACK AND HAD A KIND FACE.
REAL-LY? HE DID?
I GUESS IT'S USUALLY THE INNOCENT-LOOKING ONES WHO HIDE A CAULDRON OF BUBBLING DARK DESIRES AND EXTREME PERVERSIONS BEHIND THEIR PLACID EYES.
I-I REALLY CAN'T BELIEVE THAT YOU'RE HIS SISTER... AND YOU'RE SAYING THESE THINGS.
Whose side are you on, anyway?
YOU SEEM TO BE SUPPORTING YUKI...
...EVEN THOUGH HE KILLED YOUR BROTHER...
REALLY?
IT'S HARD TO GET AROUND THAT IT WAS MY BROTHER'S FAULT.

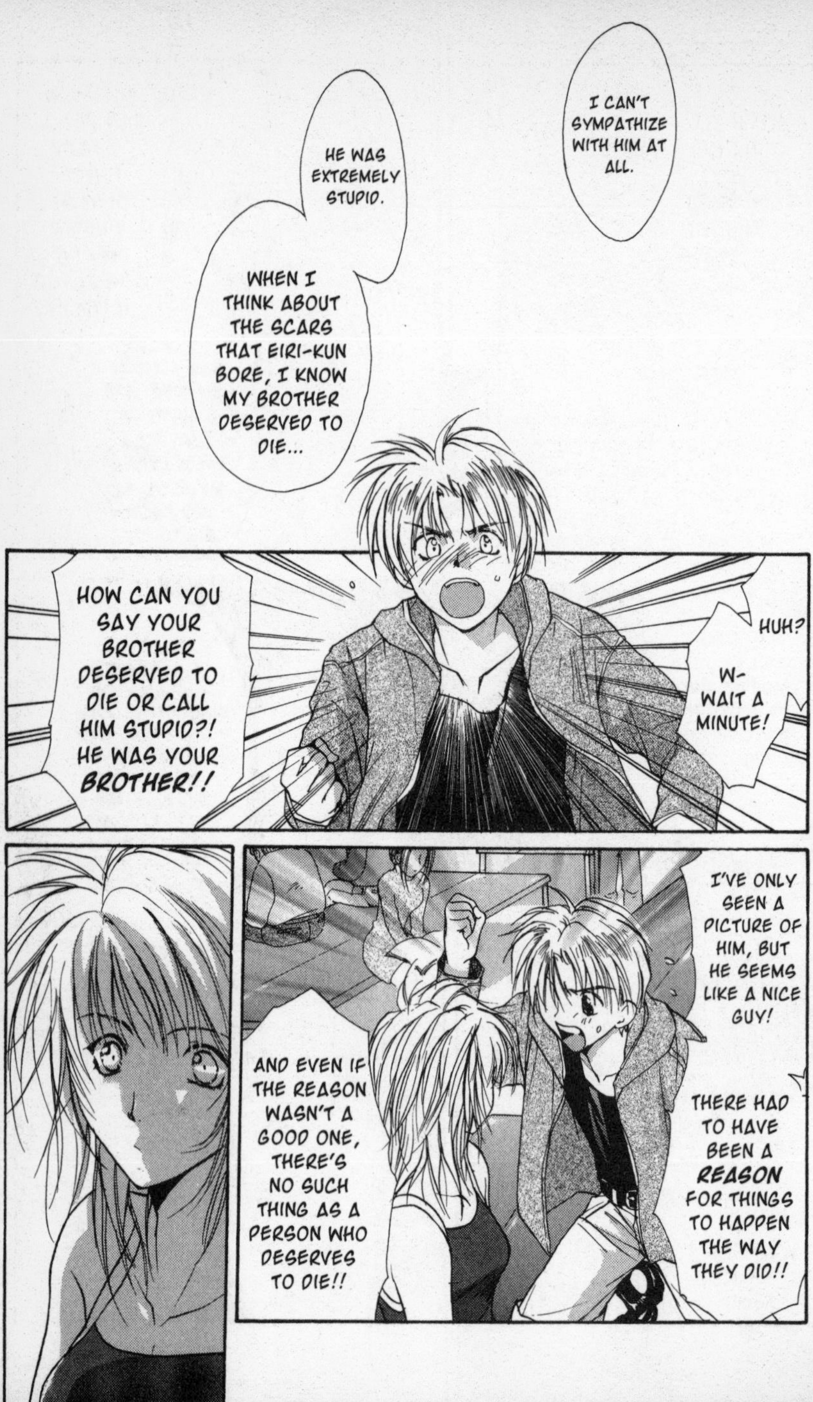
I CAN'T SYMPATHIZE WITH HIM AT ALL.
HE WAS EXTREMELY STUPID.
WHEN I THINK ABOUT THE SCARS THAT EIRI-KUN BORE, I KNOW MY BROTHER DESERVED TO DIE...
HUH?
W-WAIT A MINUTE!
HOW CAN YOU SAY YOUR BROTHER DESERVED TO DIE OR CALL HIM STUPID?! HE WAS YOUR BROTHER!!
I'VE ONLY SEEN A PICTURE OF HIM, BUT HE SEEMS LIKE A NICE GUY!
THERE HAD TO HAVE BEEN A REASON FOR THINGS TO HAPPEN THE WAY THEY DID!!
AND EVEN IF THE REASON WASN'T A GOOD ONE, THERE'S NO SUCH THING AS A PERSON WHO DESERVES TO DIE!!

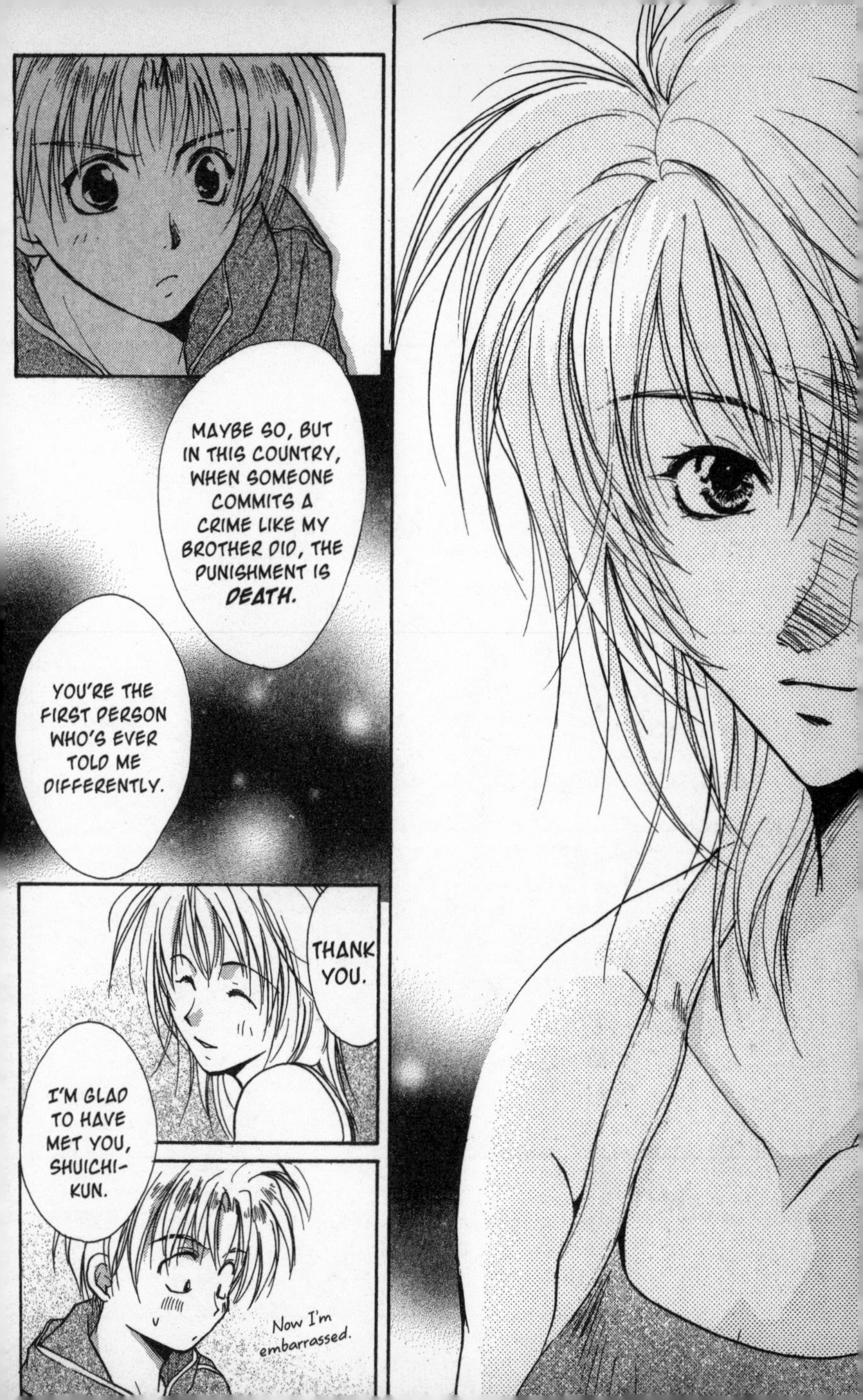
MAYBE SO, BUT IN THIS COUNTRY, WHEN SOMEONE COMMITS A CRIME LIKE MY BROTHER DID, THE PUNISHMENT IS ***DEATH.***
YOU'RE THE FIRST PERSON WHO'S EVER TOLD ME DIFFERENTLY.
THANK YOU.
I'M GLAD TO HAVE MET YOU, SHUICHI-KUN.
Now I'm embarrassed.

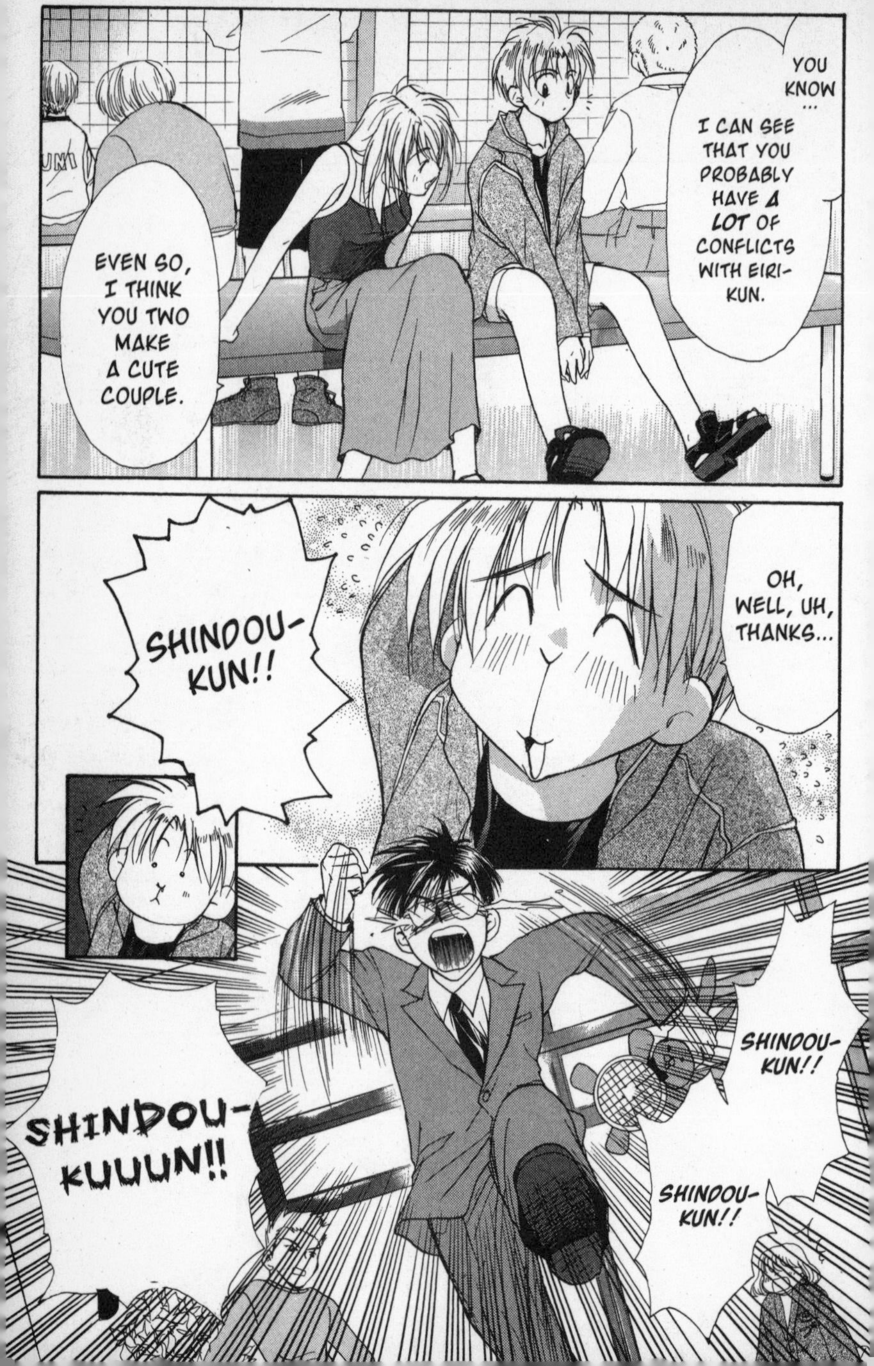
YOU KNOW... I CAN SEE THAT YOU PROBABLY HAVE A LOT OF CONFLICTS WITH EIRI-KUN.
EVEN SO, I THINK YOU TWO MAKE A CUTE COUPLE.
OH, WELL, UH, THANKS...
SHINDOU-KUN!!
SHINDOU-KUN!!
SHINDOU-KUN!!
SHINDOU-KUUUN!!

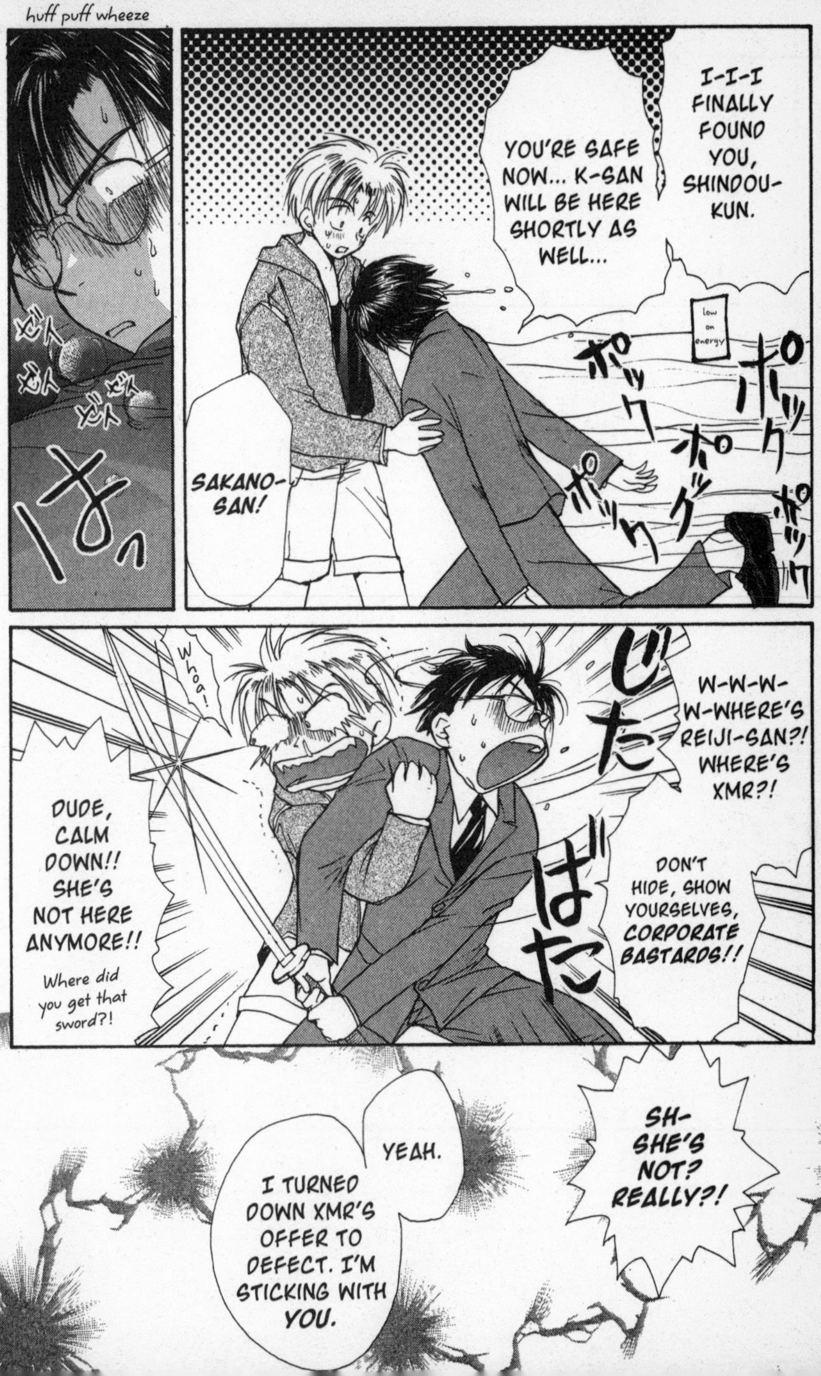
I-I-I FINALLY FOUND YOU, SHINDOU-KUN.
YOU'RE SAFE NOW... K-SAN WILL BE HERE SHORTLY AS WELL...
low on energy
SAKANO-SAN!
huff puff wheeze
W-W-W-W-WHERE'S REIJI-SAN?! WHERE'S XMR?!
DON'T HIDE, SHOW YOURSELVES, CORPORATE BASTARDS!!
Whoa!
DUDE, CALM DOWN!! SHE'S NOT HERE ANYMORE!!
Where did you get that sword?!
SH-SHE'S NOT? REALLY?!
YEAH.
I TURNED DOWN XMR'S OFFER TO DEFECT. I'M STICKING WITH YOU.

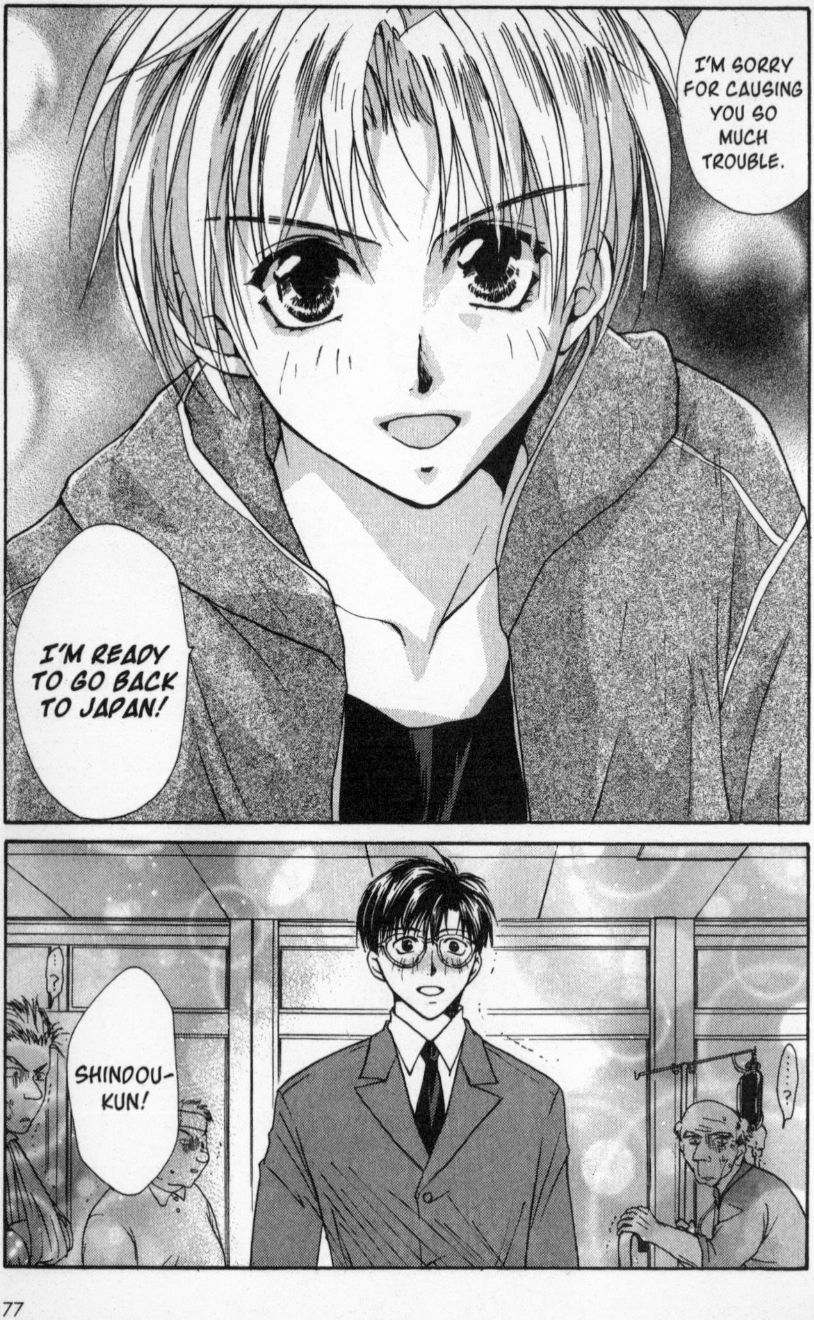
I'M SORRY FOR CAUSING YOU SO MUCH TROUBLE.
I'M READY TO GO BACK TO JAPAN!
...?
SHINDOU-KUN!
...?

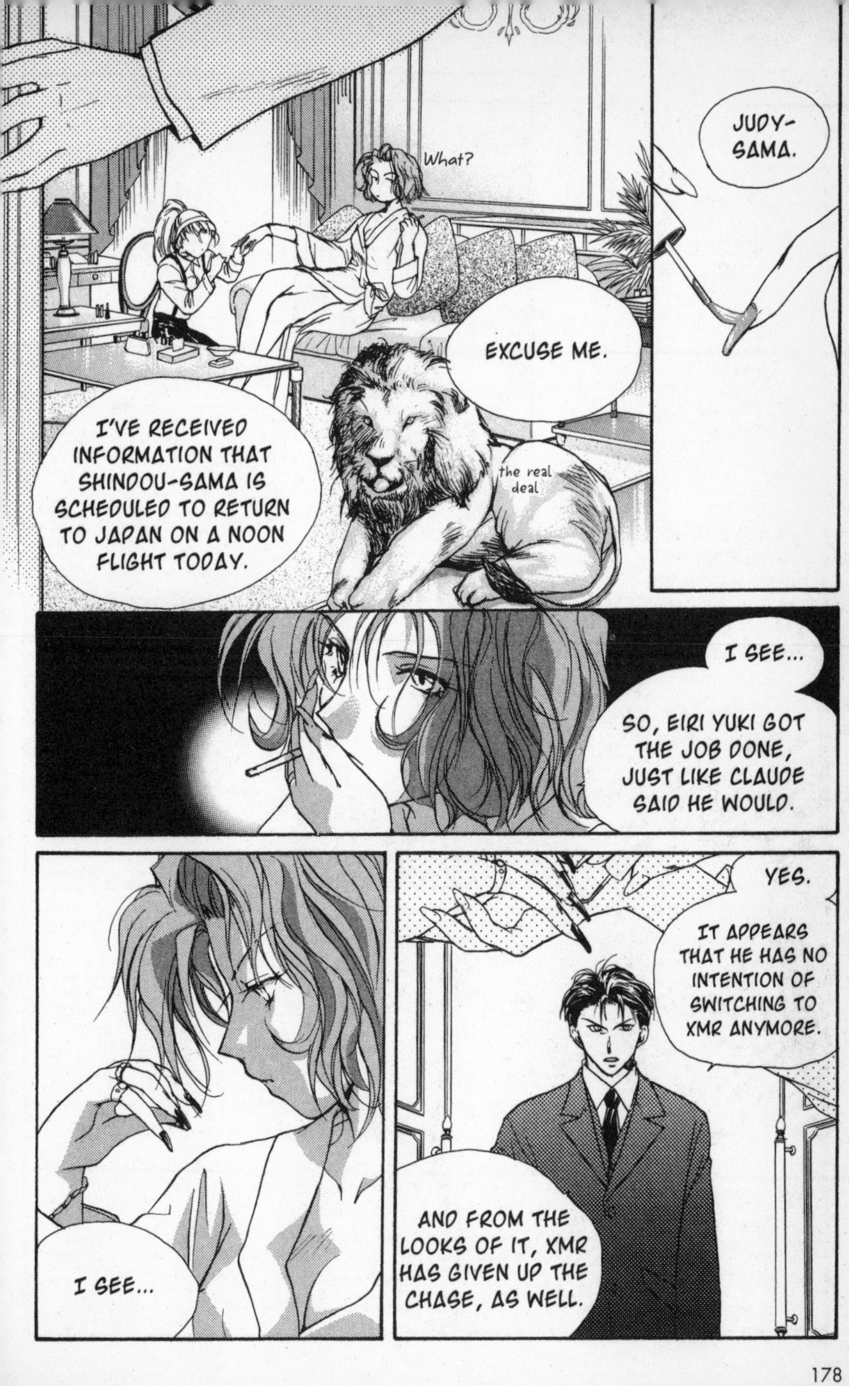
JUDY-SAMA.
What?
EXCUSE ME.
the real deal
I'VE RECEIVED INFORMATION THAT SHINDOU-SAMA IS SCHEDULED TO RETURN TO JAPAN ON A NOON FLIGHT TODAY.
I SEE...
SO, EIRI YUKI GOT THE JOB DONE, JUST LIKE CLAUDE SAID HE WOULD.
YES.
IT APPEARS THAT HE HAS NO INTENTION OF SWITCHING TO XMR ANYMORE.
AND FROM THE LOOKS OF IT, XMR HAS GIVEN UP THE CHASE, AS WELL.
I SEE...

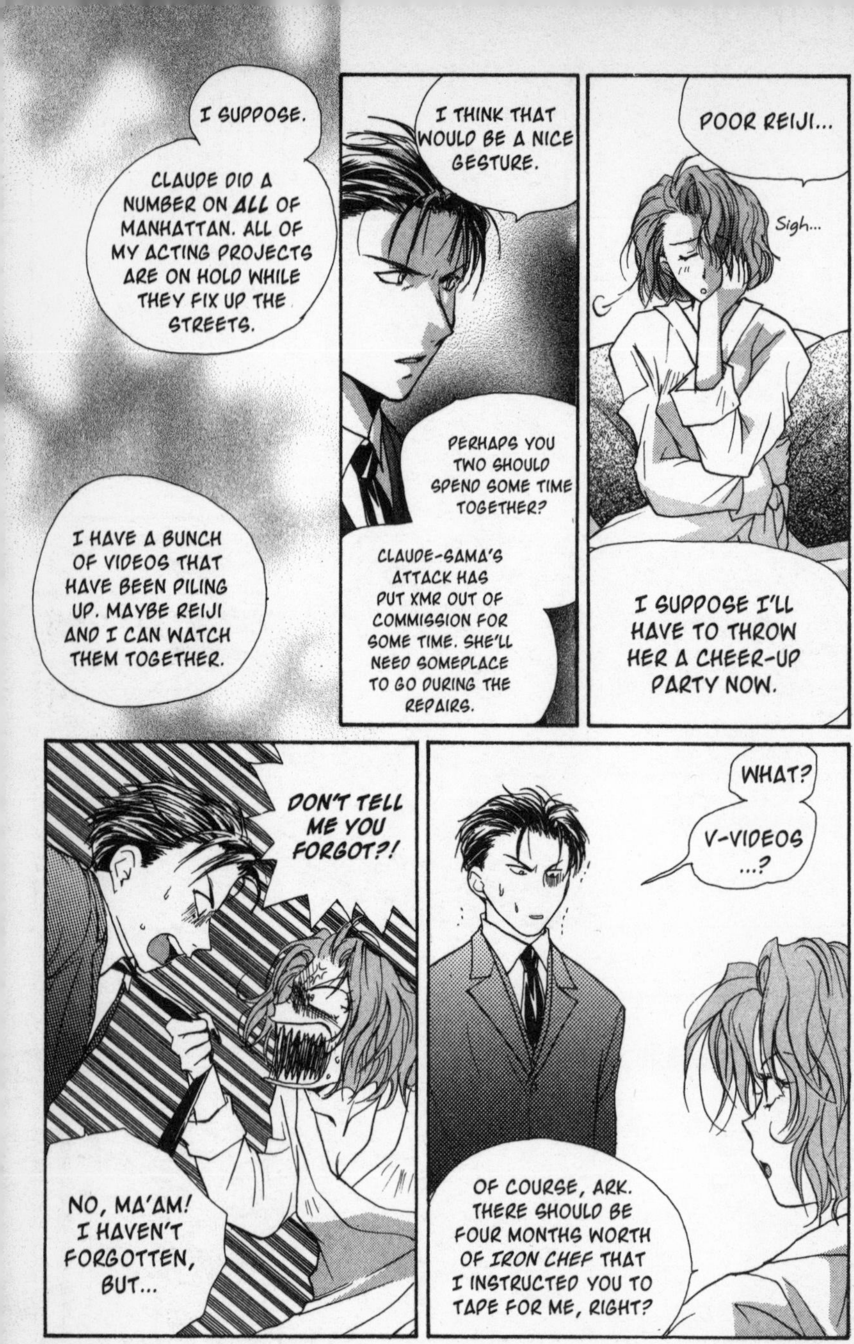
POOR REIJI...
Sigh...
I SUPPOSE I'LL HAVE TO THROW HER A CHEER-UP PARTY NOW.
I THINK THAT WOULD BE A NICE GESTURE.
PERHAPS YOU TWO SHOULD SPEND SOME TIME TOGETHER?
CLAUDE-SAMA'S ATTACK HAS PUT XMR OUT OF COMMISSION FOR SOME TIME. SHE'LL NEED SOMEPLACE TO GO DURING THE REPAIRS.
I SUPPOSE.
CLAUDE DID A NUMBER ON ALL OF MANHATTAN. ALL OF MY ACTING PROJECTS ARE ON HOLD WHILE THEY FIX UP THE STREETS.
I HAVE A BUNCH OF VIDEOS THAT HAVE BEEN PILING UP. MAYBE REIJI AND I CAN WATCH THEM TOGETHER.
WHAT?
V-VIDEOS ...?
OF COURSE, ARK. THERE SHOULD BE FOUR MONTHS WORTH OF IRON CHEF THAT I INSTRUCTED YOU TO TAPE FOR ME, RIGHT?
DON'T TELL ME YOU FORGOT?!
NO, MA'AM! I HAVEN'T FORGOTTEN, BUT...

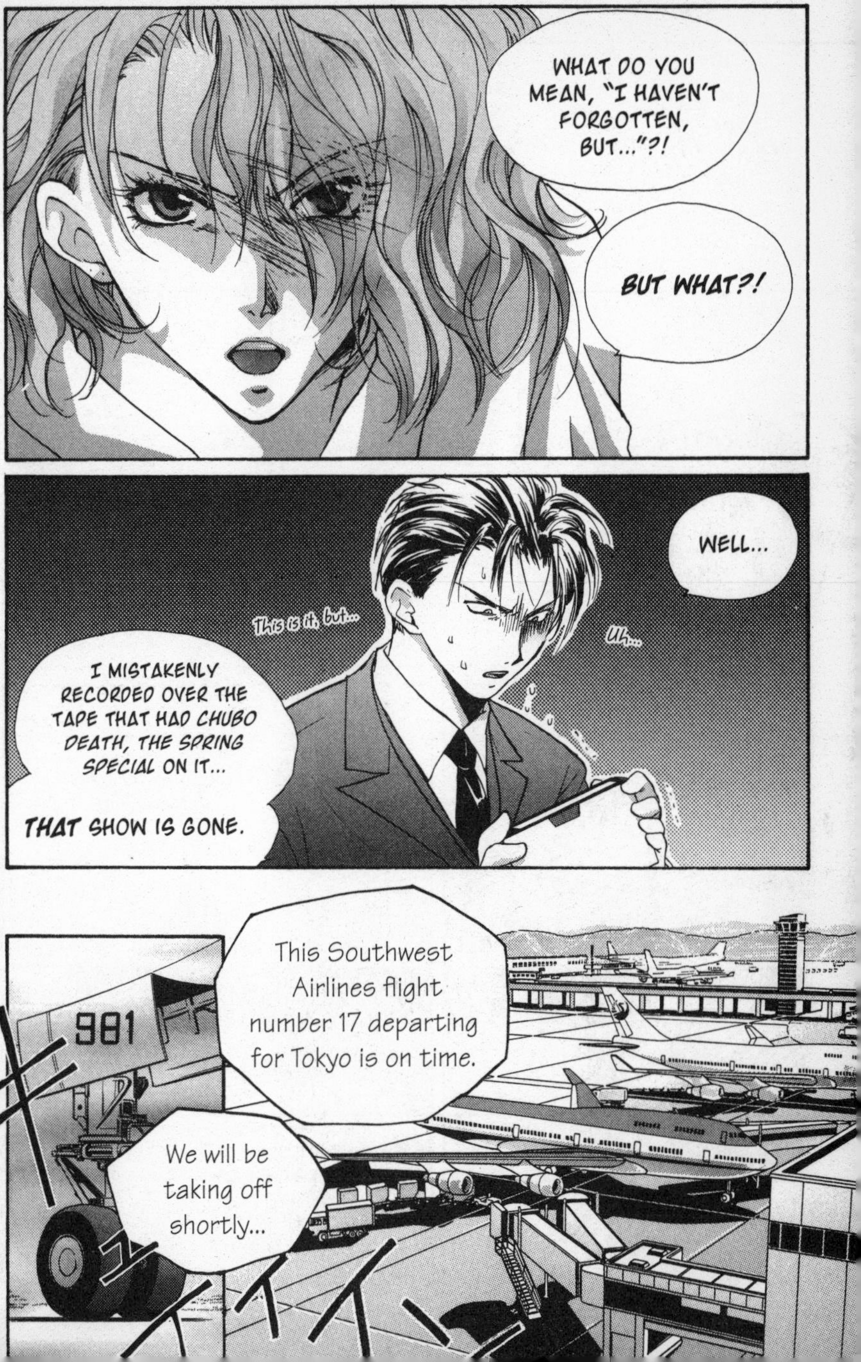
WHAT DO YOU MEAN, "I HAVEN'T FORGOTTEN, BUT..."?!
BUT WHAT?!
WELL...
Uh...
This is it, but...
I MISTAKENLY RECORDED OVER THE TAPE THAT HAD CHUBO DEATH, THE SPRING SPECIAL ON IT...
THAT SHOW IS GONE.
This Southwest Airlines flight number 17 departing for Tokyo is on time.
981
We will be taking off shortly...

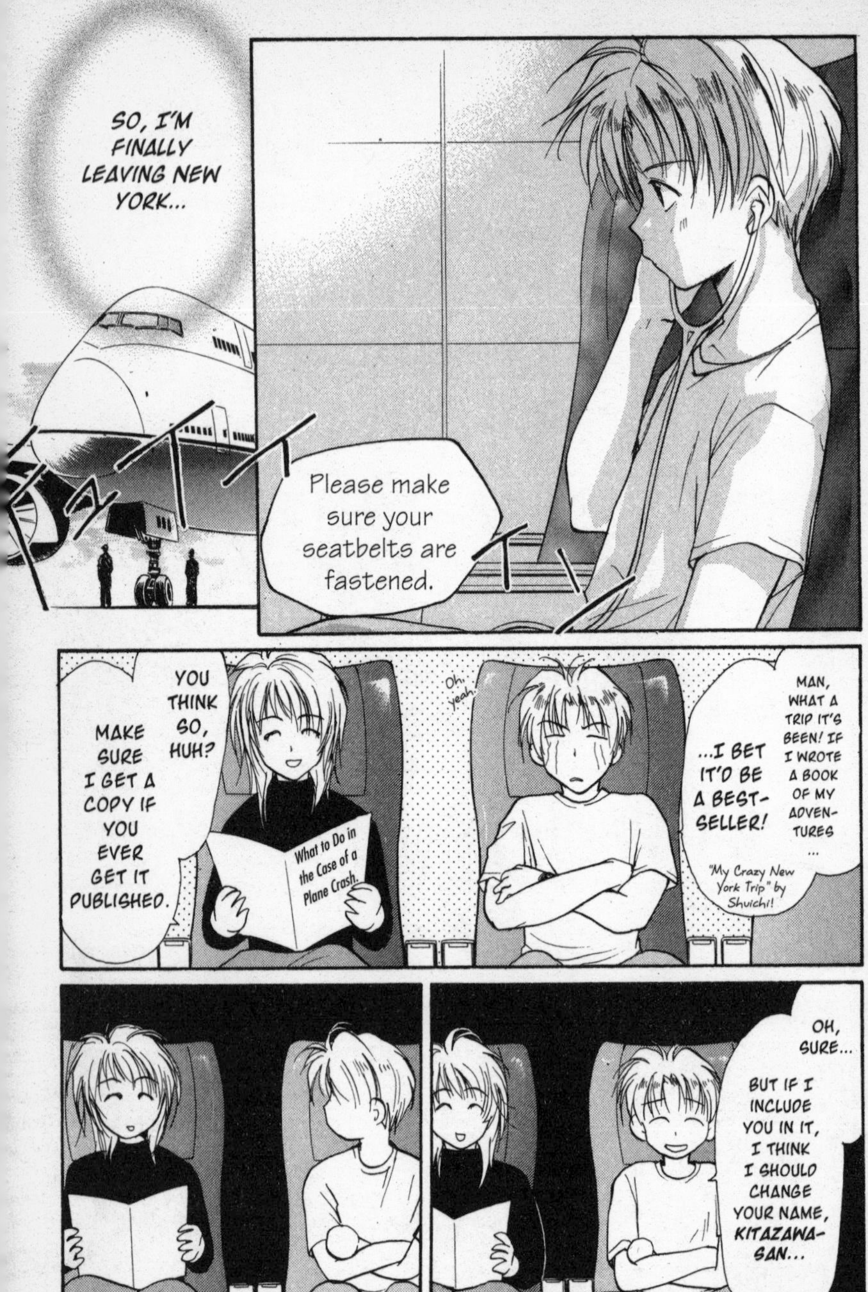
Please make sure your seatbelts are fastened.
SO, I'M FINALLY LEAVING NEW YORK...
MAN, WHAT A TRIP IT'S BEEN! IF I WROTE A BOOK OF MY ADVENTURES ...
...I BET IT'D BE A BEST-SELLER!
"My Crazy New York Trip" by Shuichi!
Oh, yeah.
YOU THINK SO, HUH?
MAKE SURE I GET A COPY IF YOU EVER GET IT PUBLISHED.
What to Do in the Case of a Plane Crash.
OH, SURE...
BUT IF I INCLUDE YOU IN IT, I THINK I SHOULD CHANGE YOUR NAME, KITAZAWA-SAN...

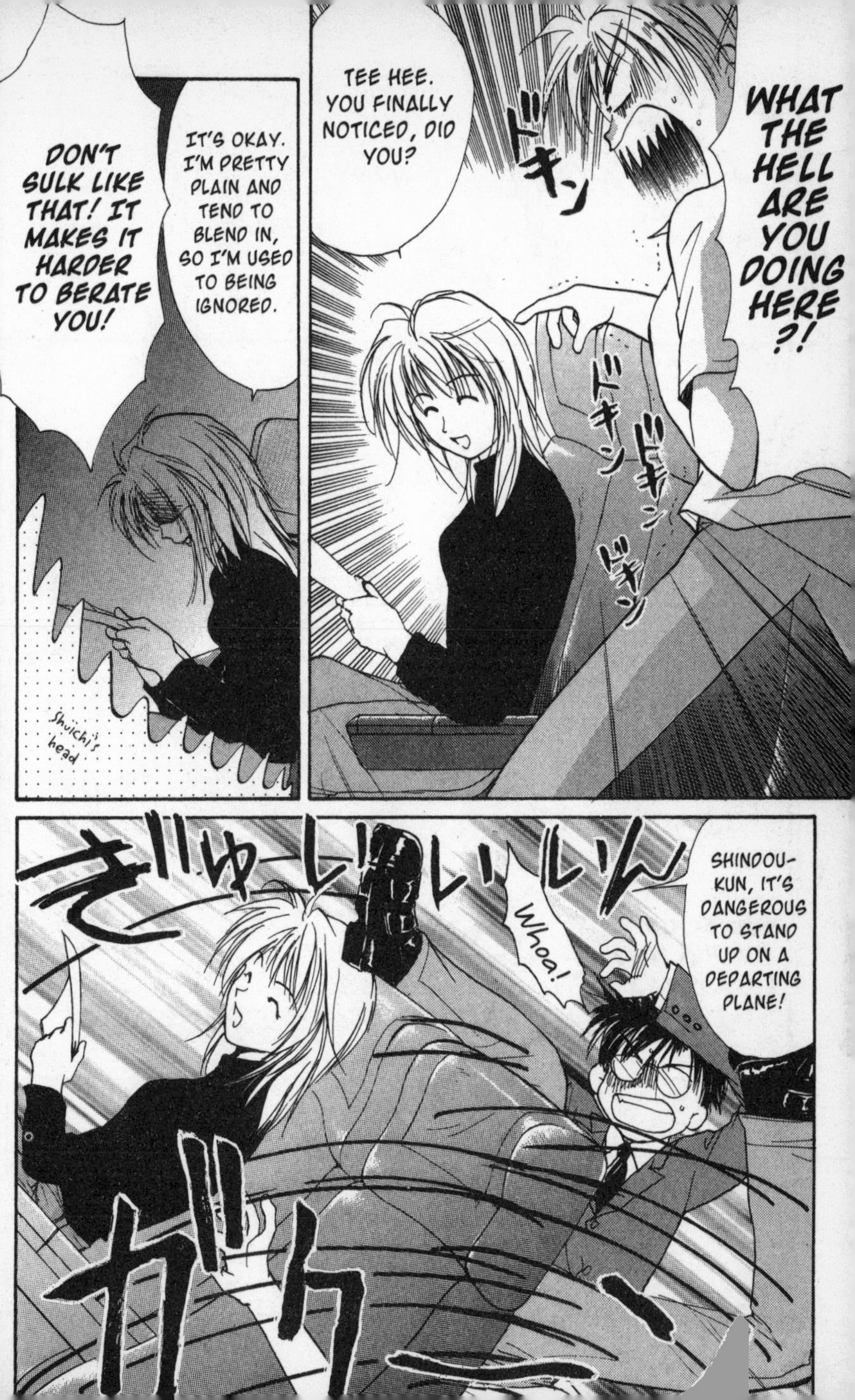
WHAT THE HELL ARE YOU DOING HERE?!
ドキン
TEE HEE. YOU FINALLY NOTICED, DID YOU?
ドキン
ドキン
ドキン
IT'S OKAY. I'M PRETTY PLAIN AND TEND TO BLEND IN, SO I'M USED TO BEING IGNORED.
DON'T SULK LIKE THAT! IT MAKES IT HARDER TO BERATE YOU!
Shuichi's head
SHINDOU-KUN, IT'S DANGEROUS TO STAND UP ON A DEPARTING PLANE!
Whoa!

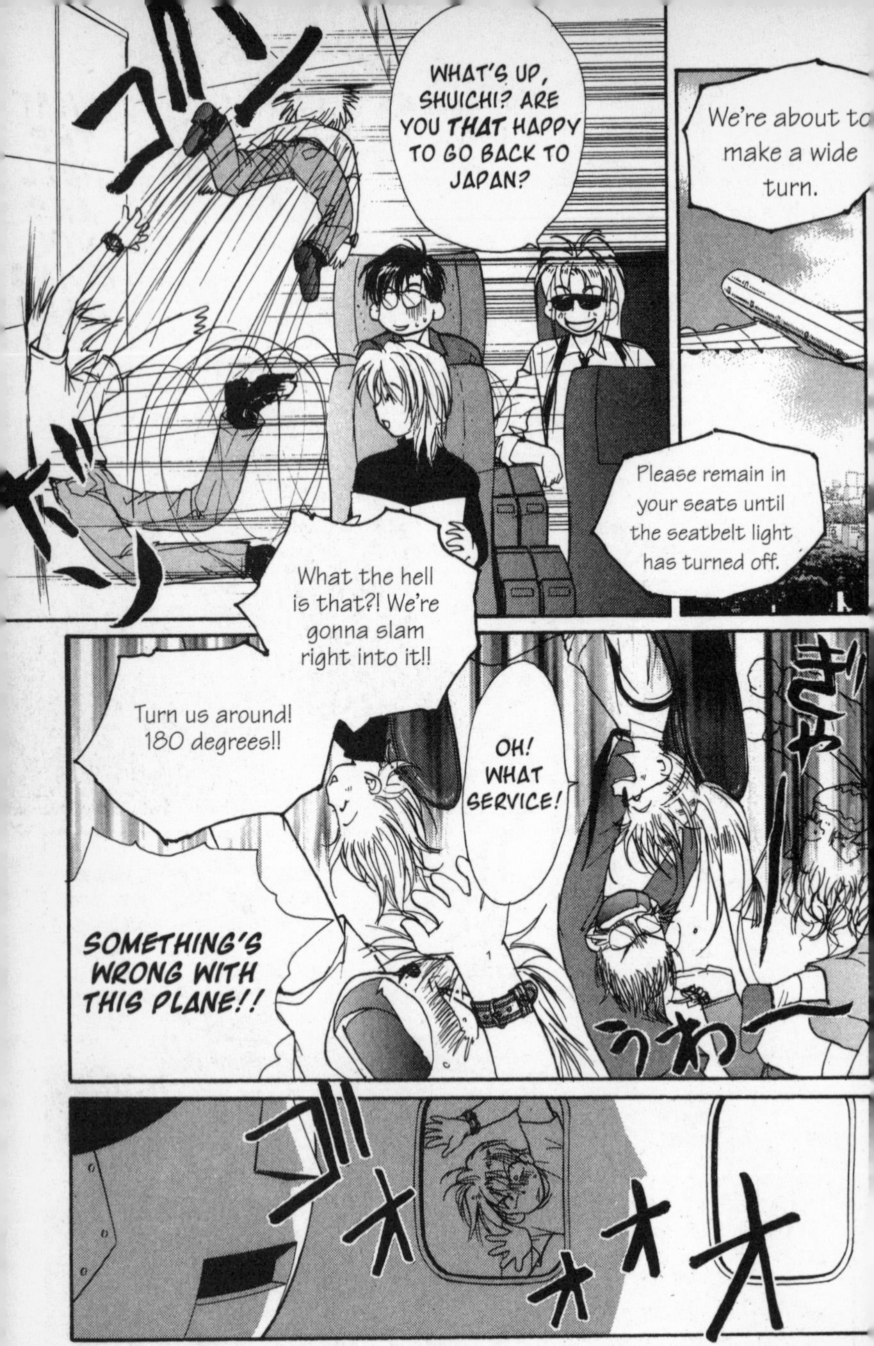
We're about to make a wide turn.
Please remain in your seats until the seatbelt light has turned off.
WHAT'S UP, SHUICHI? ARE YOU THAT HAPPY TO GO BACK TO JAPAN?
What the hell is that?! We're gonna slam right into it!!
Turn us around! 180 degrees!!
OH! WHAT SERVICE!
SOMETHING'S WRONG WITH THIS PLANE!!

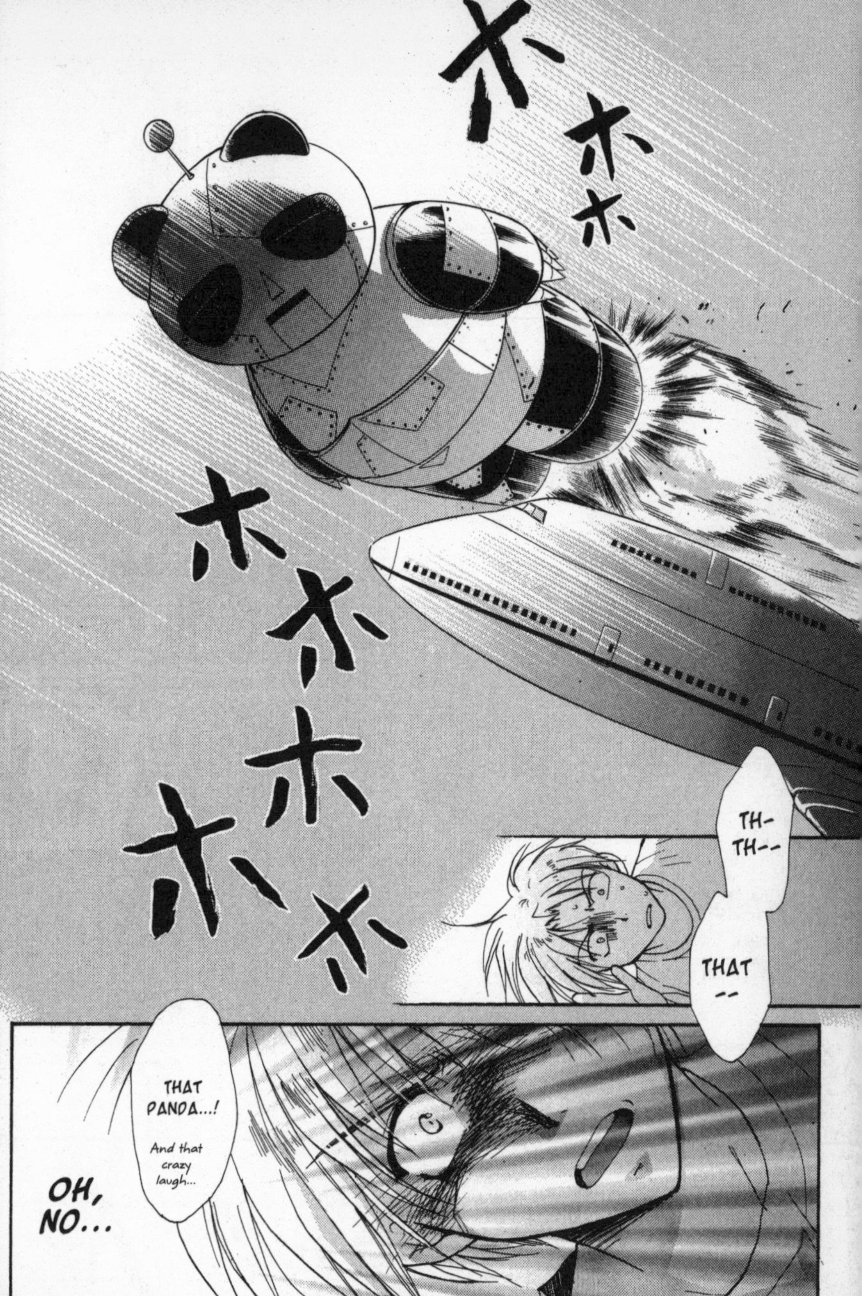
ホホホ
ホホホホホ
TH- TH--
THAT --
THAT PANDA...!
And that crazy laugh...
OH, NO...

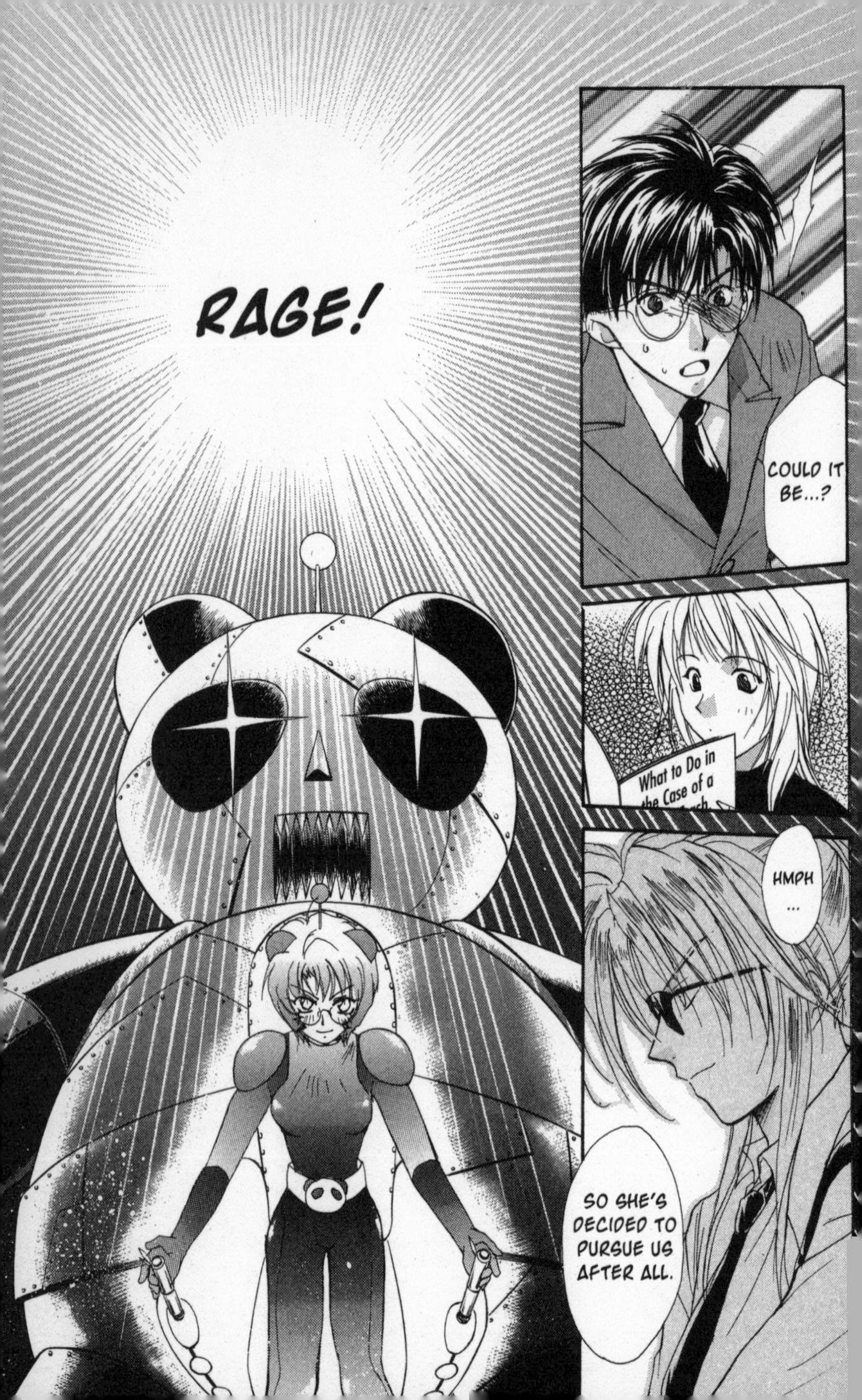
COULD IT BE...?
What to Do in the Case of a
HMPH ...
SO SHE'S DECIDED TO PURSUE US AFTER ALL.
RAGE!

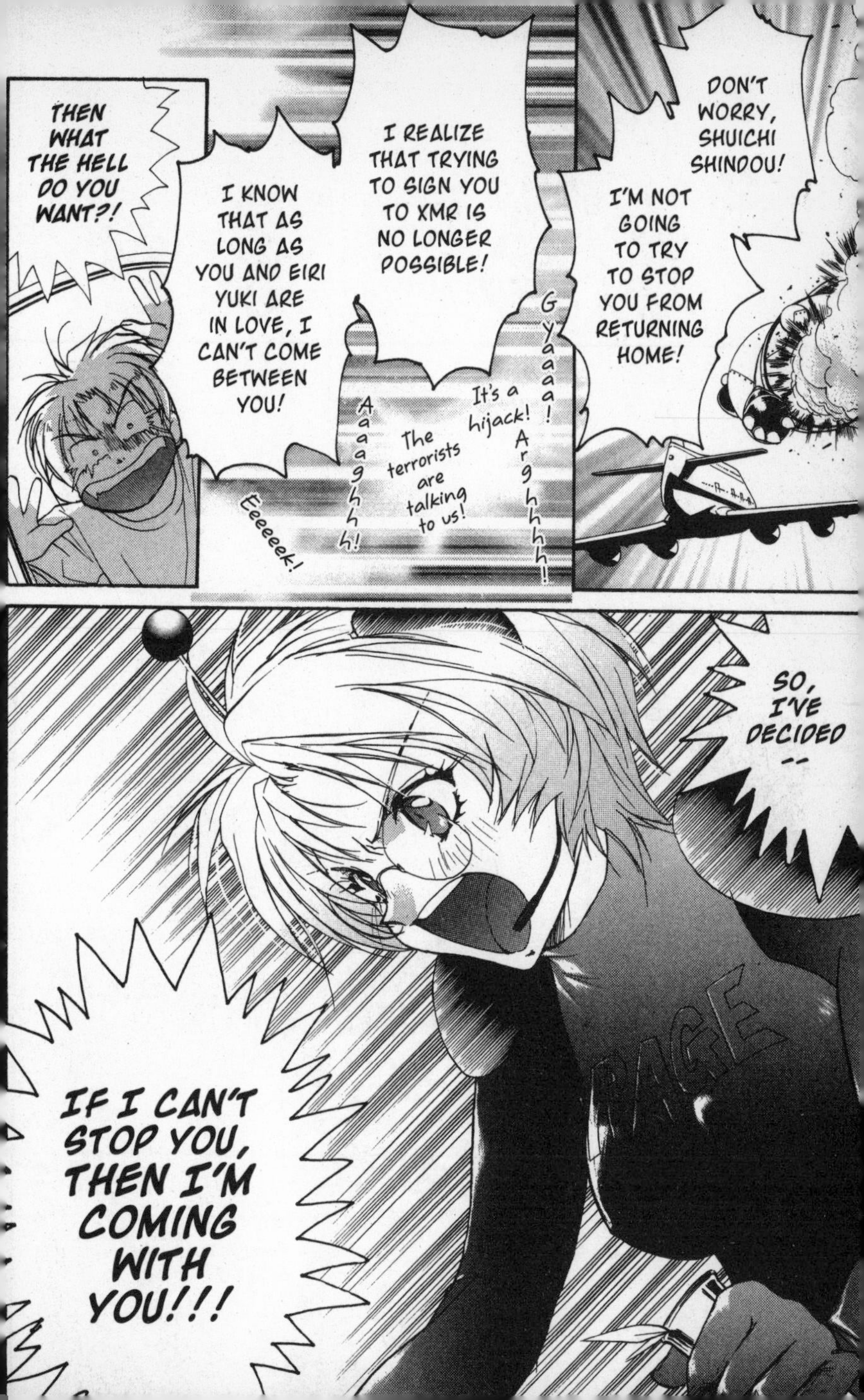
DON'T WORRY, SHUICHI SHINDOU!
I'M NOT GOING TO TRY TO STOP YOU FROM RETURNING HOME!
I REALIZE THAT TRYING TO SIGN YOU TO XMR IS NO LONGER POSSIBLE!
I KNOW THAT AS LONG AS YOU AND EIRI YUKI ARE IN LOVE, I CAN'T COME BETWEEN YOU!
Gyaaaaa!
It's a hijack!
Arghhhh!
The terrorists are talking to us!
Aaaaghhhh!
Eeeeeek!
THEN WHAT THE HELL DO YOU WANT?!
SO, I'VE DECIDED --
IF I CAN'T STOP YOU, THEN I'M COMING WITH YOU!!!

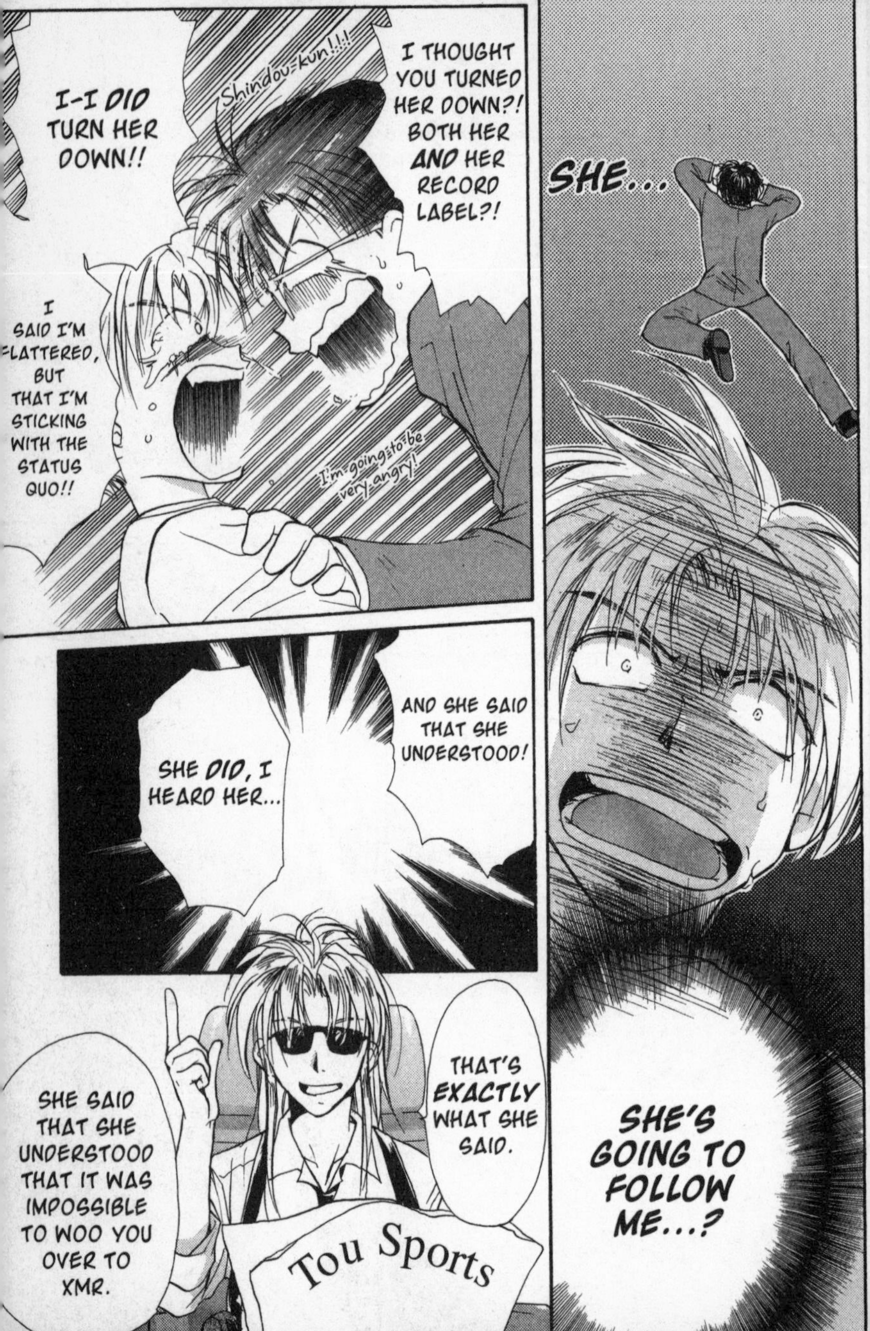
SHE...
SHE'S GOING TO FOLLOW ME...?
I THOUGHT YOU TURNED HER DOWN?! BOTH HER AND HER RECORD LABEL?!
Shindou-kun!!!
I-I DID TURN HER DOWN!!
I'm going to be very angry!
I SAID I'M FLATTERED, BUT THAT I'M STICKING WITH THE STATUS QUO!!
AND SHE SAID THAT SHE UNDERSTOOD!
SHE DID, I HEARD HER...
THAT'S EXACTLY WHAT SHE SAID.
SHE SAID THAT SHE UNDERSTOOD THAT IT WAS IMPOSSIBLE TO WOO YOU OVER TO XMR.
Tou Sports

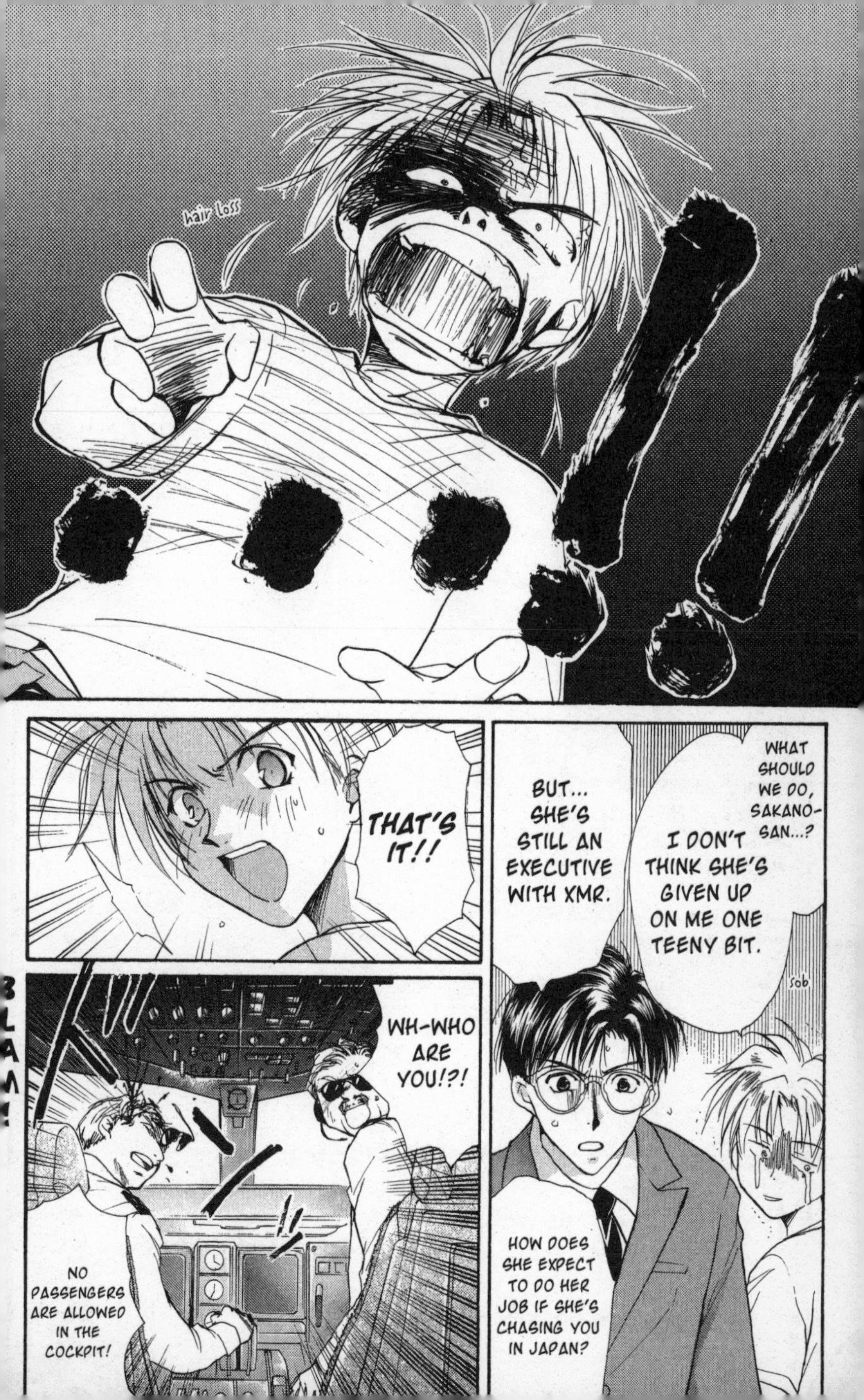
hair loss
WHAT SHOULD WE DO, SAKANO-SAN...?
I DON'T THINK SHE'S GIVEN UP ON ME ONE TEENY BIT.
sob
BUT... SHE'S STILL AN EXECUTIVE WITH XMR.
HOW DOES SHE EXPECT TO DO HER JOB IF SHE'S CHASING YOU IN JAPAN?
THAT'S IT!!
WH-WHO ARE YOU!?!
NO PASSENGERS ARE ALLOWED IN THE COCKPIT!
BLAM!

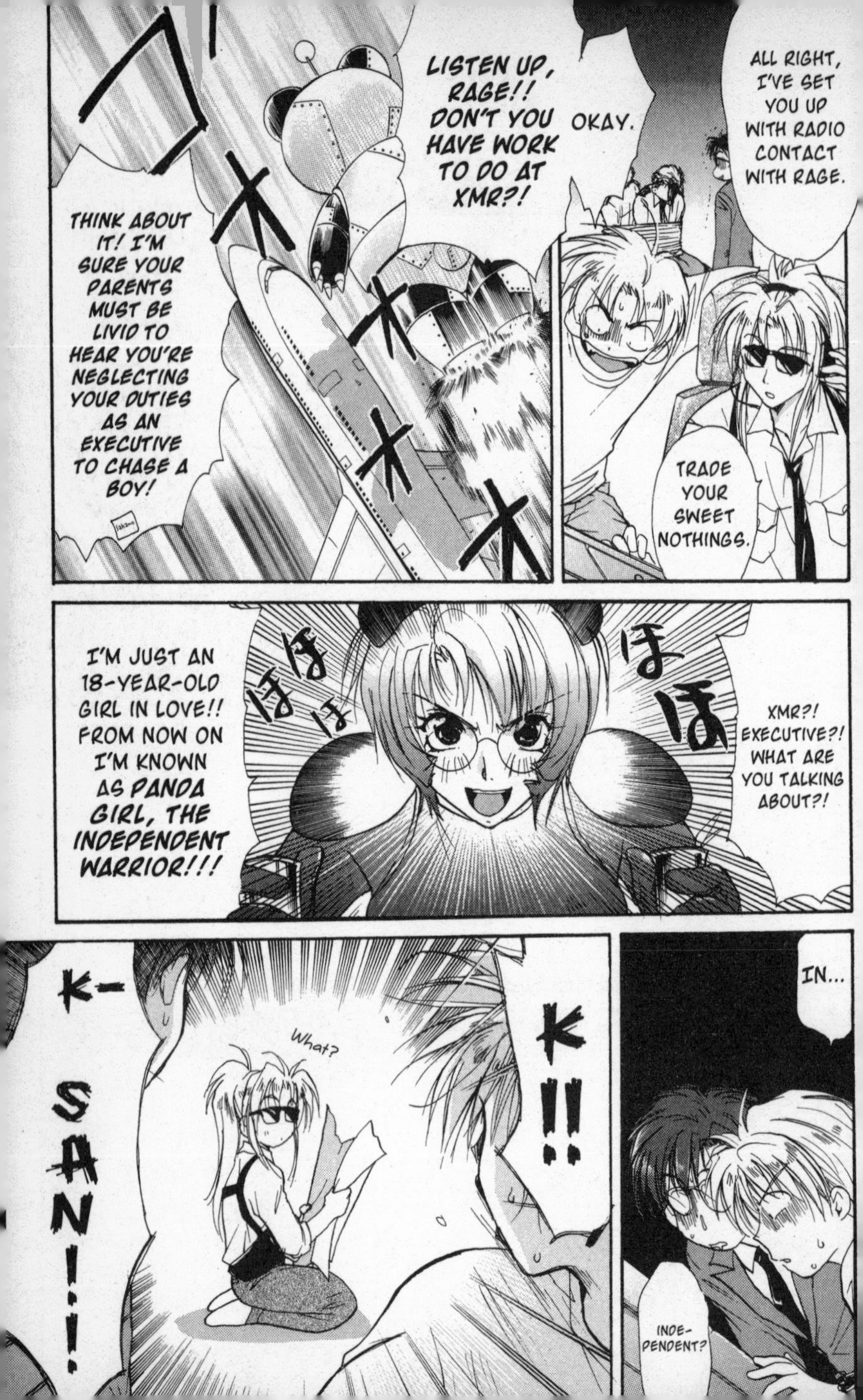
ALL RIGHT, I'VE SET YOU UP WITH RADIO CONTACT WITH RAGE.
OKAY.
TRADE YOUR SWEET NOTHINGS.
LISTEN UP, RAGE!! DON'T YOU HAVE WORK TO DO AT XMR?!
THINK ABOUT IT! I'M SURE YOUR PARENTS MUST BE LIVID TO HEAR YOU'RE NEGLECTING YOUR DUTIES AS AN EXECUTIVE TO CHASE A BOY!
XMR?! EXECUTIVE?! WHAT ARE YOU TALKING ABOUT?!
ほほ
ほほほ
I'M JUST AN 18-YEAR-OLD GIRL IN LOVE!! FROM NOW ON I'M KNOWN AS PANDA GIRL, THE INDEPENDENT WARRIOR!!!
IN...
INDE-PENDENT?
K!!
What?
K-
SAN!!!

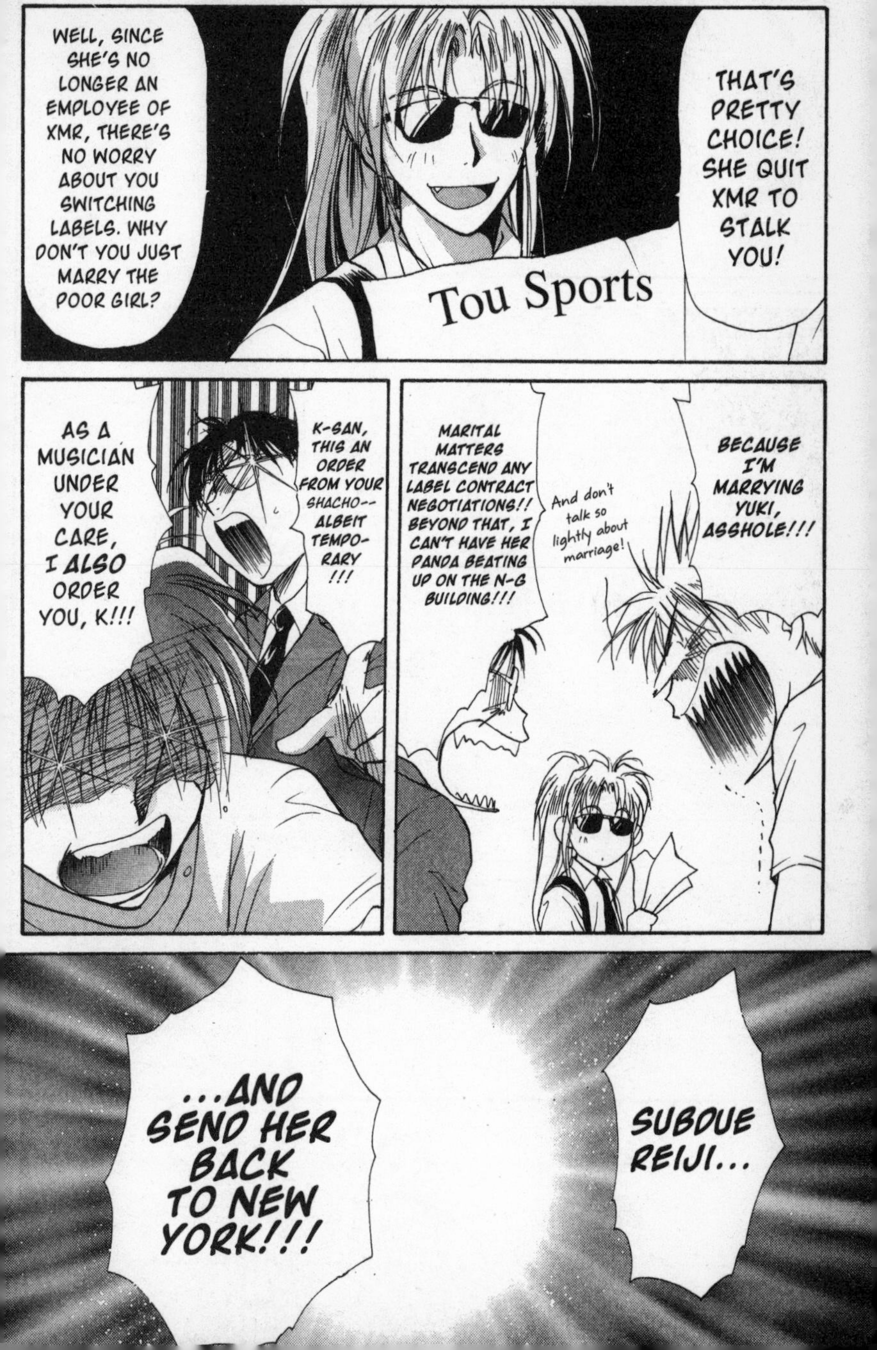
THAT'S PRETTY CHOICE! SHE QUIT XMR TO STALK YOU!
Tou Sports
WELL, SINCE SHE'S NO LONGER AN EMPLOYEE OF XMR, THERE'S NO WORRY ABOUT YOU SWITCHING LABELS. WHY DON'T YOU JUST MARRY THE POOR GIRL?
BECAUSE I'M MARRYING YUKI, ASSHOLE!!!
And don't talk so lightly about marriage!
MARITAL MATTERS TRANSCEND ANY LABEL CONTRACT NEGOTIATIONS!! BEYOND THAT, I CAN'T HAVE HER PANDA BEATING UP ON THE N-G BUILDING!!!
K-SAN, THIS AN ORDER FROM YOUR SHACHO-- ALBEIT TEMPORARY!!!
AS A MUSICIAN UNDER YOUR CARE, I ALSO ORDER YOU, K!!!
SUBDUE REIJI...
...AND SEND HER BACK TO NEW YORK!!!

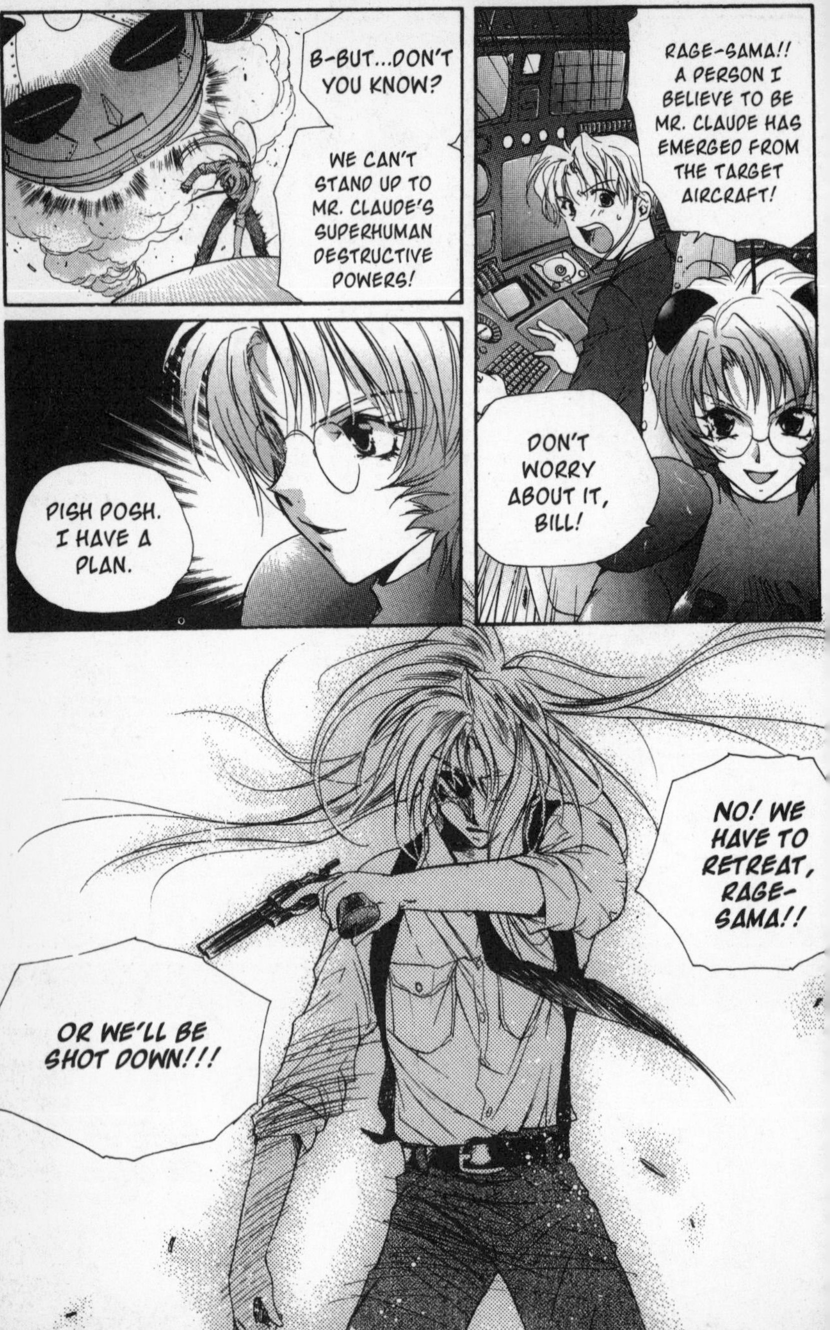
RAGE-SAMA!! A PERSON I BELIEVE TO BE MR. CLAUDE HAS EMERGED FROM THE TARGET AIRCRAFT!
DON'T WORRY ABOUT IT, BILL!
B-BUT...DON'T YOU KNOW?
WE CAN'T STAND UP TO MR. CLAUDE'S SUPERHUMAN DESTRUCTIVE POWERS!
PISH POSH. I HAVE A PLAN.
NO! WE HAVE TO RETREAT, RAGE-SAMA!!
OR WE'LL BE SHOT DOWN!!!

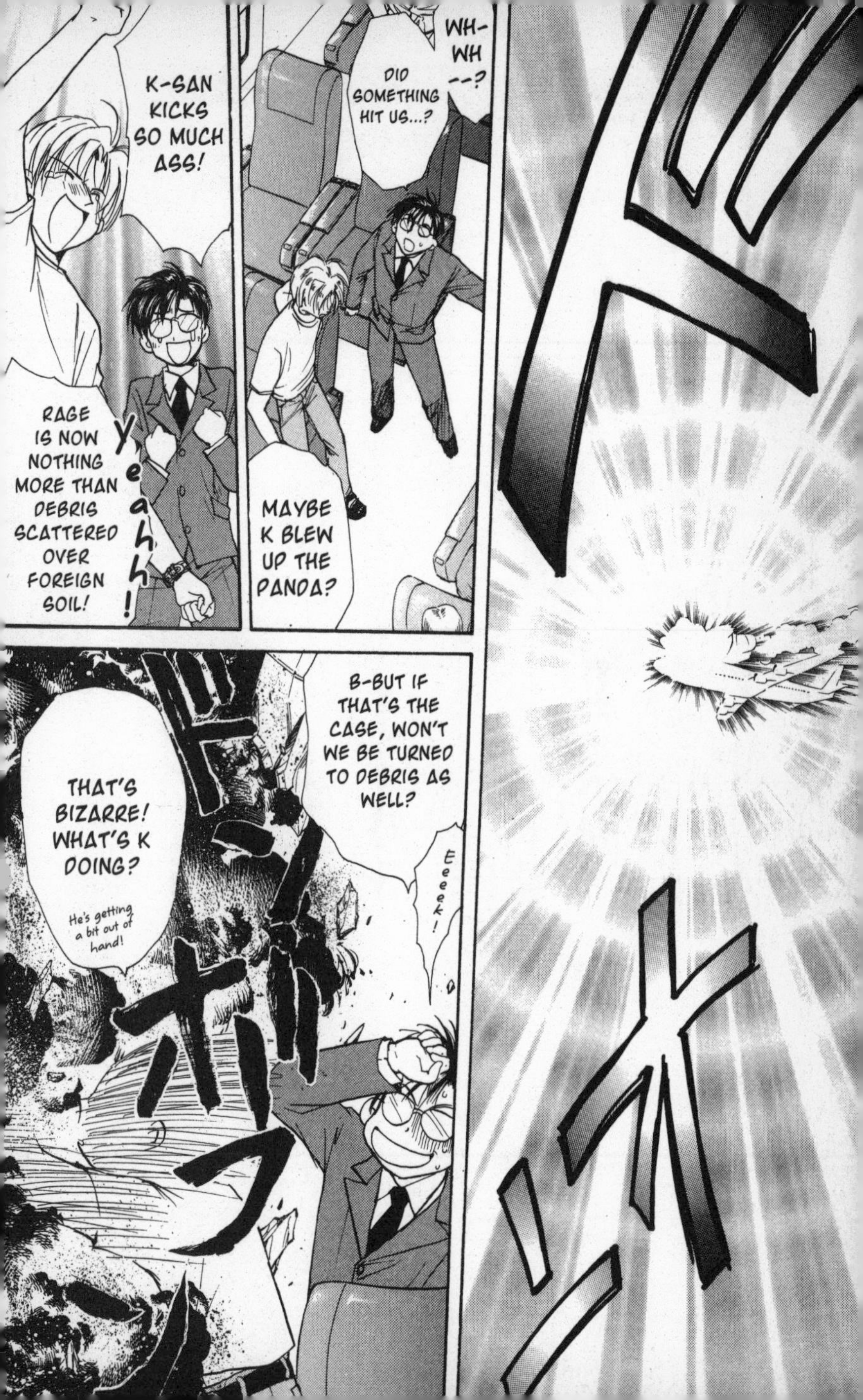
WH-WH--?
DID SOMETHING HIT US...?
MAYBE K BLEW UP THE PANDA?
K-SAN KICKS SO MUCH ASS!
RAGE IS NOW NOTHING MORE THAN DEBRIS SCATTERED OVER FOREIGN SOIL!
Yeahh!
B-BUT IF THAT'S THE CASE, WON'T WE BE TURNED TO DEBRIS AS WELL?
Eeeek!
THAT'S BIZARRE! WHAT'S K DOING?
He's getting a bit out of hand!

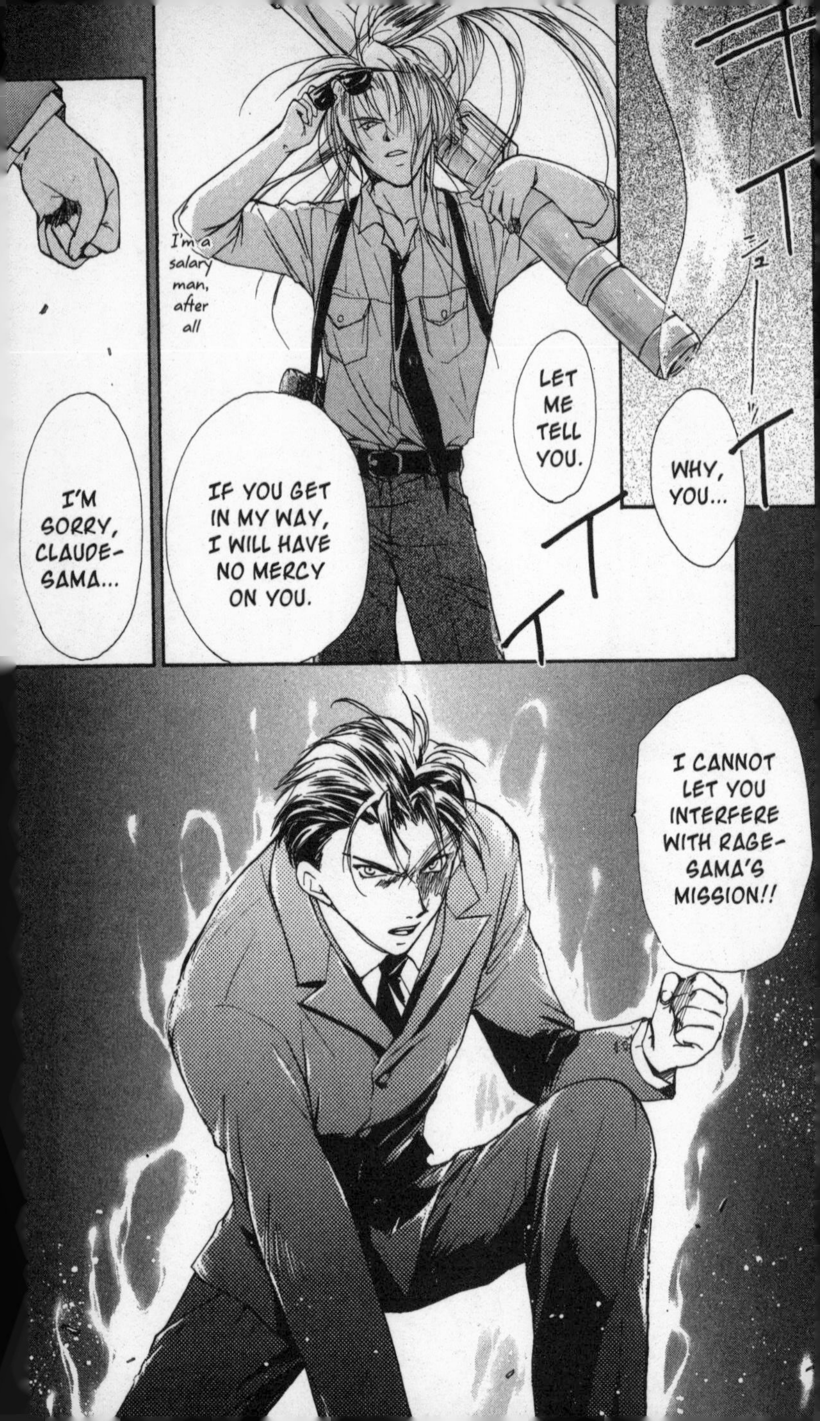
WHY, YOU...
LET ME TELL YOU.
I'm a salary man, after all
IF YOU GET IN MY WAY, I WILL HAVE NO MERCY ON YOU.
I'M SORRY, CLAUDE-SAMA...
I CANNOT LET YOU INTERFERE WITH RAGE-SAMA'S MISSION!!

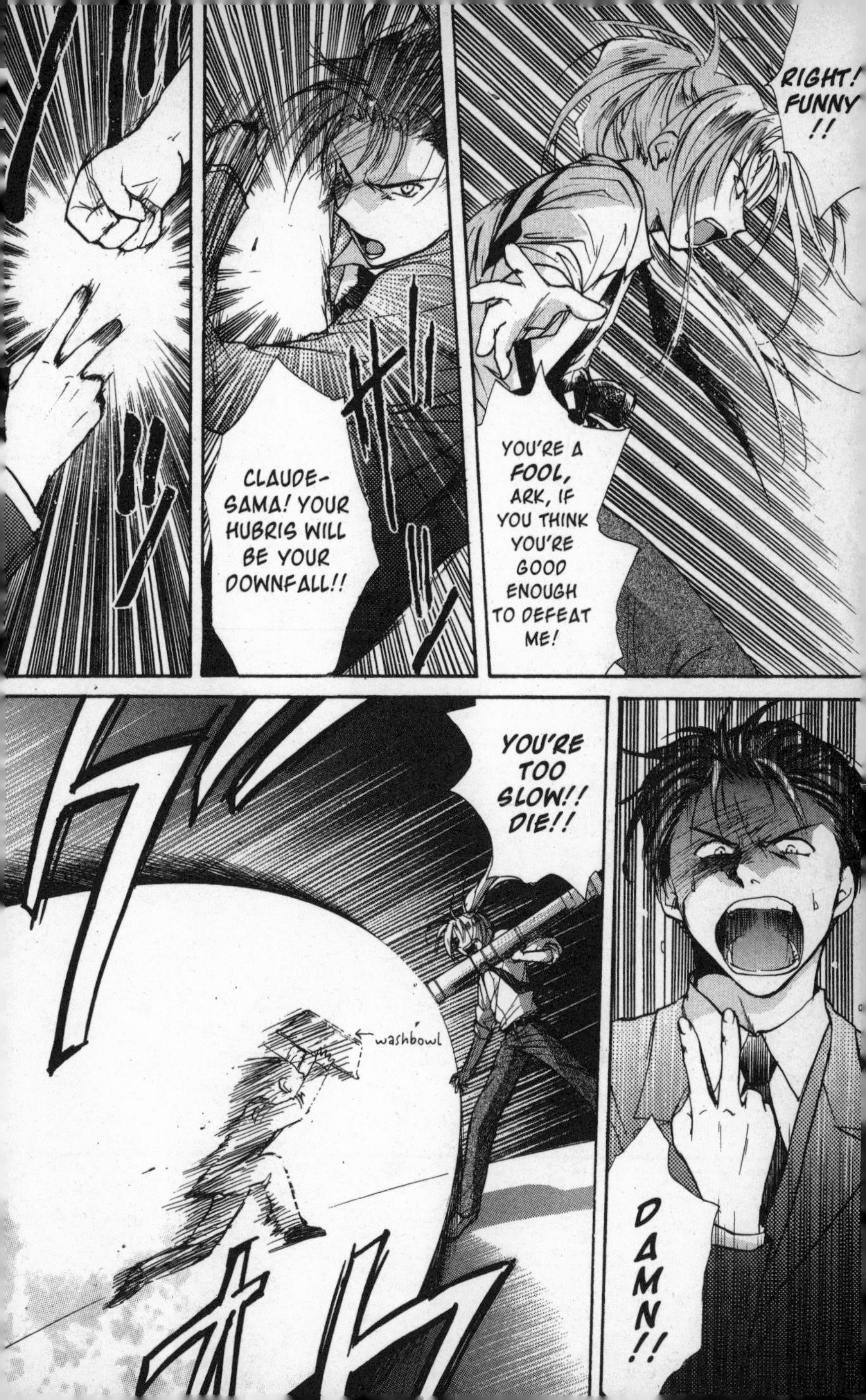
RIGHT! FUNNY!!
YOU'RE A FOOL, ARK, IF YOU THINK YOU'RE GOOD ENOUGH TO DEFEAT ME!
CLAUDE-SAMA! YOUR HUBRIS WILL BE YOUR DOWNFALL!!
DAMN!!
YOU'RE TOO SLOW!! DIE!!
washbowl

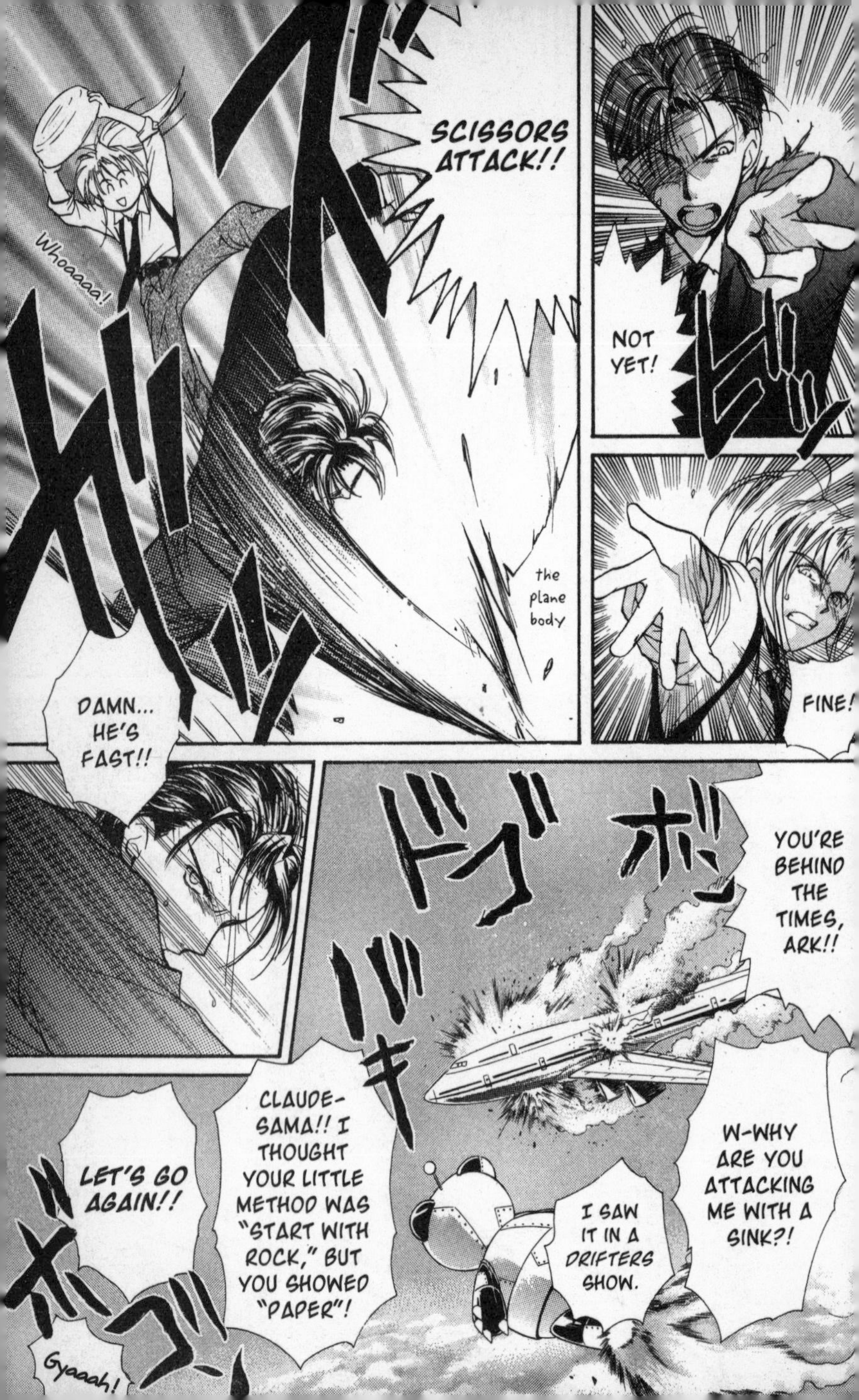
NOT YET!
FINE!
SCISSORS ATTACK!!
Whoaaaa!
the plane body
DAMN... HE'S FAST!!
YOU'RE BEHIND THE TIMES, ARK!!
W-WHY ARE YOU ATTACKING ME WITH A SINK?!
I SAW IT IN A DRIFTERS SHOW.
CLAUDE-SAMA!! I THOUGHT YOUR LITTLE METHOD WAS "START WITH ROCK," BUT YOU SHOWED "PAPER"!
LET'S GO AGAIN!!
Gyaaah!

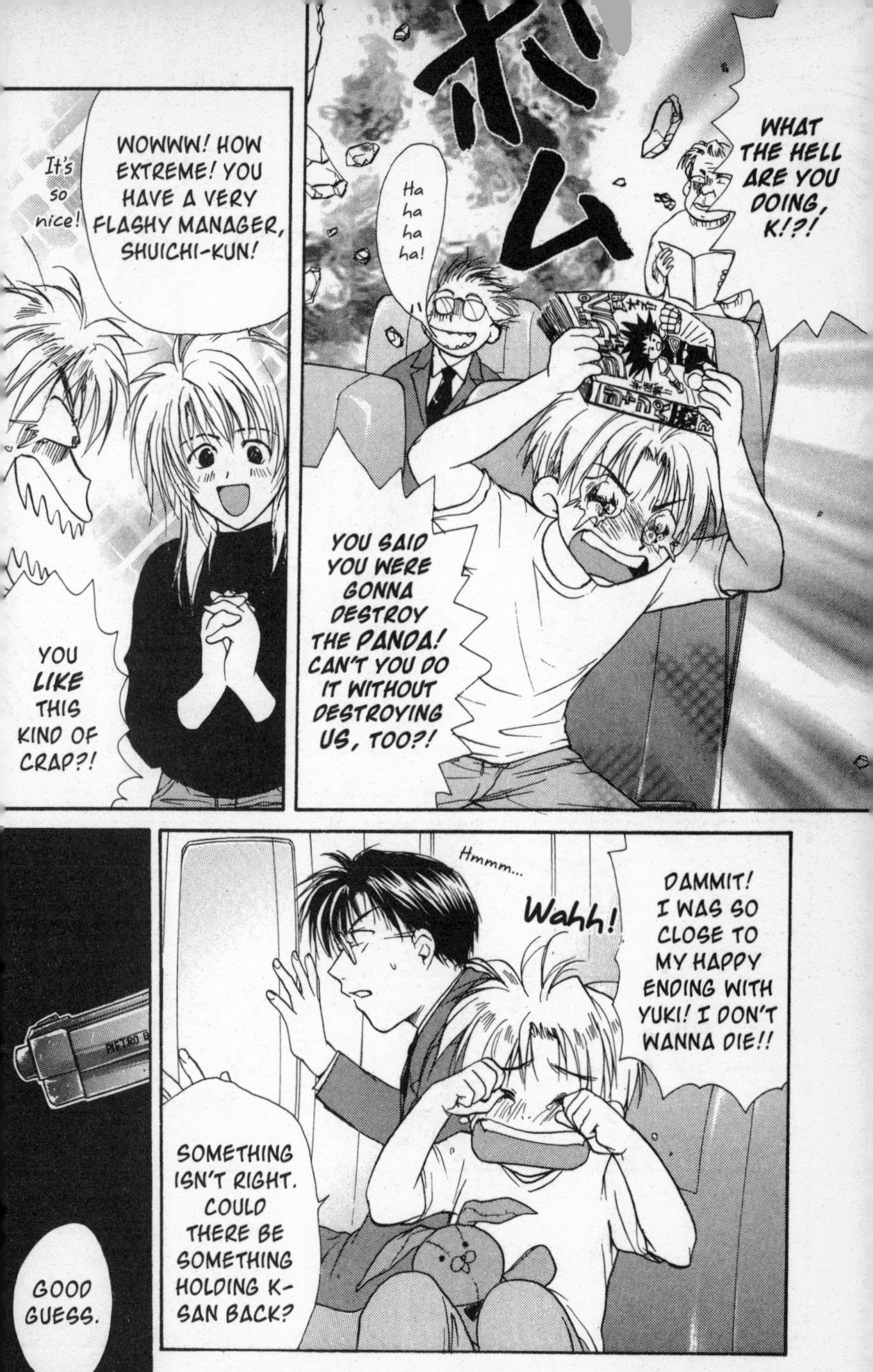
WHAT THE HELL ARE YOU DOING, K!?!
Ha ha ha ha!
YOU SAID YOU WERE GONNA DESTROY THE PANDA! CAN'T YOU DO IT WITHOUT DESTROYING US, TOO?!
WOWWW! HOW EXTREME! YOU HAVE A VERY FLASHY MANAGER, SHUICHI-KUN!
It's so nice!
YOU LIKE THIS KIND OF CRAP?!
DAMMIT! I WAS SO CLOSE TO MY HAPPY ENDING WITH YUKI! I DON'T WANNA DIE!!
Wahh!
Hmmm...
SOMETHING ISN'T RIGHT. COULD THERE BE SOMETHING HOLDING K-SAN BACK?
GOOD GUESS.

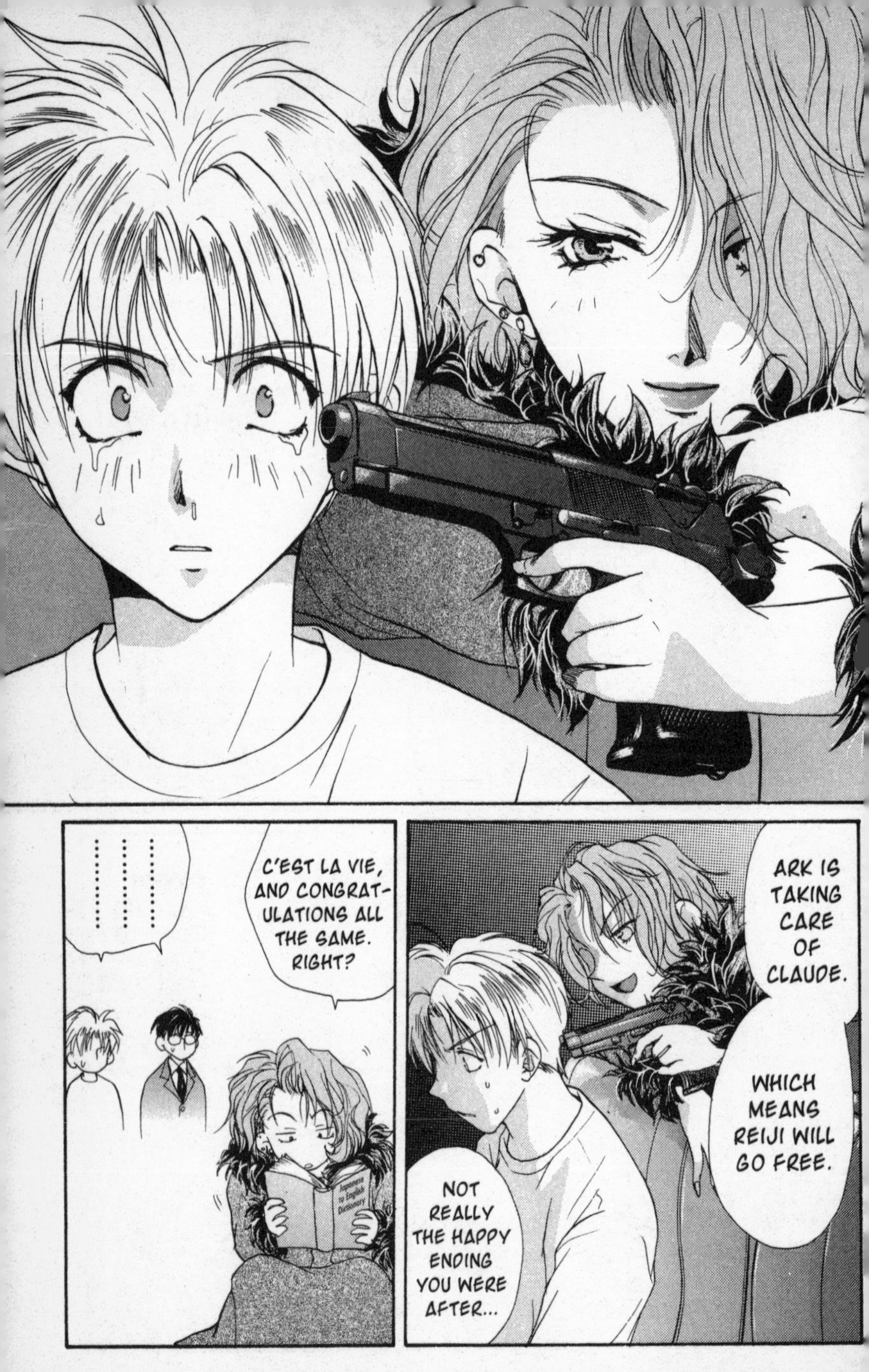
ARK IS TAKING CARE OF CLAUDE.
WHICH MEANS REIJI WILL GO FREE.
NOT REALLY THE HAPPY ENDING YOU WERE AFTER...
C'EST LA VIE, AND CONGRAT-ULATIONS ALL THE SAME. RIGHT?
Japanese to English Dictionary
......

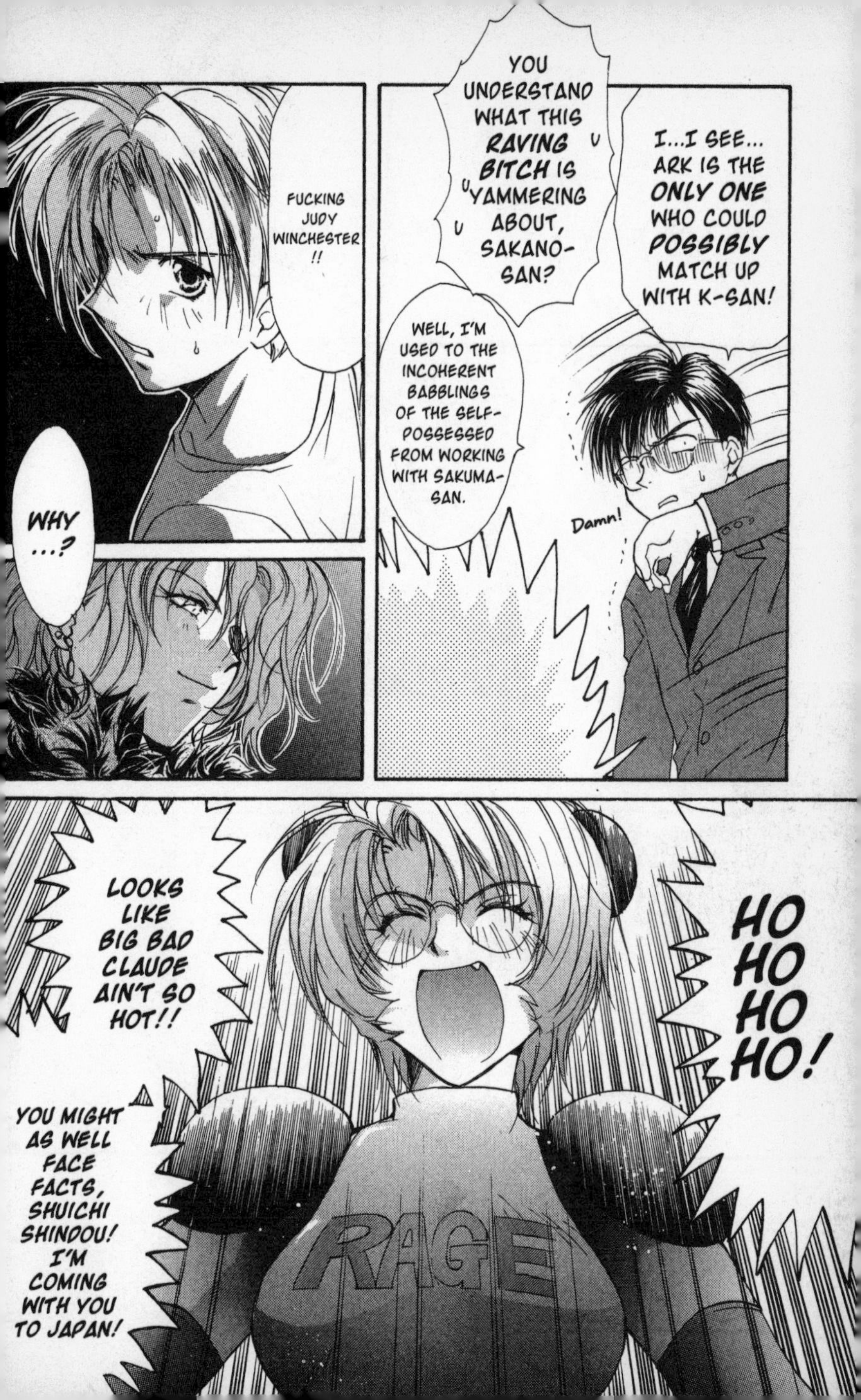
I...I SEE... ARK IS THE ONLY ONE WHO COULD POSSIBLY MATCH UP WITH K-SAN!
YOU UNDERSTAND WHAT THIS RAVING BITCH IS YAMMERING ABOUT, SAKANO-SAN?
WELL, I'M USED TO THE INCOHERENT BABBLINGS OF THE SELF-POSSESSED FROM WORKING WITH SAKUMA-SAN.
Damn!
FUCKING JUDY WINCHESTER !!
WHY ...?
HO HO HO HO HO!
LOOKS LIKE BIG BAD CLAUDE AIN'T SO HOT!!
YOU MIGHT AS WELL FACE FACTS, SHUICHI SHINDOU! I'M COMING WITH YOU TO JAPAN!
RAGE

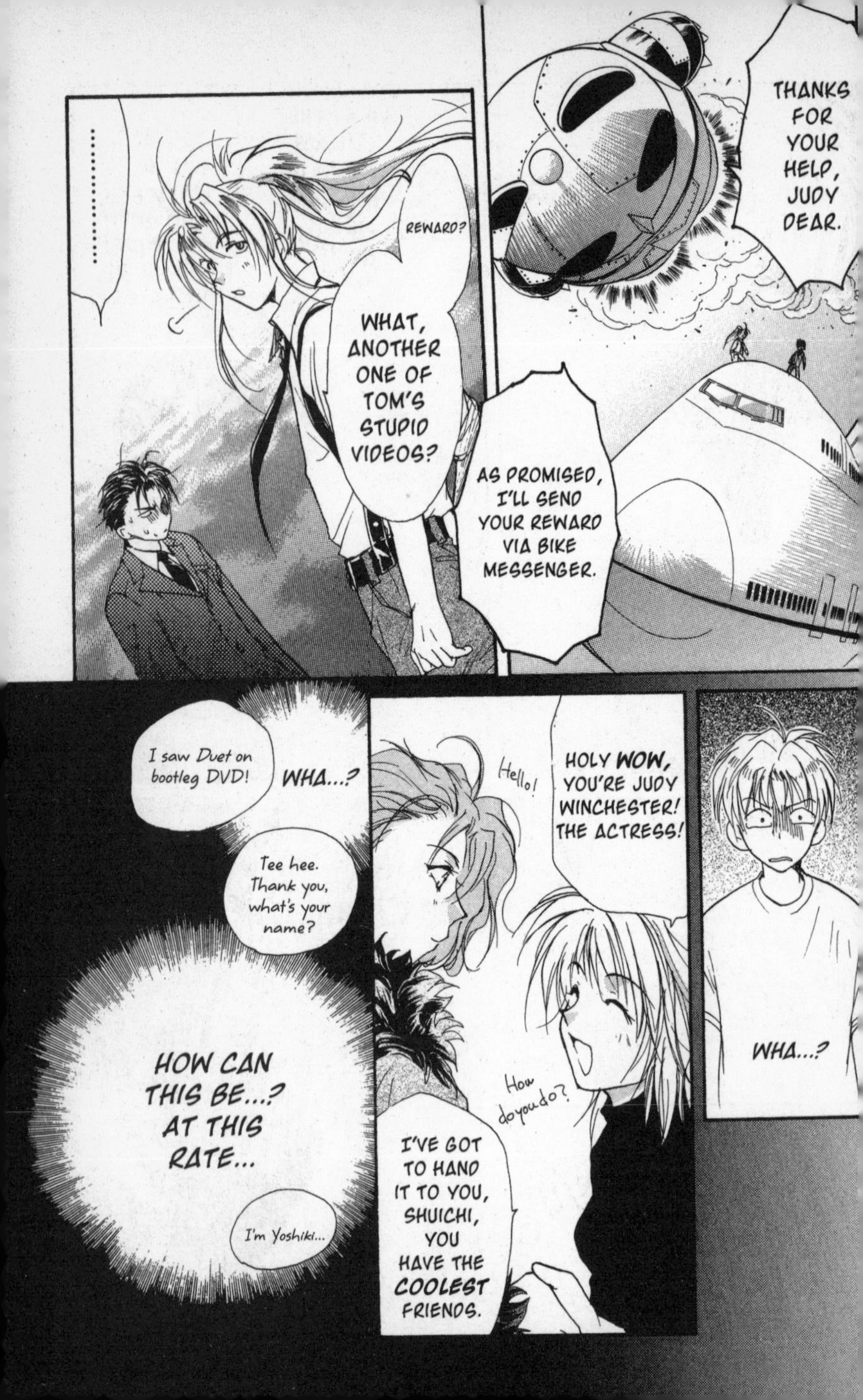
THANKS FOR YOUR HELP, JUDY DEAR.
AS PROMISED, I'LL SEND YOUR REWARD VIA BIKE MESSENGER.
REWARD?
WHAT, ANOTHER ONE OF TOM'S STUPID VIDEOS?
……
WHA...?
HOLY WOW, YOU'RE JUDY WINCHESTER! THE ACTRESS!
Hello!
How do you do?
I'VE GOT TO HAND IT TO YOU, SHUICHI, YOU HAVE THE COOLEST FRIENDS.
WHA...?
I saw Duet on bootleg DVD!
Tee hee. Thank you, what's your name?
HOW CAN THIS BE...? AT THIS RATE...
I'm Yoshiki...

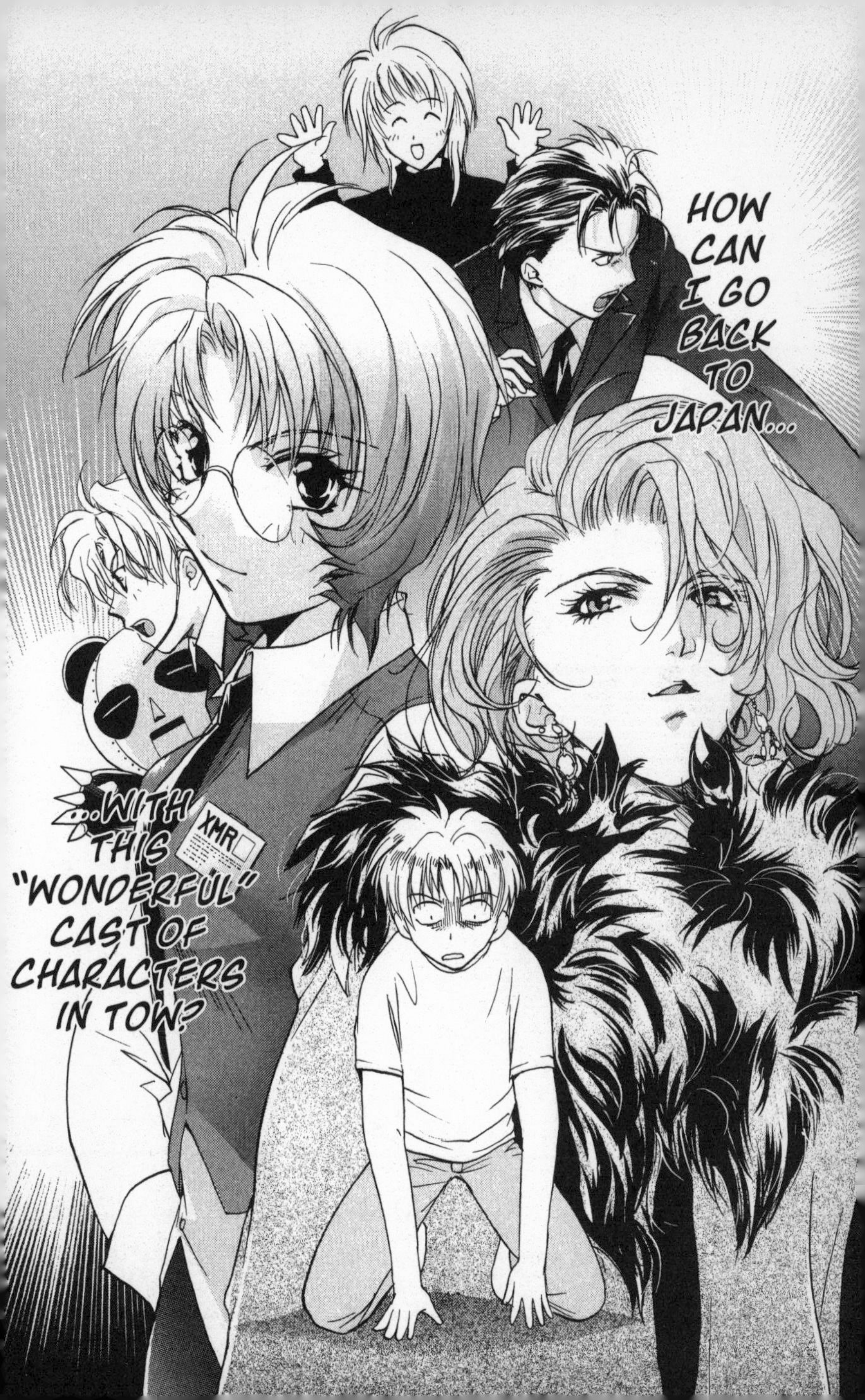
HOW CAN I GO BACK TO JAPAN...
...WITH THIS "WONDERFUL" CAST OF CHARACTERS IN TOW?
XMR

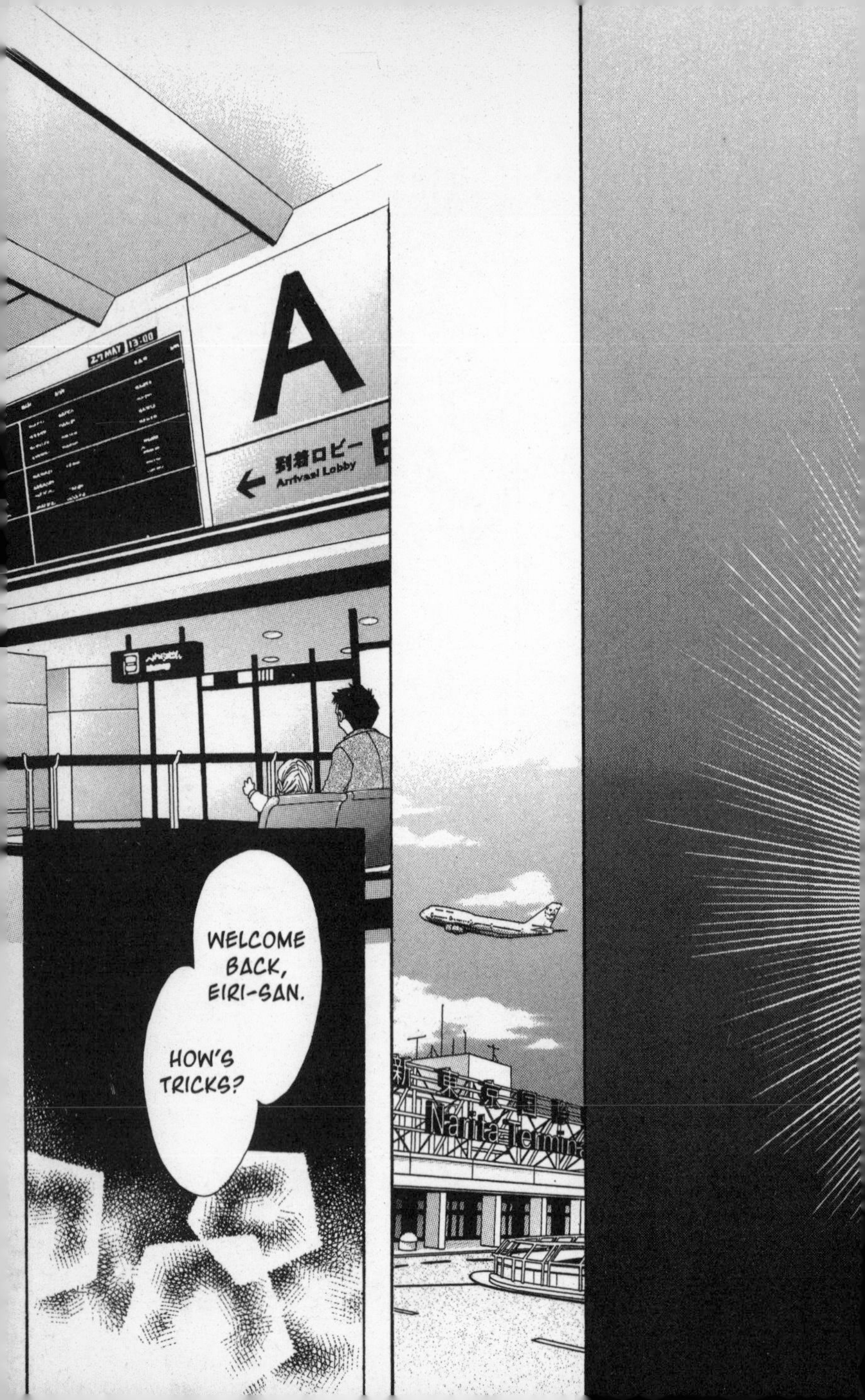
A
到着ロビー
Arrival Lobby
WELCOME BACK, EIRI-SAN.
HOW'S TRICKS?

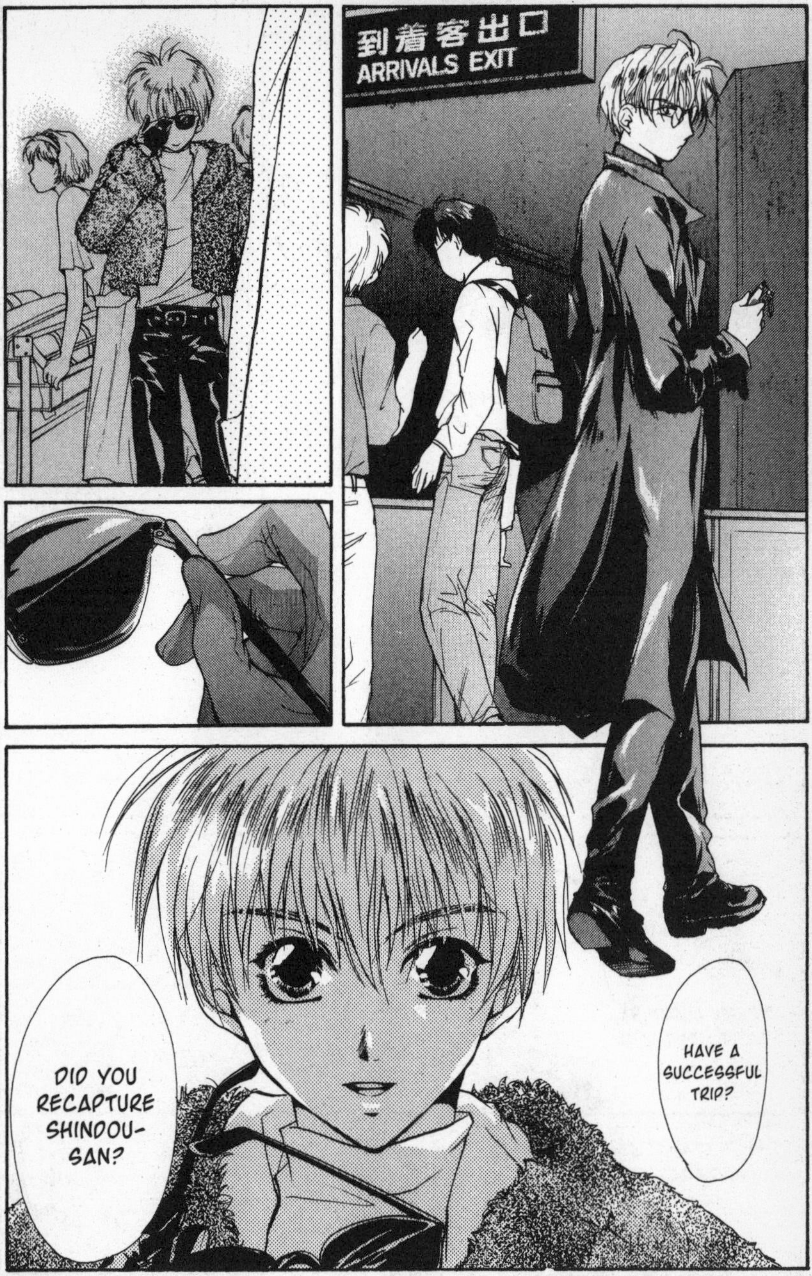
到着客出口
ARRIVALS EXIT
HAVE A SUCCESSFUL TRIP?
DID YOU RECAPTURE SHINDOU-SAN?

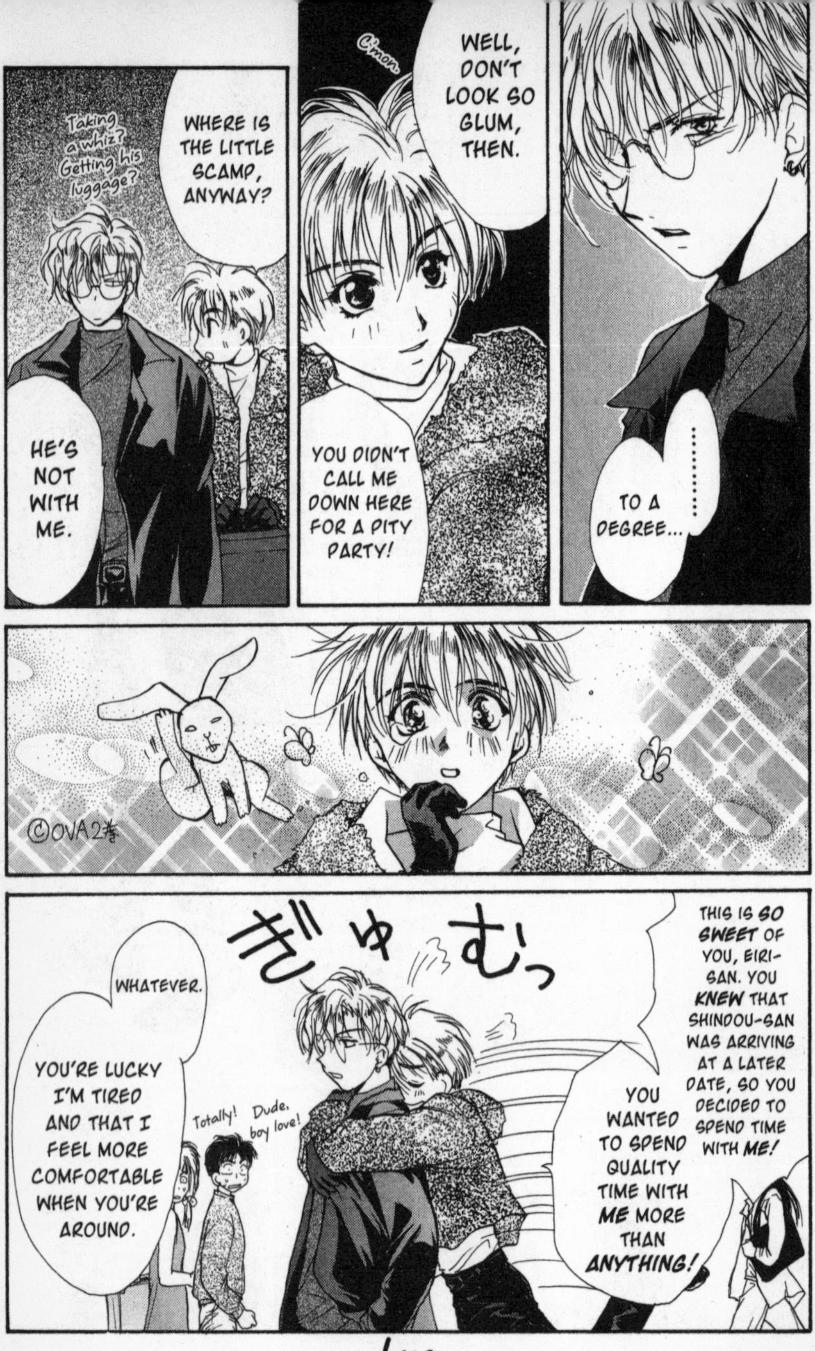

......
TO A DEGREE...
C'mon.
WELL, DON'T LOOK SO GLUM, THEN.
YOU DIDN'T CALL ME DOWN HERE FOR A PITY PARTY!
WHERE IS THE LITTLE SCAMP, ANYWAY?
Taking a whiz? Getting his luggage?
HE'S NOT WITH ME.
©OVA2巻
ぎゅむっ
THIS IS SO SWEET OF YOU, EIRI-SAN. YOU KNEW THAT SHINDOU-SAN WAS ARRIVING AT A LATER DATE, SO YOU DECIDED TO SPEND TIME WITH ME!
YOU WANTED TO SPEND QUALITY TIME WITH ME MORE THAN ANYTHING!
WHATEVER.
YOU'RE LUCKY I'M TIRED AND THAT I FEEL MORE COMFORTABLE WHEN YOU'RE AROUND.
Dude, boy love!
Totally!
hug

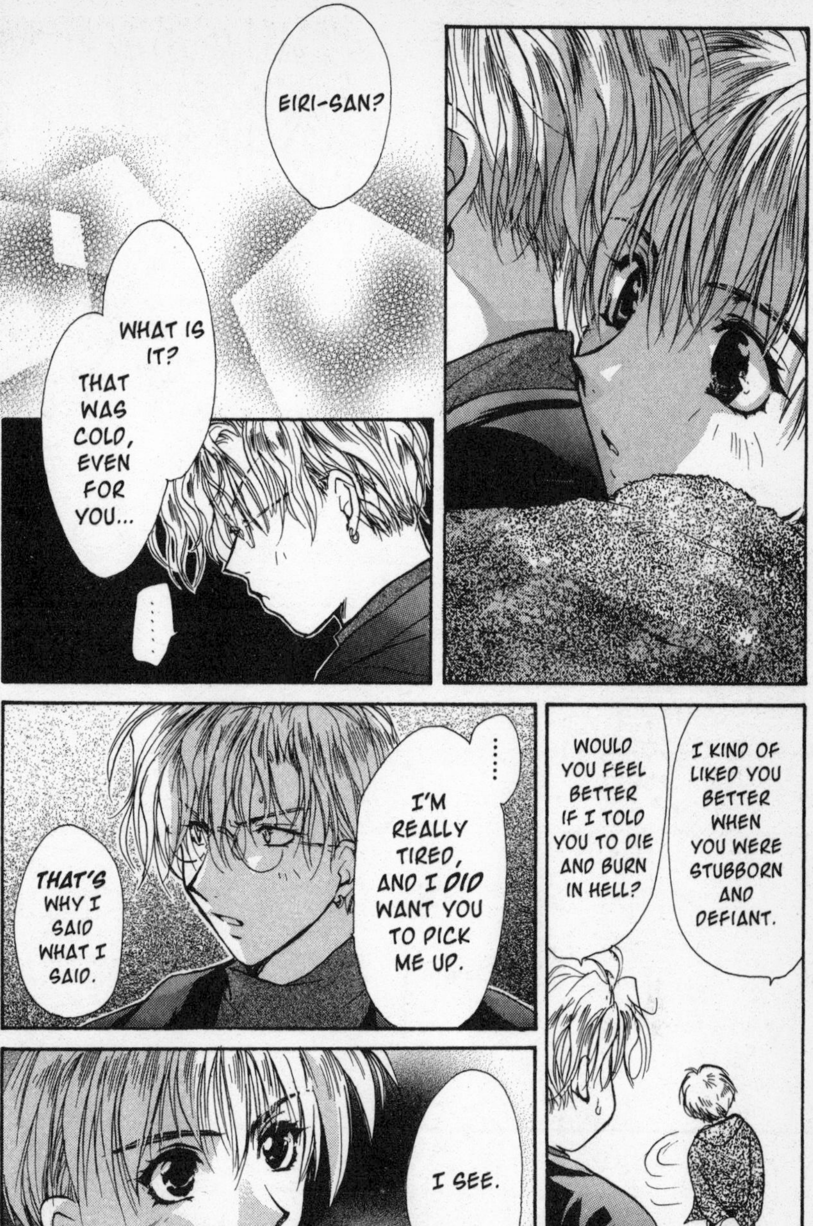
EIRI-SAN?
WHAT IS IT? THAT WAS COLD, EVEN FOR YOU...
......
I KIND OF LIKED YOU BETTER WHEN YOU WERE STUBBORN AND DEFIANT.
WOULD YOU FEEL BETTER IF I TOLD YOU TO DIE AND BURN IN HELL?
......
I'M REALLY TIRED, AND I *DID* WANT YOU TO PICK ME UP.
THAT'S WHY I SAID WHAT I SAID.
I SEE.

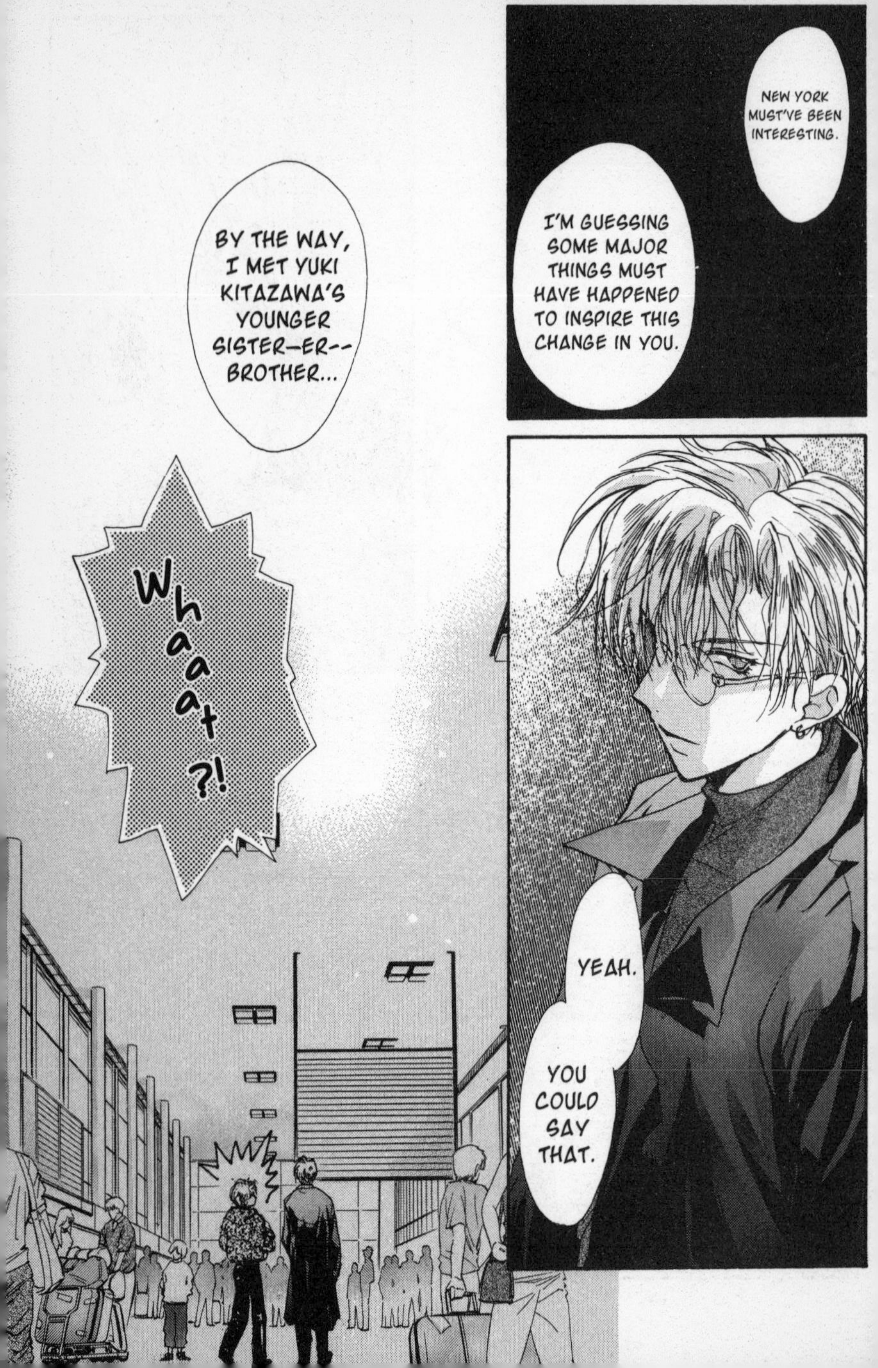
NEW YORK MUST'VE BEEN INTERESTING.
I'M GUESSING SOME MAJOR THINGS MUST HAVE HAPPENED TO INSPIRE THIS CHANGE IN YOU.
YEAH.
YOU COULD SAY THAT.
BY THE WAY, I MET YUKI KITAZAWA'S YOUNGER SISTER--ER-- BROTHER...
Whaaat ?!

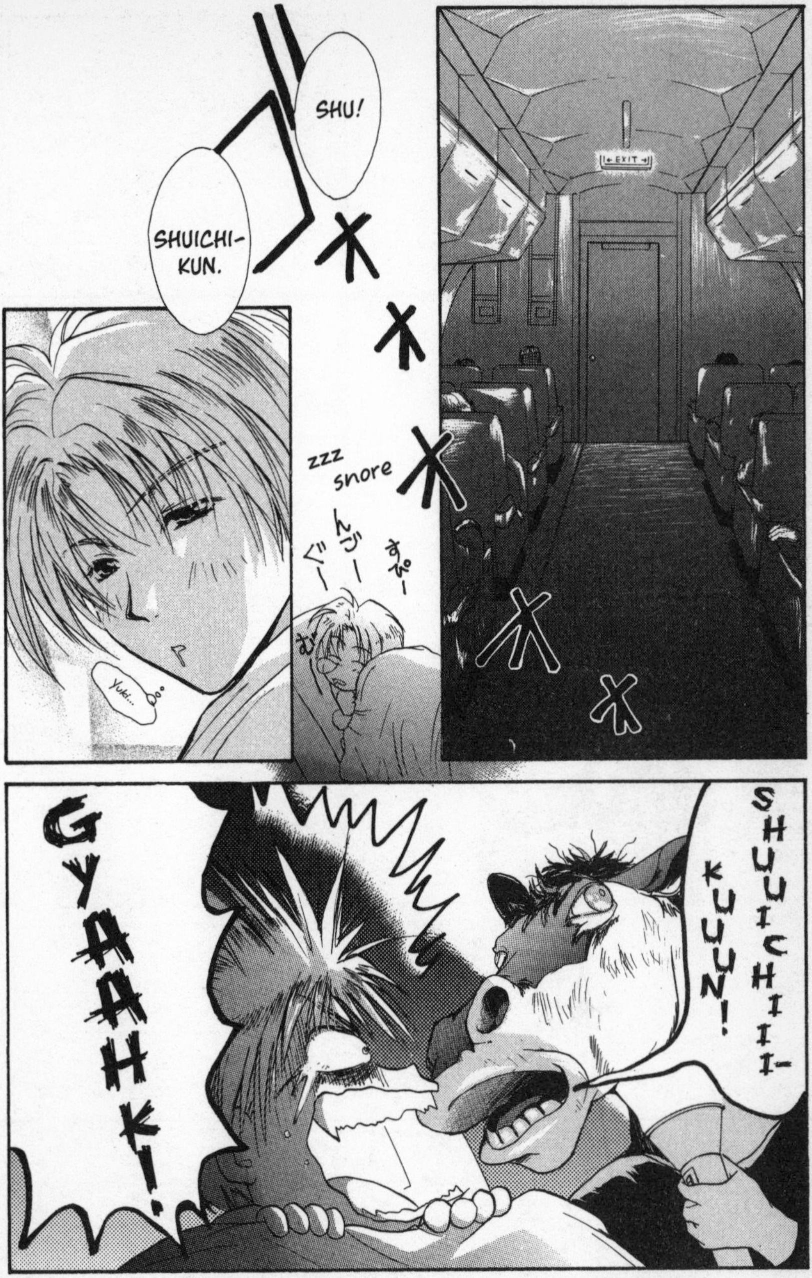
EXIT
SHU!
SHUICHI-KUN.
zzz snore
すぴー
んごー
ぐー
む
Yuki...
SHUUICHIII-KUUUN!
GYAAHK!!

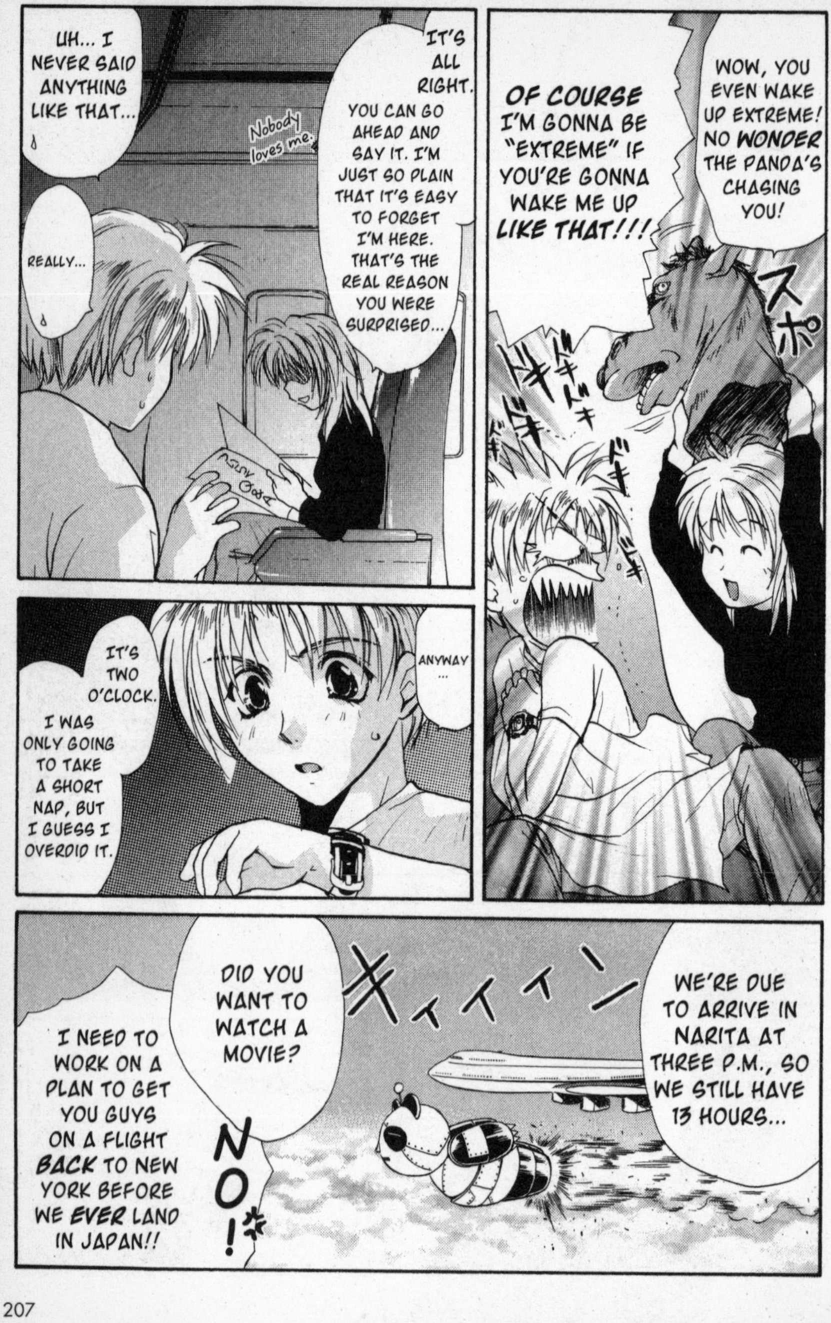
WOW, YOU EVEN WAKE UP EXTREME! NO WONDER THE PANDA'S CHASING YOU!
OF COURSE I'M GONNA BE "EXTREME" IF YOU'RE GONNA WAKE ME UP LIKE THAT!!!
スポ
ドキ ドキ ドキ ドキ ドキ
IT'S ALL RIGHT. YOU CAN GO AHEAD AND SAY IT. I'M JUST SO PLAIN THAT IT'S EASY TO FORGET I'M HERE. THAT'S THE REAL REASON YOU WERE SURPRISED...
Nobody loves me.
UH... I NEVER SAID ANYTHING LIKE THAT...
REALLY...
ANYWAY...
IT'S TWO O'CLOCK. I WAS ONLY GOING TO TAKE A SHORT NAP, BUT I GUESS I OVERDID IT.
WE'RE DUE TO ARRIVE IN NARITA AT THREE P.M., SO WE STILL HAVE 13 HOURS...
キィイイン
DID YOU WANT TO WATCH A MOVIE?
NO!
I NEED TO WORK ON A PLAN TO GET YOU GUYS ON A FLIGHT BACK TO NEW YORK BEFORE WE EVER LAND IN JAPAN!!

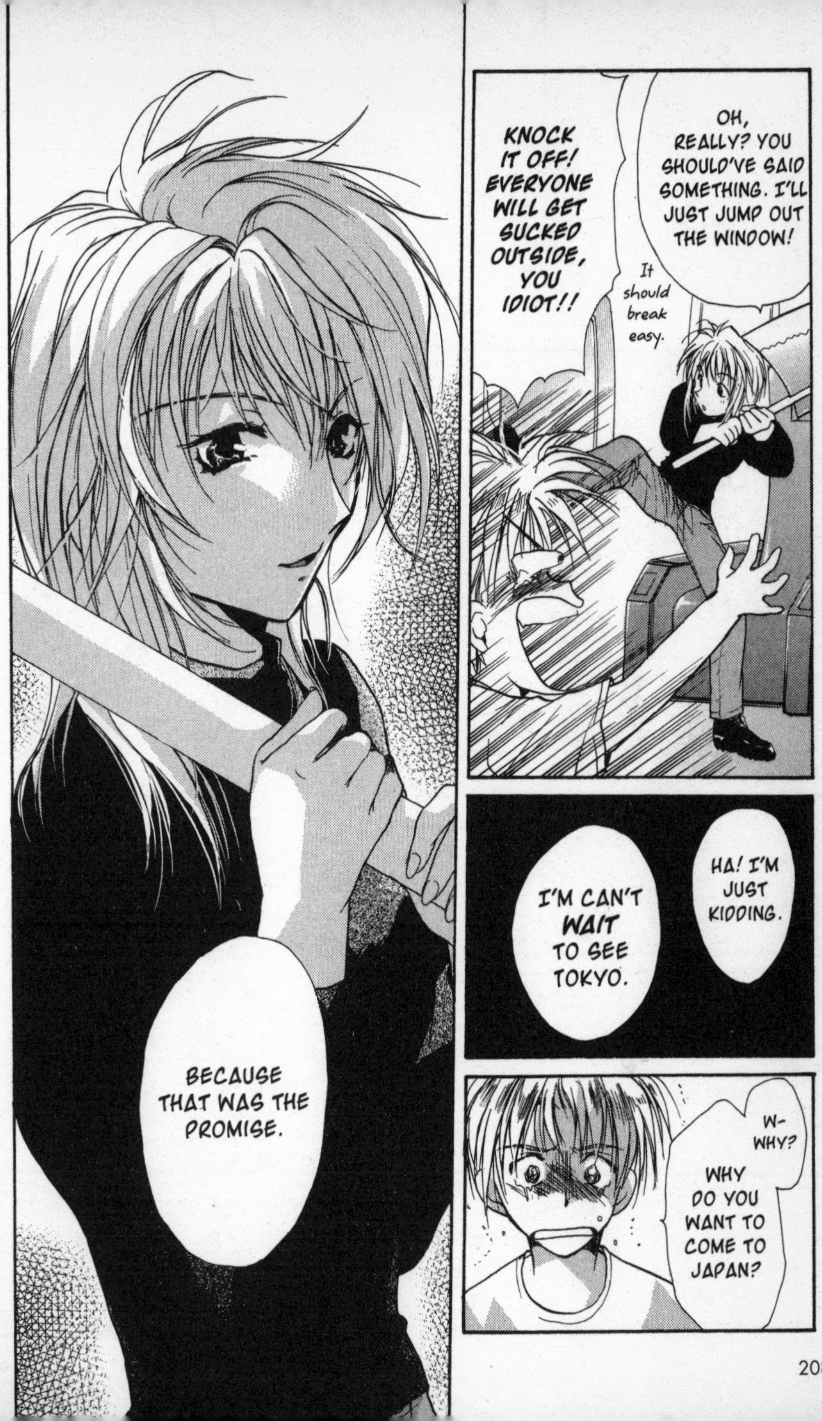
OH, REALLY? YOU SHOULD'VE SAID SOMETHING. I'LL JUST JUMP OUT THE WINDOW!
It should break easy.
KNOCK IT OFF! EVERYONE WILL GET SUCKED OUTSIDE, YOU IDIOT!!
HA! I'M JUST KIDDING.
I'M CAN'T WAIT TO SEE TOKYO.
W- WHY?
WHY DO YOU WANT TO COME TO JAPAN?
BECAUSE THAT WAS THE PROMISE.

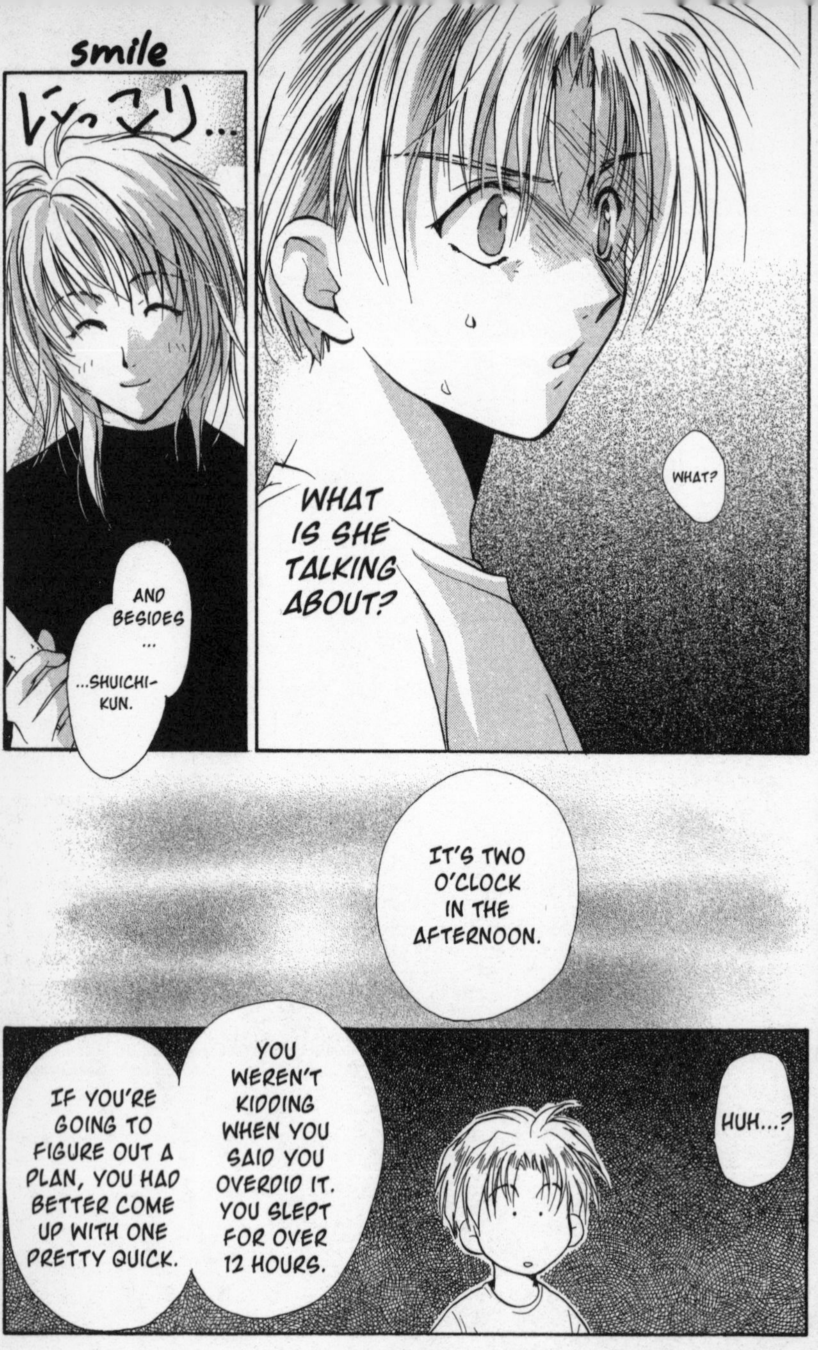
WHAT?
WHAT IS SHE TALKING ABOUT?
smile
にっこり…
AND BESIDES ...
...SHUICHI-KUN.
IT'S TWO O'CLOCK IN THE AFTERNOON.
HUH...?
YOU WEREN'T KIDDING WHEN YOU SAID YOU OVERDID IT. YOU SLEPT FOR OVER 12 HOURS.
IF YOU'RE GOING TO FIGURE OUT A PLAN, YOU HAD BETTER COME UP WITH ONE PRETTY QUICK.

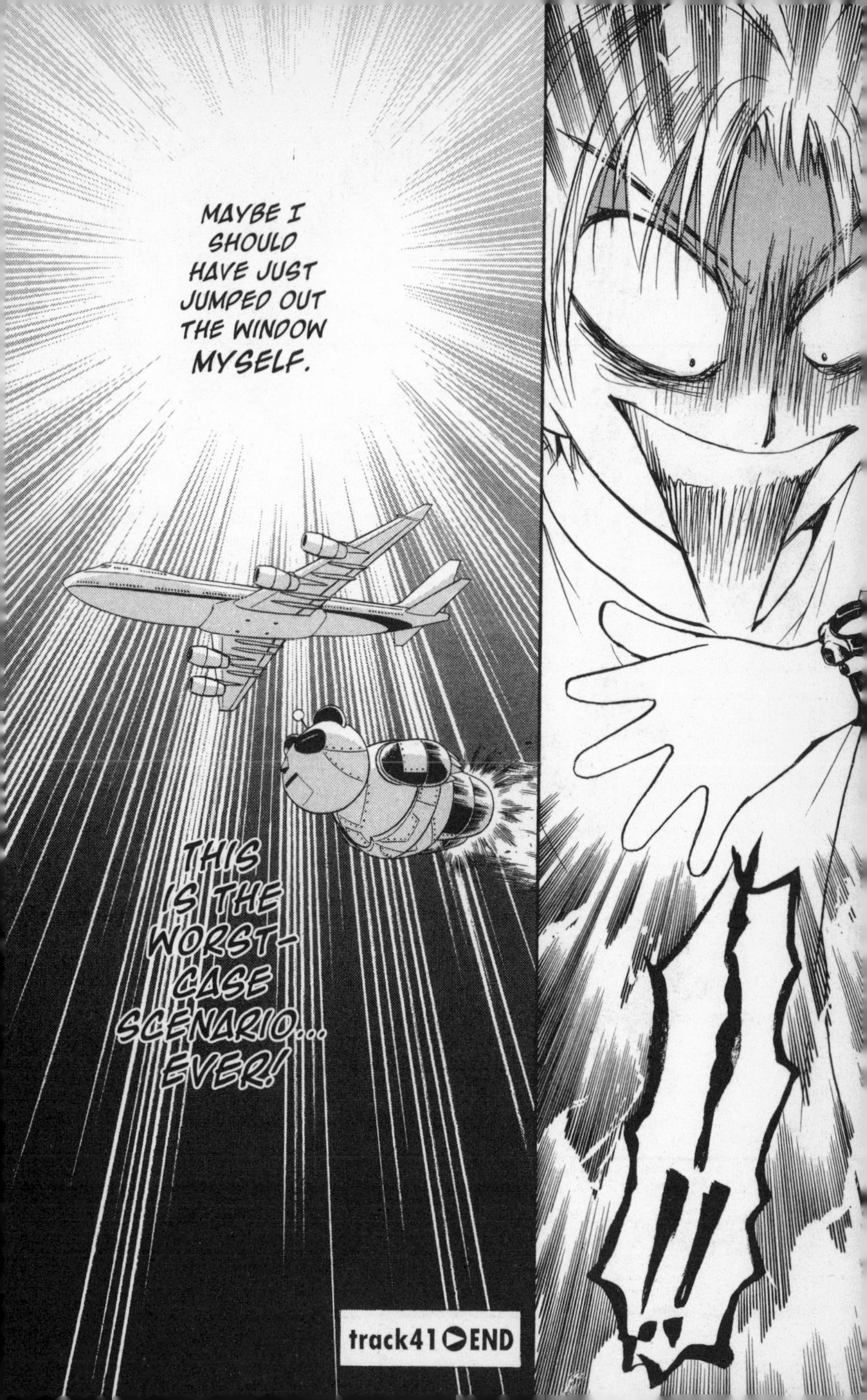
!!
MAYBE I SHOULD HAVE JUST JUMPED OUT THE WINDOW MYSELF.
THIS IS THE WORST-CASE SCENARIO... EVER!
track41 ▶END

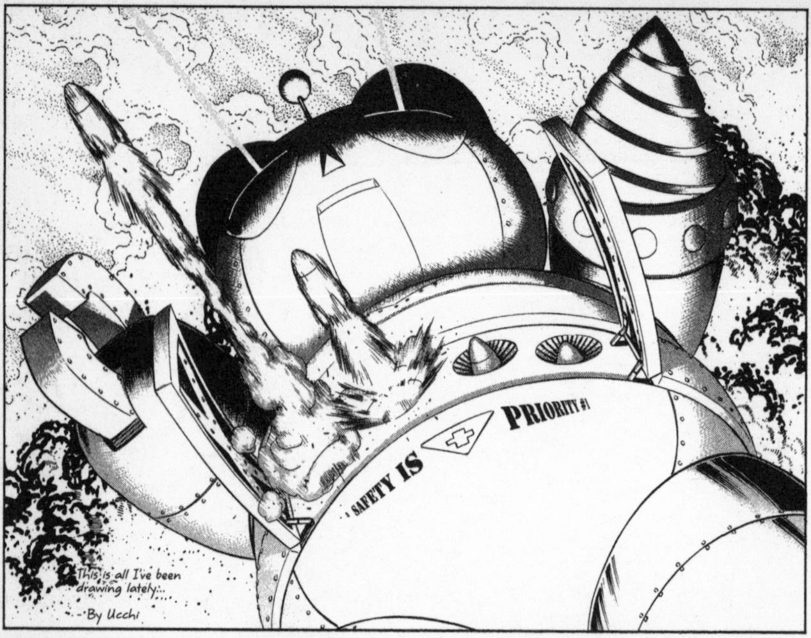
SAFETY IS PRIORITY #1
This is all I've been drawing lately...
- By Ucchi

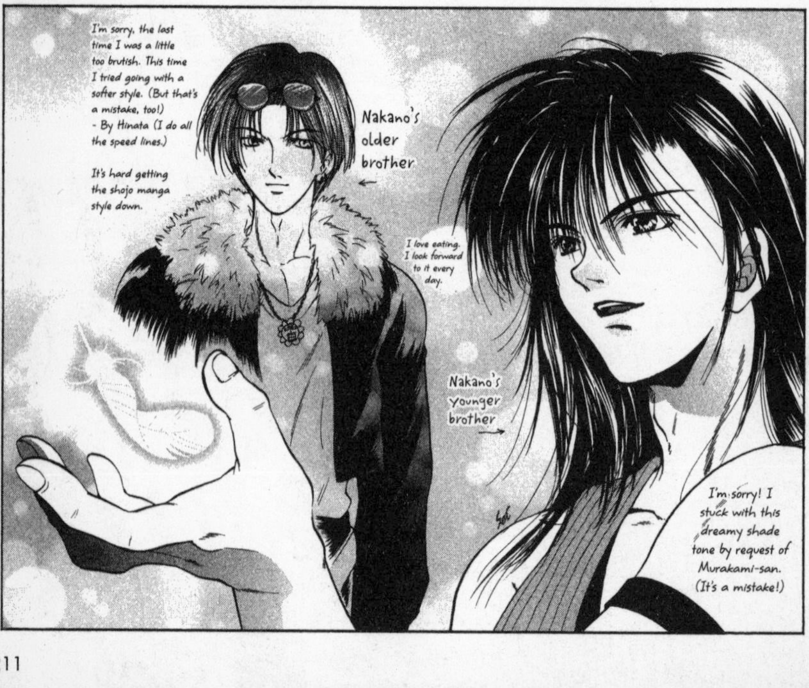
I'm sorry, the last time I was a little too brutish. This time I tried going with a softer style. (But that's a mistake, too!) - By Hinata (I do all the speed lines.)
It's hard getting the shojo manga style down.
Nakano's older brother
I love eating. I look forward to it every day.
Nakano's younger brother
I'm sorry! I stuck with this dreamy shade tone by request of Murakami-san. (It's a mistake!)

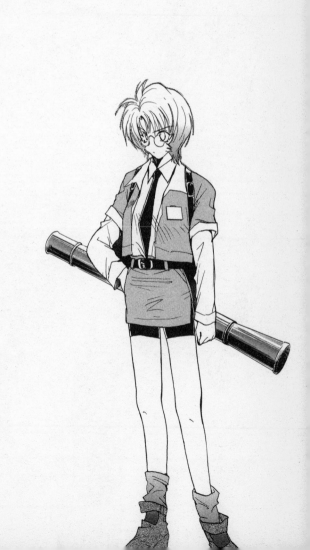

Gravitation

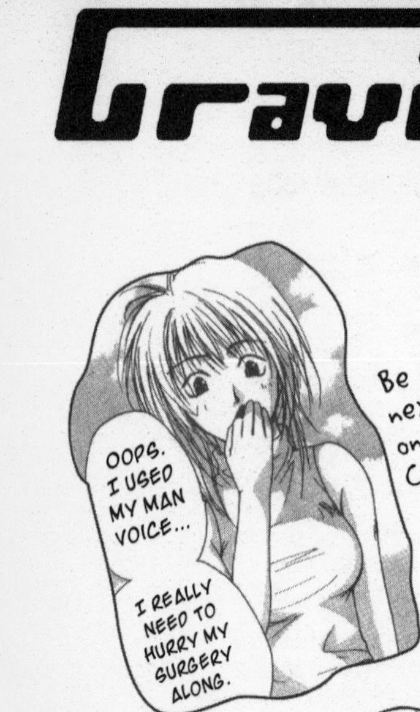
OOPS. I USED MY MAN VOICE...
I REALLY NEED TO HURRY MY SURGERY ALONG.

Be the next contestant on "The Crying Game"!

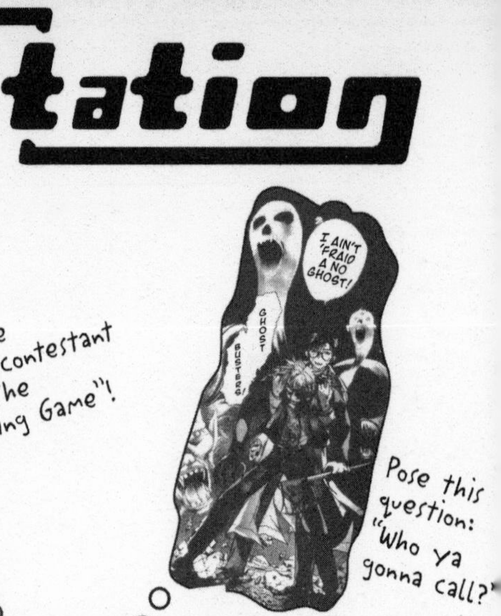
I AIN'T 'FRAID A NO GHOST!
GHOST BUSTERS!

Pose this question: "Who ya gonna call?"

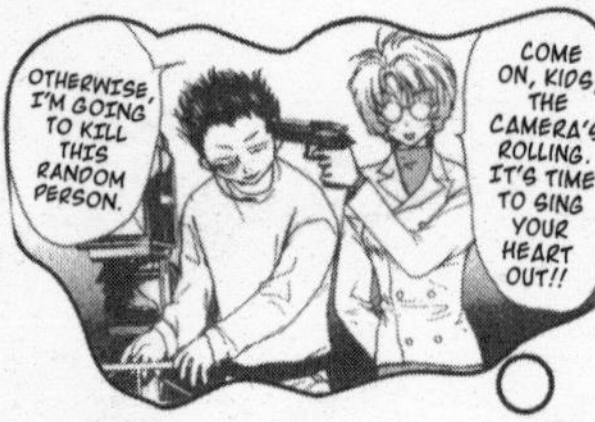
COME ON, KIDS, THE CAMERA'S ROLLING. IT'S TIME TO SING YOUR HEART OUT!!
OTHERWISE, I'M GOING TO KILL THIS RANDOM PERSON.

Increase Bad Luck's fan base by hiring Rage as the new manager!

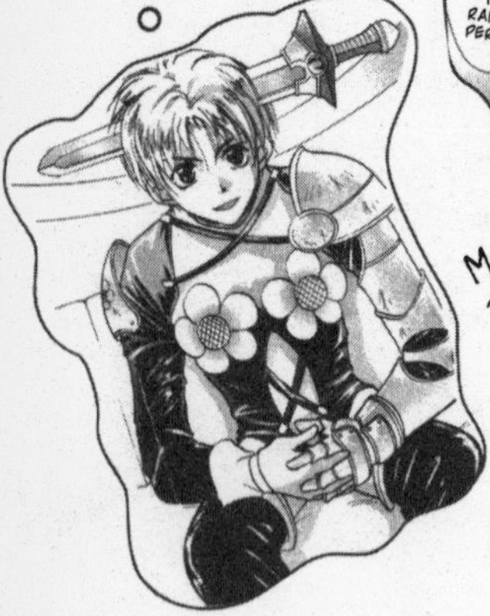

Mature as a serious artist.

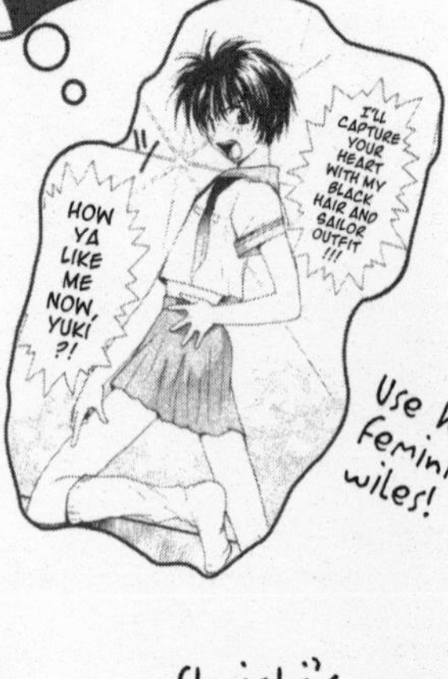
I'LL CAPTURE YOUR HEART WITH MY BLACK HAIR AND SAILOR OUTFIT!!!
HOW YA LIKE ME NOW, YUKI?!

Use his feminine wiles!

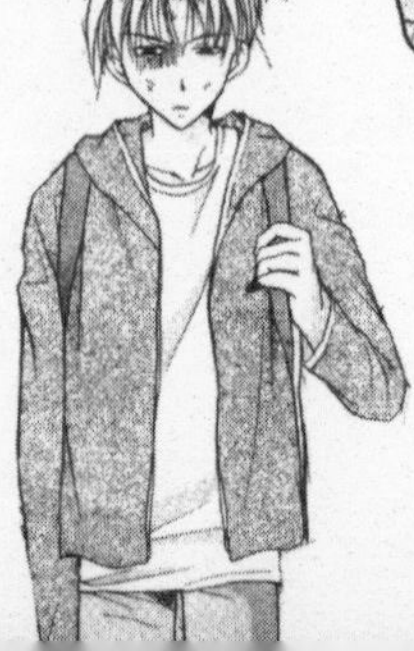

Available February 2005!

Shuichi's things to do in Volume 10...

ALSO AVAILABLE FROM ☺TOKYOPOP®

PLANETES
PRESIDENT DAD
PRIEST
PRINCESS AI
PSYCHIC ACADEMY
QUEEN'S KNIGHT, THE
RAGNAROK
RAVE MASTER
REALITY CHECK
REBIRTH
REBOUND
REMOTE
RISING STARS OF MANGA
SABER MARIONETTE J
SAILOR MOON
SAINT TAIL
SAIYUKI
SAMURAI DEEPER KYO
SAMURAI GIRL REAL BOUT HIGH SCHOOL
SCRYED
SEIKAI TRILOGY, THE
SGT. FROG
SHAOLIN SISTERS
SHIRAHIME-SYO: SNOW GODDESS TALES
SHUTTERBOX
SKULL MAN, THE
SNOW DROP
SORCERER HUNTERS
STONE
SUIKODEN III
SUKI
TAROT CAFÉ, THE
THREADS OF TIME
TOKYO BABYLON
TOKYO MEW MEW
TOKYO TRIBES
TRAMPS LIKE US
UNDER THE GLASS MOON
VAMPIRE GAME
VISION OF ESCAFLOWNE, THE
WARCRAFT
WARRIORS OF TAO
WILD ACT
WISH
WORLD OF HARTZ
X-DAY
ZODIAC P.I.

NOVELS

CLAMP SCHOOL PARANORMAL INVESTIGATORS
SAILOR MOON
SLAYERS

ART BOOKS

ART OF CARDCAPTOR SAKURA
ART OF MAGIC KNIGHT RAYEARTH, THE
PEACH: MIWA UEDA ILLUSTRATIONS
CLAMP NORTHSIDE
CLAMP SOUTHSIDE

ANIME GUIDES

COWBOY BEBOP
GUNDAM TECHNICAL MANUALS
SAILOR MOON SCOUT GUIDES

TOKYOPOP KIDS

STRAY SHEEP

CINE-MANGA®

ALADDIN
CARDCAPTORS
DUEL MASTERS
FAIRLY ODDPARENTS, THE
FAMILY GUY
FINDING NEMO
G.I. JOE SPY TROOPS
GREATEST STARS OF THE NBA
JACKIE CHAN ADVENTURES
JIMMY NEUTRON: BOY GENIUS, THE ADVENTURES OF
KIM POSSIBLE
LILO & STITCH: THE SERIES
LIZZIE MCGUIRE
LIZZIE MCGUIRE MOVIE, THE
MALCOLM IN THE MIDDLE
POWER RANGERS: DINO THUNDER
POWER RANGERS: NINJA STORM
PRINCESS DIARIES 2, THE
RAVE MASTER
SHREK 2
SIMPLE LIFE, THE
SPONGEBOB SQUAREPANTS
SPY KIDS 2
SPY KIDS 3-D: GAME OVER
TEENAGE MUTANT NINJA TURTLES
THAT'S SO RAVEN
TOTALLY SPIES
TRANSFORMERS: ARMADA
TRANSFORMERS: ENERGON

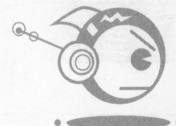

You want it? We got it!
A full range of TOKYOPOP
products are available now at:
www.TOKYOPOP.com/shop

09.21.04T

ALSO AVAILABLE FROM 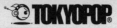 TOKYOPOP®

MANGA

.HACK//LEGEND OF THE TWILIGHT
@LARGE
ABENOBASHI: MAGICAL SHOPPING ARCADE
A.I. LOVE YOU
AI YORI AOSHI
ALICHINO
ANGELIC LAYER
ARM OF KANNON
BABY BIRTH
BATTLE ROYALE
BATTLE VIXENS
BOYS BE...
BRAIN POWERED
BRIGADOON
B'TX
CANDIDATE FOR GODDESS, THE
CARDCAPTOR SAKURA
CARDCAPTOR SAKURA - MASTER OF THE CLOW
CHOBITS
CHRONICLES OF THE CURSED SWORD
CLAMP SCHOOL DETECTIVES
CLOVER
COMIC PARTY
CONFIDENTIAL CONFESSIONS
CORRECTOR YUI
COWBOY BEBOP
COWBOY BEBOP: SHOOTING STAR
CRAZY LOVE STORY
CRESCENT MOON
CROSS
CULDCEPT
CYBORG 009
D•N•ANGEL
DEARS
DEMON DIARY
DEMON ORORON, THE
DEUS VITAE
DIABOLO
DIGIMON
DIGIMON TAMERS
DIGIMON ZERO TWO
DOLL
DRAGON HUNTER
DRAGON KNIGHTS
DRAGON VOICE
DREAM SAGA
DUKLYON: CLAMP SCHOOL DEFENDERS
EERIE QUEERIE!
ERICA SAKURAZAWA: COLLECTED WORKS
ET CETERA
ETERNITY
EVIL'S RETURN
FAERIES' LANDING
FAKE
FLCL
FLOWER OF THE DEEP SLEEP
FORBIDDEN DANCE
FRUITS BASKET

G GUNDAM
GATEKEEPERS
GETBACKERS
GIRL GOT GAME
GRAVITATION
GTO
GUNDAM SEED ASTRAY
GUNDAM WING
GUNDAM WING: BATTLEFIELD OF PACIFISTS
GUNDAM WING: ENDLESS WALTZ
GUNDAM WING: THE LAST OUTPOST (G-UNIT)
HANDS OFF!
HAPPY MANIA
HARLEM BEAT
HYPER RUNE
I.N.V.U.
IMMORTAL RAIN
INITIAL D
INSTANT TEEN: JUST ADD NUTS
ISLAND
JING: KING OF BANDITS
JING: KING OF BANDITS - TWILIGHT TALES
JULINE
KARE KANO
KILL ME, KISS ME
KINDAICHI CASE FILES, THE
KING OF HELL
KODOCHA: SANA'S STAGE
LAMENT OF THE LAMB
LEGAL DRUG
LEGEND OF CHUN HYANG, THE
LES BIJOUX
LOVE HINA
LOVE OR MONEY
LUPIN III
LUPIN III: WORLD'S MOST WANTED
MAGIC KNIGHT RAYEARTH I
MAGIC KNIGHT RAYEARTH II
MAHOROMATIC: AUTOMATIC MAIDEN
MAN OF MANY FACES
MARMALADE BOY
MARS
MARS: HORSE WITH NO NAME
MINK
MIRACLE GIRLS
MIYUKI-CHAN IN WONDERLAND
MODEL
MOURYOU KIDEN: LEGEND OF THE NYMPH
NECK AND NECK
ONE
ONE I LOVE, THE
PARADISE KISS
PARASYTE
PASSION FRUIT
PEACH FUZZ
PEACH GIRL
PEACH GIRL: CHANGE OF HEART
PET SHOP OF HORRORS
PITA-TEN
PLANET LADDER

09.21.04T

BOYS:BE™

A GUY'S GUIDE TO GIRLS

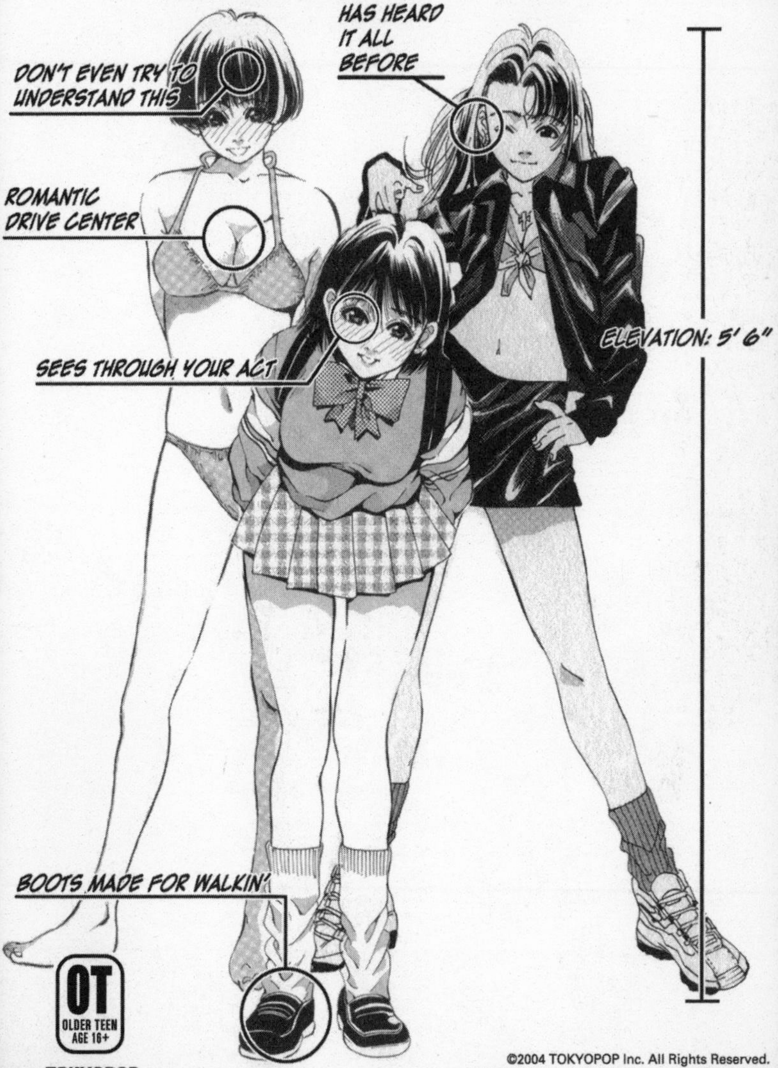

HAS HEARD IT ALL BEFORE
DON'T EVEN TRY TO UNDERSTAND THIS
ROMANTIC DRIVE CENTER
ELEVATION: 5' 6"
SEES THROUGH YOUR ACT
BOOTS MADE FOR WALKIN'

OT
OLDER TEEN
AGE 16+

www.TOKYOPOP.com

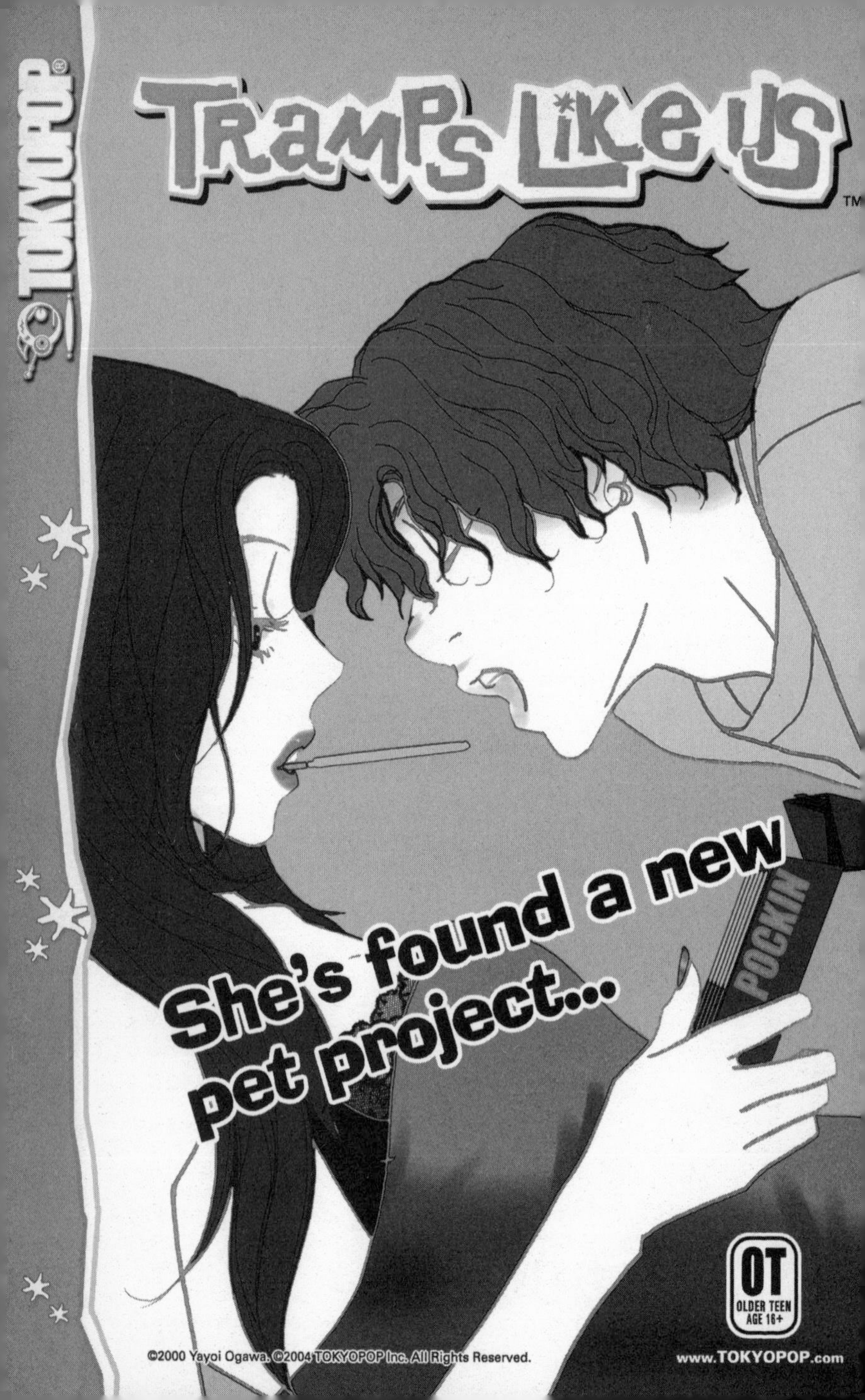
TOKYOPOP®
TRAMPS LIKE US™
She's found a new pet project...
POCKIN
OT OLDER TEEN AGE 16+
©2000 Yayoi Ogawa. ©2004 TOKYOPOP Inc. All Rights Reserved.
www.TOKYOPOP.com

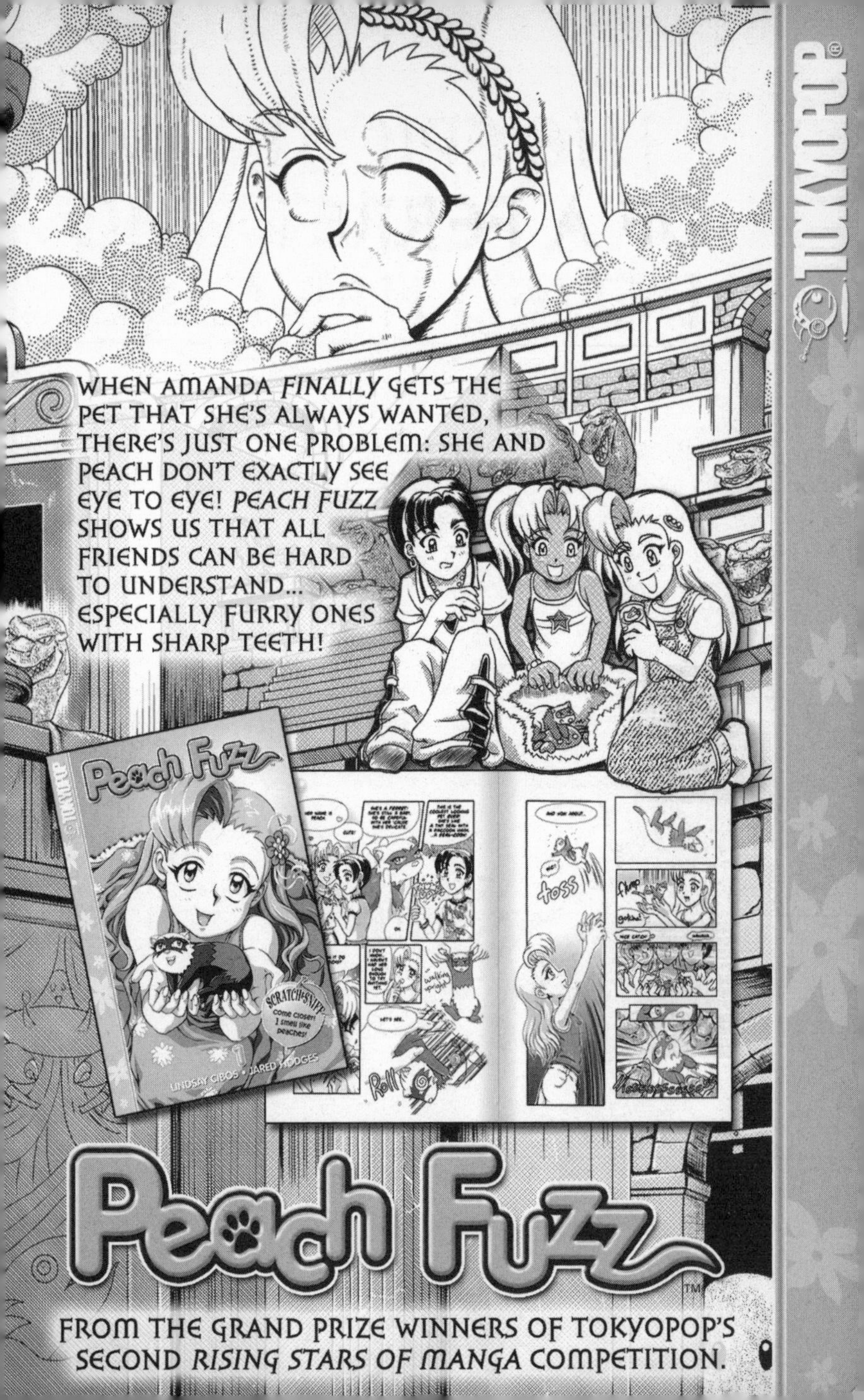
TOKYOPOP
WHEN AMANDA FINALLY GETS THE PET THAT SHE'S ALWAYS WANTED, THERE'S JUST ONE PROBLEM: SHE AND PEACH DON'T EXACTLY SEE EYE TO EYE! PEACH FUZZ SHOWS US THAT ALL FRIENDS CAN BE HARD TO UNDERSTAND... ESPECIALLY FURRY ONES WITH SHARP TEETH!
Peach Fuzz
SCRATCH-N-SNIFF
come closer! I smell like peaches!
toss
Roll
Peach Fuzz™
FROM THE GRAND PRIZE WINNERS OF TOKYOPOP'S SECOND RISING STARS OF MANGA COMPETITION.

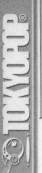

THE EPIC STORY OF A FERRET WHO DEFIED HER CAGE.

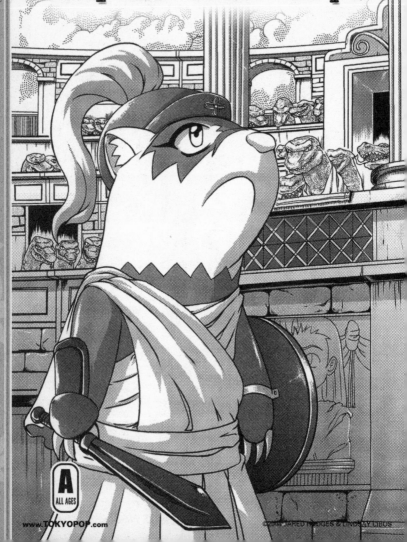

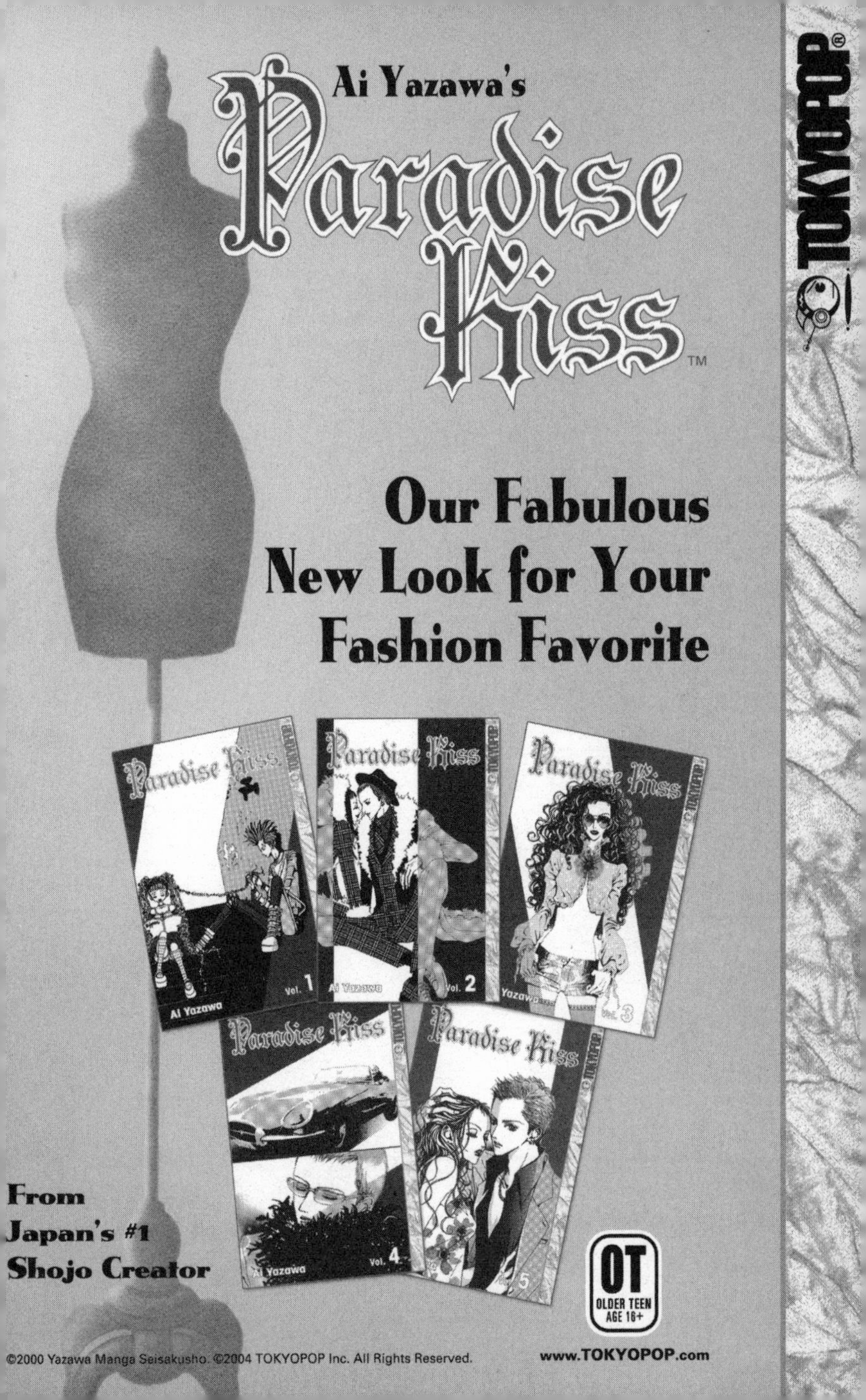
Ai Yazawa's
Paradise Kiss™
Our Fabulous New Look for Your Fashion Favorite
From Japan's #1 Shojo Creator
OT
OLDER TEEN
AGE 16+
©2000 Yazawa Manga Seisakusho. ©2004 TOKYOPOP Inc. All Rights Reserved.
www.TOKYOPOP.com
TOKYOPOP®

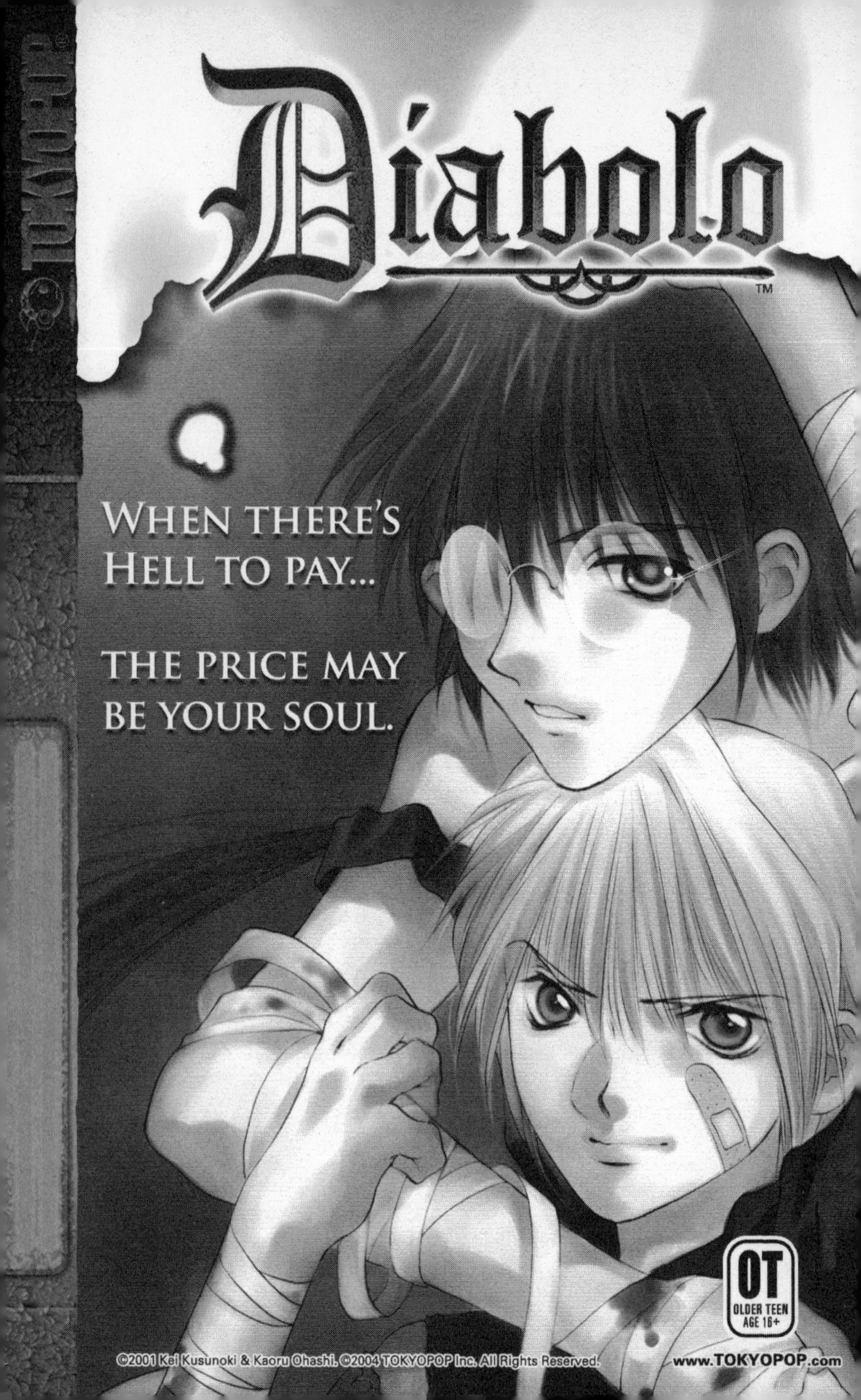
TOKYOPOP
Diabolo
TM
WHEN THERE'S HELL TO PAY...
THE PRICE MAY BE YOUR SOUL.
OT
OLDER TEEN AGE 16+
©2001 Kei Kusunoki & Kaoru Ohashi. ©2004 TOKYOPOP Inc. All Rights Reserved.
www.TOKYOPOP.com

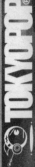

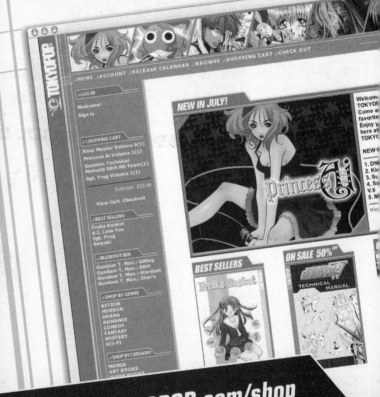
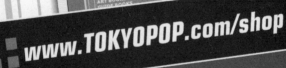

STOP!

This is the back of the book.
You wouldn't want to spoil a great ending!

This book is printed "manga-style," in the authentic Japanese right-to-left format. Since none of the artwork has been flipped or altered, readers get to experience the story just as the creator intended. You've been asking for it, so TOKYOPOP® delivered: authentic, hot-off-the-press, and far more fun!

DIRECTIONS

If this is your first time reading manga-style, here's a quick guide to help you understand how it works.

It's easy... just start in the top right panel and follow the numbers. Have fun, and look for more 100% authentic manga from TOKYOPOP®!

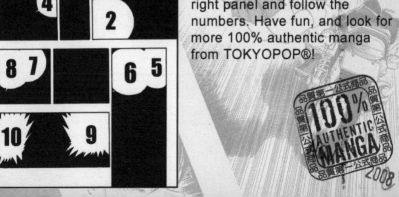